AGATHA CHRISTIE'S GOLDEN AGE

VOLUME II: MISS MARPLE AND THE OTHER GOLDEN AGE PUZZLES

JOHN GODDARD

With an Introduction by Dr John Curran

STYLISH EYE PRESS
www.stylisheyepress.com
goddard.goldenage@gmail.com

First published 2021

Hardback ISBN - 978-1-9996120-4-7
Paperback ISBN - 978-1-9996120-5-4
eBook ISBN - 978-1-9996120-6-1

Printed and bound in the United Kingdom by
www.spiffingcovers.com

Typeset in Minion Pro 12pt

Cover design and layout by www.spiffingcovers.com

*To all those who since July 2015 have
helped turn six months into six years*

Acknowledgements

Like Volume I, this companion volume is not an 'official' Agatha Christie publication in the sense of one sponsored by her estate but an independent project on which I have been working since 2005. Although I have again worked on it very largely on my own, some people have continued to provide important support to me for which I am very grateful, especially Dawn Hudson, Christopher Blain, Owen O'Rorke and Liz Bourne who reprised their original, invaluable roles, as, of course, did Spiffing Covers – James Willis, Joseph Hewes and Stefan Proudfoot, who produced another of his great dust jacket designs.

I could not be sure, when completing Volume I, whether I would be able to write this second volume or to give the same thorough analytical treatment to each novel. But I was so encouraged by the positive comments that I received, both in complimentary reviews of Volume I and in e-mails urging me to produce a second volume, that I decided to return seriously to the project and, as an ardent Christie fan, I am delighted to have done so.

For those positive comments, I would particularly like to express my appreciation to Scott Baker; Roger Lewis; Geoff Bradley; Tony Medawar; Brad Friedman; Kate Jackson; Kemper Donovan and Catherine Brobeck; Martin Edwards; Barry Forshaw; Mark Aldridge; Peter Keating; Jamie Bernthal; Christopher Chan; Kathryn Harkup; and, most of all, John Curran. Although the pandemic precluded any trip to Dublin to visit John this time around, he made a large number of helpful suggestions during our telephone and e-mail conversations and Volume II is, like Volume I, better for his advice.

John Goddard   Wimbledon, May 2021

Contents

INTRODUCTION

In 2018 John Goddard produced his first volume of *Agatha Christie's Golden Age*, analysing in forensic detail the puzzle elements in the Poirot novels published during the 'Golden Age' of detective fiction. He now presents *Volume II* in which he does the same with the non-Poirot novels of the same period, from Christie's first thriller *The Secret Adversary* (1922) to the underestimated but excellent *Towards Zero* (1944).

As previously, John adopts the approach – Solution, Plot and Clues – he used in Volume I, a highly original method which proved an accessible way for both Christie scholars and general readers to understand the novels as puzzles. After all, it is through her facility with puzzles that Christie triumphs over all other detective novelists.

Because this volume, unlike the earlier one, contains discussion of six thrillers, John also includes a welcome examination of the distinction between thrillers and detective fiction in Christie's output. And into which category does her most famous and popular book *And Then There Were None* fall? John's extended forensic analysis of this novel highlights some fascinating and hitherto neglected points.

Even seasoned Christie addicts will find much to ponder: what links *The Secret Adversary, The Man in the Brown Suit* and *The Secret of Chimneys*? What are the four reasons why murder is 'easy'? Which of *N or M?* or *N and M?* is more accurate? And what are the ages of Tommy and Tuppence?

I am delighted to write an Introduction to this significant contribution to Christie scholarship; and I hope that readers will be sufficiently enthused by it to enjoy again her remarkable output.

Dr John Curran   Dublin, May 2021

PREFACE

This is Volume II of *Agatha Christie's Golden Age.* Volume I analysed the 21 novels featuring Hercule Poirot published in the UK before 1945. This companion volume analyses all the author's other (i.e. non-Poirot) crime novels published in the UK before 1945.

There are 13 such novels covering the period from 1922 to 1944. They are listed in chronological order on the Contents page, with the year of publication in the UK and, where a novel has a different title in the United States, with that title appearing in brackets.

They comprise

- six thrillers
- three Jane Marple detective stories
- two detective stories with other amateurs as the main sleuths
- one Superintendent Battle detective story
- *And Then There Were None*, the author's most popular masterpiece.

As in Volume I, each novel is analysed in a commentary by reference to the three puzzle elements of Solution, Plot and Clues. In view of the encouragingly positive feedback which I have received about that structure, I see no need to adjust it here. The reasons for adopting it are fully explained in Volume I (from p.35) and are not repeated here save that it may help readers to repeat that I defined the three elements as follows:

1. Solution: Creation of an ingenious and satisfying solution involving a clever and convincing murder plan and a credibly motivated but unexpected murderer.
2. Plot: Presentation of the murder and its suspects, clues, detection and solution in a well-paced, tightly-constructed plot, which engages, mystifies and deceives the reader until the denouement.
3. Clues: Detection of the solution through an assessment of fairly presented but imaginative clues which intrigue or deceive the reader.

Before the novels are analysed in the commentaries, there are three chapters. The first is about Jane Marple; the second is about Tommy and Tuppence Beresford, who appear in two of the thrillers; and the third is about the thrillers more generally.

Tommy and Tuppence are the author's best-known sleuths after Poirot and Jane Marple and, since only 13 novels are analysed in this volume (compared with 21 in the first), there is space for rather more detailed pen portraits of them, and of Jane Marple, than there was for Poirot in Volume I.[1] Hence the first and second chapters.

Both Miss Marple and Tommy and Tuppence appeared in a number of short stories during the Golden Age and, although there are references to those stories in the two chapters, the short stories are again not analysed in this volume. This is because, as I explained in Volume I (p.24), the solution in a short story occurs so relatively soon after the problem is posed that there isn't sufficient space or time for the same level of ingenuity, complexity, mystification, misdirection or detection as in a novel. As Agatha Christie herself said, "The short story technique, I think, is not really suited to the detective story at all" (*An Autobiography*, Part

VII section Three).

Since the thrillers comprise nearly half the novels in this volume, the third chapter is about the thrillers more generally. That chapter looks at the essence of thrillers, contrasting them with the author's detective novels and indicating why readers should not expect the same standards of plotting, clueing or solution from them.

There is, I believe, no need for an introductory chapter about *And Then There Were None*, even though it is the author's most popular work, since it is a stand-alone novel. It is, however, discussed in the chapter about thrillers.

Similarly, there is no introductory chapter for the three detective stories *The Sittaford Mystery, Murder is Easy* and *Towards Zero* since they, too, are stand-alone novels. The amateur sleuths in the first two novels are single-appearance detectives. Although the main detective in the third novel, Superintendent Battle of Scotland Yard, does feature in three other novels in this volume, two of them are thrillers (*The Secret of Chimneys* and *The Seven Dials Mystery*) and he appears only at the very end of *Murder is Easy*, in which he is not the main detective. He also appears in one other Golden Age novel, *Cards on the Table*, but that is a Poirot novel and so again he is not the main detective there.

It is notable that in nearly all the novels, the principal protagonist, or one of the principal protagonists, is a woman – not just in the case of Jane Marple (three times) and Tuppence Beresford (twice) but also Anne Beddingfeld, Lady Eileen 'Bundle' Brent (twice), Emily Trefusis, Lady Frances Derwent, Bridget Conway and Vera Claythorne.

The exception is the Battle novel, *Towards Zero*. This was published in the UK in July 1944 (and in the United States a month earlier) and it is my final Golden Age novel. When I started on the present volume, I was not sure when Agatha Christie's Golden Age should come to an end: perhaps in 1942, which is where Volume

I ended, or perhaps as late as the end of 1945. In the event, I have ended it prior to *Death Comes as the End*, which was published in the United States in October 1944 and in the UK in March 1945.

That novel was set in ancient Egypt at the suggestion of a close friend of the Christies, Stephen Glanville, who was Professor of Egyptian Archaeology at UCL at the time. As such, it was a highly innovative experiment and turned out to be a forerunner of the numerous historical crime puzzles that have appeared since.

But, even though it is a closed circle family mystery, it does not feel like a Golden Age puzzle. This is not just because of the unusual setting but also because the story has very little ingenuity and almost no clues or detection. Unlike *And Then There Were None*, where the closed circle reaches a mystifying zero, the Egyptian household circle does not reach zero but simply gets smaller and smaller, as the suspects are gradually eliminated from suspicion (literally, with seven murders) until the murderer is exposed and killed.

The author says in *An Autobiography* (Part X section Three) that she was "bullied" into writing the novel by Glanville and that he "argued with me a great deal on one point of my denouement, and I am sorry to say that I gave in to him in the end. I was always annoyed with myself for having done so ... I still think now, when I re-read the book, that I would like to re-write the end of it – which shows that you should stick to your guns in the first place, or you will be dissatisfied with yourself. But I was a little hampered by the gratitude I felt to Stephen for all the trouble he had taken, and the fact that it had been *his* idea to start with".[2]

Despite her annoyance, the novel which annoyed her the most was, as we saw in Volume I (p.133), *The Mystery of The Blue Train*. That 1928 novel must, as a matter of chronology, fall within her Golden Age since the Golden Age of detective fiction in the UK is generally regarded as being roughly the period between 1918 and 1945. However, a cut-off date close to 1945 needs to be chosen for concluding her Golden Age. In view of her dissatisfaction with the denouement of *Death Comes as the End*, she would, I think, have been rather surprised if I had concluded it with a cut-off date which placed that novel within it. So, with it, her Golden Age comes to an end.

After that, she was to write a further 31 crime novels, a number of which still have a Golden Age feel, although, as I said in Volume I (p.16), there was greater inconsistency in the 1940s in the quality of her work (meaning her work as puzzles) than in the previous decade. I cited *The Hollow* (1946) as an example because it is weaker on clues and detection than one would expect from a Poirot puzzle. Even the author herself regarded it as "in some ways rather more of a novel than a detective story", adding that it "…was a book I always thought I had ruined by the introduction of Poirot" (*An Autobiography*, Part IX section Five).

However, the characterisation in the novel is excellent, perhaps her best ever, and I fully appreciate that many of her readers derive their pleasure as much from factors such as characterisation, setting, humour and atmosphere as from the puzzle elements on which my analysis focuses – and sometimes more so.

Indeed, I think that after the War it was those factors, rather than attempts to adapt to a more modern age, that enabled her new books to sustain her popularity – at a level unmatched by other Golden Age writers – among crime readers who were perhaps no longer sufficiently satisfied by the supremacy of the puzzle elements which had symbolised Golden Age detective fiction. Her popularity in the UK was also sustained by Penguin's mass publication of paperback editions, starting in 1948 with ten of her pre-War novels in a total printing of one million copies. And her UK readership – of books both Golden and Modern – expanded again from 1962 with the Fontana paperback editions fronted by Tom Adams' brilliant covers.

Although her comments about *Death Comes as the End*

and Poirot 'ruining' *The Hollow* suggest that she wasn't pleased with her work at that time, this is by no means to say that she stopped writing good puzzles after the War. In fact, two of the novels published shortly after *The Hollow* would get into my overall Christie 'top ten'. The website accompanying Volume I (*Stylish Eye Press*) identified seven Poirot Golden Age novels as being in my Christie 'top ten' but did not identify the other three. I have received various requests to name the others and they are *And Then There Were None* (1939), *Crooked House* (1949) and *A Murder is Announced* (1950). The *Stylish Eye Press* website has been updated for Volume II but readers who might like to see an analysis of the latter two novels will have to wait a while for *Agatha Christie's Modern Age.*[3]

I suspect that all three of those novels would probably get into the 'top ten' of quite a lot of Christie aficionados. Two such aficionados, Kemper Donovan and Catherine Brobeck, have been reviewing the author's novels (in chronological order) and ranking them in their *All About Agatha* podcasts. I mention this not only to compliment them on their very engaging and insightful reviews but also because of a point that occurred to me when I listened to their podcast about *Lord Edgware Dies* (1933). That novel falls easily within my 'top ten' because, even though the murderer is really rather obvious in retrospect, it has two of the author's best clues and an intricate murder plan which I still remember amazing me when I was starting to read her books as an 11-year-old.

Some suspects in that novel are actors and in the podcast Kemper and Catherine say that they seem to have commented, in almost every podcast, on stories which have 'actors, actors, everywhere'. They warn us that we need to be 'very, very suspicious of anything that actors are doing' and be 'on our guard'.

Those warnings are entirely reasonable since they had by that stage reviewed six novels and three short stories which featured actors. However, the 'actor' warning is an example of seasoned

Christie readers having an advantage over newcomers. That is because they will often recognise a situation in a novel as one which she has used in other stories and then treat that situation, rightly or wrongly, as a signpost to the solution in the novel they are now reading.

Those readers will therefore be wary not only of actors (*Edgware; Tragedy*) but also – taking just a handful of examples – of love triangles (*Nile, Evil*); the time of death (*Christmas, Appointment*); obvious suspects who have a good alibi (*Styles, Library*); intended victims who survive (*Peril, Buckle*); and people helping the detective (*Ackroyd, ABC*). I have cited only two novels for each example, although many more could be given, and in fact, a number of those novels feature more than one of those situations.

The relevance of all this is that it occurred to me when I heard the 'actor' warning that I should clarify one element of my definition of 'Clues'. I said in Volume I (p.46) that I am analysing each novel *individually*. So I assess clues as they appear in the *novel being analysed* and do not treat signposts from other novels (which some readers may not have read) as clues, even though seasoned readers understandably do so.

Finally, I ought to refer to *Curtain* (1975) and *Sleeping Murder* (1976) which, despite being the last two Christie novels to be published, were in fact written in the 1940s but held in reserve by her. It seems clear that *Curtain* was written in about 1940 (during the Golden Age) but there is a well-reasoned disagreement among Christie scholars as to whether *Sleeping Murder* was written at about the same time or much nearer the end of the decade (after the Golden Age). I am not going to contribute here to that debate. All I think I ought to clarify at this stage is that, even if the novels were *written* during the Golden Age, they fall outside the scope of my two volumes because they were not *published*, or therefore known to readers, within it.

CHAPTER 1

Miss Jane Marple

Miss Jane Marple appears in 12 novels and 20 short stories published between 1927 and 1976. She lives in the village of St Mary Mead, which is in Downshire in *The Murder at the Vicarage* (her first novel) but in Radfordshire in *The Body in the Library* (her second). She is described by the Vicar, Leonard Clement (narrator of *The Murder at the Vicarage*), as "a white-haired old lady with a gentle, appealing manner". She is well-bred and ladylike but of limited means, though able to afford a maid.

Readers of that first novel, published in October 1930, could fairly assume that it marked her debut unless they had come across any of the 12 short stories which were published in magazines between December 1927 and May 1930, starting with *The Tuesday Night Club*. Those short stories did not appear in book form until 1932 when they were, with a further short story, collected together in *The Thirteen Problems*.[1] As explained in the Preface, the short stories are not analysed in this volume. Only the Golden Age novels are analysed – namely, *The Murder at the Vicarage*, *The Body in the Library* and *The Moving Finger*, which are abbreviated in this chapter to *Vicarage*, *Library* and *Finger*.

It appears from *An Autobiography* that the author had three sources of inspiration for the character of Miss Marple.[2] First, she thinks it possible that Miss Marple arose from the pleasure she had taken in portraying Caroline Sheppard in *The Murder of*

Roger Ackroyd (1926). Caroline had been her favourite character in the book – "an acidulated spinster, full of curiosity, knowing everything, hearing everything: the complete detective service in the home".

Second, she says that Miss Marple was the sort of old lady who would have been like some of her grandmother's Ealing cronies – old ladies whom she had met in so many villages where she had gone to stay as a girl.

Third, she says that, although Miss Marple was not in any way a picture of her grandmother, they had one thing in common, which was that, despite her grandmother being a cheerful person, she always expected the worst of everyone and everything, and was, with almost frightening accuracy, usually proved right. And, indeed, in *Vicarage,* the first thing we learn about Miss Marple is that (according to Griselda, the Vicar's wife) "She's the worst cat in the village. And she always knows every single thing that happens – and draws the worst inferences from it".

That is true. But she can also make us smile with observations that are humorous or which sound genuine but which are not, one suspects, entirely sincere. Thus, in her very first short story *The Tuesday Night Club* she thinks that forming a club would be "very interesting especially with so many clever gentlemen present". And she continues with the 'gentlemen' theme in *Vicarage*, for example: "Gentlemen require such a lot of meat, do they not? And drink." (chapter 17); "Gentlemen are so clever at arranging things" (chapter 30); and, best of all, "Gentlemen always make such excellent memoranda" (when she knows that Clement's schedule in chapter 26 focuses on two suspects who do not fit her theory).

And she can look at herself humorously. Thus, in chapter 30 Clement likes her "humorous perception of her own weakness" when she says that the murderers realised that, once she had seen them go into the studio, she wouldn't leave her garden until they came out. After all, he knows that "Miss Marple sees everything" (chapter 2) and he even refers to "the danger point of Miss Marple's garden" (chapter 3).

In chapter 26 she explains to him why she is so interested in the murder: "…my hobby is – and always has been – Human Nature. So varied – and so very fascinating. And, of course, in a small village, with nothing to distract one, one has such ample opportunity for becoming what I might call proficient in one's study. One begins to class people, quite definitely, just as though they were birds or flowers, group so-and-so, genus this, species that. Sometimes, of course, one makes mistakes, but less and less as time goes on. And then, too, one tests oneself. One takes a little problem – for instance the gill of picked shrimps that amused dear Griselda so much – a quite unimportant mystery but absolutely incomprehensible unless one solves it right … It is so fascinating, you know, to apply one's judgment and find that one is right … I have always wondered whether, if some day a really big mystery came along, I should be able to do the same thing. I mean – just solve it correctly".

We will look in a moment at how she solves her mysteries but it is first worth mentioning the "little problem" that amused Griselda since it relates to Miss Marple's first ever reference to an incident from village life in *The Tuesday Night Club*. It concerns two gills of picked shrimps (meaning ones that have had their heads and shells removed) which disappeared after being purchased at Elliot's by Mrs Carruthers. Miss Marple refers to it as an "unsolved mystery" but suggests that there are all kinds of explanations for it. Frustratingly, however, she is interrupted by her nephew Raymond before she can let us know what the explanations are or tell us the solution to this first mystery.

Despite that, the mystery is nevertheless referred to again fleetingly in later stories. Thus, in the tenth Problem, *A Christmas Tragedy*, Sir Henry Clithering jokingly mentions the "epic of the shrimps". In *Vicarage* Griselda alludes to it in chapter 11, when she says "I wish you'd solve the case, Miss Marple, like you did the time Miss Wetherby's gill of picked shrimps disappeared" – this is presumably the same incident, although the lady and the number of gills are different. And in *Sleeping Murder* (1976) Raymond gives examples of the kind of problems his aunt adores in chapter 3, including "Why a gill of pickled shrimps was found where it was" (he means 'picked', not 'pickled').

Turning, then, to how Miss Marple solves her mysteries and problems, a short section on her detection methods was included in Volume I (from p.22) simply to compare her methods with Poirot's. However, for this volume, a more extended section is now appropriate, small parts of which inevitably duplicate the section in Volume I.

She starts by collecting the facts. She then produces a theory and works back to the facts to check that they fit and, if they do, the theory has to be the right one. She says in *Vicarage* chapter 26, "Each thing has got to be explained away satisfactorily. If you have a theory that fits every fact – well, then, it must be the right one".

But how does she produce her theory in the first place? Sometimes, but rarely, she uses logic. For example, she produces a genuinely good logical analysis in relation to the timing of the 'Protheroe note' clue supposedly written at 6.20 pm in *Vicarage*. However, on other occasions when she presents her ideas in a way that *sounds* logical, this does not always withstand scrutiny.

For example, with her 'unreal letters' clue in *Finger*, she concludes that the anonymous letters were just a smoke screen, written by a *man* because of their style (not pointed enough) and their content (not enough knowledge or gossip). This sounds quite logical but a few paragraphs later she says that the letters represented a *woman's* mind. And in *Library* she suggests that the body in the burnt-out car is Pamela Reeves because she would have had to pass through Danemouth to get home after the Girl Guide rally. Again, that sounds quite logical but, really, she is jumping to a conclusion because she hasn't been told where the car was, let alone that it was near Danemouth, or even that the body was a girl (and in fact she turns out to be wrong).

She would appear more logical if she took us more carefully through the murderer's planning in her explanations. So, sticking with *Library*, she doesn't explain why the two murderers drugged Pamela instead of murdering her straightaway or why the body in the library was wearing a shabby white dress rather than the better pink one or why Ruby Keene was instructed to change out of the pink dress in her room before going to Josie Turner's room. These all have good logical answers when we think about them, as she leaves us to do, but one feels that she should have explained them herself.

If, therefore, it is rare for her to produce her theories with genuine logic, how does she do so? Mainly, the answer lies in two special talents – an instinct for recognising evil and a thorough appreciation of human nature.

The first talent, her instinct for recognising evil, is honed by a mistrust of almost everyone. This is borne out partly by the comments of other characters in the novels. Thus, in *Vicarage* Clement says that she "systematically thinks the worst of everyone"; in *Library* Clithering says she has "a mind that has plumbed the depths of human iniquity and taken it as all in the day's work"; and in *Finger* Maud Dane Calthrop describes her as knowing "more about the different kinds of human wickedness than anyone I've ever known".

It is also borne out by the comments Miss Marple makes about herself. Thus, in *Vicarage* she says "I always find it prudent to suspect everybody just a little" and later "...there's a lot of wickedness in the world. A nice honourable upright soldier like you doesn't know about these things, Colonel Melchett". In *Library* she murmurs "One does see so much evil in a village" and she extends the comparative innocence of soldiers to policemen when saying "The truth is, you see, that most people – and I don't exclude policemen – are far too trusting for this wicked world. They believe what is told them. I never do. I'm afraid I always like to prove a thing for myself".

Her most important quotation in this context is her earlier comment in that novel that "...everybody has been much too *credulous* and *believing*. You simply cannot *afford* to believe everything that people tell you. When there's anything fishy about, I never believe anyone at all!" The quotation is important because she was giving us a clue not to trust Josie's (false) statement that the body in the library was Ruby's.

Her second talent, a thorough appreciation of human nature (a "hobby" in fact, as we saw earlier from her long quotation about it), is honed by careful observation (her garden overlooks the Vicarage) and by an impressive recollection of village gossip, enabling her, as she says in *Vicarage*, "to compare people with other people you have known or come across". Thus, when Clement warns Redding not to underestimate the detective instinct of village life, he says that "There is no detective in England equal to a spinster lady of uncertain age with plenty of time on her hands" – although Gill rather belittles Clement's warning (p.203) as "a classic justification" for the existence of elderly amateur female sleuths such as Miss Marple by saying that, in the real world, this is "nonsense" since crimes are solved by the police, not little old ladies.

Be that as it may, Miss Marple is able, with her second special talent, to explain the likely behaviour of a particular person (such as a suspect) by reference to the comparable way in which someone else (such as a villager) had behaved in the past. As she tells Clithering in *Library*, "Human nature is very much the same anywhere, Sir Henry".

With these two special talents, she is able to draw parallels between village life and the more significant crimes she is detecting and so sometimes (but not always) to solve murders by using village analogies – that is to say, by using, as Professor Bargainnier puts it (p.74), "analogical reasoning" (meaning reasoning by analogy). As we are told in *Library*, she "had attained fame by her ability to link up trivial village happenings with graver problems in such a way as to throw light upon the latter" and later by Clithering that she has "an interesting, though occasionally trivial, series of parallels from village life".

These village analogies may reflect (a) the appearance or character traits of villagers or (b) acts of minor wrongdoing committed by them or (c) relationships between them. But it is usually hard to know whether the village analogy actually *prompts* her idea or simply *reinforces* an idea that has already occurred to her. Either way, the analogy may be used to give readers a clue when it is too early to reveal the actual idea itself or to explain a conclusion she has reached.

The best Golden Age novel for village parallels is *Library*. The main parallel she draws there is between the body in the library and Edie Chetty, so giving us clues about fingernails, teeth and clothing – the 'fingernails' clue being the most important one in the novel.

She also compares, albeit in more throwaway fashion, Josie to Jessie Golden, an ambitious young woman, who married the "son of the house", just as Josie turns out to be married to Mark Gaskell; and she compares Mark to Mr Cargill, the builder, who was able to explain his bills away "plausibly", just as Mark "plausibly" persuades Pamela to come for a screen test. And she tells us of Tommy Bond putting a frog in a school clock, which is analogous to Basil Blake putting the body in the library by way of a prank to annoy Colonel Bantry.

However, she also has a couple of village parallels relating, not to the murder plan or to clues, but to the relationship between young women and older men, which Peter Keating analyses (from p.126) and describes as a major theme ignored by commentators. She refers in chapter 8, in the context of Conway Jefferson and Ruby, to the village parallels of Mr Harbottle and Mr Badger and to the tale of King Cophetua and the Beggar Maid. And the background, of course, is the body of a young girl found in the library of Colonel Bantry who is sometimes "a little silly about pretty girls who come to tennis".

Although *Library* is therefore relatively rich with parallels, this is not really the case with the other two novels. In *Vicarage* Miss Marple may have been convinced that Hawes, the curate, was the thief because he reminded her so much of the organist who took the money for the choirboys' outing. And she may have thought that the person pretending to be Dr Stone was an imposter because he reminded her of the woman who pretended to represent Welfare and of the man who pretended to be a Gas Inspector. But she does not draw any village parallels to identify Lawrence Redding or Anne Protheroe as the murderers or to work out how they committed the murder.

And, similarly, in *Finger,* she does not draw any village parallels to identify Richard Symmington as the murderer or to work out how he murdered his wife, Mona. She does not even draw any village parallels about anonymous letter writers or about the typical style or content of anonymous letters (despite being so clear about this with the 'unreal letters' clue).

Perhaps most noticeably of all, she draws no parallels about Symmington's motive – based on his love for the much younger Elsie Holland – or, therefore, how she knows that "gentlemen, when they fall in love at a certain age, get the disease very badly" or that Symmington "hadn't really the strength to fight his madness" (chapter 14). This is a little surprising in view of the equivalent parallels which, as we have just seen, she draws in *Library.* Maybe she felt that she had already said enough there about the 'Cophetua complex' and didn't want to rehearse it again with Symmington and Elsie – or Jerry and Megan.

So, if it is rare for her to use genuine logic or village parallels to make the key deductions, how does she boost her two special talents? The answer is that she also jumps to correct conclusions, which can only be put down to intuition.

Intuition had been explained by Poirot in *The Murder of Roger Ackroyd* (1926): "Women observe subconsciously a thousand little details, without knowing that they are doing so. Their subconscious mind adds these little things together – and they call the result intuition" (chapter 13). It is also explained by Miss Marple in *Vicarage* where she discusses it with Clement (chapter 11), indicating that, if one thing reminded you of another, this was "really what people call intuition" and that this was "a very sound way of arriving at the truth".

She went on to explain that "Intuition is like reading a word without having to spell it out. A child can't do that because it has had so little experience. But a grown-up person knows the word because they've seen it often before." And she agreed with Clement's summary of her point "…if a thing reminds you of something else – well it's probably the same kind of thing" (chapter 11).

In *Library*, when Jefferson assumes that Miss Marple uses "Woman's intuition", Clithering responds "No, she doesn't call it that. Specialised knowledge is her claim" (chapter 8). His response is a reference back to the short story *Death by Drowning*, the last of *The Thirteen Problems*. There, Miss Marple says that "It's very difficult to understand what you might call specialised knowledge", which enabled her to identify a murderer because, several years before, a man called Peasegood had left turnips instead of carrots when he came with a cart and sold vegetables to her niece.

In *Murder is Easy*, which could have been an ideal setting for a Miss Marple novel, Luke Fitzwilliam refers to "guesswork" (chapter 17). He says that "Every man should have aunts. They illustrate the triumph of guesswork over logic. It is reserved for aunts to *know* that Mr A. is a rogue because he looks like a dishonest butler they once had."

Whether intuition derives from specialised knowledge or from years of experience or from being reminded of something similar or from subconscious observation or simply from guesswork, there are occasions where it is the only way of explaining an inference which Miss Marple has correctly drawn.[3]

Thus, as early as chapter 6 in *Vicarage* she is "quite *convinced* I know who did it. But I must admit I haven't one shadow of proof" and, as we later learn in chapter 30, she was referring (correctly) to Redding and Anne. And in *Finger*, one could reasonably assume, when re-reading chapter 10 (her first appearance in the novel) and chapter 14 (her explanations), that she had actually solved the puzzle before even appearing in the story (having had the background from Maud), particularly since, as she says in chapter 14, the very first person one thinks of in such a case is the *husband*.

In *Library* there can be no doubt that she had managed to work out by the end of chapter 8 (and perhaps well before) how the body came to be in the library. She doesn't tell us at that point *how* this happened. But it is clear, from her later analysis, that she already knew by then that a "very careful plan" was made to implicate Blake and that it "went wrong because human beings are so much more vulnerable and sensitive than anyone thinks" (chapter 8).

We are perhaps meant to assume from her later analysis that what she had been hinting there was that Blake, who was vulnerable to an accusation of murder by his wife and sensitive to Bantry's sneering, moved the body from his own cottage to the library in order to play a prank on Bantry. Although we had known by then that Bantry wouldn't hear a good word about Blake and that the body was dressed for a party of the sort which Blake gave, it is hard to attribute the extensive inference which Miss Marple draws from those facts to anything other than intuition.

Of course, readers do not necessarily have her intuition, or her instinct for evil or her knowledge of village life, and can therefore find themselves regularly mystified (even in retrospect) by her knowing what is going on much earlier than seems justified by the available information.

So, with her detection technique being so opaque, what she tends to do, in order to keep readers engaged in trying to solve the puzzles, is to *give* clues to them *herself*. She does so (a) where the facts themselves had seemed to give no hint of a clue or (b) where they had given a hint but not in a sufficiently suggestive way for readers to realise that they were getting a clue without a prompt from her. Thus, to continue with the example about how the body came to be in the library, she essentially gives us three clues.

First, in chapter 1, she "understood" what Dolly Bantry meant when saying that the dead girl in the library "doesn't look real at all" and she "nodded her head" at Dolly's comment that "It just isn't *true!*". What she is doing there, with this 'unreality' clue, is hinting that the body shouldn't have been in the library at all, which she reinforces in chapter 8 by telling us that a "very careful plan" went wrong.

Second, in chapter 4, when indicating that she has an "*idea*" why the body was in the library, she refers to Tommy Bond and the new schoolmistress who went to wind up the clock and a frog jumped out. She is hinting, with the 'frog' clue, that the body was put in the library as the result of a prank.

Third, in chapter 8, when referring to the "very careful plan" going wrong, she says, as we have just seen, that it did so because human beings are so much more vulnerable and sensitive than anyone thinks. She seems to be hinting, with the 'vulnerable' clue, that, in considering who might have caused the "plan" to go wrong, we need to look for a character who is vulnerable and sensitive, namely Blake.

Looking beyond this example more generally at her technique of giving clues to readers, she does this in various different ways (with just one instance of each). She does so

- expressly (the 'no Elsie letter' clue in *Finger* being "*very important*" and "the most interesting thing I've heard yet");
- by telling us that she's just had an idea without telling us what it is (the 'plant pot' clue in *Vicarage*);
- by a more oblique remark (the 'credulous' clue in *Library*);
- by her manner (nodding, smiling and seeming pleased with the 'telephone message' clue in *Finger*);
- with a village parallel (the 'fingernails' clue in *Library*);
- by agreeing with a remark by another character (the 'unreality' clue in *Library*); or
- by prompting another character to give us the clue (the 'smoke' clue in *Finger*).

The overall result of her style of detection is that she usually has a very plausible theory rather than any proper evidence of the murderer's guilt. What this means – in each of the three novels considered in this volume – is that a trap needs to be set for the murderer.

Thus, in *Vicarage*, because "there's no proof – not an atom", a trap is set for Redding – a pretence by Haydock that he had been seen transposing Hawes's cachets – into which Redding falls by discussing the matter with Anne. In *Library*, because Miss Marple wants to be "doubly sure", a trap is set for Josie – a pretence that Jefferson is going to make a new will – into which she falls by trying to kill him. And in *Finger*, because there's "no evidence", a trap is set for Symmington – a pretence that Megan Hunter saw him tamper with Mona's cachet – into which he falls by trying to kill her.

It is perhaps notable in this last example that Miss Marple is prepared to use Megan, a girl of only 20, to bait the trap and that, when Jerry Burton tries to interfere and later tries to reprimand her, she looks at him sternly and says: "Yes, it was dangerous, but we are not put into this world, Mr Burton, to avoid danger when an innocent fellow-creature's life is at stake. You understand me?". Jerry understood, thus concluding Miss Marple's role in the novels of Agatha Christie's Golden Age. But the best Miss Marple novel was still to come – *A Murder is Announced* (1950).

CHAPTER 2

Tommy And Tuppence Beresford

Tommy Beresford and Tuppence Cowley's first novel is *The Secret Adversary* (1922). Tuppence's real name is Prudence but chapter 1 tells us that she is known to her intimate friends as Tuppence "for some mysterious reason".

The Secret Adversary is a thriller set in 1920 when Tommy and Tuppence are probably aged 25 and 19 respectively, as explained in the section at the end of this chapter. Despite the age difference, they had been childhood friends – "Tuppence and I have been pals for years. Nothing more", says Tommy. However, he goes on to say "Darling Tuppence, there was not a girl in the world to touch her!" and later, when he thinks she's dead, he says "…but I *loved* her. I'd have given the soul out of my body to save her from harm" (chapters 18 and 21).

At the end of the novel they decide to marry and have done so by the time of their next book, *Partners in Crime* (1929), which, as a collection of short stories, is not analysed in this volume.[1]

Their other Golden Age novel is another thriller, *N or M?* (1941). It is set in 1940, by which time they have twin children, Deborah and Derek. There were two later Beresford novels – *By The Pricking of My Thumbs* (1968) and *Postern of Fate* (1973).

Turning from the stories to the characters themselves[2], Tommy has a shock of exquisitely slicked-back red hair. His face is ugly – or, rather, pleasantly ugly – nondescript, yet unmistakably the face of a gentleman and sportsman. Tuppence, who is of medium height and slight build, has no claim to beauty, but there is character and charm in the elfin lines of her little face, with its determined chin and large wide-apart eyes that looked mistily out from under her straight black brows, and she has black bobbed hair.

She is the fifth daughter of an Archdeacon in Suffolk. She left home early in the First World War and came up to London where she worked for three years, 1915 to 1918, in various capacities. Initially she was a nurse in an officers' hospital where, in the ninth month, she came across her wounded childhood friend Tommy, now a Lieutenant, whom she had not seen for five years. At the end of the year she left the hospital and became the driver of, successively, a trade delivery van, a motor-lorry and a General. Then she entered a government office but was released after the Armistice.

Meanwhile Tommy, after his hospitalisation in 1916, had gone out to France again. Then he was sent to Mesopotamia where he was wounded for the second time and went into hospital there. Finally, he got stuck in Egypt until the Armistice, after which he was demobbed. At some stage while in France, he was "with the Intelligence", as he puts it. He must also have been promoted to Captain at some point since he is referred to by that rank in *N or M?* (chapters 1, 9 and 11 twice). But there is no reference to that promotion in *The Secret Adversary*, in which, when comparing his War to Tuppence's, he says "There's not so much promotion in mine".

When they meet at the start of *The Secret Adversary*, not having seen each other "for simply centuries", they have both spent months looking for a job. Although their opening words to each other sound upbeat – "Tommy, old thing!" and "Tuppence, old bean!" – they both desperately need money but their efforts to get it by orthodox methods have failed.

So, says Tuppence, "...suppose we try the unorthodox. Tommy, let's be adventurers!". She pursues the idea further, asking Tommy: "Shall we form a business partnership?", to which Tommy responds "Trading under the name of The Young Adventurers Ltd? Is that your idea, Tuppence?". Indeed it is. They plan to place a newspaper advertisement saying "*Two young adventurers for hire. Willing to do anything, go anywhere. Pay must be good. No unreasonable offer refused*" – although in fact their first adventure starts before they place the advertisement, which later leads to them working for 'Mr Carter'.

As characters, they are both very engaging. Although this is mainly because of their interplay with, or thoughts about, one another, they have different personalities, making, as Carter puts it, "a pretty pair working together. Pace and stamina".

Tommy is not distinguished by any special intellectual ability. He says "I'm a bit of an ass, as you know" and reckons he's "not a very brainy sort of chap". He might be slow in his mental processes but he is very sure and it is quite impossible to lead him astray through his imagination because he hasn't got any – making him difficult to deceive. He worries things out slowly and, once he's got hold of something, he doesn't let go. He is emphatically at his best in a 'tight place' and he brightens at the thought of an encounter with his fists, which is infinitely more in his line than a verbal encounter.

Tuppence is quite different – with more intuition and less common sense, and she is optimistically given to overlooking the disadvantages and difficulties which Tommy sees. She is described as "one in a thousand!" for the smart way she inveigles herself into an assignment which Tommy is given in *N or M?*, although she does concede in *The Secret Adversary* that "I've always thought I was so much cleverer than Tommy – but he's undoubtedly scored over me handsomely". She relied a good deal on his judgment – there was something so eminently sober and clear-headed about him, and his common sense and soundness of vision were so unvarying, that without him Tuppence felt much like a rudderless ship.

In *N or M?* Tommy thinks that his life with Tuppence had been and would always be "a Joint Venture" (chapter 3). But by then, when they are eager to assist with the Second World War effort, it seems that neither is wanted in any capacity because they are too old (Tommy being 46 and Tuppence probably 39) and that their joint venture is no longer so much fun. Tuppence remembers in chapter 4 what "fun" it was and how "excited" they were when hunting down Mr Brown in *The Secret Adversary* and wonders why it isn't the same now. Tommy replies that "This is the second war we've been in – and we feel quite different about this one" because, explains Tuppence, "we see the pity of it and the waste – and the horror. All the things we were too young to think about before".

The Beresfords' Ages

It is helpful, in establishing the ages of Tommy and Tuppence, to work out when their books are set because information about their ages in one book can then be used to establish or confirm their ages in others.

(i) *The Secret Adversary*: In chapter 4 Carter tells Tommy and Tuppence that the draft treaty came into being in the "early days" of 1915 and, 11 paragraphs later, that "five years ago, that draft treaty was a weapon in our hands; today it is a weapon against us"; and in chapter 25 Jane refers to "Five years! Five long years!" as the period for which she has pretended to lose her memory since the sinking of the *Lusitania* on 7 May 1915. So, the story is set in 1920. And, if the references by Carter and Jane to "five years" literally mean five years from, respectively, the early days of 1915 and 7 May 1915, then we are talking about spring 1920 (as confirmed by *N or M?* – see below). At the end of the book, Tommy and Tuppence decide to get married.

(ii) *Partners in Crime*: Chapter 1 says that the book starts six years after their marriage. So, if they were married reasonably soon after deciding to wed – in, say, the summer of 1920 – the book very probably starts towards the end of the summer of 1926. Indeed, the magazine story of 24 September 1924 (titled *Publicity*), on which chapter 1 is based, actually says that the marriage took place four years ago; and so the author, in deliberately changing four years (in the magazine story) to six years (in the novel), clearly intended it to be set in 1926. Chapter 1 also tells us that the book will cover a period of about six months and by chapter 21, which is near the end of this 23-chapter book, it is Christmas. So the six-month period very probably runs from about August 1926 to January 1927.

(iii) *N or M?*: In chapter 1 we are told that it is the spring of 1940. So that is clear. But *N or M?* also helps us with *The Secret Adversary* because Grant says to Tommy that it is "over 20 years since you worked for the department". Since he was doing "pure office work" (rather than work for the "department") when he was "more or less in the Secret Service" at the start of *Partners in Crime*, Grant must be referring to *The Secret Adversary*. And, since he says "over" 20 years, *The Secret Adversary* cannot have been set later than the early spring of 1920.

Of course, one accepts that the author may not have intended the degree of precision indicated above but, whether she did or not, the dates of 1920 (first half), 1926 (second half) and 1940 (first half) fit together very well for Tommy and Tuppence.

Turning, then, to their ages, the books tell us the following:

(i)   *The Secret Adversary*: We are not told how old Tommy and Tuppence are – only, at the start of the book, that their "united ages would certainly not have totalled forty-five".

(ii)   *Partners in Crime*: Chapter 2 tells us that Tuppence is not "a day over twenty-five"; and Chapter 7 tells us that Tommy is 32.

(iii) *N or M?*: Chapter 1 tells us that Tommy is 46 (which fits precisely with *Partners in Crime*, assuming that he was already 32 in the spring of 1926).

What this means in relation to *The Secret Adversary* is that in 1920:

(a)   Tommy, who was 46 in spring 1940, would have been 25 or 26, depending on which month he was born; and

(b)   Tuppence, who was not "a day over twenty-five" in *Partners in Crime* (set in 1926) could not have been older than 18 or 19 six years earlier, depending on which month she was born.

Those conclusions make sense of the assertion in *The Secret Adversary* that the united ages of Tommy and Tuppence "would certainly not have totalled forty-five". One's instinct is to bring their ages as close together as mathematically permitted by the data, meaning that:

(a)   Tommy is 25 at the start of *The Secret Adversary* (and not 26 until, say, May 1920 or 46 until May 1940); and

(b)   Tuppence is 19 (and still 19 in August 1920 so that she is not over 25 by August 1926, meaning that she would be 39 in May 1940).

This gives a united age of 44 in the early days of 1920.[3]

Finally, in *N or M?* Tommy and Tuppence have twin children, Deborah and Derek. We are not told their ages. We know, however, that *Partners in Crime* ends with Tuppence being pregnant and, since there are no references to any other children in *N or M?*, the twins were presumably the result of that pregnancy. As noted earlier, *Partners in Crime* appears to end in January 1927. So the twins must have been born after the spring of that year, meaning that by spring 1940 they can only have been 12. However, Deborah works in the coding department and Derek in the Royal Air Force in *N or M?*. That cannot be right.

CHAPTER 3

Thrillers

Thrillers and detective stories are two different types of crime fiction.

Detective stories are cerebral – requiring brainwork and intellect – and involve detectives, whether they be amateurs or policemen or a combination of both, seeking, usually, to solve murder puzzles. As I explained in Volume I (p.39), quoting Rodell (chapter 3), "It is the detection, then, which is of prime importance in a detective story: the unravelling of the puzzle." The detective story's success as a puzzle depends on the ingenuity of the crime and solution and on the plotting and clueing of the story.

Thrillers are not generally cerebral. They classically comprise heroes hunting for, and/or being hunted by, villains. Those villains may be murderers or master criminals or conspirators engaged in crime or politics or espionage, while the heroes may not be detectives at all but adventurers who enjoy sleuthing or innocent people who are caught up in events beyond their control. The essence of a thriller is the physical danger posed to the hero by the villain and a thriller's success depends more on the menace, excitement and suspense generated in overcoming that danger than on ingenious solutions, tight plotting or deceptive clueing.

As a result, the author found thrillers easier to write. She refers in *An Autobiography* to "...the light-hearted thriller, which is particularly pleasant to do" and contrasts this with "the intricate detective story with an involved plot which is technically interesting and requires a great deal of work, but is always rewarding".[1]

Readers should not therefore expect the puzzle elements of the author's thrillers to exhibit the same high standards which she set for her detective stories. Indeed, the 1928 'rules' of detective fiction considered in Volume I (from p.32) were not intended to apply to thrillers. Thrillers often had an international element and Van Dine's Rule 19 says: "International plottings and war politics belong in a different category of fiction – in secret-service tales, for instance". Five of the author's six thrillers analysed in this volume involved international plotting or war politics and, although the other, *Why Didn't They Ask Evans?*, is a domestic thriller, it does have foreign elements.

The first of those six thrillers was *The Secret Adversary* (1922), which featured Tommy and Tuppence. The author says in *An Autobiography* that "It was fun, on the whole, and much easier to write than a detective story, as thrillers always are". But it does anticipate a device which she was to use to use from time to time in her detective stories – the villain being someone who appears to be helping the sleuths.

Her second thriller was *The Man in the Brown Suit* (1924), which is notable because some of the chapters are diary extracts written by the person who turns out to be the master criminal. So, again, the thriller anticipates a device – that of the narrator as murderer – which the author was to use so successfully two years later in a detective story *The Murder of Roger Ackroyd*. Whether or not that device constituted 'cheating' in *Ackroyd* was carefully analysed in Volume I and, even though it was deployed much less extensively in *The Man in the Brown Suit*, I will also consider the 'cheating' issue in the commentary on that novel.

Her final thrillers of the decade were *The Secret of Chimneys* (1925) and its successor, which included some of the same characters, *The Seven Dials Mystery* (1929). They were again, as she says in *An Autobiography*, of "the light-hearted thriller type ... always easy to write, not requiring too much plotting and planning". Both *The Secret Adversary* and *The Man in the Brown Suit* had had elements of humour and the author continued to write amusingly in *The Secret of Chimneys* and *The Seven Dials Mystery*. However, both those stories are ludicrously unbelievable.

The next thriller, *Why Didn't They Ask Evans?* (1934), was less overtly comic, instead having a much more intriguing central mystery than any of its predecessors. Even the title makes you want to know what the story is about. It feels more cerebral than the other five thrillers and its main mystery (Carstairs' dying words about why Evans wasn't asked) could have been converted into a good detective story. But, even as a thriller, the coincidences in it mean that the plot does not feel as satisfying as it should.

Finally, the author came full circle in her sixth Golden Age thriller with a wartime spy story, *N or M?* (1941), in which Tommy and Tuppence make a comeback. With its wartime setting, the story is more serious than its predecessors. But it too relies overly on coincidence.

Indeed, there are quite a few coincidences in the thrillers. This can be frustrating but, as indicated earlier, loose plotting is more forgivable in thrillers than in detective stories – especially where the purpose of a coincidence is simply to get the story underway and not to assist in solving the puzzle. Thus, for example, the overheard conversations which occur early in *The Secret Adversary* and *The Man in the Brown Suit*, although hard to believe, are plotting devices which we accept for launching the stories, just as we also accept the coincidence that the two parcels are in the hands of the same person at the start of *The Secret of Chimneys*.

But the coincidences in *Why Didn't They Ask Evans?* – such as Carstairs and Frankie visiting the same solicitor; and "Mrs Templeton" being in the photograph on the piano – are of significant assistance in reaching the solution. So are the coincidences in *N or M?* – such as Tuppence being seen in Leahampton by someone known to her daughter; and later naming a book which conceals a list of German supporters. As such, the coincidences in those two stories feel much less acceptable.

Two years prior to *N or M?* the author published her most popular masterpiece *And Then There Were None* (1939). The murderer in that novel, Wargrave, says in his confession that he enjoys reading every kind of detective story and thriller. But which is this? Although the first victim, Marston, says "Whole thing's like a detective story", it is not because no one is a detective in the traditional sense and there is in fact little detection, although more cerebral readers will, of course, treat the story as one for exercising their brainpower to try to solve the apparently insoluble mystery.

Equally, while the story undoubtedly has a thriller's menace, excitement and suspense, it doesn't feel like a classic thriller because there's no hero to overcome the physical danger posed by the villain. Even Vera Claythorne, who seems to be the main character until the solution, is clearly no 'hero' because she intentionally allowed a young boy to drown. Therefore, although the novel is noticeably nearer to being a thriller than a detective story despite the cerebral element, it is probably best described as a 'murder mystery', which is why I refer to analysing six thrillers, not seven, in this volume.

Certainly, the brilliantly clever plotting of that novel puts it in a different category from the other six thrillers. It is well worth quoting here from the author's own comments in *An Autobiography* about writing the novel. She says that she had written it "...because it was so difficult to do that the idea had fascinated me … I wrote the book after a tremendous amount of planning … I knew better than any critic how difficult it had been … I don't say it is the play or book of mine I like best, or even that I think it is my best, but I do think in some ways that it is a better piece of *craftsmanship* than anything else I have written". She also noted that, after converting it into a play, there was never any suggestion, when she saw it performed, of "…the whole thing being too ridiculously thrillerish".

Finally, putting the thrillers into the context of the author's work in the Golden Age, she wrote nine crime novels during the 1920s. As we have seen, four were thrillers, as was the Poirot novel, *The Big Four*, while the other four novels were Poirot detective stories. So she was dividing time pretty evenly between thrillers and detective stories.

Of the 1920s thrillers analysed in the first four commentaries in this volume, *The Man in the Brown Suit* is, in my view, the best (despite the author saying she considered it "rather patchy" in *An Autobiography*). Although it has the most complex plot, its intricacies have, generally speaking, been more clearly and convincingly dovetailed than in the other thrillers. It is also the most readable of the four because of Pedler's engaging writing style and Anne's plucky narrative. And, of course, although there are surprises among the other thrillers, the one in this novel – the 'diarist as murderer' device – is the most striking.

As the author moved on from the "light-hearted" thrillers into the 1930s and 1940s, the "intricate" detective stories at which she excelled, especially those of Hercule Poirot, became very much her main focus. Although she did continue to write the occasional thriller, her special talent of puzzle construction – mingling detection with deception so skilfully – was not as well developed in the thrillers and, if she had written only those, we would probably not remember her today.

1

The Secret Adversary

Solution

Agatha Christie's second novel is a thriller set in 1920, shortly after the First World War, in which readers are introduced to Tommy Beresford and his equally penniless friend, Prudence Cowley (known as Tuppence). They are a captivating young couple, aged probably 25 and 19 respectively, as explained in the chapter about them.

Tuppence suggests to Tommy that, since the orthodox ways of making money have failed, they should try the unorthodox and become adventurers. Her idea is that they should form a business partnership trading under the name of The Young Adventurers Ltd. When she receives her first proposition, she refuses to proceed unless Tommy is also involved. By chapter 4 they are both working for a man known as Mr Carter, whom Tommy recognises from his time in Intelligence during the War.

Their adventure involves the hunt for a secret two-page draft treaty which was handed by a special messenger, Danvers, to an American girl, Jane Finn, on the *Lusitania* after it was torpedoed off the coast of Ireland on 7 May 1915. Danvers was killed but Jane, who was not, had vanished, along with the treaty.

Five years have passed and, although the treaty might have been a vital weapon for the Allies during the War, it would now be seen, if it were found and published, as a gigantic blunder. It might even bring about another war. If the Bolsheviks, who are manipulating the Labour Party leaders, can locate it, the Labour leaders will broadcast it throughout England and public opinion will swing to the Labour extremists and revolutionaries.

Behind the Bolsheviks is a master criminal with "possibly the finest criminal brain of the age". He is known as 'Mr Brown' but his real name is unknown. He controls an organisation with spies everywhere and probably seeks "supreme power for himself of a kind unique in history" (chapter 4).

Carter instructs Tommy and Tuppence to *"Find Jane Finn"*, the main puzzles being: (1) Which of the characters is 'Mr Brown'? (2) Where is the treaty, if it still exists? (3) Where is Jane, if she is still alive? (4) Who killed Mrs Marguerite (Rita) Vandemeyer, a member of Mr Brown's gang, before she could betray him (chapter 13)?

As for puzzle (1), we assume that Mr Brown is not going to be Tuppence, Tommy or Carter. We also assume (again correctly) that Mr Brown is not one of the minor suspects, namely Kramenin the Russian (a senior gang member, who is perhaps too obvious anyway with his title of Number One) or Boris Ivanovitch (another Russian member, who is followed by Tommy to the gang's "evil-looking" house in Soho) or Edward Whittington of the Estonia Glassware Co. (another member, whose meeting with Tuppence in chapter 2 initiates the adventure) or Dr Hall (the principal of a sanatorium in Bournemouth where Jane is detained).

So it is clear by no later than chapter 13 (out of 28) that there are only two suspects for the role of Mr Brown, particularly since they are the only two people present (besides Tuppence) when Rita Vandemeyer dies. They are Julius Hersheimmer, an American millionaire, who claims to be Jane Finn's cousin, and Sir James Peel Edgerton MP, the most celebrated King's Counsel in England and a possible future Prime Minister. In fact, Mr Brown turns out to be Edgerton but it is not until the denouement that readers can be certain that he, rather than Julius, is the villain.

At the end, we see extracts from his diary which explain his motivation – a craving for absolute power and a wish to apply his exceptional brain power in the criminal field where the standard was low but the opportunities were extraordinary. However, there is nothing particularly ingenious in the solution that Mr Brown is Edgerton rather than Julius.

Puzzles (2) and (3) – the whereabouts of Jane and the treaty – are best considered together. Jane is still alive. She had sailed on the *Lusitania* in order to take up a hospital post in Paris, having studied French in America. After it was torpedoed and Danvers had given her an oilskin packet containing the treaty, the rescued passengers were taken to Ireland and then by boat to Holyhead in Wales. As a precaution, Jane opened the packet, substituted blank paper, sewed it up again and put the two-page treaty inside a magazine which she carried in her bag.

On the boat to Holyhead, a woman (Rita Vandemeyer) was keen to befriend Jane. Then Jane saw her talking to some queer-looking men. And later, on the train from Holyhead to London, Jane was knocked out and kidnapped by Rita and other gang members. She woke in a squalid, windowless room in a house in Soho which had four battered old pictures on the wall representing scenes from *Faust*, Gounod's 1859 opera. The gang were very angry because the packet contained blank paper. What could she do?

First, she pretended she had lost her memory and started babbling in French. She played the part convincingly, appearing unable to remember her name, the oilskin packet or anything else. Second, on noticing that the magazine was still in her bag, she waited until the early hours of the morning and hid the treaty inside one of the four pictures, between the picture itself and its brown-paper backing.

The gang decided to keep Jane alive because she might recover her memory and remember where she had hidden the treaty. So, they watched her for weeks, regularly questioning her. Then they took her back to Ireland, and over every step of the journey, in case she had hidden the treaty *en route*. Then she was sent to Dr Hall's sanatorium in Bournemouth. And the years went on.

Now, five years after the sinking of the *Lusitania*, she is taken back to Soho where Tommy, having been seized after following Boris to the "evil-looking" house, is being held captive. Jane serves his meals, introducing herself as a French girl called 'Annette'. After a few days, she saves his life by helping him escape, but without revealing her true identity or escaping herself.

The gang, knowing that Tommy will tell Carter about the house, clear out, taking 'Annette' to a house called Astley Priors in Kent where they are also holding Tuppence, who had been lured there earlier with a telegram purporting to have come from Tommy. In chapter 24 Julius rescues Tuppence and 'Annette', who confirms that she is really Jane.

However, before the rescue is complete, Tommy appears and tells Tuppence and Jane to take the train to London and go straight to Edgerton where they will be "safe". As Julius tries to prevent them going, Tommy aims a revolver at him, making readers doubt that the rescue was genuine and creating the impression that Tommy thinks that Julius is really Mr Brown.

In fact, Tommy has a different purpose. But, before we learn it, Tuppence and Jane arrive at Edgerton's house. Jane tells him that the treaty is still inside the picture. So the three of them go to the Soho house where, after pocketing the treaty, Edgerton reveals that he is Mr Brown. However, as he is about to shoot the two girls, he is overpowered by Tommy and Julius. Tommy's real purpose had been to get to the house, with Julius, before Edgerton and lie in wait for him – although, when their grip on Edgerton slackens, he raises his signet ring to his lips and poisons himself with cyanide concealed inside.

Although the summary so far provides the solution to most of the story, there is still puzzle (4), the murder of Rita Vandemeyer before she can betray Mr Brown. However, we cannot assess Edgerton's ingenuity in murdering her because we are not told how he carried it out. Nor are we told definitively that she was murdered. All of which makes the episode very odd.

It begins in chapter 12, by which time Tuppence, who suspects Rita's involvement, has managed to get a job as her house-parlourmaid at her second floor flat in a mansion block, South Audley Mansions. In chapter 12 Tuppence, Edgerton and Julius decide that they will pay a surprise visit on Rita at 10 pm. However, before then, Tuppence, returning from her 'afternoon out', learns from Albert, the lift-boy at South Audley Mansions, that Rita is packing because she is about to leave the flat and has ordered a taxi.

So Tuppence asks Albert to telephone Julius and Edgerton and ask them to come to the flat at once (not waiting until 10 pm). She then goes up to the flat, wondering how to detain Rita until the two men arrive. She tries to persuade her to identify Mr Brown and the two men arrive just after Rita has agreed to do so for £100,000. Their arrival causes her to shriek in terror and faint.

Edgerton and Tuppence carry her to her bed while Julius fetches a glass of brandy from the dining room. He hands this to Edgerton. As Tuppence lifts Rita's head, Edgerton tries to force a little of the spirit between her closed lips. Rita opens her eyes feebly and Tuppence then holds the glass to her lips. Rita drinks before falling back with a groan, still alive but with her eyes closed.

Tuppence tells Julius and Edgerton that Rita had been willing to disclose the identity of Mr Brown but had been very frightened in case her intended betrayal had been overheard ("Even the walls might have ears", she had whispered). They decide that she must be safeguarded. But, when Rita hears that Julius and Edgerton are to split the vigil overnight, her face has an expression of mingled fear and malevolence and she struggles to say to Tuppence "Don't – leave – sleepy – Mr – Brown".

So Tuppence insists on sitting up with Julius and Edgerton. As Rita sleeps, Tuppence locks Rita's bedroom door, having checked that there is no hiding place in the room, and takes the key. Julius goes to reassure Albert and then to the larder for food while, as far as we know, Edgerton remains with Tuppence. The three of them then spend the night in the boudoir, apparently awake together, while Rita is in the bedroom.

At 7 am Tuppence makes tea and unlocks the bedroom door. She finds that Rita has been dead for some hours and notices that her little bottle of chloral sleeping draught, which had been three parts full, is now empty. A doctor, hastily summoned and sensing an odour of chloral, accepts that she had accidentally taken an overdose.

If, however, it had been administered by someone other than Rita, we get no indication of how this might have been done other than in the brandy, which led to her falling back with a groan and closing her eyes. But Julius poured the brandy and, because he and Tuppence were present while it was given to Rita, Edgerton never had an opportunity to add any sleeping draught to it from the little bottle. And, as far as we know, he was then with Tuppence until she made the morning tea. So he must have murdered Rita with real ingenuity.

Presumably, he did kill her because it would seem too coincidental for her to die by suicide or by chance when she was about to betray him. Julius thinks it a "sure thing" that Mr Brown did it and he says that Tuppence and Edgerton also think so.

But how? Since we are not told, we can only speculate. Once Julius brings the brandy, Edgerton (who has been handed the glass by Julius) tries to force a little of the spirit between Rita's closed lips. This seems to be his only opportunity. But one cannot work out how he can have accessed the bottle of chloral or added it to the brandy, unseen. Maybe – somehow – he managed to slip some poison from his signet ring into the brandy, with no one noticing his sleight of hand or an odour of cyanide.

If, however, Rita was murdered after her bedroom door was locked, while Tuppence, Julius and Edgerton spent the night apparently awake together, no one else could have entered the bedroom through the door or through the window, whose balcony only went as far as the boudoir, where they were. Since, as Tommy later says, "Mr Brown hasn't got wings", Julius asks "How about some high-class thought transference stunt? Some magnetic influence that irresistibly impelled Mrs Vandemeyer to commit suicide?".

Unfortunately, readers waiting for the ingenious solution to be revealed will be disappointed since there is simply no explanation of how the murder took place, let alone confirmation that there was a murder. Although Tommy says in chapter 18 "I think the gifted young detectives must get to work, study the entrances and exits, and tap the bumps on their foreheads until the solution of the mystery dawns on them", this never happens.

Plot

The short Prologue, in which Jane Finn is given the draft treaty on the sinking *Lusitania* in May 1915, provides a promising start. Chapter 1 then moves us forward to London in 1920 and introduces us to Tuppence and Tommy, whose interplay provides engaging reading. However, they don't actually see as much of each other as we might expect during their adventures because, after the first six introductory chapters, they do not appear together again until the end of chapter 24 (out of 28).

Nevertheless, their separation is a successful plot device because it results in Tuppence sharing the adventures with Tommy so that they have equally significant roles, although it is Tommy who spots the identity of Mr Brown while Tuppence admits that she never suspected it (chapter 27). However, apart from quite a well thought-out denouement, the separation is really the only notable achievement in plot construction, which is understandable since the story comprises a series of episodes and there are only two suspects. Of course, the murder of Rita is a genuinely mystifying episode but it is ultimately an unsatisfactory one because we are not given the solution.

The adventure starts in a contrived way when Whittington overhears Tommy and Tuppence discussing their wish for adventure and offers Tuppence a job. When he asks Tuppence her name, she says hastily that it is Jane Finn, a name mentioned to her by Tommy, who heard two people in the street talking about someone of that name. One of them turns out to have been Whittington. So the adventure is initiated by the coincidence of Tommy overhearing Whittington, and Whittington later overhearing Tommy and Tuppence. Of course, this seems hard to believe but we accept the coincidence as a device for doing no more than getting the story underway.

The plot then moves forward, episode by episode, at a readable pace and with unusually regular descriptions of the food eaten by the main characters. The adventure starts in earnest when Whittington and Boris are followed as they leave Rita's mansion block: Julius follows Whittington to Dr Hall's sanatorium in Bournemouth where Jane is detained under the watchful eye of Nurse Edith before she is moved that night to the gang's house in Soho; and Tommy follows Boris to the Soho house, where he is captured and held before escaping some days later with help from 'Annette'. Meanwhile Tuppence, aided by Albert, becomes Rita's house-parlourmaid.

After Rita's death, Tuppence is lured to Kent by a telegram purporting (falsely) to come from Tommy, which reads "Come at once, Astley Priors, Gatehouse, Kent. Great developments –

Tommy". When Tommy and Julius learn that she had received a telegram, they go to her room and find it in the grate where she had thrown it after crumpling it up into a ball (chapter 18). Tommy smoothes it out. It reads "Come at once, Moat House, Ebury, Yorkshire, great developments – Tommy", as a result of which Tommy and Julius are lured to Yorkshire (not Kent).

It would seem that the original telegram had been altered because Edgerton later says (chapter 22) "Very simple and very ingenious. Just a few words to alter, and the thing was done". However, the alteration doesn't look "very simple", or even plausible. Although the beginning and end of the telegram remained the same (except the capital G of 'Great'), the key part (the address) was altered in its entirety and not even by words of the same length, which surely Tommy or Julius would have noticed. Perhaps, therefore, although this is not suggested in the story, the original telegram had not been altered but replaced with a second telegram containing the Yorkshire wording by one of the gang who had gone into Tuppence's room after she had left.

Whatever the explanation, Tommy and Julius waste a week in Yorkshire looking for Tuppence. They are then sent on a second wild goose chase to Holyhead by a girl, found by Edgerton, who pretends to be Jane Finn and tells them that she hid the draft treaty there. They do find the oilskin packet but it contains only a sheet of paper which reads "With the Compliments of Mr Brown", suggesting that he has got to the treaty first.

One does wonder about the purpose behind these two wild goose chases to Yorkshire and Holyhead. One can understand Edgerton imprisoning Tuppence in Kent (so that, if Tommy had learned anything at the Soho house, he could be silenced with a threat of violence against her) but his purpose in luring Tommy and Julius away is a lot less clear.

On the Yorkshire trip, they find Tuppence's brooch, and later her coat is washed up on the coast, making it look as if she has drowned. Perhaps Edgerton's thinking – though we are not told – is that, when he finally disposes of Tuppence (as we later learn he intended), her disappearance will attract no scrutiny if she is already thought to be dead.

As for the Holyhead trip, Tommy later suggests (chapter 22) that Edgerton's purpose in making it look as if Mr Brown had got to the treaty first (even though he hadn't) was to make Carter think that "the game was up". But what advantage would Edgerton get from this? Perhaps the answer – though again we are not told – is that Carter would then stop looking for the treaty. But that wouldn't help Edgerton find the treaty himself.

Earlier (chapter 21), Julius had wondered *how* Mr Brown might have got to the treaty first. Since he and Tommy had been directed to Holyhead by (so they thought) Jane, he asks "Do you reckon there was a dictaphone in Jane's room?" (chapter 21). This reminds us that he had said in chapter 13, in relation to Rita's remark about the walls having ears, that "Maybe she meant a dictaphone". One assumes that, on these two occasions where Julius refers to a dictaphone, he meant to refer to a hidden *microphone*, enabling someone outside Jane's room or Rita's flat to hear what was said inside.[1]

The final episode starts after Edgerton has apparently helped Tommy to locate Tuppence by advising him to ask Carter to obtain a copy of the *original* telegram sent to her. Carter does so and it contains the original Kent wording (chapter 22), prompting Edgerton to make his comment about how easily it could have been altered and prompting Tommy to go to Kent. Tommy later says that he had been suspicious of Edgerton but that his help "almost disarmed me, but not quite". So perhaps Edgerton's purpose in helping Tommy was to disarm him – but again we are not told.

The episode itself is, however, quite well constructed. After Tommy has arrived in Kent, he interrupts Julius's rescue attempt, as we saw earlier, and sends Tuppence and Jane *back* to Edgerton.

This results in Edgerton telling them that Julius is Mr Brown and brilliantly explaining how Julius had planned for Jane to lead him to the treaty, when in fact Edgerton smugly knows that Jane is about to lead *him* to the treaty.

That is quite clever because what Edgerton does not know in his smugness is that he has been tricked, in this game of relying on Jane to locate the treaty, because Tommy has sent Jane to him for the very purpose of leading him to the Soho house where he will be lying in wait with Julius.

Clues

Generally speaking, with one reasonably memorable exception, the clues in this story are, as one might expect from a thriller, not very imaginative. They tend to be quite simple or obvious or, conversely, too difficult to spot or interpret. They start with "two distinct clues" identified by Tuppence as she and Tommy begin the search for Jane.

In fact, these are not clues in the puzzle-solving sense but ideas about how to begin. Thus her first 'clue' is to look for Whittington, having met him in chapter 2. Tommy says (rightly) "I don't call that much of a clue" and "…it's about a thousand to one against your running against him by accident". In fact, however, they do find him by accident when they see him leave Rita's flat (and he is then followed by Julius to the Bournemouth sanatorium).

They locate the flat with Tuppence's second 'clue', which is the name 'Rita' mentioned by Whittington in chapter 2 (when asking Tuppence whether it was 'Rita' who had been blabbing). Tuppence "reasons" that 'Rita' was a passenger shadowing Danvers on the *Lusitania*. So, this 'Rita' clue sets Tommy and Tuppence searching for female survivors from the *Lusitania* living in London and thus to Marguerite Vandemeyer.

Although Rita is killed before providing any information, the name 'Marguerite' does provide a clue to puzzle (2), Jane's hiding place for the treaty inside one of the four pictures depicting scenes from the opera *Faust*. Since the opera is based on the German legend of a scholarly man who sells his soul to the Devil in return for power and pleasure, some readers may in retrospect regard the opera as a pointer towards Edgerton.

The picture in question is that of the character Marguerite with her casket of jewels and, as Tommy is escaping from the house, 'Annette' (Jane) says, in a clear voice which gets louder, "I want to go back to Marguerite. To Marguerite. *To Marguerite*". Although Tommy later supposes that she meant she wanted to go back to Marguerite Vandemeyer, Edgerton points out that she always signed herself 'Rita' (not Marguerite) and that all her friends spoke of her as 'Rita'.

In fact, 'Annette' had hoped that Tommy would think of the picture of Marguerite with her casket of jewels (chapter 25). Although he didn't think of it while escaping, he later remembered her shouting and thought of the picture – although this was a "guess", as he admits to Carter (chapter 22).

Readers would do very well to "guess" correctly in relation to the 'Marguerite' clue since the picture of her with her box of jewels is referred to only once (when the scenes in all four pictures are mentioned at the end of chapter 16). Indeed, it is one of the *other* pictures, that of the Devil and Faust, that is referred to on three more occasions (in chapter 17) – when Tommy unhooks it; when 'Annette' sees it next morning against the wall (and her look of terror changes to relief, presumably on seeing that he has not chosen the picture with the treaty in it); and when Tommy hits a gang member with it while escaping.

Having escaped, Tommy wants to find Tuppence and is told by a page-boy at the Ritz that she has taken a taxi to Charing Cross. This is obviously a clue that she's taking a train to the south-east – in fact to Astley Priors in Kent, where the solution to puzzle (3) is to be found because Jane is also there.

However, Tommy dismisses the 'Charing Cross' clue as a mistake for King's Cross when he sees the altered version of the telegram with the Yorkshire wording. He says, "Boy must have made a mistake. It was King's Cross, not *Charing Cross*". Edgerton later describes the page-boy's statement as "the one important clue they overlooked" but few readers would have overlooked what the page-boy had *actually* said.

On returning from Yorkshire, Tommy meets the fake Jane, who sends him to Holyhead with Julius. When they return, Julius realises that she was actually Nurse Edith, who had been at the Bournemouth sanatorium.[2] Edith had, when pretending to be Jane, spoken with "the slight warmth of the Western accent". Tommy found this (American) accent "vaguely familiar", which we assume is meant as a clue. But a clue to what?

The only girl of significance he has met in the story is 'Annette' but, for him to be reminded of her, she too must have spoken with a slight American accent. However, Tommy, like the reader, believes that 'Annette' is French and, indeed, she spoke either in French or in "soft, broken English". So, is it now being suggested (even though it was not at the time) that 'Annette' had in fact spoken with a slight American accent? If so, one would have expected Tommy to make much more of this 'Western accent' clue because it would have pointed strongly to her being Jane. But, as with the 'Charing Cross' clue, he dismisses it too quickly, thrusting "the impression aside as impossible".

The main clueing interest is in puzzle (1), the identity of Mr Brown, which includes puzzle (4), the death of Rita. In chapter 12, before Albert had asked Edgerton and Julius to come at once to Rita's flat (because she was planning to leave), they had agreed with Tuppence to come to the flat anyway at 10 pm to pay a surprise visit on Rita. It is really this 'surprise visit' clue which starts one thinking that Mr Brown must be either Julius or Edgerton because only one of them can have warned Rita that they would be coming to the flat at 10 pm and advised her that she should leave it before they arrive.

When they do so, earlier than Rita had expected, she gives her shriek of terror and faints. By the time she says to Tuppence "Don't – leave – sleepy – Mr – Brown", it is pretty obvious from this 'Don't leave' clue that there are only two suspects, even though Tuppence doesn't seem to realise this.

But which of the two is Mr Brown? Right from Julius's first appearance (chapter 5) he has seemed to be entirely on Tommy and Tuppence's side and, subject only to his duplicity about Jane's photograph (discussed below), this is the case pretty much throughout. He therefore seems a most unlikely suspect – not that Christie readers would be deterred by that from suspecting him. But, even by chapter 13, we already have a number of minor clues which suggest that Mr Brown is more likely to be Edgerton than Julius.

First, Carter says "I have every reason to believe he is an Englishman" (chapter 4). Second, Julius has been tricked (chapter 5) into giving his photograph of Jane *to* Mr Brown – a police imposter called 'Inspector Brown' – and so, if he is telling the truth about what happened, he cannot be Mr Brown himself. Third, the German gang member tells Number Fourteen that he will have "the best legal talent" to defend him if charged with murder (chapter 8). Fourth, Tuppence reads kindliness in Edgerton's glance but also "something else more difficult to fathom" (chapter 10). Fifth, and more significantly, Edgerton is quite insistent that Tuppence should not go back to Rita's flat before 9.30 pm on the night of the surprise visit "on any account" and should instead have a good dinner, "a really good one, mind" (which would give Rita time to pack her belongings and leave).

On the other hand, we cannot acquit Julius at that stage. Edgerton is after all a celebrated K.C. and possible future Prime Minister. Moreover, when Boris had suggested to Rita that she should end her relationship with Edgerton because Edgerton "can smell a criminal!" (chapter 10), she had replied that Edgerton "suspects nothing", which plainly suggests that she does not think he is Mr Brown. So he too seems a most unlikely suspect – though again Christie readers would not be deterred by that.

Then we come to Rita's death where the only tangible clue is the 'empty bottle' clue, which does not implicate one of Edgerton or Julius more than the other – although we do note that it was Julius who brought in the brandy and left Tuppence's presence twice, which Edgerton did not. We are also slightly troubled by Julius's pause before he denies having found anything in Rita's safe. But, although he turns out to have lied (because he found Jane's photograph there), Tuppence makes a bit too much of being unconvinced by his denial – twice in chapter 15 – with the result that we rightly think that it is probably a red herring in relation to the identity of Mr Brown.

In chapter 17 a genuinely strong pointer that Edgerton is Mr Brown is given to the astute reader when the gang, who have been holding Tommy captive at the Soho house for some days, tell him one evening that they are going to kill him. That is because Mr Brown has somehow found out who Tommy really is and has therefore seen through the bluff with which he has successfully kept himself alive over those days. But how has Mr Brown suddenly become aware of this because Tommy has given no clue to his identity and his disappearance has not become public?

To answer this, readers must show unusual patience in working back through a number of earlier chapters. Those who do will realise that Tommy was seized on a Wednesday and that it is a Sunday evening when the gang say they will kill him (which, for less patient readers, is confirmed two chapters later when Julius reckons that someone put the gang wise "not earlier than Sunday afternoon"). Those who work back will also establish that Sunday afternoon was when Tuppence and Julius first met Edgerton and told him their tale.

With the decision to kill Tommy coming soon after that meeting, this 'Sunday' clue makes it pretty clear that Mr Brown found out about Tommy when he was told the tale. Julius, we know (chapter 6), had learned "the whole history of the joint venture" before Tommy was even captured and so could have had him disposed of well before Sunday. The astute reader will therefore conclude that Mr Brown is Edgerton by chapter 17.

Other readers will probably think the same soon afterwards, either when Edgerton is "too wary to be drawn" on how he found the fake Jane (chapter 19) – which is unconvincingly explained away by Tommy as a "foible of the legal mind" – or when he offers Tommy a post in the Argentine (chapter 21), presumably as a ploy to get him out of the way.

However, our confidence in the conclusion is rather dented by the next clue, the photograph of 'Annette' found by Tommy in Julius's writing table. Up to that point, Tommy has "no doubt about her being one of the gang" and so it is suspicious that Julius should have a photograph of a gang member. But readers will remember that the only photograph which Julius had mentioned having was one of Jane. So, they will assume, rightly, that the photograph in the writing table, thought by Tommy to be of 'Annette', is in fact of Jane and that they are therefore one and the same.

But, if so, that is just as suspicious because Julius had told Tommy and Tuppence that he had given his only photograph of Jane to the police (the fake 'Inspector Brown'). So, if he still has it, it seems that he had lied about giving it to the police. In fact, however, the 'Annette photograph' clue is a red herring because he did not lie. He did surrender the photograph but, as noted earlier, he found it again in Rita's safe, although he claimed to have found nothing there simply because he did not want it taken from him again.

The final clue, which is in a note to Tommy, is the most

memorable. After he has arrived in Kent, he manages to signal his presence to Tuppence while she is held at Astley Priors. In response, he receives a note, apparently from her, in chapter 23 telling him that she and Annette are being taken from Astley Priors to Holyhead. The note is in Tuppence's handwriting but signed "Twopence". Tommy later says that she would "never" spell her name that way but that anyone who had not seen it written might easily do so.

So the 'Twopence' clue reveals that the note is a trick and Tommy, spotting it as such, pretends to go away, as the note had intended him to, but doubles back. He is therefore present, after Tuppence and Jane have been rescued by Julius, to send them both to Edgerton and thence to the Soho house where Edgerton is exposed.

But how does Tommy know which of Edgerton or Julius was responsible for the trick? The answer is that he knows that Julius had seen the correct spelling of 'Tuppence' in a note which she had sent him in chapter 15, and which he showed to Tommy in chapter 18. Edgerton, however, had never seen Tuppence's name written down, which neatly distinguishes him from Julius. A possible criticism of the clue is that Julius could still be Mr Brown if the note had been forged by a gang member of his who had not been given his guidance on the spelling.

Nevertheless, this 'Twopence' clue is a good one, the best in the book. Indeed, since readers are never told why Prudence Cowley was nicknamed "Tuppence", some may even wonder whether she was given the nickname so that the clue could be used. For those who don't spot the clue, the author gives a cheeky little prompt four chapters later, just to stimulate awareness of the difference between 'Tuppence' and 'Twopence', when Tuppence says to Julius "I could see at the time you didn't care a twopenny dip for me!".

2

The Man In The Brown Suit

Solution

This is a thriller in which the heroine, Anne Beddingfeld, who narrates most of the story, has adventures in England, on board the *Kilmorden Castle* and in South Africa and Rhodesia.

The complicated story poses so many questions that one needs to focus on the four main puzzles: (1) Who is 'the man in the brown suit'? (2) Who is the 'Colonel', the main villain of the story? (3) Who tries to kill Anne twice? (4) Who commits the only murder by strangling Nadina with a cord at Sir Eustace Pedler's empty property, the Mill House in Marlow, on 8 January 1922?

Puzzle (1) is to identify the man in the brown suit who visits the Mill House after Nadina and emerges minutes later. Next day, when she is found strangled, he is assumed to have murdered her and the *Daily Budget*'s war-cry is '*Find the Man in the Brown Suit*'.

In fact, Anne had seen him before, at Hyde Park Corner tube station (although he then wore a dark overcoat over his brown suit). His arrival on the platform had caused another man (Mr L. B. Carton) to step back in shock and be electrocuted by the live rail. Claiming to be a doctor, the man in the dark overcoat examined the dead man and took from his pocket a roll of film and a note with '1 7·1 22 *Kilmorden Castle*' on it. But he dropped the note when leaving and Anne picked it up.

Because of the dark overcoat, we do not know then that the 'doctor' is the man in the brown suit. But, when Anne learns that the dead man also had in his pocket a house-agent's order to view the Mill House, this gives her a connection between (a) the dead man (and therefore the 'doctor' who tended him) and (b) the murder of Nadina (and therefore the suspect in the brown suit). So she investigates at the Mill House and by sailing on the *Kilmorden Castle* to Cape Town on 17 January.

The puzzle of the man in the brown suit does not actually last long because by chapter 15 (out of 36) Anne has established that he is Harry Rayburn, who is also on the *Kilmorden Castle*, as Sir Eustace Pedler's second secretary. However, she believes he didn't kill Nadina because, if he had strangled her, he would have used his bare hands, not cord.[1] Nevertheless, that is not the end of puzzle (1) because, although we know which character he is *physically*, his real identity remains a mystery until much nearer the end, even after he and Anne have fallen in love and (in chapter 27) decided to marry.

By chapter 16, Anne has guessed that Rayburn's name is really Lucas, one of two young prospectors (Lucas and Eardsley) whose story is told on the *Kilmorden Castle* by Colonel Race. They claimed to have discovered diamonds in British Guiana, South America before the War but their claims were regarded as fantasy when they were found with diamonds stolen from De Beers in Kimberley, South Africa. Although they avoided trial because of the influence of Eardsley's very wealthy father, they were disgraced, after which Eardsley was killed in the War.

In fact – as readers (though not Anne) largely know from the Prologue – the De Beers robbery was committed, under orders of the 'Colonel', by Carton, a diamond sorter there. The stolen diamonds were then substituted for the young prospectors' South American diamonds by Carton's wife, Anita Grünberg (later called Nadina), who pretended to hand them all to the

'Colonel' but held some back.

In chapter 26 Rayburn admits to Anne that he is Lucas, who, although reported 'Missing, presumed killed' during the War, went to South Africa, becoming Harry Parker. Recently he came across Carton, who told him about Nadina holding back some diamonds and said that she might be willing to sell them to him. Lucas realises that, if he can buy them, the story of a substitution will be believed, the 'Colonel' will be suspected and he and Eardsley will be cleared.

Carton cables Nadina in Paris to tell her of this possible deal with Lucas. But she uses it to demand a "staggering price" for the diamonds from the 'Colonel' and, it seems, they agree to meet at the Mill House. The night before leaving Paris for the meeting, she tells Count Sergius Paulovitch (in the Prologue) that the 'Colonel' will have to deal not just with her but her husband – and he, Carton, arrives from Cape Town on the *Kilmorden Castle* on 7 January.

Next day Lucas, who (suitably disguised) had followed Carton onto the ship in Cape Town, trails him to a house-agent in Knightsbridge. Nadina, having also arrived in England on 7 January, goes to the house-agent too. She (as Mrs de Castina) and Carton, who show no signs of recognising each other, receive separate orders to view the Mill House. When they leave the house-agent, Lucas follows and, after seeing Nadina enter her hotel, he trails Carton, hoping he will get the diamonds.

But Carton is electrocuted at Hyde Park Corner station after recognising Lucas, who searches him and takes the roll of film and the note. He then removes his make-up (and dark overcoat), returns to Nadina's hotel and follows her to the empty Mill House where he is seen in his brown suit. He enters only three minutes after her but finds her dead. There is no sign of anyone, or of the diamonds. He then lays low during the *Daily Budget*'s war-cry before his return trip on the *Kilmorden Castle* with Pedler (and Anne).

Although there is skill in the plotting of these revelations, there is no real ingenuity in Lucas turning out to be the man in the brown suit. But there is a twist. In chapter 34 Anne learns that he is not Lucas but the other prospector, John Eardsley (it was Lucas who was killed in the War). He had told Carton that he was Lucas because Nadina would not have dealt with Eardsley, the only man she feared, and he hadn't told Anne his real name because he wanted her to care for him without regard to the Eardsley fortune.

Since Eardsley, the man in the brown suit, has by now had three other names (Rayburn, Lucas and Parker), it may be clearer to refer to him henceforth as Eardsley rather than by the false names variously used in the book.

Puzzle (2) is to identify the 'Colonel', who controls an organisation of international crooks and has planned robberies, forgery, espionage, sabotage and assassination. He is supplying arms for a revolution in South Africa while also trying to recover Nadina's diamonds before Eardsley.

There are various suspects for the role of the 'Colonel', all on the *Kilmorden Castle* bound for Cape Town on 17 January, namely Eardsley himself; Sir Eustace Pedler; Guy Pagett, his principal secretary; Reverend Edward Chichester (who is really a former quick-change music-hall artiste, Arthur Minks, who also plays Count Sergius Paulovitch as well as a night stewardess and Pedler's third secretary, Miss Pettigrew); Colonel Race, whose rank makes him an obvious suspect but who is really a Secret Service man hunting the 'Colonel'[2]; and a society lady, Suzanne Blair, who befriends Anne (but is probably not the 'Colonel' herself since the Prologue suggests he is a man).

We assume that, as the main villain, the 'Colonel' is responsible, though perhaps not personally, for trying to kill Anne twice and for killing Nadina. So, identifying him should also help solve puzzles (3) and (4).

As for puzzle (3), Anne is personally targeted twice. First, she is on deck after midnight when an assailant grips her throat (chapter 16). Half choking, she bites and scratches him. Before he can throw her overboard, Eardsley rescues her, striking the attacker, who runs off. They pursue him round to the starboard side where they find Pagett collapsed. Their assumption, which is repeated for us in chapters 18, 20, 23 and 26, is that he attacked her.

Second, after the ship has arrived, Anne, lured by a fake note, slips out of her hotel at night to meet Eardsley near the Victoria Falls on the Zambesi River (chapter 24). On the way out she passes Pedler's room and hears him dictating to Pettigrew. Then, on the path, a man emerges from the shadow behind her. She runs, with him pounding behind, her eyes fixed on the white stones showing her where to step in the darkness. And then her foot feels nothing as she falls down a ravine. The stones outlining the path had been taken up and balanced on bushes growing over the edge so that she would think she was on the path when she was really stepping into nothingness. However, she is caught by a tree overhanging the ravine and is again rescued by Eardsley.

In chapter 32 we get the answers to puzzles (2), (3) and (4). The 'Colonel' is Pedler. He had murdered Nadina, having briefly nipped over to England from "wintering on the Riviera". And he had personally carried out the attempts on Anne's life – he apologises for trying to throw her overboard and admits that he was not dictating in the hotel when she fell down the Falls, saying that Minks (as Pettigrew) had imitated his voice creditably. There is no ingenuity in the first attempt beyond Pedler hitting Pagett as he runs (to make it look as if Pagett was the assailant struck by Eardsley) but the imitated dictation and stone relaying are quite clever elements of the second.

However, his motivation for the attacks is unclear. If, as Chichester says in chapter 19, the 'Colonel' wants "information" from Anne, why try to kill her? In chapter 21 she thinks that some "knowledge", which she was thought to have, made the 'Colonel' anxious to remove her. But what 'knowledge' is this? Of course, as Anne says, "I, and only I, know that the murderer was not Harry Rayburn" (chapter 23) but no one – not even Pedler – is aware that *Anne* knows this apart from Suzanne. Tantalisingly, in chapter 32, Minks asks Anne in Pedler's lair "Perhaps, Miss Beddingfeld, you can guess why we required your presence here?" But she doesn't guess and this is never clarified.

There are three other unsatisfactory issues relating to Pedler's guilt. One, after the first attempt, he shows no signs of being bitten or scratched. Two, both attempts involve running, making him a most unlikely suspect, given the comments throughout about his girth and lack of fitness. Three, and even more surprising, is that both attempts and Nadina's murder are personally committed by a man who, so we had been told, does not do things personally. Thus, Paulovitch had said that the 'Colonel' has organised his crimes "without committing himself" and is an apostle of the maxim "If you want a thing done safely, do not do it yourself!" (the Prologue).

Moreover, Anne had heard that he "took no part in these things himself … limited himself to directing and organising … the brain-work – not the dangerous labour – for him" (chapter 21). And Pedler himself records that he has no desire to participate in sensational happenings and hates being involved (chapter 8). Even after admitting his guilt, he says "I never made the mistake of trying to carry out my schemes myself".

Looking at the identity of the 'Colonel' more generally, it is a surprise when he is suddenly revealed as Pedler in chapter 32, not just because of the three issues but because he tells part of the story. While 28 of the 36 chapters are written by Anne, extracts from his diary comprise the other eight chapters (8, 12, 13, 17, 22, 28, 29 and 31). So, to that limited extent, he can be regarded as the narrator and that is the most ingenious and satisfying aspect of his villainy. Whether it is cheating is considered in the Plot section.

Finally, as to Nadina's murder, he has a dual motive. As he explains (chapter 32) "Nadina both thwarted me and threatened me". She thwarted him by retaining some of the diamonds and she threatened him by demanding the "staggering price" for them, failing which she would sell them back to Lucas.

As for the murder itself, we are only told that Nadina is strangled with a piece of black cord, having evidently been caught unawares. So there is no murder plan to assess, although Pedler deserves credit for sending Pagett to Florence (so he thinks), so that he can nip over from Cannes to Marlow unnoticed and commit the murder. Although Eardsley calls the murder a "master-stroke" by the 'Colonel', in removing his blackmailer *and* providing a suspect (chapter 26), he overdoes the praise because Pedler had not planned for Eardsley, in his brown suit, to be a suspect.

Plot

In the Prologue, set in Paris, the 'Colonel' and the diamonds are discussed by Nadina and Paulovitch, both of whom use various names in the novel. The author then skilfully mingles the developing story with revelations not only of recent events leading to Nadina's murder but also of other events years before.

She does so by interweaving the plucky, melodramatic narrative of her enterprising and intelligent heroine with Pedler's diary extracts. Pedler writes in a marvellously readable way, with a sort of airy geniality and disdainfully affected boredom and, were he in a better-known story, he would be one of the author's most memorable characters. But even he was unable to recover the diamonds from Nadina at the Mill House. So, where were they?

Carton had them on him when he sailed to England on the *Kilmorden Castle*, arriving on 7 January. They were in a little yellow cylindrical tin used to store rolls of Kodak film. The roll had been removed and was in his pocket. He gave the tin to a steward, who was paid to drop it into cabin 71 at 1 am on 22 January on the *Kilmorden Castle*'s voyage back to Cape Town (the voyage on which Anne and the others sail) and he gave the ship's wireless operator a note for cabling this information to Nadina (i.e. '1 71 22 *Kilmorden Castle*'). The steward was told that a lady would be occupying the cabin. The lady, called Mrs Grey, would have been Nadina (had she not been murdered).

Quite what Carton's purpose was in doing this (and putting such trust in a steward) is not made clear. One can see why (as chapter 27 says) he and Nadina wanted to prevent the diamonds being seized and why the 'Colonel' was unlikely to guess that they were with a steward. But, if Nadina hoped, as she says in the Prologue, to sell the diamonds to the 'Colonel' (rather than Eardsley), it seems odd that she can't access them for him until she sails to Cape Town. Perhaps she planned to tell the 'Colonel' at the Mill House that, if he agreed the price, he would get them on board ship.

Be that as it may, after her murder, neither Eardsley nor Pedler know where the diamonds are. And yet both of them end up on 17 January sailing to Cape Town on the *Kilmorden Castle*, which is exactly where the diamonds are (in the tin held by the steward). So, how does that happen?

In Pedler's case, there are two reasons. One is that he "managed" (chapter 32) to get a "copy" of the wireless message sent by Carton to Nadina (how? when killing her?), which he "took" to be a meeting with Eardsley on the *Kilmorden Castle*. The other is that he is conveniently asked by Augustus Milray to deliver some confidential papers to the South African Prime Minister.

As for Eardsley, when Carton and Nadina got orders to view the Mill House, he "leaped to the conclusion" (chapter 26) that the house-hunting was a pretext for meeting Pedler and that he must be the 'Colonel'. Then he "overhead a conversation between two middle-aged gentlemen in the street, one of whom proved to be Sir Eustace Pedler" (the other being Milray). He later approached

Pedler and, by pretending to come from Milray, was allowed to travel to South Africa as Pedler's second secretary (using the name Harry Rayburn). Although the plotting of the overheard conversation is unconvincing, more leeway is allowed to loose plotting in thrillers than in detective stories – the more so where, as here, the conversation does not lead directly to any insights which would help explain the answers to the puzzles.

Its result is that Eardsley (who saw Carton's original note, taken from his pocket) is on the *Kilmorden Castle* with Pedler (who had got his "copy"), where they are joined by Anne (who had picked up the note dropped by Eardsley at the station) and by Minks, who (as Paulovitch in the Prologue) saw the cable which Nadina received from Carton and decided to go for the diamonds himself (as Reverend Chichester).

However, although the four of them saw Carton's message, the wireless operator had transmitted it as '1 7·1 22' (instead of '1 71 22', as Carton had intended). This was because, due to a flaw in the paper on which his note was written, it looked as if there was a dot after the 7. Carton must have given the operator his original note to copy on to a cable form and never read the copy. The flaw/dot causes the four people who see the note or cable to think that Carton is referring to cabin 17 (not cabin 71) at 1 am on 22 January.

The original occupant of cabin 17 plays no part in the story and disembarks at Madeira. After that, there is an argument between Anne, Pagett (directed, we later find, by Pedler) and Chichester about who should have the cabin. Anne is given the cabin but an attempt is made to get her to vacate it by putting the nauseous-smelling drug asafoetida inside. This (unsuccessful) attempt is presumably made by Chichester, rather than Pedler, since afterwards (in chapter 11) Pedler hands him a note (quoted in chapter 12) warning him not to "play a lone hand" – the note no doubt being written by Pedler himself because he uses the same 'lone hand' expression in chapter 32.

Then at 1 am Eardsley bursts into the cabin, saying "They're after me". Anne notices "a nasty deep wound" under his left shoulder blade, which, oddly, we do not hear of again. Nor are we told who stabbed him. But, when Pedler says "Minks muffed it" (chapter 32), he is presumably referring to this.

Also during "the middle of the night" – presumably at 1 am – the steward, as planned, delivers the film tin with the diamonds to cabin 71, into which Suzanne had moved when the intended occupant, Mrs Grey (Nadina), did not show. He puts his arm through the ventilator and drops the roll of film (as the author calls it in chapter 11, although she means the tin, not the roll) onto Suzanne's tummy. Suzanne, having earlier lost a roll of film, isn't suspicious about one being returned to her (in that way, at that time, which is surprising). Then, after seeing the diamonds in the tin, she hides them in, we later learn, a wooden giraffe, which she and Anne recover much later (chapter 35).

By then we have had Pedler's two attempts to kill Anne (chapters 16 and 24); her escapes from Pedler's henchmen (chapters 19 and 27); and her arrival at Pedler's lair (chapter 32) where, after exposing him, she lets herself be tricked into summoning Eardsley. When he arrives, she whips out a pistol, which she had found in her sponge-bag to her "utter amazement" (and to ours since it was not there when her luggage was searched on her arrival). She holds it to Pedler's head. Although he says that she and Eardsley are outnumbered by his men, Race arrives with his people and Pedler's game is up.

Although the pistol and some other points remain unexplained, the story is on the whole quite impressively constructed, given its large number of events and admirably fast pace. The plot interconnects coherently, not just episodically, and bears close examination pretty well, with the main mystification element – the identity of the 'Colonel' – resulting in a surprise.

THE MAN IN THE BROWN SUIT

Although the story is complicated, it is enjoyable, with Pedler's diary extracts the highlight.

Which brings us to the key plotting issue of whether the author cheats with those extracts, in allowing a diarist, as part-narrator, to be the villain since, although the extracts seemingly reflect Pedler's thoughts and deeds, they in fact conceal his villainy. Of course, Pedler is not a narrator in the sense of a person who is telling a story (such as Dr Sheppard in *The Murder of Roger Ackroyd*, published two years later) since the extracts comprise only eight of the 36 chapters. That person is Anne, who supplements her narrative with the extracts, and, as far as we know, there were no complaints of cheating which had the strength of feeling recorded by a few people about *Ackroyd*, in which the murderer being the narrator was the novel's key feature.

Where there was criticism, it was mild. Thus *The Observer* wrote "...giving alternate passages from the diaries of the heroine and of Sir Eustace Pedler is not altogether justified by the glimpses it gives of that entertaining but disreputable character" (7 September 1924). And *The New Statesman* seems impressed rather than critical: "It is remarkable especially for a brand new device for concealing the villain's identity to the very end" (11 October 1924).

Nevertheless, some readers may feel that having the villain as a diarist (even if only for under 25% of the chapters) is *of itself* cheating because a villainous diarist cannot be completely honest about his thoughts or deeds. A second category of readers might claim that there has been cheating if there are *particular* abuses of plotting or clueing in the diary extracts.

As with *Ackroyd*, readers in the first category have simply been outwitted. A villainous diarist is not obliged to be completely honest. If Pedler had revealed his real thoughts or deeds, this would have undermined much of the suspense, excitement or menace generated by the thriller and his omissions cannot *of themselves* seriously be regarded as cheating. Indeed, the author has played fair by flagging Pedler's reticence in chapter 13 where he says, "I may commit indiscretions but I don't write them down".

However, as the second category might claim, it could be cheating if the extracts mislead by abuses of plotting or clueing, meaning do the extracts either (1) lie to us or (2) omit events which, without revealing Pedler's role as the villain, ought fairly to have been mentioned contemporaneously?

As for issue (1), Pedler does not lie to the *reader* by asserting, as a fact, something that is untrue. Instead he lies to *other characters*, which is not cheating. Thus, he does not say as a fact that he asked for cabin 17 because he "happened to observe it was vacant" (chapter 12) but says this to Pagett. And he does not say as a fact that he presumes that Anne is in bed or out for a stroll (chapter 28) but says these things to Suzanne.

However, there are a couple of instances where the issue of lying arises when he is not speaking to someone else but recording his thoughts for the reader of his diary. First is his comment in chapter 8 that he has no desire to participate in sensational happenings and hates being involved. When we learn that he is the 'Colonel' and has committed murder, it seems he was lying. But perhaps he *does,* truthfully, hate having to participate or get involved personally, even though he finds himself doing so.

Second, in chapter 28 he writes "As I remarked once before [in chapter 8], I am essentially a man of peace". Here he seems to be claiming (untruthfully) to disavow violence. But, if one looks back at chapter 8 and to his liking for being at sea because it is "peaceful" (chapter 12), he may just mean 'peace' in the sense of 'calmness', rather than 'non-violence'.

As for issue (2), if one accepts that a murderer-diarist cannot be expected to tell the whole truth, there do not seem to be any illegitimate omissions from the diary. So, overall, there are no definite abuses of plotting or clueing.

However, before leaving the topic of cheating, the 'rules' of detective fiction should perhaps be mentioned (because they were in the *Ackroyd* commentary) even though, as we saw in the Thrillers chapter, they were intended to apply to detective stories rather than thrillers. If they did apply here, only Knox's Commandment No. 1[3] would be relevant, prohibiting an author from implying an attitude of mystification in the character who turns out to be the criminal.

Under that 'rule' Pedler would not be entitled to think, for example, '*I wonder who murdered Nadina?*'. Nevertheless, in his diary he records exclaiming to Pagett: "Why in *my* house? Who murdered her?" (chapter 8). If the 'rule' applied, it may be arguable that it is not breached since Pedler is just recording what he asked Pagett. But there is a stronger argument that, in recording the questions *in his diary*, he is implying (even expressing) an attitude of mystification to anyone who reads it – not just the person (Pagett) to whom he was speaking – and that this amounts to cheating, even without a 'rule'.

By contrast, when he asks Anne and Suzanne why a strange woman was murdered in his house (chapter 20), this seems more permissible because his attitude of mystification is in *Anne's* narrative. He is not addressing the reader through his diary but just pretending mystification to Anne and Suzanne.

However, there are other occasions, all in diary extracts, where he implies an attitude of mystification without addressing anyone other than readers of his diary, namely: (i) "Who is this fellow Chichester, I wonder?" (chapter 12); (ii) "What else would you think if a man [Pagett] comes to you with a lump the size of an egg on the side of his head and an eye coloured all the tints of the rainbow?" (chapter 17, after suggesting that Pagett had been in "a drunken brawl" when he himself had hit Pagett after trying to throw Anne overboard); (iii) Miss Pettigrew is "Probably one of Pagett's Italian friends he has palmed off on me" (chapter 22); (iv)

"Where did the girl go? … Then where the devil is she?" (chapter 28, after Anne has fallen down the ravine), and (v) "Where the devil did she go that night, that's what I'd like to know" (chapter 29).

Looking at these five examples in retrospect, the first three seem to breach the 'rule' because, dealing with them in order (i) Pedler presumably knew that Chichester was Minks by chapter 11 when he gave the 'lone hand' note to *Chichester* because in chapter 32 he refers to stopping *Minks* from playing a lone hand; (ii) Pedler knows full well that he himself had hit Pagett when running off after his attempt to throw Anne overboard; and (iii) Pedler must have known that Pettigrew was Minks by chapter 24 when Pettigrew imitated his voice, although one assumes that he would have known throughout.

Examples (iv) and (v) probably do not breach the 'rule' because they can fairly be read as 'Where is she *now*?' (which he does not know) rather than 'What *caused* her to disappear?'. Breach (ii), however, which is clear, cannot be dismissed as insignificant because it relates directly to puzzle (3) and, like Pedler's questions to Pagett about the murder, it implies mystification in a way that feels like cheating, irrespective of a 'rule'.

Clues

The word 'clue' first occurs in chapter 3 when the *Daily Budget* of 10 January refers to the (then) unidentified body at the Mill House, saying "The police are reported to have a clue". We are never told what this "clue" is but, since the Mill House caretaker reveals at the inquest that the bronzed man seen there had worn a brown suit, presumably that is it. Puzzle (1) then is: who is he?

Anne thinks that he is connected with the 'doctor' who examined the dead man at the tube station for a combination of reasons, which perhaps flow most logically in the following chain of reasoning. First, the dead man had in his pocket a house-agent's order to view the Mill House. Second, both the dead man and the man in the brown suit were evidently Englishmen from abroad because they were tanned and because the dead man's coat reeked of moth balls (the 'moth balls' clue) whereas most men in England wear their winter coats before January, meaning that the smell should have worn off by then.

Third, the note dropped by the 'doctor' which Anne picked up (with '1 7·1 22 *Kilmorden Castle*' on it) *also* smelled of moth balls. Since the 'doctor' did not smell of them, or examine the dead man like a real doctor, he must have pretended to examine him and taken the note. So, the 'moth balls' clue is a double one, also suggesting a connection between the dead man and the 'doctor' – explaining the dead man's shock (when recognising the 'doctor') – and therefore suggesting (because of the first two reasons) a connection between the man in the brown suit and the 'doctor'.

Fourth, Anne spots that the differences in appearance between the man in the brown suit and the 'doctor' were all of non-essential items (coat, glasses, beard) and that the latter had a shiny chin, perhaps because removing the beard had left traces of spirit gum. So, they might even be the same man.

But, despite this logical reasoning, none of these clues actually identifies the man in the brown suit. However, his connections with the dead man and the 'doctor' are enough for her to want to visit the Mill House and to interpret the note with '1 7·1 22 *Kilmorden Castle*' on it.

"Here was the clue to the mystery", she says about the '*Kilmorden Castle* note' clue (chapter 6) and it is the most examined clue in the book. She solves one element of it on realising by chance, when passing a shipping office (chapter 7), that the '*Castle*' is not a castle but a ship. As for the numbers, she tries various interpretations and seems dim to us because the numbers surely mean 17 January 1922, which is the day when the *Kilmorden Castle* is to return to Cape Town. On realising this, she buys a ticket.

However, the author has tricked us since the interpretation is not as obvious as we thought. After finding the asafoetida in cabin 17, Anne wonders why someone wants her to vacate it and she reinterprets the numbers, with 17 meaning cabin 17 (not 17 January) and 1 being the time and 22 the date. Perhaps something will happen on 22 January at 1 am in cabin 17, which is when the wounded Eardsley bursts into her cabin.

But next day, after spotting the flaw in the paper, Suzanne correctly suggests that it refers to cabin 71, not 17, by which time the tin has been delivered by the steward to her in cabin 71. When she and Anne find the diamonds inside, this 'diamonds' clue explains, she says, what "all these people are after".

The tin had originally contained the roll of film taken by Eardsley from Carton's pocket. Later he dropped the roll while at the Mill House, which Anne visits before sailing. She finds it and records elatedly "I had got my clue!" (chapter 7). This 'roll of film' clue helps her, not because of its contents (the film is unexposed) but in two other ways.

First, she notices that a minute shred of cloth, caught on the edge of the roll, smelled strongly of moth balls. Ignoring whether a 'minute' shred could smell so noticeably, particularly when the films had "a strong smell of their own", she concludes from the 'moth balls' clue (which has now become a triple one) that the roll had been in the dead man's pocket. Since he had not been in the Mill House, it must have been dropped by the man in the brown suit. So he must have been the 'doctor' who took it from the dead man's pocket and at last we know for certain that the 'doctor' is the man in the brown suit.

Second, just as Anne and Suzanne have worked out that the appointment at 1 am on 22 January in cabin 71 was with Nadina, Anne suddenly pronounces that the reason why Nadina could not travel was that she was the unidentified woman killed at the Mill

House. Anne thinks this because she remembers the 'roll of film' clue found there and "connects" this with the roll of film (again, in chapter 14, the author means the tin) passed through the ventilator to Suzanne, which she thinks was meant for Nadina. When Pedler learns (chapter 22) that Anne has identified the dead woman as Nadina, he accepts that her guess is right, adding "but to call it a deduction is absurd".

Similarly, Anne and Suzanne's reasons for thinking (rightly) in chapter 15 that the man in the brown suit is Eardsley are not very compelling. Suzanne simply "surmises", albeit most impressively, that, in order to get out of England, the man in the brown suit might have induced Pedler to bring him on board as his secretary and might then have entered Anne's cabin at 1 am on 22 January because he had misread the '*Kilmorden Castle* note' clue.

Anne never explains her thinking, although she did fall silent when told (chapter 13) that Pedler had engaged Eardsley (as Rayburn) just before sailing. Later, in chapter 26 Eardsley refers to the overheard conversation which led to his engagement and says that it "gave me my clue". It's not clear what "clue" he has in mind. Perhaps he just means that the conversation gave him the 'idea' to pretend to have come from Milray when seeking the engagement.

Our only pointer to Anne's thinking is her reluctance in chapter 15 to tell Suzanne that the word for a human head whose breadth is more than 75% of its length is 'brachycephalic'. She had told us in chapter 4 that the 'doctor' had a brachycephalic head and, since she concludes that he is the man in the brown suit, the latter's head must have been brachycephalic too. What we must assume (since we are not told) is that, when Eardsley burst into her room, Anne noticed that his head was brachycephalic. Unless this explains her thinking, it's hard to see the purpose of the 'brachycephalic' clue.

From that moment, Eardsley is assumed to be the man in the brown suit, which he admits in chapter 18. As to his true identity, Anne thinks (chapter 16) that he is one of the two young prospectors. We are not told why but perhaps her clue is that he looked profoundly moved when Race told their story. Of the two, she assumes he is Lucas, presumably because Race had said that Eardsley was killed in the War. There are no clues to her finding out later that he is also known as Harry Parker (chapter 25) or that he is in fact Eardsley (chapter 34) since he simply tells her.

However, she later thinks that she did have clues about Eardsley – "discrepancies" in the tale he told her in chapter 26 when claiming to be Lucas – namely, "an assurance of money, the power to buy back the diamonds of Nadina, the way in which he had preferred to speak of both men from the point of view of an outsider".

The last point is not much of a clue, since he explains why he is telling the tale that way. But the 'wealth' clues are rather good because he openly tells us that Lucas had always been poor and yet it doesn't occur to us how odd it is that later in the tale he talks about himself (as Lucas) buying back the diamonds from Carton. Eardsley, on the other hand, knew he would be a millionaire when his wealthy father died, as he had done a month earlier.

Turning to puzzle (2) – identifying the 'Colonel' – Pedler's diary is the most important clue. There are two main elements. First, as noted earlier, he very fairly says that he may commit indiscretions but doesn't write them down – so indicating that he may have omitted thoughts or deeds. And, second, is his comment that he has no desire to participate in sensational happenings and hates being involved. We have already noted this in two contexts (guilt and cheating), but in this third context (clueing) Pedler's comment resonates with the 'Colonel' not doing things personally – so indicating that they are both of the same mind about getting personally involved.

There are other Pedler 'diary' clues – he was in South Africa during the De Beers robbery (chapter 13); he knows that

Johannesburg will be unpleasant to visit soon (chapter 22); he is stared at by a government official who says that the person behind the strikes is in Johannesburg (chapter 29); and he makes an "involuntary exclamation" after learning that Eardsley and Pettigrew have gone into Agrasato's curio-shop (a rendezvous for the revolutionaries) and then adds, after going in there himself, "That is where I made a mistake" (chapter 31). So, when Eardsley tells Pedler that he had himself provided "the clue of your whereabouts" (chapter 33), the "clue" is presumably his "mistake" in going into the shop because this helps Race find his lair.

There are also some minor clues which are not from Pedler's diary, including that the 'Colonel' is an Englishman (chapter 14); Anne thinking that Race told the story of the young prospectors for its effect on Pedler (chapter 15); Anne referring to criminals being "cheerful fat men like Sir Eustace" (chapter 20); and Pedler's dislike of talking about how he makes his money (chapter 23). Moreover, as noted earlier, Eardsley "leaped to the conclusion" that Pedler was the 'Colonel' after Carton and Nadina obtained their house-agent's orders.

As for puzzle (3) – the two attempts on Anne – Pagett was sure that the man who tried to throw Anne overboard had been, as he says to Pedler, coming down the passage "from your cabin" before adding that the only two cabins down that passage were "yours and Colonel Race's" (chapter 17). Although this 'cabin' clue also implicates Race, it really points at Pedler. There are no clues against him relating to the attempt on the ravine path.

Finally come the clues relating to puzzle (4), Pedler's murder of Nadina. The most obvious one is that he owns the Mill House – the 'Marlow house' clue – making Anne think (chapter 11) that his presence on the *Kilmorden Castle* seemed something of a coincidence. However, the clue she gives when asked when she suspected Pedler is the 'Marlow recognition' clue.

This starts with her guessing that, when Nadina was

murdered, Pagett was in Marlow – not Florence where Pedler had sent him. She tricks Pagett with a question about the Duomo being a river in Florence, when it is really a Cathedral, and he falls for it, so indicating that he has never been to Florence (chapter 16). Emboldened by this 'Florence' clue, she pretends that she recognised him in Marlow. His reaction makes her "pretty certain" (chapter 26) that he was there, which he admits in chapter 30.

This 'Marlow recognition' clue is clever because at first it looks like a clue against Pagett. But, when he admits to being in Marlow, he adds that he hopes that Pedler had not recognised him there. This means, as Anne spots, that Pedler must have been in Marlow *as well* as Pagett, which is confirmed in chapter 31 when Pedler says that Pagett, by telling Anne this, has "blinking well torn it". The cleverness of the clue is improved by Anne misdirecting us away from its significance by repeatedly trying to get Pagett to answer the (irrelevant) question of *why* he went to Marlow.

This very good 'Marlow recognition' clue is the best in a book which has a decent number of clues of a reasonable standard for a thriller. Some enable Anne to demonstrate admirably logical thinking, although at other times her conclusions are assumptions or hunches. And not even the clever 'Marlow recognition' clue is determinative because it does not actually show that Pedler murdered Nadina. Indeed, he points this out.

So, at a gesture from Race in chapter 33, Minks steps forward in order to confirm that he (as Paulovitch in the Prologue) had learned from Nadina that Pedler was going to meet her at the Mill House. However, Minks never actually makes this point. He does say that Nadina told him her "purpose" but she never referred to a meeting at the Mill House. So Minks does not in fact provide the final link in the clueing chain, although it is clear from Pedler's reaction to Minks that he knows his game is up.

3

The Secret Of Chimneys

Solution

This is a thriller, not a detective story, although Superintendent Battle of Scotland Yard features regularly from chapter 11 (out of 31).[1] He is investigating the murder of Prince Michael Obolovitch of Herzoslovakia at 'Chimneys', the country home of the Marquis of Caterham and his daughter, Lady Eileen Brent (nicknamed Bundle), at which much of the action occurs.

The story is the first of two thrillers to feature Bundle and Superintendent Battle (the other being *The Seven Dials Mystery* published four years later). Although Bundle is the heroine in the latter novel, she does not feature significantly in the present one, hardly appearing in the first half. Virginia Revel is the most significant female character and she marries the story's main character, Anthony Cade.

Chimneys is the setting for an extended weekend house party, starting on Thursday 7 October, at which the British government (in the form of George Lomax and his assistant, Bill Eversleigh) hope that the pro-British Prince Michael will grant oil concessions to British companies in return for a loan from a British syndicate, represented by the financier Herman Isaacstein. This loan would assist Prince Michael's claim to the throne of Herzoslovakia, which had become a republic about seven years before, following a revolution in which King Nicholas IV had been assassinated. The other house guests are Virginia, a family friend, who had been in Herzoslovakia with her late husband just before the revolution, and an American, Hiram P. Fish, who is apparently there to view Lord Caterham's rare first editions.

Since the story is rather convoluted, it is best to focus on the four main puzzles: (1) What is the secret of Chimneys? (2) Which of the characters is 'King Victor', the notorious Parisian jewel thief and, more particularly, is he Anthony Cade? (3) Who murdered Giuseppe Manelli at Virginia's house in London? (4) Who shot Prince Michael in the Council Chamber at Chimneys?

As to puzzle (1) – the secret of Chimneys – we know from chapter 3 that there had been some "unfortunate disappearance" there of an item (we are not told what) which was never recovered. We also know from chapter 2 that Count Stylptitch, the former Prime Minister of Herzoslovakia, who had died two months ago, had said that "he knew where the Koh-i-noor was".

Therefore, when Lomax and Battle talk of the Koh-i-noor and its disappearance in chapter 14, with Chimneys being one of four places where it might have been concealed, no ingenuity is required to assume that the "secret" of Chimneys is that it is the hiding place of that precious diamond.[2] Although various other "secrets" are revealed in the story, particularly as to certain characters' true identities, these are not secrets *of Chimneys*.

It was about seven years before that the diamond had been hidden there by Queen Varaga of Herzoslovakia, who had stolen it during a royal visit which she and her husband, King Nicholas IV, had made to England. On that visit, they were guests at Chimneys, home of the then Foreign Secretary, the previous Marquis of Caterham.[3]

Before her marriage, Varaga had been a Parisian music-hall actress, Angèle Mory, who was an associate of the notorious jewel thief known as 'King Victor'. She had been bribed by a revolutionary organisation in Herzoslovakia, the Comrades of the Red Hand, to infatuate King Nicholas IV and decoy him to a spot agreed with them. However, she was more ambitious than they had expected and betrayed them, captivating the King, who fell in love with her. She married him and became Queen Varaga.

Despite her marriage, Varaga kept in with King Victor, stealing many stones from the Herzoslovakian Crown Jewels and replacing them with paste substitutes. She sent coded letters to him in Paris, written in the name Virginia Revel, whose husband was then at the British Embassy in Herzoslovakia.

After she had stolen the Koh-i-noor, hidden it at Chimneys and replaced it with a substitute fashioned by King Victor, he intended to retrieve it in due course. The British authorities hoped that this would result in him leading them to the diamond but, before this could happen, he was arrested in Paris and imprisoned for seven years. The police had hoped to find the coded letters at his house since these might indicate the location of the diamond but they had been stolen.

About a fortnight after the royal visit, the Herzoslovakian revolution took place. The Comrades of the Red Hand, who had been furious at Varaga's betrayal and tried twice to kill her, finally worked up the aristocratic and reactionary populace in Herzoslovakia to such a pitch that they stormed the palace, murdered the King and Queen (so we are told in chapters 1, 6, 15 and 19 twice) and proclaimed a republic.

Then a few months ago, King Victor was released from prison and, after spending time in America, came to England where his men managed to recover Queen Varaga's stolen coded letters. Battle reckons that coded instructions for finding the diamond had been in her last letter (headed 'Chimneys') and that the men had decoded it and knew where to look.

However, after three failures looking in the Council Chamber at Chimneys at night (during the first of which Prince Michael is murdered), the letters appear in Anthony Cade's room at Chimneys on Monday 11 October. Battle reckons that King Victor had decided, after the three failures, to let the authorities decode the letters and lead him to the hiding place.

So Battle has Varaga's 'Chimneys' letter decoded. In it she says that they were "double crossed" by S (Count Stylptitch, the Herzoslovakian statesman, who had also stayed at Chimneys during the royal visit). She says that he had removed the diamond from her hiding place and hidden it himself. She couldn't find it in his room but had found a memorandum, which she thought referred to it. It included the word "Richmond" and Battle suggests that a portrait of the Earl of Richmond in the Council Chamber is what prompted the crooks to treat the Chamber as the "starting point" for their search. This Richmond memorandum is indeed a clue leading to the diamond, which is not in the Council Chamber but buried in the rose garden under a bush.

As to puzzle (2) – the identity of King Victor – we are for much of the story encouraged to believe that he must be Anthony Cade, who had arrived in London from South Africa on Tuesday 5 October. He had travelled under the name of his friend Jimmy McGrath, who had asked him to undertake two tasks since he was unable to go to London himself.

The first was to deliver a parcel containing the *memoirs* of Count Stylptitch (not to be confused with his Richmond *memorandum*) to the publishers Balderson & Hodgkins by 13 October, the Count having entrusted the task to Jimmy who had rescued him from an attack in Paris by King Victor's men four years before. The second was to deliver to Virginia a parcel of letters (in fact the coded letters) which appeared to have been written by her. These had been stolen from King Victor by a Herzoslovakian called Dutch Pedro, who had given them to Jimmy for saving his life in Uganda.

As we later learn, after Anthony's various adventures at

Chimneys and elsewhere, he is not King Victor. Instead, he turns out in chapter 29 to be Prince Nicholas Obolovitch of Herzoslovakia, the next in line to the throne after Prince Michael, who was his cousin.

King Victor, whose real name we never learn, turns out to be a Frenchman pretending to be Monsieur Lemoine of the Sûreté. Battle had been expecting Lemoine in England on the trail of King Victor but the real Lemoine was kidnapped by King Victor's men and held at his headquarters in Dover. King Victor takes his place but, rather than going to see Battle at Chimneys when arriving on the day after Prince Michael's murder, he books in to the Jolly Cricketers in the nearby village. He then searches the Council Chamber on two nights (the second and third unsuccessful attempts) but is caught on the second night, which is when he claims to be Lemoine. He succeeds with this pretence until chapter 28.

Puzzle (3) is the murder of Giuseppe Manelli, a waiter at the hotel where Anthony stays on arriving in London. Battle thinks that Manelli was employed, either by King Victor or the Comrades of the Red Hand who were working with him, to steal Count Stylptitch's memoirs from Anthony because they might reveal the diamond's location (although in fact they do not).

Instead, after a struggle with Anthony on 6 October, Manelli mistakenly steals the parcel containing the coded letters rather than the parcel containing the memoirs. He wrongly thinks that they are compromising letters which can be used to blackmail Virginia, which is what he tries to do, not realising that she did not write them.

Next day he is found shot at Virginia's house. Battle says that the Comrades believed that he had, in using the letters for his own ends, double-crossed them and executed him as a traitor. He also says that King Victor's men took the letters from him, which was when they were recovered, and decoded them.

Meanwhile, Anthony, who wanted to retrieve the letters stolen by Manelli, had located Virginia's address. He arrived there as she found Manelli's body. The letters had gone but in Manelli's pocket was a scrap of paper saying "Chimneys 11.45 Thursday –", which is where Virginia was going for the weekend house party.

Anthony too had been invited that day to Chimneys, by the British government, who thought he was Jimmy McGrath. They wanted to ensure that there was nothing in the memoirs, which they knew he was bringing to England, that might embarrass completion of the oil deal with Prince Michael. Anthony had declined the invitation (chapter 7) on the grounds that he had already handed the Count's memoirs to a representative of the publishers.

We learn in chapter 15 that a trick had been played on him since the person who collected the memoirs from him was not from the publishers but was Prince Michael himself (before his murder) who, according to Baron Lolopretjzyl from the Loyalist party of Herzoslovakia, had then burned them. So Anthony now appears to have lost both the memoirs (given to Prince Michael) and the letters (taken by Manelli). Despite declining the invitation to stay at Chimneys, he nevertheless decides to stay at the Jolly Cricketers.

Although there is no ingenuity in the simple shooting of Manelli, the clever element of this murder is that under King Victor's direction he is shot in Virginia's house in order to incriminate her. The purpose is to prevent her going to the house party at Chimneys where she might recognise the murderer of Prince Michael, given that (as we are told in chapters 6, 15 and 24) she had been in Herzoslovakia for two years before the revolution and has "an excellent memory for faces" (chapter 6). It is, however, a little disappointing that a key feature of this cleverness, namely how Manelli got into Virginia's house, which is asked twice by Virginia and Anthony in chapter 8, is never answered.

Puzzle (4) is the murder of Prince Michael, who comes to Chimneys in the late afternoon of Thursday 7 October. That night at 11.45 he is shot with a revolver in the Council Chamber. His body is found at 7.45 next morning.

Oddly, no one inside Chimneys heard the shot, even though Anthony had heard it since, before going to the Jolly Cricketers, he had stopped outside Chimneys, prompted by the scrap of paper in Manelli's pocket. He was on the terrace at 11.45 and, after the shot, he had seen a light go on in a first-floor window. Next morning, he goes to Chimneys and says that he had heard the shot. He is then invited to move there from the Jolly Cricketers.

In chapter 14 Battle tells him that the first question is always "motive" – who benefits by Prince Michael's death? "We've got to answer that before we can get anywhere", he says with apparent significance. In chapter 16 Anthony, in effect, replies by asking him who is next in line for the throne because this seems "important". Although this looks like a good question, it is, as a pointer to motive, rather irritating in retrospect because Anthony (being next in line himself) is well aware that this succession motive is not "important" at all.

The murderer turns out to be the children's French governess at Chimneys, obtained from an agency two months before. She had come, under the name of Mademoiselle Geneviève Brun, with references from the Comtesse de Breteuil with whom she had lived for ten years. In fact, the real Mademoiselle Brun had been kidnapped on the way to her new post, and the governess who had arrived at Chimneys, using her name, was the actress Angèle Mory, otherwise known as Queen Varaga.

Although we had been told on no less than five occasions (noted earlier) that Queen Varaga had been murdered in the revolution, we had been told on one of them that her body was "horribly mutilated and hardly recognisable" (chapter 19). In fact, as we learn when Anthony provides his explanations (chapter 28), the "unrecognisable" body (which is a bit different from "hardly recognisable") of Queen Varaga was not hers. She had escaped to America and spent years lying low in fear of the Comrades of the Red Hand. Then, after King Victor was released, the two of them planned to recover the diamond from Chimneys together.

So she came as governess and, prompted by Count Stylptitch's memorandum, which she had seen seven years before, took the Council Chamber as her starting point. No murder plan needs to be analysed for Prince Michael's murder because there isn't one. He just comes unexpectedly face to face with her in the Council Chamber as she searches for the diamond (we are never told why *he* was there). With exposure and disgrace staring her in the face, she shoots him and puts some notepaper, which bears the design of the Comrades of the Red Hand, under his body. So her simple, impromptu motive does not have the significance that Battle had expected in chapter 14.

Plot

Chimneys is not described, this being "superfluous" since descriptions of it can be found in any guidebook and it is No. 3 in *Historic Homes of England* (chapter 10). Although Anthony does not come to Chimneys until the end of chapter 9, nearly all the action in the remaining 22 chapters happens there.

However, the story begins in Bulawayo (now in Zimbabwe, which was Southern Rhodesia when the novel was published). There Anthony is asked by Jimmy McGrath to go to London to deliver the two parcels. It is extraordinary that Jimmy should be in possession in Bulawayo of two entirely separate parcels (Count Stylptitch's memoirs and Queen Varaga's coded letters) which might contain clues to the location of a diamond hidden seven years before in England.

It seems particularly odd that Count Stylptitch does not send his memoirs straight to his publishers in London instead of sending them from his home in Paris to Jimmy McGrath in Bulawayo for delivery to London. Since Jimmy asks why in chapter 2, as does Lomax in chapter 3, we think this will be answered at some stage. But it never is and we just have to accept that Jimmy having both parcels is the starting point of the story, even though this is, as Battle says in chapter 20, a "very odd coincidence".

As noted earlier, the plot is rather convoluted. This may not seem apparent on a casual reading because the story moves at a lively pace throughout and never requires readers to pause and wonder how events, whether in the past or present, fit together coherently. The lively pace is assisted by a number of dramatic episodes including Anthony's struggles on his arrival in London, first with a Comrade of the Red Hand and later with Manelli; the disposal of Manelli's body; Anthony's visit to King Victor's headquarters in Dover; and two 'midnight adventures' in the Council Chamber.

The first of these takes place in chapter 17 (entitled "A Midnight Adventure") on the night of Saturday 9 October, two nights after Prince Michael is murdered during the first unsuccessful attempt to find the diamond. Having heard a noise, Virginia wakes Bill Eversleigh so that they can investigate "queer things" going on in the Chamber. They enter the darkened room and see silhouetted against the Richmond portrait a man holding a torch, gently tapping the panelling. Bill struggles with him but the intruder, unidentifiable in the darkness, escapes through a French window. That is the second unsuccessful attempt.

The second midnight adventure takes place in chapter 18 (entitled "Second Midnight Adventure") when, on Sunday 10 October, Bill and Virginia, with Anthony this time, hide in the Chamber, believing that the intruder will return. It is after 2.30 am when a man steps through the French windows into the Chamber. He goes over to the same bit of panelling that he had examined the night before and Anthony jumps on him (foiling the third attempt to find the diamond). The intruder is then revealed as Monsieur Lemoine of the Sûreté, although, unknown to us, he is in fact King Victor.

He admits that he was the man with whom Bill struggled during the first midnight adventure. But he pretends that he had slipped into the Chamber from the terrace after seeing someone tapping the panelling, and that Bill and Virginia had then burst in, with Bill mistaking him for the intruder in the darkness. He claims that, after struggling with Bill, he had escaped through the window, having no wish as yet to reveal his identity as Lemoine.

Although the plot is rather convoluted, the interweaving of the four main puzzles is quite impressive. But the construction is too loose in too many areas, with so many puzzles and solutions – not just the main four – that the plot lacks focus. It is also difficult to engage with any of the characters because we get the viewpoint of so many of them (even of Lord Caterham, who has no role in any of the puzzles) that none of them, not even Virginia, is given the chance to charm us.

There are also two other key weaknesses. One is that beyond generating an interest in who Anthony really is and whether he is part of the answer to any of the four main puzzles (in fact, he is not), no real feeling of mystification is engendered by any of them.

The other is that the story is so implausible that readers have to suspend disbelief completely at certain events. These include the episode in which Virginia pays the blackmailing Manelli for letters she didn't even write and then, after finding him dead in her house, allows Anthony, whom she has only just met, to dispose of the body while she goes to the Chimneys house party. Her extraordinary behaviour is matched by Anthony's comical disposal plan, which includes him taking the body to Paddington Station in a car which he had, completely unknown to readers, acquired earlier in the day (chapter 9).

The story also contains other bits of nonsense such as the

housemaid's failure to spot Prince Michael's body in the Council Chamber until she had polished half the floor and the decision to wait until after lunch before pursuing the important revelation that there is a secret passage out of the Council Chamber.

We are also left unsure about Anthony's story in chapter 12 where he tells Battle "the truth – with one trifling alteration, and one grave suppression". The alteration is presumably him saying that he got the scrap of paper (with "Chimneys 11.45 Thursday –" on it) from Manelli during his struggle with him at his hotel rather than from his dead body at Virginia's house. We also initially assume that the grave suppression may relate to other aspects of the death of Manelli and disposal of his body. However, when we learn at the end that Anthony is Prince Nicholas, this must surely be what he suppresses. But we are never told.

Similarly frustrating is a point in Constable Johnson's list in chapter 10 of the ten people who had arrived at the railway station on Thursday and were "there for Chimneys". One is "a young Army chap" but readers who are waiting for him to appear will be surprised because he never does. Although Prince Michael had an equerry, Captain Andrassy, he had remained in London (chapters 11 and 14) and did not come to Chimneys until after the murder.

The denouement occurs at Chimneys where, at Anthony's (Poirot-like) invitation, many of the main characters are assembled in the Council Chamber. Anthony even suggests that King Victor might be "settling down somewhere in the country where you can grow vegetable marrows" (as Poirot is to do in the author's next story). Brun and Lemoine are unmasked and during a struggle with Boris, Prince Michael's valet, Brun is shot as her pistol goes off.

There is also a nice twist explaining why Anthony had replied to the Baron in chapter 15 that he had "good reasons" for believing that the memoirs had not been burnt (by Prince Michael), namely that they had never been out of his control. He had guessed that the man from Balderson & Hodgkins would not be authentic and he had made up a dummy package. He put the real package in the hotel safe and handed the dummy to Prince Michael. So, on Wednesday 13 October he was able to deliver the real memoirs to the publishers.

An oddity of this twist is that there is no reference to Prince Michael realising that he had received a dummy package. It is not as if he can just have burned the memoirs without checking them because the Baron says that his purpose was to read them before putting them on the fire. So one wonders what Prince Michael thought when he opened the package and why, after collecting it at 9 am on Thursday, he did not pursue Anthony's deception before going to Chimneys by the 5.40 train.

Clues

Since this is a thriller which just unfolds, it is understandable that the identification of clues is, with the exception of the 'Virginia recognition' clue, generally too easy. But even some of these obvious clues are never properly explained and, although we do get an explanation of the main tangible clues relating to the diamond's location, they would be impenetrable without it.

This book is the author's third thriller. In the first we searched for the secret adversary known as 'Mr Brown'. In the second we searched for the man in the 'brown' suit. And here Prince Michael is murdered by Mademoiselle 'Brun' (the French for brown), not that this is seriously intended as a clue.

Anthony "suspected her from the first" (chapter 28) and says in chapter 15, when told by Bundle that Brun has been with them for two months, "I smell a rat". One wonders why he smells a rat about Brun by that stage. We are not told then but three chapters later he does list his clues.

First, she is the most unlikely person. Second, when the light went on in an upstairs room after Prince Michael was shot ("the only clue of any kind that I've got" – chapter 15), it was her room. Third, she had only been at Chimneys a short time. Fourth (although this happens after he had 'smelled a rat'), he had "found a suspicious Frenchman spying round the place" (Lemoine) and decided that he and the French governess were in league.

Despite those clues, Anthony changes his mind in chapter 18 because she seems "so absolutely the governess". The clue which points him back towards her is said in chapter 28 to be that she was recognised by Virginia. What he says there is that Virginia "had definitely recognised the woman" (after he had mentioned her being the Comtesse de Breteuil's governess) and that her face being "familiar to Mrs Revel" was what enabled him to see the daylight.

If Virginia had recognised Brun as the Comtesse's governess, this would provide no clue because she would be the genuine article. So, what Anthony must mean is that Virginia recognised Brun from her time in Herzoslovakia (even if unable to place her as Queen Varaga). However, this 'Virginia recognition' clue doesn't work because Anthony does not properly record what Virginia had said in chapter 22.

What she had actually said was that she knew the Comtesse quite well and fancied that she had come across Brun at her chateau and also knew her face quite well. The key point is that she is plainly referring to having known the face of the *real* Mademoiselle Brun *at the chateau* whereas Anthony's argument is based upon her knowing the face of the *imposter* Brun *at Chimneys*. But Virginia does not say she recognised the imposter's face, let alone that she knew her from Herzoslovakia.

The clue does, however, lead Anthony to reason correctly that the plan to prevent Virginia going to Chimneys (by murdering Manelli at her house) was prompted by a concern that she might spot Brun's true identity as the only member of the house party (other than Prince Michael and Boris) to have been to Herzoslovakia. As he points out in chapter 28, on the day when another Herzoslovakian, Baron Lolopretjzyl, visited Chimneys (Friday 8 October), Brun retired with a convenient migraine (chapter 16).

There are other clues relating to Prince Michael's murder, none pointing to Brun. First, under his body is the notepaper bearing the design of the Comrades of the Red Hand but Battle dismisses this red herring as having been put there to suggest the obvious solution (chapter 14). Second, the light may not have gone on in Brun's room after the shot because, looking at Chimneys from a different angle, it could have gone on in Fish's room (chapter 18). Third, the revolver is found in the suitcase of the financier, Herman Isaacstein, having been put there by Brun "to confuse the trail".

Last is the scrap of paper in Manelli's pocket saying "Chimneys 11.45 Thursday –". Since we are specifically reminded just before the shot that this is "the time mentioned on the scrap of paper", the scrap must surely be a clue. However, we are never told why Manelli had it on him. Indeed, the 'Manelli scrap' clue is a complete curiosity because the murder at 11.45 was not planned for that time: Brun came across Prince Michael "when she least expected it" and shot him (chapter 28).

So, the clueing of puzzle (4), Prince Michael's murder, is not impressive. The same can be said of puzzle (3), Manelli's murder, where we know almost immediately that the two clues – a fake telegram sending Virginia's staff to her bungalow in Datchet and a pistol engraved with the word "Virginia" – are aimed at framing her. There are no real clues to the true culprits. However, the attempted framing leads Battle (chapter 20) and Anthony (chapter 28) to conclude that "some abler intelligence" than the Comrades (King Victor) directed operations.

As to puzzle (2), King Victor's identity, a series of red herrings point repeatedly towards Anthony. His life story before coming to Bulawayo a month ago (chapter 21) is hardly known and he is so obviously clued as King Victor that, if this was his true identity, the story would have hardly any mystification at all.

The clues abound from the opening of the book, with him being called "Gentleman Joe" by Jimmy. Why "Joe"? Is Anthony a false name? We never learn why Jimmy calls him Joe but we do learn in the first two chapters that some relevant events occurred seven years ago in addition to the revolution in Herzoslovakia. It was when Anthony last saw Jimmy, when Anthony was last in England and when King Victor was sent to the prison. When Jimmy mentions King Victor, Anthony says "What?" and wheels round suddenly. Could he have been the imprisoned King Victor during those years? It seems unlikely given that he has such a deep tan.

What we know about King Victor is that his father was Irish (or English) and his mother French; that he speaks at least five languages; that he has a genius for impersonation; that he has never been known to take a life; that he pretended to be Prince Nicholas (Anthony's true identity) in America after his release from prison, obtaining a haul of dollars on account of supposed oil concessions; and that he is now reckoned to be in England.

What we know about Anthony is that he doesn't like "regular" work; that his few old friends would be unlikely to recognise him; that he speaks Italian to Manelli; that he says "we criminals have to be so careful"; that he is squeamish about blood; that he only half-answers Virginia's question about whether he has been steeped in crime before; that he has a revolver; that, according to Battle, you can't mistake the face of a man who has led a life of daring and adventure; that he has spent most of it looking for trouble and taken many risks; and that he has abandoned an unknown "trade" on principle.

As we have seen, however, it transpires that he is not King Victor but Prince Nicholas ("the trade of royalty"), a role he had abandoned because he had democratic ideas and did not believe in kings and princes. We had wondered whether he had a Herzoslovakian connection ever since he "looked up sharply" when Jimmy first mentioned Herzoslovakia, repeated the words "with a curious ring in his voice" and then, while trying to dismiss his knowledge as being "only what everyone knows", seemed remarkably knowledgeable about recent Herzoslovakian political history.

Nevertheless, it was by no means clear that he was a prince, even though there are some clues. The first is that, on being told he has the manners of a "gentleman", he vaguely remarks that "Kind hearts are more than coronets". Later clues are that Anthony and Prince Nicholas both went to Oxford; that Anthony and Prince Nicholas had been socialists; that Herzoslovakian princes are educated in England; that Anthony is amazed when told that King Victor had pretended to be Prince Nicholas in America; that he says, in response to being shown an anonymous note saying *"Look out for Mr Cade. He isn't wot he seems"* (whose authorship is strangely never revealed), "I am really a king in disguise"; and that Boris tells him, after Prince Michael's death, that he will now serve him as his master, a clue repeated three chapters later by Battle when wondering why Boris had done this.

This 'Boris' clue is a strong pointer to Anthony's identity and as such perhaps the best in the book. But even this clue is not very satisfactory because we are given no inkling why or how Boris selects Anthony – other than "instinct" (chapter 30). It seems unlikely that he actually recognised him as Prince Nicholas, partly because his old friends were unlikely to do so and partly because Virginia didn't, which seems surprising given her time in Herzoslovakia and her "excellent memory for faces". The key element of the 'Boris' clue is that, surprisingly, Anthony does not ask Boris why he has chosen him – probably meaning that he knows that Boris has made the right choice – and simply mutters that it's "damned awkward – just at present".

If Anthony is not King Victor, then the next series of red herrings points most obviously to the American, Hiram Fish. We know that King Victor has come recently from America. We also know that Fish is "interested in crime"; has "a wide experience" of burglars; is still dressed just after the first midnight adventure; lets Caterham do all the talking about rare books; asks Caterham to show him the secret passage in the Council Chamber; and is presumably the person who dropped a match which is found there, given that Anthony later asks him for a match and puts it carefully in his pocket. Things look pretty black for Fish when Anthony finds him at the house in Dover holding an automatic before we learn that he is a Pinkerton's agent trailing King Victor.

When King Victor is revealed to be a Frenchman impersonating Lemoine, we wonder if we should have read something into his initial appearance in chapter 15 when he is found suspiciously kneeling on the ground by the boathouse at Chimneys listening to conversations (Anthony with Virginia, then with Bundle) not meant for his ears.

A more obvious clue appears to be a scrap of paper given to Anthony by Boris (chapter 22) showing the address in Dover of King Victor's men and the Comrades of the Red Hand. Since Boris tells Anthony that the 'Dover scrap' clue was dropped by "the foreign gentleman", and Anthony supposes that he is referring to the person pretending to be Lemoine, this is a clear clue against that person *if* he was the foreign gentleman meant by Boris – although Virginia suggests that Boris was referring to Isaacstein. Lemoine, having denied dropping it (chapter 23), later admits that he did drop it but *only* after coming across it where Anthony had lately passed along (chapter 25), although this does not seem at all convincing because of his original denial.[4]

Finally, as to puzzle (1), the "secret" of Chimneys (the location of the Koh-i-noor), this is where the main tangible clues in the book are found. The first is Varaga's coded letter headed

'Chimneys' whose decoded message reads:

> *"Operations carried out successfully, but S double-crossed us. Has removed stone from hiding-place. Not in his room. I have searched. Found following memorandum which I think refers to it:* RICHMOND SEVEN STRAIGHT EIGHT LEFT THREE RIGHT".

So Varaga, having found the memorandum indicating where Stylptitch had hidden the diamond, returned to Chimneys seven years later as Mademoiselle Brun and searched in the Council Chamber, prompted by the word 'Richmond' and the Richmond portrait. But, despite this 'Richmond memorandum' clue, the villains had been unable to find the diamond.

However, unknown to them, but known for years to Bundle, there was, to the side of the portrait, a concealed spring causing a section of panelling to swing inward revealing a secret passage. Battle takes seven straight paces into the passage, looks eight bricks up from the bottom on the left-hand side and then three bricks to the right of that. He pulls the brick out and thrusts his hand into the small cavity behind (chapter 23).

But there is no diamond there. Instead, there are "three articles" – described in the narrative as "a card of small pearl buttons, a square of coarse knitting, and a piece of paper on which were inscribed a row of capital E's!".[5] Anthony reckons that Stylptitch suspected that his memorandum had been read and had removed the diamond and re-hidden it in a different place; and that that place was again clued by the Richmond memorandum, but this time read in conjunction with the three articles which Stylptitch had substituted for the removed stone.

A reader would need to be particularly astute to interpret the 'Richmond memorandum' clue and the 'three articles' clue as skilfully as Anthony then does in chapter 27 – indeed, one cannot imagine any reader interpreting it. He says that in Stylptitch's memoirs ("which I happen to have read") there is a reference to a "flower" dinner which everyone attended wearing a badge representing a flower. He says that Stylptitch wore "the exact duplicate of that curious device we found in the cavity in the secret passage. It represented a rose. If you remember, it was all *rows* of things – buttons, letter E's, and finally rows of knitting". Anthony suggests that, since the books in the library are arranged in rows, and there is a book there called "The Life of the Earl of Richmond", one should start at this book and, using the numbers to denote shelves and books, find the stone hidden in a dummy book or in a cavity behind a book.

In fact, Anthony has tricked the reader or, rather, Brun who goes to the library to look at the books and is thereby exposed. This is because, as he reveals in chapter 29, the Count's "device" (as he again, oddly, describes the three, apparently separate, articles) stood not for "rows" but a "rose". Thus, if one goes to the rose garden and, standing with one's back to the sundial, takes seven paces straight forward, then eight to the left and three to the right, one comes to some bushes of a bright red rose called Richmond where, if one digs, as Battle and others do, the diamond is to be found (chapter 31).

It is very unusual that a clue, the 'Richmond memorandum' clue (clue one), whose purpose is to direct people to the cavity where the 'three articles' clue (clue two) is found, is then again used as a separate clue (clue one repeated) – thereby locating the diamond in the rose garden. It is impressive of Anthony to imagine that the clue can have worked in this unusual double way. It is also impressive that Fish had, as Anthony puts it, "tumbled to the same idea" (of the diamond being in the rose garden) and gone there in chapter 23 – although we are not told his chain of reasoning for 'tumbling' to it.

However, the real criticism of this clueing relates not to the

'Richmond memorandum' clue (although it is not clear why one would *start* at the sundial in the rose garden) but to the conundrum posed by the 'three articles' clue. It is not so much that we had no idea that the memoirs referred to the representation of a rose but, rather, that the articles themselves cannot fairly be said to point us to "rows" or "rose".

When the articles are found in the cavity, there is no reference in the narrative (quoted earlier) to "rows" in relation to the buttons or the knitting. And, when Battle then goes on to summarise his finding – "A bit of knitting, some capital E's and a lot of buttons" (chapter 23) – he does not even refer to "rows" in the context of the capital Es. So, no one could be expected to interpret the meaning of the three articles (or "device") either as "rows" or "rose".

It is noteworthy, in retrospect, that Anthony and Jimmy mention "rows" (meaning arguments) three times in chapter 1, including Anthony having "an absolute instinct for rows". It is also noteworthy, again in retrospect, that Anthony dismissed his pretence at being Jimmy as unimportant by reference to Shakespeare's remarks about "the nomenclature of roses".[6] However, it is almost impossible to believe that the author thought that any reader would spot these references as intending to assist interpretation of the 'three articles' clue.

4

The Seven Dials Mystery

Solution

This is the second of two thrillers to feature Lady Eileen Brent (nicknamed Bundle) and Superintendent Battle of Scotland Yard – the first being *The Secret of Chimneys* published four years earlier. Bundle, the heroine of the story, is the daughter of the Marquis of Caterham who owns the country house 'Chimneys'.

The puzzles appear to be: (1) Who killed Gerry Wade at Chimneys? (2) Who killed Ronny Devereux? (3) Who attempted to steal the plans of an invention from Terence O'Rourke at Wyvern Abbey, shooting Jimmy Thesiger in the arm while escaping? (4) Who tried to murder Bill Eversleigh (by poisoning him with hydrochloride of morphia) and then Bundle (by knocking her on the head with a sandbag)?

These are hardly separate puzzles since the answer to all of them seems obvious – the Seven Dials Society, a mysterious organisation of seven individuals who meet at the Seven Dials Club at 14 Hunstanton Street in an area of London called Seven Dials, near Tottenham Court Road.

When they meet, each of the Seven Dials, numbered 1 to 7, wears a face mask made of a round piece of material, with two slits for eyes. On each mask there is a clock face. The hands on the clock face of No 1 point to one o'clock and so on.

Since the answer to all the main puzzles seems so obvious, the overriding puzzle is therefore: who *are* the Seven Dials, which really means who is No 7? As Jimmy Thesiger says (chapter 25), "No – the others don't count. It's No 7 with his own ways of working that frightens me".

So it is a real surprise when No 7 is revealed as Superintendent Battle in chapter 31 – implausibly until it transpires that the Seven Dials Society is not a villainous group but a band, working under Battle's guidance, of amateur secret service workers.

The Seven Dials are: No 1 – Gerry Wade, replaced after his murder, by an actress, Babe St. Maur, who pretends to be Countess Anna Radzky; No 2 – Ronny Devereux, replaced, after his murder, by Bundle (chapter 33); No 3 – Bill Eversleigh, whom Bundle agrees to marry; No 4 – Hayward Phelps, an American journalist; No 5 – Count Andras of the Hungarian Embassy; No 6 – Mr Musgorovsky, a Russian who runs the Seven Dials Club; and No 7 – Superintendent Battle.

Battle himself appears in under 5% of the story until chapter 20 (out of 34). He has no apparent role in the detection of the murders of Gerry Wade and Ronny Devereux but he is much involved in investigating the attempted burglary at Wyvern Abbey (chapters 20–24) and explaining the crimes (chapters 32 and 33).

It transpires that the Seven Dials Society are in pursuit of a dangerous crook who has already stolen two inventions (chapter 32). So we have a second overriding puzzle: who is this dangerous crook (if he is not in fact No 7)? The answer is Jimmy Thesiger, which is another genuine – but also unlikely – surprise given the limited clueing of him. He is the answer to puzzles (1) to (4) because he kills Gerry and Ronny; he attempts to steal the plans from O'Rourke, shooting himself in the arm; and he later tries to kill Bill, then Bundle. He is assisted in some of this villainy by Loraine Wade, who is a sort of half-sister to Gerry.

Looking at the four puzzles individually, puzzle (1) is Gerry's murder on 22 September during a weekend house party hosted by Sir Oswald and Lady Coote at Chimneys. Sir Oswald, who owns England's biggest steel works, has been renting Chimneys for nearly two years from the Marquis of Caterham, although he will be handing the house back to the Caterhams in a week's time. The Cootes' guests at the house party are Gerry, Bill Eversleigh, Ronny Devereux, Jimmy Thesiger and three girls, Helen, Nancy and Socks. Also present are Rupert 'Pongo' Bateman (Sir Oswald's secretary) and Chimneys' new German footman, Bauer.

When Gerry is not down for breakfast on the first two mornings of the house party until 11.30 and 11.40 respectively, some other guests plan to wake him early on the third morning by placing a number of alarm clocks (the old word 'alarum' is used) in his room, timed to go off one after the other from 6.30. Accordingly, six of them (Bill, Ronny, Jimmy, Helen, Nancy and Socks) go into Market Basing and purchase one alarm clock each plus two more to represent Bateman and Lady Coote's participation in the plan.

Since they cannot put the clocks in Gerry's room until he is asleep, it is after 1.45 am that the clocks are placed quietly by Bateman in Gerry's room while the others, pyjamaed and dressing-gowned in the corridor, hand him the clocks two at a time. Despite the clocks going off with vigour, Gerry is still not down for breakfast by 12.20 when Tredwell the butler reveals that he has died in his sleep. The doctor blames an overdose of chloral, taken for sleeplessness, since an empty chloral bottle is by the bed, along with a glass and bottle of water for dissolving the chloral.

Bundle thinks that he had taken an overdose by mistake. But we naturally suspect foul play, particularly as Ronny and Loraine are incredulous about Gerry taking a sleeping draught. Our suspicions deepen when we learn that seven of the eight alarm clocks are found mysteriously arranged in a row on the mantelpiece in Gerry's room, with the eighth found on the lawn outside where it had been thrown from the window.

After the Cootes have returned Chimneys to the Caterhams, Bundle finds jammed in the desk of her bedroom (which Gerry had used) an unfinished letter written by him to Loraine on the night of his death with the sinister suggestion (as Bundle describes it) that she should "forget what I said about the Seven Dials business. I thought it was going to be more or less of a joke, but it isn't – anything but". Towards the end of the letter he says, "I'm sleepy. I can't keep my eyes open".

As we suspected, Gerry was murdered. But there was no real ingenuity. Jimmy slipped the chloral into a whisky which Gerry drank before retiring to bed, which is why he was sleepy. Later, with everyone asleep (and presumably after Bateman had placed the clocks), Jimmy put the bottle of water, glass and empty chloral bottle by Gerry's bedside and probably pressed his fingers round the glass and bottle, unaware of the letter.

As to motive, Battle suggests that Gerry (as No 1) had worked out "that Mr Thesiger was the man". But how did Jimmy *know* that Gerry had worked this out? The answer, Battle explains (chapter 33), is that Gerry was devoted to Loraine and told her "more than he should have done". But, because she was in turn "devoted body and soul" to Jimmy, she passed Gerry's "information" on to him. One assumes that this "information" was that Gerry was one of the Seven Dials, who were on Jimmy's tail.

Puzzle (2) is the murder of Ronny Devereux who, like Gerry, was one of the Seven Dials (No 2). As Bundle is driving to London, Ronny reels out of a hedge onto the road in front of her. She swerves but, looking back, sees him lying on the road. She jumps out of her car and kneels beside the prone figure who manages to say "Seven Dials … tell…" followed by "Tell … Jimmy Thesiger…" before his body goes limp. In fact, Bundle's car had not hit him. He had been shot with a rifle. But why?

All we are told by Battle (chapter 33) is that Ronny, who was suspicious about Gerry's death, reached the same result as him ("namely, that Mr Thesiger was the man") and, being attracted (like Gerry) to Loraine, had probably warned her against Jimmy. So Ronny in turn was silenced – and died trying to send word to the Seven Dials that Jimmy was his murderer. We cannot assess the ingenuity of the murder since we are not told anything about the rifle shooting.

We do, however, get quite a lot of detail with puzzle (3) in which Jimmy tries to steal the plans of a secret invention during a house party at Wyvern Abbey hosted by George Lomax, the Under Secretary for Foreign Affairs. The invention, by a German called Eberhard, is a patent process for making steel wire as tough as a steel bar and should be worth millions.

The aim of the house party, being attended by Lomax, Eberhard, Sir Stanley Digby (British Air Minister), Terence O'Rourke (his secretary), Sir Oswald, Lady Coote and Bateman is to enable the British government, to whom Eberhard must have offered the invention, to take the expert opinion of Sir Oswald who has been testing it out at his steel works. The other guests are a Hungarian Countess, Anna Radzky; Bill Eversleigh (Lomax's assistant); and Bundle and Jimmy (who have managed to get themselves invited). In order to prevent the theft of Eberhard's plans, the guests are watched over by Battle, who is dressed as a footman (at least in chapter 16).

However, an attempt is made to steal the plans. Having doped O'Rourke's whisky, Jimmy creeps downstairs and into the library just before 2 am and locks the door. He goes out through one of the library's French windows onto the terrace where he climbs up the ivy in order to get into O'Rourke's bedroom (the door to which is locked). He gets the plans and throws them down to Loraine on the terrace and she runs off with them but, unfortunately for her and Jimmy, straight into Battle.

Meanwhile Jimmy, unable to leave O'Rourke's bedroom via the locked door, climbs down the ivy and goes back into the library.

Then, in order to provide a realistic suspect for the burglary, he makes a considerable noise in the library, knocking furniture about so that he can pretend to have fought a "hefty man" whom he had seen climbing down the ivy while he was standing by the French window.

To make this fictitious fight appear more realistic and dangerous, Jimmy fires two shots. He fires the first with a Colt .455 blue-nosed automatic, which he bought openly the day before, and claims to have shot at the hefty man as he was escaping. He fires the second, using his left hand (gloved, so as to avoid fingerprints), into the fleshy part of his right arm with a small Mauser .25 pistol, which he had in his pocket but which he says was fired at him by the hefty man. Jimmy then throws the Mauser onto the lawn as if the hefty man had hurled it there and pulls off the left glove with his teeth (being unable to use his right arm), throwing it into the fire grate where it is later found nearly burnt.

When Battle hears the shots and runs round the terrace, he sees Jimmy lying in a pool of blood by the threshold of the French window. When he goes through the window into the library to unlock the door, the other guests who have been pounding on it, fall into the room. From their reaction to Jimmy's limp figure, it appears that his clever theatrics have been successful.

As for Loraine running off with the plans, she claims that, having learned from Jimmy on the telephone that it might be dangerous at Wyvern Abbey (chapter 15), she was keen to see what was going on. On coming up to the terrace, something fell at her feet. She picked it up and saw a man climbing down the ivy. She ran off, as though panic-stricken, but straight into Battle. Her story sounds just about plausible. But the burglary has failed.

Puzzle (4) occurs in the context of Bundle and Loraine agreeing to meet Jimmy and Bill at the Seven Dials Club. Before the meeting Bill, who (unknown to readers) is No 3 – and therefore in pursuit of Jimmy – goes to Jimmy's rooms in Jermyn Street and pretends that he has papers throwing suspicion on him (not that readers know anything at that stage about Bill meeting Jimmy). Bill's purpose is to see whether Jimmy will try to kill him. Jimmy then gives Bill a whisky doctored with hydrochloride of morphia. Bill pours it into a jar but acts as though it is taking effect. When Jimmy sees this, he admits everything, telling Bill that he will be the third victim.

Jimmy then drives the apparently drugged Bill from Jermyn Street to the Seven Dials Club where he lures Bundle on the telephone, suggesting she bring Loraine with her, by pretending that Bill has the "most amazing story" to tell. When they get there, she is prompted by Loraine to go to a room where Jimmy, hiding behind the door, knocks her unconscious with a sandbag. But, although he says that she won't come round because he has hit her with all his might, this further murder attempt also fails because she does come round. Jimmy is then caught, along with Loraine, by Battle's men who had followed him from Jermyn Street to the Club.

There is no ingenuity with these simple murder attempts but Loraine's role, as with her role in the attempted robbery at Wyvern Abbey, makes one wonder whether she knows that Jimmy's villainy extended to the murders of Gerry and Ronny. The key paragraph is in chapter 3 when she is told of Gerry's death: "The incredulity in her voice was plain. Jimmy gave her a glance. It was almost a glance of warning. He had a sudden feeling that Loraine in her innocence might say too much".

On the one hand, the "glance of warning" suggests knowledge but the other evidence ("incredulity" and "innocence") suggests that Gerry's death came as a surprise. And that is what one would expect because, just as Gerry was "very devoted" to her, she was "very devoted" to Gerry (chapter 3). Similarly, on being told of Ronny's death, her lips parted in surprise and a look of fear and horror came into her face (chapter 7). However, we cannot be certain about the extent of her knowledge.

Plot

This is the last of the early thrillers. It engages us from the start when Jimmy races down the stairs at Chimneys and collides with Tredwell, the butler. It intrigues us by the end of chapter 3 with the mystifying rearrangement of the seven clocks in Gerry's room. And it continues at a good pace, with Bundle having a likeable pluckiness and with the true identity of No 7 providing a suitably mystifying puzzle.

It is an easy, effortless and at times humorous read, uncomplicated by sub-plots or events from the past. As such, the plot appears to have a rather loose, simple structure. However, this is to undervalue the cleverness of scenes such as Loraine's visit to Jimmy in chapters 8 and 9, the Seven Dials meeting in chapter 14, Jimmy's vigil in chapter 18 and his chat with Loraine in chapter 25. Only when we know the true roles of the participants do we realise that the words used in those scenes do not mean what they had appeared to mean.

However, there is a significant flaw in all this cleverness, which is that the author has not built into it sufficient clueing for us to feel satisfied by her surprising solution that Jimmy is the villain and that the masked members of the Seven Dials Society are not the villains – but amateur secret service workers, with a police Superintendent as No 7.

Furthermore, after we learn that Battle is No 7, the remainder of the story is rather frustrating. What we hope is that we can then follow the Seven Dials' hunt for the dangerous crook. But only a few sentences later, before we can even start to assess the impact of this dramatically changed situation, we learn that the crook is Jimmy and that he has already been arrested.

And then, after learning who the other Seven Dials are and that Jimmy is the dangerous crook (chapter 32), we wonder why the Cootes had invited Nos 1, 2 or 3 to Chimneys at the start of the book. But nothing is said to explain this or to explain why they had invited a group of youngsters (including also Helen, Nancy and Socks) or, more importantly, why they had invited Jimmy.

Also curious, for three reasons, is the meeting of the Seven Dials in chapter 14. First, No 6 cannot understand why he has not had No 2's report. No one says that this is explained by Ronny (No 2) being dead and yet the Seven Dials know he is dead because they talk about his inquest. Perhaps they simply didn't know that No 2 was Ronny (because of his mask) – although, as we shall see, Ronny knew that Gerry was one of them.

Second, with regard to Ronny's inquest, No 4 says that reports about local lads practising with rifles have been spread everywhere, to which No 6 says "That should be all right then". This makes sense when we regard the Seven Dials as Ronny's murderers because they would naturally wish to encourage a verdict of accidental death. However, when we later learn that they are the sleuths, it is not obvious why they would want to spread such false rumours about the death of one of their members.

Third, it is odd, with Bundle and Bill being, rather engagingly, such good friends (and even agreeing to marry), that she does not recognise his voice as No 3's as she eavesdrops on the meeting. Indeed, she is "dumbfounded" when learning (chapter 32) that he is No 3. Although No 3 only says a dozen words and is "indistinct", the voice is said to be "unmistakable" and she had, only the night before, been out with him (when he had spoken at length). It is also strange, with Battle having said that news of Ronny's death would appear in the papers that day (chapter 10), that they do not discuss it over their dinner.

Similarly unexplained is the small bottle of white powder which Jimmy finds (so he claims) at Letherbury, the house rented by the Cootes after returning Chimneys to the Caterhams. He refuses to tell Bundle and Loraine where he found it but, assuming it is sinister, it seems to be a clue. But it is never referred to again and it is not clear why it was mentioned at all.

There is also an unrealistic aspect to Bundle's sandbagging. Although Jimmy thought he had killed her, Battle says (chapter 33) that she had been saved partly because he had used his wounded arm: "He didn't realise it himself – but it had only half its usual strength". How could he not have realised this?

Finally, there is the occasional use of a rather conversational style of writing which reads as if the author were speaking to us. Examples are at the start of chapters 7 (when Bundle motored up to town "this time without adventures by the way"); 8 ("We must at this point go back to some 20 minutes earlier"); 10 ("Now it may be said at once that in the foregoing conversation each of the participants had, as it were, held something in reserve"); and 18 ("Our chronicle must here split into three separate and distinct portions"). Although not at all unpleasant, the style is rather at odds with the rest of the novel.

Clues

The least satisfying aspect of the clueing is that there is almost nothing to enable us, even in retrospect, to identify Battle as No 7 or the Seven Dials as sleuths, while the persistent misdirection about Jimmy's character makes it most unlikely that he could be a villain. Even accepting that one doesn't expect the same standard of clueing in a thriller as in a detective story, the clues against him are, generally speaking, not fairly presented (such as the otherwise clever 'Tell Jimmy' clue) or unconvincing. Although there is one potentially excellent clue (the 'bitten glove' clue), the author disguises a key piece of information (the teeth marks) too heavily for us to interpret it.

We assume, not least from the book's title, that the principal clue about Gerry's murder is going to be the "mystery" (as Bundle puts it in chapter 4) of the seven clocks arranged on the mantelpiece in his room, with the eighth one found on the lawn, after being thrown out of the window

While Bundle is puzzling about this 'clocks' clue, she finds Gerry's unfinished letter telling Loraine to forget about the Seven Dials business. This 'Gerry letter' clue is the first pointer to the Seven Dials and she says to Jimmy and Loraine in chapter 9, after discussing the 'Gerry letter' clue and 'clocks' clue, "Don't you see! *Seven Dials*! … It can't be a coincidence".

So, with no one admitting to having arranged the clocks, we look back to recall whose idea it was to buy them. In fact it was Bateman who suggested buying one clock; Bill who suggested that *all* six people going into Market Basing should buy one; Ronny who suggested getting one for Bateman; and Bill who suggested getting one for Lady Coote. Jimmy did not have a role.

Despite this build-up, the 'clocks' clue turns out to be very disappointing since the clocks' apparently mystifying arrangement is not intended to provide a clue, in the form of, say, a coded message, to the identity of Gerry's murderer. They were, so Battle explains (chapter 33), arranged on the mantelpiece after Gerry's death by Ronny (who threw the eighth out of the window to leave seven) merely as a symbol that the Seven Dials would avenge the death of one of their members. So Ronny must have known that Gerry was one of the Seven Dials and he watched eagerly to see if anyone was perturbed on seeing the seven clocks.

Battle assumes that Jimmy, who had noticed that there were seven clocks, rather than eight, had a bad five minutes at times thinking of them. And in chapter 9 Jimmy says "Somehow those clocks have always given me the shivers. I dream of them sometimes" and he shivers in chapter 18 when recalling them. But he also asks himself, before shivering, why they had been placed there, which is a fair question because the idea that they would effectively convey the message intended by Ronny is by no means convincing. And, since Jimmy did not appreciate their purpose, why was he shivering? Readers may wonder whether he is worried because they provide a clue against him. In fact they do not. It is only his worrying about them that does.

The first clue, as far as Battle is concerned (chapter 33), is Ronny's dying plea "Seven Dials … tell…", followed by "Tell … Jimmy Thesiger…". Battle says that Bundle interpreted the plea as meaning that Ronny was sending word to Jimmy that the Seven Dials had killed him. After all, she was already suspicious about Seven Dials in view of the 'Gerry letter' clue. And our suspicions about them are reinforced by two letters posted from the area of Seven Dials – a warning letter to Lomax about his house party at Wyvern Abbey (chapter 6), which was in fact sent to him to ensure that he would ask Battle to attend; and a letter to Gerry with a list of names and dates (chapter 8).

However, since Battle knew that an interpretation which implicated the Seven Dials could not be right, he knew that it was the Seven Dials (not Jimmy) to whom Ronny wanted to send word ("Seven Dials … tell…") – and that what he wanted to say was *about* (not for) Jimmy ("Tell … Jimmy Thesiger…").

This 'Tell Jimmy' clue is clever for various reasons. First, given our suspicion about the Seven Dials, we do not naturally interpret Ronny's words correctly or even appreciate that they are ambiguous. Second, the words misdirect us *away* from thinking of Jimmy as a villain. Third, the punctuation allows for enhanced misdirection: thus in chapter 15 Bundle says that the words were "Seven Dials. Tell Jimmy Thesiger" – so she interprets the dying words by putting the full stop before (not after) the word "Tell". Fourth, if one interprets the words correctly, it is a pretty compelling pointer towards Jimmy.

Having said this, the clue is not presented fairly because, after Ronny has said "tell" for the first time, Bundle asks "Who am I to tell?" and it is at this point that Ronny says "Tell … Jimmy Thesiger". So we are unambiguously directed to believe that it is

Jimmy who needs to be told. While we do not mind being tricked by Bundle *misinterpreting* the punctuation (since it is for us to spot that *she* is wrong), the misdirection built into the clue *itself* by Bundle's intervening question and Jimmy's answer is not fair. The author should have been braver in realising that the clue would be clever enough without them.

Nevertheless, even Battle does not regard the 'Tell Jimmy' clue as decisive because Ronny and Jimmy were close friends. But he does refer to two other factors implicating him. One is that two previous thefts of secret inventions must have been committed by someone who could hear, as Battle puts it, all the Foreign Office's chit-chat, which Jimmy, as a friend of both Ronny and Bill, could do. But this 'Foreign Office' clue is not fair because it is only a few lines before Jimmy's exposure that we are even told of these thefts.

The second factor implicating Jimmy is that it was very hard to find out how he could live at an expensive rate (with a manservant, Stevens, and his wife who cooked) when the income left to him by his father was small. This 'expensive rate' clue is also unfair because, although we are told that Jimmy doesn't have a job (chapter 7) and has never done an honest day's work in his life (chapter 25), we are never told that the income from his father was small.

Even though Battle therefore relies on three unfairly presented clues (the 'Tell Jimmy', 'Foreign Office' and 'expensive rate' clues), his own suspicions about Jimmy are "distinctly shaken" by the supposed fight. But he remains suspicious about it because none of his men saw the hefty man departing – although perhaps another ground for suspicion is that, although the fight is *heard* (by Bundle, Countess Radzky and the "several people" who fell into the room when the library door was unlocked), no one actually *sees* the fight.

Battle is also suspicious because of a "suggestive point" made by Countess Radzky, who is in the library at the time of the supposed fight but cannot see what is going on because she is hiding behind a big screen. She says (chapter 22) that she hears a man enter the room, turn on the lights and cross to the French window, then recross the room, turn the lights out and lock the library door, and then go back to the window for a second time. She says that, as the minutes then passed by with no further sound, she was almost sure that he had gone out through the window before the fight started.

Battle says that her story "agreed perfectly" with Jimmy's (not quite, if one studies the text in chapter 18, though close enough) but that there was a "suggestive point" – namely, that, if Jimmy had stayed in the room (rather than gone out through the window), she could hardly have helped hearing his breathing if she was listening for it and so he supposes that Jimmy *had* gone outside, giving himself the chance to climb up and down the ivy.

This 'breathing' clue sounds quite clever but it is hardly convincing because it is really only "suggestive" if Jimmy had claimed that he had *not* gone outside. But he had not claimed this in chapter 21 when responding to questions from Battle, who didn't actually ask him what he did when he went over to the window for a second time.

In fact, readers (and Battle) had already been told what he claimed to have done when going back to the window because in chapter 20 he had said that he saw the hefty man climbing down the ivy. To have seen this, he must have been outside. So there was no need for a "suggestive point" to make us think he had gone out – we could have deduced this already.

But the clue that turns up to clinch matters is the 'bitten glove' clue – "the burnt glove in the fireplace with the teeth marks on it", as Battle describes it in chapter 33. He had told us in chapter 23 that the pistol with which Jimmy was apparently shot had no fingerprints since the man who handled it wore gloves. So, when Battle shows us a burnt glove, blackened and charred, towards the end of that chapter, we know that this is a clue. But what does it tell us? There are two key points.

The first is that the glove was a left-handed glove, suggesting that the hefty man was left-handed. But how do we know that the glove was left-handed since we are not actually told this when Battle refers to the glove in chapter 23? What we are told then is that he tried it on Jimmy's hand – but not which one – and that it was large (well chosen by him to fit a hefty man) – although it cannot have been so large as to preclude squeezing the trigger of the Mauser pistol, which we are told was small.

In chapter 28 Bundle remembers that, when Battle tried the glove on Jimmy's hand (on the morning after the supposed fight), his right hand was by then in a sling, which leads Jimmy to recall that the glove which Battle tried on him was a left-handed glove. The prompting of Jimmy's memory in this way is contrived because Bundle introduces the point by the device of asking him "Didn't you say he tried it on your hand?". In fact, Jimmy had not said this.

Nevertheless, ignoring this contrivance, the key point is that we know by chapter 28 that the glove is left-handed. This casts suspicion on Sir Oswald, who is ambidextrous, O'Rourke who deals cards with his left hand and Bateman who plays tennis left-handed. Indeed, Battle says that the glove pointed straight to Bateman if it hadn't been for one thing.

That one thing is the second key point – the teeth marks. Since normally one would remove a left-handed glove with one's right hand, "only a man whose right hand was incapacitated would have needed to tear off that glove with his teeth", explains Battle. The only person whose right hand was incapacitated was Jimmy and therefore he must have been wearing the left-handed glove. Why was he? So that he could shoot himself in the right arm without leaving any fingerprints on the weapon, thereby corroborating his story of the fight.

That reasoning gives this 'bitten glove' clue the capacity to be an excellent one. The beauty of it is not so much that it is of itself decisive of the villain (as it is) but rather that the conclusion derived from it (that teeth marks on a left-handed glove mean that only a man whose right hand was incapacitated could have worn the glove) is not at all obvious when one is simply told that the glove had teeth marks on it, but yet is obvious when one thinks about it.

The reason for the clue having the 'capacity' to be excellent – rather than actually being excellent – is that it is not until chapter 33 (*after* Jimmy has been exposed) that Battle expressly refers to the glove "with the teeth marks on it". What he says, when he first displays the glove (chapter 23), is that it was "in the grate – nearly burnt, but not quite. Queer; looks as though it had been chewed by a dog" and, when Bundle later refers to the glove (chapter 28), she doesn't refer to the teeth marks at all.

By not referring to them, the author goes too far in concealing the very core of the clue. As with the 'Tell Jimmy' clue, she should have been braver, in this case by letting Battle say that the glove had teeth marks on it instead of disguising them by saying that it looked as though it had been "chewed" by a dog, which conveys the impression of a far more mangled item than Jimmy would have created by simply tearing off the glove with his teeth. Nevertheless, despite the excessive disguise, this is the best clue in the book.

We also get a related supplemental clue, prompted by Battle noticing a dent in the lawn where the pistol had landed after Jimmy had thrown it. Battle asks Sir Oswald to throw the pistol from the terrace and it lands a good ten yards further than the dent. Battle comments (in chapter 33) that a man who is right-handed doesn't throw as far with the left hand. What we are perhaps supposed to deduce from this 'dent' clue – but Battle does not make this clear – is that the pistol was thrown by someone who did not use his normal throwing hand. If so, that implicates Jimmy because he is right-handed (chapter 27) but could not have used that hand. However, this is unconvincing since, even if Jimmy had been able to throw the pistol with his right hand, he might still have thrown it ten yards less than Sir Oswald who threw the pistol with a powerful sweep of his arm.

Although the 'bitten glove' clue is the best one, the most obvious aspect of the clueing – or, rather, misleading clueing – of Jimmy is that we are persistently conditioned to believe that he cannot be the villain. This starts at the outset when chapter 1 begins "That amiable youth, Jimmy Thesiger…" and continues in that vein. Jimmy is "a fair, cherubic young man" (chapter 1), an "amiable, pink-faced young man" (chapter 16) and a "pleasant and engaging youth" (chapter 18) with a "cherubic pink face" (chapter 25).

He is not only portrayed as nice but as caring (his concern for Loraine and, after time, Bundle); patriotic (singing Rule Britannia and therefore unlikely to steal an invention being evaluated by the British government); and not clever enough to be the villain ("the usual complete young ass" in chapter 14). And there are various occasions where we participate in his thoughts or feelings and so are led to sympathise with him as a sleuth.

The effect of all these 'Jimmy' clues is to make readers feel, when they learn in chapter 33 that Battle has never met "a more utterly depraved and callous criminal", that his comment is completely contrary to the psychological profile of Jimmy which has been created and therefore dissatisfyingly hard to accept.

This is not to say that there are no other clues pointing to him but they are all minor such as Ronny's belief (mentioned at least three times) that Jimmy has brains; Bill's similar view that Jimmy has "more brains than you'd think"; Jimmy being described as a liar "of the most unblushing order" in chapter 12 (but so is Bundle); and Jimmy saying "Oh, I was born to be hanged" in chapter 27 (although he is simply responding to Lady Coote's exaggeration).

Indeed, most of the clues (and Jimmy's thoughts and feelings) which turn out to be clues to his villainy are just as compatible with him being a sleuth. So it is only in retrospect that we realise their true meaning – such as his taking the trouble to find out that Gerry, although at the Foreign Office, had been out of England from 1915–1918 and was therefore probably in the Secret Service (chapter 9); purchasing an automatic (chapter 15); attempting to get invited to Letherbury, the Cootes' newly rented house (chapter 25); being on the wrong side of Sir Oswald and Bateman, which is as much a clue against them if he's a sleuth (chapter 25); using skeleton keys to search Sir Oswald's desk at Letherbury (chapter 27); and sending his manservant Stevens out for cigarettes during the discussion in which he poisons Bill (chapter 29).

The first clue we have against Loraine (other than Jimmy's attraction to her, which is perhaps a clue for anyone who suspects Jimmy) is her "meekness" in agreeing in chapter 9 not to participate in the adventure at Wyvern Abbey, which Bundle regards as "highly suspicious". If Bundle's attitude is a clue against Loraine, it seems neutralised by the fact that she *does* then participate.

What creates greater suspicion about Loraine is a textual clue at the start of chapter 10. We are told that each of Bundle, Jimmy and Loraine had been holding something in reserve and so we wonder what this is. In Bundle's case, we quickly learn that she had a "fully-fledged plan" which involved visiting Battle at Scotland Yard. In Jimmy's case, the position is rather vague – he had "various ideas and plans" connected with the party at Wyvern Abbey which he had no intention of revealing to Bundle – but this reticence is not clearly a clue against him. However, in Loraine's case, chapter 10 actually questions whether she was "perfectly sincere in her account of the motives which had led her to seek out Jimmy Thesiger" and, although we therefore wait for an explanation of her true motives, it never comes.

The main behavioural clue against her is her arrival on the terrace at Wyvern Abbey just as the papers fall at her feet. And this seems to be supported by another textual clue when she runs off with them "as though panic-stricken" straight into Battle. One wonders if the words "as though" suggest that she was not *in fact* panicked by a man climbing down the ivy. However, we are misdirected away from her by her almost plausible explanation, the credit she gets for saving the plans and Battle's theory that they were thrown to her by the burglar who thought she was someone else.

Readers are also unlikely to spot her as Jimmy's accomplice because, although we know that he is attracted to her and even suggests marriage, we get no real clue that *she* is "devoted body and soul" to him. This is particularly unsatisfactory given that it is, crucially, the passing on of information by her, as a result of that devotion, that leads to the murders of Gerry and Ronny.

Indeed, when it comes down to it, the only factor against Loraine which is not counteracted by an innocent explanation is one which Battle gives in chapter 33 – that "She's got bad blood in her – her father ought to have seen the inside of a prison more than once". However, even the most alert reader would have done very well to spot the clueing of this hereditary factor, which occurs just once, in chapter 6, where her father is described as "a perfect blackguard" and "rascally". Such a reader would do better still to deduce that this 'blackguard' clue means that she had inherited sufficiently bad blood to assist Jimmy.

Finally, as for Battle, there is no real clueing of his role as No 7 or of the Seven Dials being an organisation for good rather than evil. We do get a clue that Countess Radzky is No 1 when Bundle spots that below Radzky's right shoulder blade there is a small black mole which she had seen on No 1's back when eavesdropping at the Seven Dials meeting. But the nearest one perhaps gets with Battle is that his eyelids flickered and he looked taken aback when Bundle mentioned Seven Dials in chapter 10; and that in chapter 22, after she had told him that Radzky was No 1, he hemmed and hawed and said that that he knew all about her and wanted her left alone. But these clues are very slight, if they can be counted as clues at all.

Perhaps the most imaginative 'Battle' clues are ones which, as mere retrospective verbal ones, are probably not intended as clues at all, namely Jimmy's question in chapter 18 as to whether No 7 is disguised as a servant at Wyvern Abbey (and, as noted earlier, Battle is disguised as a footman there) and Bundle's comment in chapter 24: "In fact there is only one person I am really sure isn't No 7 … Superintendent Battle".

5

The Murder At The Vicarage

Solution

This is the first Jane Marple novel, set in her village of St Mary Mead in Downshire. Her house is next to the Vicarage and, as a "noticing kind of person" (chapter 30), she keeps an eye on people approaching it from the lane and entering its garden through the back gate to gain access via the French window in the study, instead of the front door.

The victim of the murder at the Vicarage is Colonel Lucius Protheroe, wealthy magistrate and churchwarden. He is found by the Vicar, Leonard Clement (the story's narrator), at about 6.45 on a Thursday evening sprawled across the writing table in the Vicarage study, shot through the head.

He had arrived at 6.15 to discuss some missing church collection money with Clement. But Clement had been called to a dying parishioner at about 5.30 and did not return until 6.45. In fact, the call was a hoax to remove him so that Protheroe could be shot at about 6.20.

The immediate suspects are Protheroe's second wife, Anne, and her lover, Lawrence Redding, an artist using a studio in the Vicarage garden. However, by chapter 12 (out of 32) both seem to be above suspicion. It is the creation, and then elimination, of suspicion against them that is the essential cleverness of the murder plan because it is in fact Anne, aided by Redding, who shoots Protheroe with Redding's pistol.

Readers know of Redding and Anne's relationship because on the day before the murder Clement finds them kissing in the studio. Shortly after that, Anne, whom we know to be "fed up to the teeth" with Protheroe (chapter 1), tells Clement that she is "dreadfully unhappy" and wishes Protheroe were dead. She impresses Clement as a woman who would stick at nothing and is "desperately, wildly, madly in love" with Redding. Her motivation and probable guilt could hardly be more plainly conveyed.

As for Redding, he tells Clement, after dinner that day, that Anne is one of the truest and most loyal women that ever lived. He is not described as having her desperation but he says "If I had a penny in the world I'd take her away without any more ado" (chapter 4). Clement begs him to leave St Mary Mead because, when Protheroe finds out, things will be infinitely worse for Anne.

By the following afternoon, so we are told in chapter 30, the crime had been planned to the smallest detail. At about 3.45 Clement finds Redding waiting for him at the Vicarage. Redding says that he will say goodbye to Anne that evening (at 6.15 in the studio, we later learn) and probably leave next day.

Once Clement has been lured away at 5.30 by the hoax call (made by Redding, sounding like a woman), Anne comes down the lane, passing Miss Marple's garden shortly before 6.20. The murder plan depends importantly upon the murderers being seen by Miss Marple, who can act as a witness. Anne speaks to her to show that she is her normal self and to allow Miss Marple to confirm later that she didn't have a pistol: it wasn't in a handbag (she didn't have one) and it couldn't have been hidden on her, given the revealing dress she wore.

She tells Miss Marple that she is calling for her husband at the Vicarage so that (after his 6.15 meeting with Clement) they can go home together – which she later pretends she said because she "had to say something" rather than admit she was meeting Redding at the studio at 6.15. This supposed meeting with her husband enables her to explain why, after then going into the Vicarage garden by the back gate, she goes round the corner of the Vicarage to the French window of the study, so disappearing from Miss Marple's sight. She later claims to have looked through it but, because she had not seen him (as she would not have done since the writing table was in the corner), she had hurried back across the lawn to the studio for her meeting with Redding.

In fact, she had entered the study through the French window, come up behind the "slightly deaf" Protheroe, shot him with Redding's Mauser .25 pistol (which was already hidden in the study, with a silencer), come out like a flash and – seen again "almost immediately" by Miss Marple – gone down the garden to the studio to meet Redding. She was out of Miss Marple's sight for such a short time that, as Miss Marple explains in chapter 30, "nearly anyone" would swear that there couldn't have been time for her to shoot Protheroe.

Miss Marple then sees Redding come along the lane to the back gate and go into the studio where, he claims, he and Anne said goodbye to each other. About ten minutes later, just after 6.30, she sees them leave and stroll along the lane to the village, with a natural demeanour, smiling and talking and appearing very happy and not at all as if they have just committed a murder.

For the next ten minutes they set up alibis. Having been joined by Dr Stone as they walk to the village, they talk by the Post Office for a few minutes. Anne goes into Miss Hartnell's house and remains there until 7 pm. Redding goes to the Blue Boar with Stone, leaving at 6.40 to go to the Vicarage because, he explains, he wanted someone to talk to after saying goodbye to Anne, although in fact he was going there to carry out some final murder plan tasks.

He enters the Vicarage through the open front door, just after seeing Clement far away on the footpath returning (from the hoax call) at about 6.45. Before Clement arrives, he carries out the tasks in the study in a couple of minutes.

First, he puts on the writing table a forged note, "dated" (meaning 'timed at') 6.20, apparently begun by Protheroe just before he is shot, which reads "Dear Clement, Sorry I cannot wait any longer, but I must…" before the writing tails off. The note seems to implicate Anne because of her being seen near the study by Miss Marple just after 6.20 but, since the time is written in a different ink and handwriting from the body of the note, which is not even in Protheroe's handwriting, it will be seen as a clumsy attempt to incriminate Anne by someone who had killed Protheroe at, say, 6.30 but knew that Anne had been there just after 6.20.

Second, he notices a letter actually being written by Protheroe, in relation to the missing collection money, accusing "an ordained priest of the church" of being the culprit. Redding removes this unexpected bonus, which may come in useful later in implicating the 'priest' in Protheroe's murder.

Third, he alters the clock on the writing table to 6.22 to accord with the time of death suggested by the forged note and overturns it (as if Protheroe had done so when falling forward) so that it stops at that time. But he knows that the clock is kept quarter of an hour fast, and so also knows that overturning it will be seen as part of the attempt to incriminate Anne because, unknown to the clumsy incriminator, the 'real' time when the clock stopped at its adjusted time of 6.22 would have been 6.07 when Protheroe had not yet arrived.

Fourth, he pockets his Mauser .25 pistol left by Anne and then leaves the Vicarage, acting distraught as he passes the arriving Clement. The reason he had waited, before entering the Vicarage until he saw Clement returning, was that he wanted to be seen by him leaving in a distraught state. As Miss Marple explains, a murderer who has committed a crime would try to behave naturally – so Redding (who will shortly pretend, unconvincingly, that he murdered Protheroe at 6.45) does the opposite, by appearing distraught, so helping his pretence look unconvincing.

At 10 pm that evening, he goes into the police station with his pistol (having discarded the silencer). He pretends that he came to the Vicarage at about 6.45 to see Clement, that he found Protheroe, that they quarrelled and that he shot him with his Mauser pistol, on which only his fingerprints are later identified (after he has wiped off Anne's). Next day, Anne too claims to have shot him, saying she had hated him for a long time. However, in order to make their confessions appear to be a pretence, their answers to questions about how they each committed the murder are (deliberately) unconvincing.

Anne claims to have used her husband's pistol, which she had brought to the Vicarage, but Miss Marple says she can't have brought it and Protheroe's valet says he didn't have a pistol. And Redding could not have killed Protheroe at 6.45 because the effect of Dr Haydock's comments in chapters 5, 7 and 18 is to put the time of death at 6.35 at the latest. Nor could he have done so before 6.35 because he had been in the village near the Blue Boar at 6.10 (before Protheroe was even at the Vicarage) and was then seen by Miss Marple coming along the lane to the studio and departing ten minutes later.

Their combined confessions comprise a sort of joint double bluff – telling the truth (that they are murderers) while hoping that people will think they are bluffing. Although perhaps not strictly a double bluff because, individually, they didn't tell the truth (since Redding didn't shoot Protheroe and Anne used Redding's pistol), the ploy works. It seems that Redding had only confessed to protect Anne because, having found Protheroe dead at 6.45, he feared that she had shot him with the pistol from his cottage; and that she had only confessed because he had been so "noble" in accusing himself.

So, with Redding having an alibi and Anne seeming to be

the victim of clumsy attempts to incriminate her at about 6.20, when no shot was even heard, their unconvincing confessions are dismissed, putting them above suspicion.[1]

Who else, then, might have killed Protheroe – taking Redding's pistol (since he doesn't lock his cottage) and entering through the Vicarage's open front door (since, says Miss Marple, no one else came down the lane)? In chapter 9 she "can think of at least seven people who might be very glad to have Colonel Protheroe out of the way" but doesn't give any names then or when asked in chapter 11, suggesting that Clement should be able to think of them himself. He can only think of Lettice, Protheroe's daughter by his first marriage, who comes into money on her father's death.

Lettice does later turn out to be Miss Marple's third suspect "wanting freedom and money to do as she liked" and she is, like Anne, "fed up to the teeth" with Protheroe (chapter 1). We find out in chapter 22 that her alibi – that she did not return from a tennis party on the afternoon of the murder until 7.30 – may not be true because she left early. So she appears to have motive and opportunity, but neither as clearly as Anne.

When Miss Marple, having again declined to name the seven suspects in chapter 26, finally does so in chapter 30, it seems an odd list, in terms of both who is, and who is not, on it. It would be very surprising if any reader came up with exactly the same list, either when first thinking about it in chapter 9 or even when returning to it in chapter 30.

First is Archer, a poacher jailed by Protheroe, but now released. Protheroe had told Clement that Archer had vowed vengeance, so it is strange that Clement doesn't think of him in chapter 11. But he is never a realistic suspect. Nor is her second choice, Mary, the Vicarage servant, despite her going out with Archer and being in the Vicarage at the time of the murder.

Third is Lettice, while fourth is Dennis, Clement's young nephew, who is infatuated with her. Miss Marple refers to a tennis racquet seen by Mrs Price Ridley's maid lying on the grass by the Vicarage gate which, she says, made it look as if he had got back earlier from the tennis party than he had said. But her suggestion to Clement about his motivation ("Whatever the motive – for Lettice's sake or for yours, it was a possibility") is most uncompelling.

Fifth and sixth come Hawes, the curate, and Clement himself because one of them must have stolen the collection money and feared exposure by Protheroe. Hawes acts nervously throughout the story and Miss Marple says she was always convinced (rightly) that he was the thief.

In chapter 27 he rings Clement saying "*I want to confess*". Clement rushes to him and finds him asleep, an empty cachet box beside him. On the floor is a crumpled, unfinished letter to Clement, which turns out to be Protheroe's accusation against "an ordained priest of the church". This suggests that Hawes, fearing exposure by Protheroe, had murdered him, removed the letter and then taken an overdose out of remorse. In fact, Redding had visited Hawes earlier, substituted a harmful cachet and put the letter into his pocket.

Clement, Melchett (the Chief Constable), Haydock and Miss Marple all seem to assume that Hawes wanted to 'confess' to the murder. However, since Miss Marple knows by then that he didn't commit it, her interpretation is that he felt he must confess to the theft, but found the letter after innocently taking the harmful cachet and "in his disordered state" was impelled to confess "the whole thing", not just the theft. In the event, his life is saved by Dr Haydock.

Clement, Miss Marple's sixth suspect, starts the story by saying "Anyone who murdered Colonel Protheroe would be doing the world at large a service". He had been offended by Protheroe's comments about the collection money and was rumoured by Mrs Price Ridley to have been at fault for objecting to any inquiry into it. We do not rule him out simply because he is the narrator (so, when he says something "truthfully", such as in chapter 21, we wonder if he is not being truthful elsewhere) but he never seems a realistic suspect.

Seventh is Clement's much younger wife, Griselda, who had returned from London unexpectedly early, giving her the opportunity to commit the murder. Moreover, Clement had received two anonymous letters – one suggesting that she was "Carrying On" with Redding; and the second saying she had left his cottage at 6.20 on the fatal day, causing Clement to envisage Protheroe learning of an intrigue between her and Redding but being shot by her with Redding's pistol before he could reveal it. In fact, she may, as Miss Marple suggests, just have been using the cottage with Dennis to telephone Mrs Price Ridley abusively at about 6.30 to silence her rumours.

Beyond Miss Marple's suspects there are at least two others who might have killed Protheroe – Dr Stone and Mrs Lestrange. Stone, an archaeologist working on Protheroe's property, had had several disputes with him, including, as Miss Marple knows (chapter 2), a serious quarrel shortly before the murder. In chapter 21 he is confirmed as an imposter – being a cracksman who had studied Stone's subject and was really after Protheroe's silver. His secretary, Gladys Cram, also acts suspiciously and is seen by Miss Marple leaving a suitcase in the woods at night. This is found by Clement, with silver objects inside, but she is never a realistic suspect.

Mrs Lestrange had arrived mysteriously in St Mary Mead and visited Protheroe the night before the murder, when she had argued with him "hammer and tongs" and said "*By this time tomorrow night, you may be dead*" (chapter 19). Protheroe's butler, Reeves, had even "got the sack" for letting her in and so he is another person with a grudge against Protheroe.

Although Mrs Lestrange is Inspector Slack's main suspect,

readers should realise that the mystery about her is that she is Protheroe's first wife (Lettice's mother). Redding remembers her as "dangerous" (chapter 4) but the context in which he might previously (and surprisingly) have met her is not clarified. In fact, she had only come to St Mary Mead, with a month to live, to ask to see Lettice and was helped by Haydock, an old friend. When Protheroe refused, she met Lettice at 6.15, which is why Lettice left the tennis party early.

After Protheroe's death, Haydock was frightened that Mrs Lestrange had killed him – which explains why he looks "grey and old" on realising that Redding could not have done it, and later looks worried, upset, harried, rattled and haggard in chapters 8, 14, 16 and 25 – even though he is "not a man who ever shows his feelings" (chapter 29). Indeed, his appearance may cause readers to wonder if he too should be on the lengthy list of suspects.

Although the list is lengthy, the only people on it who are perhaps credible suspects (Hawes, Stone and Mrs Lestrange) are almost too suspicious as they conceal their secrets. So, despite Anne and Redding's ploy of unconvincing confessions and Clement being "convinced" that Anne is "a very honest woman" (chapter 22), they will remain under scrutiny from readers, who will be well aware of her obvious mixed motivation of love (of Redding) and hate (of Protheroe) and be wary of her disappearance from Miss Marple's sight.

There is therefore no great surprise in her being the murderer. As Miss Marple says, "…it is so often the obvious that is true" (chapter 30), although she is talking there about Redding whose motivation is more clinical. We know that, if he had a penny in the world, he would take Anne away without more ado. But he doesn't have a penny. And because he would never run away with "a penniless woman" it was, from his point of view, as Miss Marple explains, "…necessary that Colonel Protheroe should be removed – and so he removed him. One of those charming young men who have *no* moral sense".

Miss Marple even regards him as "the murderer" (chapter 29) because Anne was completely under his thumb and "would do anything he told her" (chapter 30). While this may have been so, it was Anne who shot Protheroe and she must have agreed the murder plan. So it doesn't seem right that Redding should alone be tarred as "the murderer".

For readers who think, in relation to the *whodunnit*, that Anne's guilt seems compelling and Redding's complicity likely, there are still three stumbling blocks to solving the *howdunnit*.[2] First, where and when does Anne get the pistol, since she didn't bring it? Second, why was no shot heard at about 6.20 which is the only time when she could have shot Protheroe? Third, why was a sound like a shot heard at about 6.30 when the murderers have an alibi? Until they can be answered, even readers who suspect Anne and Redding have to keep open the possibility that the villain is to be found elsewhere.

The answer to the first stumbling block – that Anne didn't have a pistol – is that, when Redding called at the Vicarage, knowing that Clement was out (until about 3.45), he brought it with him and hid it in a plant pot for Anne.

The answer to the second one – why no shot was heard at 6.20 – is that a silencer was used. This is thought "quite likely" in chapter 7 but dismissed, not only by Melchett but also by readers, who will think it lacks the ingenuity sought in detective fiction, particularly as genuine mystification had seemed promised by it being "amazing" that no one, not even Miss Marple, had heard a shot (chapter 7) and yet "somebody *must* have heard it" (chapter 12), especially Mary because "If there was a shot she'd have heard it" (chapter 18).

Readers are also regularly directed away from a murder time of 6.20 by the third stumbling block of a shot being heard by Miss Marple, Mary and Mrs Price Ridley at about 6.30. Miss Marple *thinks* it came from the woods but it could have come from the Vicarage study. In fact, the shot was manufactured by Redding in the woods. He suspended a large stone above picric acid crystals (which explode if a weight is dropped on them), one of which is later found by Clement. He then lit a fuse, which would, says Miss Marple, take about 20 minutes to burn through so that the stone would fall, causing an explosion at about 6.30.

In fact, the 'fuse' must have taken longer than Miss Marple's 20 minutes since Redding was by the Blue Boar at 6.10 (chapter 11). And, although Clement's schedule in chapter 26 says that Redding, Anne and Stone's evidence seemed to point to a shot being heard before 6.30–6.35, one wonders what 'evidence' from Stone he means since Stone says he didn't hear a shot (chapter 17). However, the main issue about the 'shot' is whether this rather unreliable addition to the murder plan was needed at all.

Miss Marple says it was "absolutely necessary" because "otherwise suspicion of Mrs Protheroe might have continued" (chapter 30). But it's hard to believe that Redding needed to worry about mere "suspicion" when there is, as Melchett says, "no proof – not an atom" for Miss Marple's solution and when there are so many other suspects, one of whom might simply have used a silencer at 6.30 (as Anne had done at 6.20).

Apart from the suspended 'shot', the *howdunnit*, with the pistol (and silencer) already in the pot, is quite clever, albeit requiring speed and nerve by Anne. And it has been constructed really cleverly, combining further simple, but reliable, elements: the hoax call; the revealing dress; the clumsy incrimination with the note and clock; the alibis; the distraught acting after waiting for Clement; and the unconvincing confessions.

However, its principal cleverness comes in the murderers' well-calculated reliance on being seen by the "noticing" Miss Marple, who "always sees everything" from her garden (chapter 2). She confirms that Anne had no gun or handbag and was quite her normal self, that she hurried back across the lawn almost immediately, that Redding then came down the lane and that, when they emerged from the studio after ten minutes, they appeared to be very happy. Ironically, it is, as we shall see later, in their apparently clever behaviour that Miss Marple finds the best clues.

Plot

This novel, published in 1930, was the author's first for the Crime Club, an imprint of William Collins & Co. Ltd., her publishers since 1926.[3]

It is set entirely in St Mary Mead. Although the murder occurs at the Vicarage, Miss Marple's house is also a key location because of the comings and goings relating to the murder being seen and timed from "the danger point of Miss Marple's garden" (chapter 3).

The significance of the plot's geography is emphasised by having three plans – Plan A (the Vicarage and Miss Marple's house), Plan B (the study) and Plan C (the village). Indeed, it would be reasonable to wonder, with the plot being so dependent upon the curiosity of the person living next to the Vicarage, whether Miss Marple was created as a "noticing" character in order to enable the plot to work – although that is not the case because she had already appeared in 12 short stories, as explained in the chapter about her.

The strength of the story comes not in providing a surprising solution to the puzzle but in creating a classic village setting inhabited by a cast of memorable characters, which the author conjures wonderfully well, helped by Clement's easy, sometimes humorous narrative style.

The only issues with his narrative come towards the end where Miss Marple's solution and explanations, and her trap for Redding, feel rather hurried, especially when contrasted with the rest of the story which has unfolded at a pretty leisurely pace because of all its sub-plots and suspects. In particular, she suddenly names Redding as "the murderer" at the end of chapter 29. It would have been much better to finish the chapter two lines earlier, enabling us to gather our thoughts before revealing his guilt in the next chapter.

Although very little of the story focuses on her actually solving the puzzle, the plot is very well constructed on the whole. It coherently interweaves five sub-plots (the missing collection money; Mrs Lestrange; the anonymous letters; the call to Mrs Price Ridley; and Dr Stone), as well as an impressively large number of suspects, into the main murder plot and it provides readers with elements of mystification (the three stumbling blocks) – although those who think that there are too many sub-plots and suspects may find it overlong.[4]

Some readers may also feel that there is a small weakness in each of the five sub-plots. First, as to Hawes's theft of the collection money, it's a little hard to believe that, even in his "disordered state", he would feel "impelled" to react to a letter accusing him of theft by confessing to a murder he didn't commit. Second, the solution to Mrs Lestrange's sub-plot is very obvious. By chapter 19, when we learn that Protheroe had said to her "You shall not see her – I forbid it", all readers must surely realise (even though Slack and Clement do not) that she is his first wife and wants to see her daughter.

Third, there is a strange omission relating to the two anonymous letters sent to Clement about Griselda. We never learn who wrote them. Fourth, as to the abusive telephone call to Mrs Price Ridley, the second of the two letters had described "in detail" Griselda leaving Redding's cottage at 6.20 (chapter 30). So how can Miss Marple say that "Dear Griselda sent that call" (chapter 30) – which we know was put through at *6.30* from Redding's cottage (chapter 17) – if she had already left it by 6.20?

Presumably the letter was wrong.

Fifth, as to Stone's theft of Protheroe's silver, although Clement finds Miss Cram's suitcase in the woods with silver objects inside, we never learn, despite Slack commissioning an expert in chapter 25, whether they are Protheroe's objects (which had been stolen, then substituted by replicas) or the as yet unsubstituted replicas.

There is another minor point relating to Miss Cram. When Miss Marple says that she saw Stone join Redding and Anne in the lane just after 6.30, she thinks she saw Miss Cram join them. However, in chapter 25 Miss Cram says that Miss Marple "has been mistaken once, remember, when she said she saw me at the end of the lane". But we don't "remember" because no one had ever confirmed that Miss Marple was wrong.

Finally, reverting to the main plot, there are two small points concerning Anne. While she is with Clement on the day before the murder, she suddenly looks at the study window, saying she thinks she heard something. He looks out but no one is there. Yet he thinks that he, too, had heard someone. This intriguing event is not referred to again – even though we assume (wrongly) that it relates to the murder plan, perhaps allowing Anne to hide the pistol. Then at the inquest (chapter 18) she says she arrived at the Vicarage at about 6.15 to meet her husband – not at about 6.20 (the actual time). We learn later in the chapter that she had been "told" (by the police?) to suggest this. Why?

Clues

A reader who pauses about three-quarters of the way through the novel (perhaps chapter 24 out of 32) may feel that there hasn't yet been a memorable clue to the murderers beyond their obvious relationship and motivation. Melchett does say in chapter 12 that "the clock, the note, the pistol – they don't make sense as they stand" but the 'clock' clue and the 'Protheroe note' clue just seem to be clues to a clumsy attempt to incriminate Anne while the pistol doesn't even seem to be a clue because it could have been brought to the study by, he says, "almost anyone".

In fact, as we shall see, there are various clues, with the 'plant pot' clue being reasonably memorable and the 'handbag' and 'happy demeanour' clues being good and imaginative. Those two are, however, easily missed, partly because they are not obviously clues – requiring, rather, behavioural interpretation – but mainly because the story's real focus is on the geography of the village and the style of the person who turns out to be the detective.

We know nowadays that this is a 'Miss Marple story' but many original readers would have assumed, unless they had read the short stories, that Clement will solve the case. He reads detective stories, is present at some significant events, thinks about the 'clock' clue, is with Melchett and Slack at some interviews and visits the woods twice to carry out detective work.

On the first visit he meets Redding, apparently doing the same, and suggests that Redding is "that favourite character of fiction, the amateur detective". However, it is Clement who more clearly fits this role, describing his success in finding the picric acid as "Sherlock Holmes's secret" and even saying "I think each one of us in his secret heart fancies himself as Sherlock Holmes".

We do get a hint that Miss Marple may have a detection role when Clement says in chapter 4 (not referring specifically to her but to the detective instinct of village life) that "There is no detective in England equal to a spinster lady of uncertain age with plenty of time on her hands".

Indeed, she produces a genuinely good piece of analysis in chapter 11 in relation to the 'Protheroe note' clue, supposedly written by him at 6.20 in which he says that he "...cannot wait any longer...". Since he had been told by Mary (only five minutes before) that Clement wouldn't be back before 6.30 and had appeared willing to wait, why would he write impatiently at 6.20? Miss Marple's clever reasoning makes Clement think that

Protheroe wasn't shot while writing the note at 6.20, but at 6.30 with the murderer putting 6.20 on the note – though the real answer is that Protheroe didn't write it at all.

However, beyond this, her role as the person who's going to solve the puzzle is not clear before chapter 26 – only three chapters before she names Redding as "the murderer". Although she says in chapter 6 that she is "quite *convinced*" that she knows who did it, we regard her only as a well-informed and insightful observer or as a witness. Indeed, after her clever analysis in chapter 11, she appears in only four of the next 14 chapters.

Beyond minor contributions in those, she doesn't change our view about her role until explaining her interest in the murder in chapter 26. She says that she had always wondered whether, if a really big mystery came along, she could solve it. Only then do we start to realise that Clement is nearer to a Watson or Hastings figure and that Miss Marple, although not detecting in the traditional sense or classic style (or even, it seems, at all), may solve the case.

We learn in chapter 30 that, when she was "quite *convinced*" as early as chapter 6 that she knew who did it, she was thinking of Redding (and of Anne, who was under his thumb). We know that she was aware by then of their relationship – even before Clement found them kissing in the studio – because in chapter 2 she thought that there was something between Redding and "another person" – meaning Anne (not Griselda).

Since she was "quite *convinced*" about Redding, it is odd that she seems "very surprised" when told in chapter 6 that he had been arrested. But she is then told that he has confessed, whereupon she says she has been "sadly at sea" because the confession just proves "that he had nothing to do with it". Although she does not explain her reasoning clearly, she does say that young men are "often prone to believe the worst" and so presumably she had cleverly concluded (six chapters before Redding even claims this) that he had only confessed because he believed that Anne had done it – meaning that he couldn't have done it himself.

She says in chapter 30 that the confession had "upset all my ideas and made me think him innocent – when up to then I had felt convinced that he was guilty". On hearing of Anne's confession, she was "almost sure" that that wasn't true either (chapter 9) and, because she liked them both, was relieved when learning that they had "both confessed in the most foolish way".

The irony of all this is that Miss Marple's first conclusion in a novel – that Redding (and Anne) were guilty – appears to have been wrong (though we later find out that it was correct) while her second conclusion (that Redding and Anne were innocent after all because of their confessions) is treated as correct for most of the book (but turns out to be wrong).

In chapter 26 she says, "I think, on the whole, one theory fits nearly everything. That is if you admit one coincidence – and I think one coincidence is allowable". Her theory only fits "nearly" everything because of "one flaw in my theory – one fact that I can't get over. Oh! If only that note had been something quite different –". So her theory has a "coincidence" and a "flaw".

Dealing first with the "flaw", we naturally assume that it must relate to the 'Protheroe note' clue because of her wishing it was "something quite different" in the very next sentence after mentioning the flaw. In fact, this juxtaposition of the flaw and the note turns out to be misdirection – and rather unfair because it is so blatant – since Miss Marple had something else in mind. However, the unfairness does not last long because at the end of the chapter she says she "never" thought the note was "the real note" – so the note can't be the flaw because she has already taken its falseness into account.

So what is the flaw? Whatever it is, it seems that she finds the answer to it in the short period between the misdirecting juxtaposition and the end of chapter 26 because, as she leaves the study, she says "An idea has just occurred to me. I must go home and think things out thoroughly. Do you know, I believe I have been extremely stupid – almost incredibly so". So what "idea" could have occurred to her in that short period?

In chapter 30 she explains that, on leaving the study, she had "noticed the palm in the pot by the window – and – well, there the whole thing was! Clear as daylight!". She had overcome her flaw – namely, that Anne didn't have a pistol – by realising that it had been hidden earlier by Redding in the plant pot.

In providing the answer to this *howdunnit* stumbling block, the 'plant pot' clue is the most memorable in the book. It is also well concealed because, before the idea occurs to Miss Marple, her conversation with Clement about the plant changes to a discussion about Lettice and Mary, and so we think that that discussion (rather than the plant) prompts the idea.

A possible criticism of the clue is that we are not actually told in chapter 26 about a 'pot' (in which to hide the pistol) – just that, on leaving the study, she "felt the rather depressed-looking plant that stood in a stand". But one can fairly argue that, if there was a plant, there must have been a pot and, anyway, Plan B (the study) does show a 'Tall Stand With Pot On It'.[5]

Turning to Miss Marple's "coincidence", she explains in chapter 30 that this was the abusive call to Mrs Price Ridley (which had nothing to do with the murder) being put through at the same time as the fake shot (engineered by Redding). She says "it led one to believe that the two must be connected" – meaning that its relevance to the murder plan would need to be explained (until one realised that it was just a coincidence). However, it is doubtful that many readers would have made such a 'connection' instead of just regarding the call (rightly) as a red herring.

A more notable coincidence occurs when Clement finds a crystal of picric acid used for the fake shot at the very spot where he finds Miss Cram's suitcase. He doesn't know what it is but later Haydock thinks it looks like picric acid, which he says is an explosive. Clement says "Yes, I know that" (which is remarkable) but, in case readers start to wonder if it caused the fake shot, Clement misdirects us "...but it's got another use, hasn't it?". Haydock says, "It's used medically – in solution for burns" – so the 'picric acid' clue has us thinking about burns rather than explosives.

However, even readers who are not misdirected away from the explosive nature of the clue would do well to work out how Redding engineered the fake shot, despite one further clue – a large stone, which Clement sees Redding carrying on his first visit to the woods. Redding is in fact removing the stone but says to Clement, "No, it's not a clue, it's a peace offering". He claims he wants an excuse for calling on Miss Marple and has heard that she likes rocks or stones for her Japanese gardens.

In chapter 30 she explains that the 'stone' clue "put me on the right track!" because "It was the wrong sort of stone for my rock gardens!". This is unconvincing because Redding could innocently have chosen the wrong stone as a gift. Moreover, how could readers spot his error, given that Miss Marple "was much pleased" with the stone when it was presented (chapter 16)?

Similarly unconvincing is the clueing of the unheard shot at 6.20, with the silencer possibly being clued by a sneeze heard by Mrs Price Ridley's maid. In chapter 30 Miss Marple wonders "if, possibly, the sneeze that the maid, Clara, heard might have actually been the shot? But no matter". One doubts if readers would have interpreted the 'sneeze' clue as a silenced shot and her concluding words "But no matter" show how weak the clue is.

It is also Clara who, according to Miss Marple in chapter 30, saw the tennis racquet lying on the grass, carelessly flung down (chapter 25), which, she says, made it look as if Dennis got back early from the tennis party. But this 'discarded racquet' clue is unsatisfactory because we are never told that the racquet is his. Moreover, we have known since chapter 22 that it was Lettice who left the tennis party early, leaving Dennis there for another quarter of an hour, so that it could have been her racquet flung down on the grass as she hurried to meet Mrs Lestrange.

The clueing of Anne comes primarily from her mixed motivation of love and hate and from her (limited) opportunity. However, there is an additional, more imaginative clue – the 'handbag' clue. In chapter 9 Miss Marple says that Anne couldn't have hidden a gun in her handbag because she wasn't carrying one; and the grocery and fish shop, where Anne had been just before, agree she didn't have one. The point, as Miss Marple explains, is that going to the village without a handbag was "really a *most* unusual thing for a woman to do". So why did she? The answer is that it was part of the murder plan for Miss Marple to *notice* that she had nothing in which to conceal a gun.

A potential clue against Anne is her blue lapis lazuli earring found on the study floor two days after the murder. However, since it can hardly have been missed by Slack (who was on his hands and knees in chapter 5), it must have been dropped *after*, not during, the murder and so be a red herring. In fact, it was planted by Lettice to incriminate Anne for whom she had a mutual dislike.

Although Anne's share in her husband's estate does not seem to provide a motive directly for *her*, his wealth is nevertheless relevant to Redding's motivation, as we know from his comment that, if he had "a penny in the world", he would take her away – the 'penny' clue. To be able to do so, he would need the penniless Anne to acquire Protheroe's wealth.

In addition to his relationship with Anne and the pistol being his, we have the 'amateur actor' clue – that he was a "good amateur actor" (chapter 4). This may have helped him when lying to Clement about his intentions or adopting a woman's voice for the hoax call (as Miss Marple suggests) or acting distraught or making his unconvincing confession.

Finally, there is a particularly good clue against both Redding and Anne. When they leave the studio at about 6.30 and stroll down the lane, they are smiling and appear to be very happy, quite unlike people who have just committed a murder. However, that was their mistake because, if they had really just said goodbye to each other, as Redding says they had (chapter 12), their demeanour would have looked very different. But, because of the murder, they dared not appear upset. Their happy demeanour, despite the apparent ending of their relationship, was "their weak point", as Miss Marple says, and, although it had appeared to be a clever part of their murder plan, the 'happy demeanour' clue is the best and cleverest clue against them.

6

The Sittaford Mystery

Solution

This is a detective story in which the murder of Captain Joseph Trevelyan RN (retired), the owner of Sittaford House, is investigated, at least officially, by Divisional Inspector Narracott, who appears in nearly all the early chapters following the murder. After chapter 10 (out of 31), however, he appears only irregularly because the detection is then mainly carried out by Emily Trefusis, with some assistance from a journalist, Charles Enderby.

Trevelyan had built Sittaford House ten years ago in the remote, tiny village of Sittaford, perched up on the fringe of Dartmoor, together with a row of six bungalows along the lane from the house. But he was not living at Sittaford House when he was murdered on Friday 14 December, having rented it to a Mrs Willett and her daughter, Violet, who had recently arrived from, we are told, South Africa. They wanted a house on Dartmoor for the winter and made him an attractive offer. So he moved out and rented a small house called Hazelmoor in the town of Exhampton, six miles away in the valley below.

That Friday, Sittaford was almost completely cut off by the snow which had fallen for the last four days. During the wintry afternoon, with more snow due, six of the inhabitants of Sittaford were participating in a séance (or 'table-turning', as it is usually called in the novel) at Sittaford House – namely, Mrs Willett and Violet; Major John Burnaby from bungalow No. 1 – the nearest one to Sittaford House; Mr Rycroft from No. 3; Mr Ronnie Garfield, the nephew of the invalided Miss Percehouse from No. 4; and Mr Duke from No. 6 – the last bungalow in the row. Neither Miss Percehouse herself nor the invalided Captain Wyatt from No. 2 nor Mr or Mrs Curtis from No. 5 were present.

During the séance (in which the number of rocking movements made by the table represented the letter of the alphabet which the "spirit" wanted to communicate) the table suddenly began to rock violently. It spelled "TREVELYAN – DEAD – MURDER". Mr Rycroft noted that it was 5.25.

Major Burnaby didn't believe in "this tommy rot" but still wanted to check that Trevelyan, six miles away in his rented house, was all right. Burnaby and Trevelyan were old friends, as is emphasised regularly by phrases such as "my best friend", "friends of a lifetime", "thick as thieves", "such pals", "two of a kind" and "like as two peas" (chapters 8, 13 and 23).

For years Burnaby had visited Trevelyan every Friday just as Trevelyan had visited him every Tuesday. Burnaby had continued to do this, despite Trevelyan living in Exhampton, because he thought nothing of walking the six miles there and, most impressively, six miles back, up the "steep ascending slope" (chapter 4). Both he and Trevelyan had been great athletes (we don't know Burnaby's age but Trevelyan, who was 60, looked only 51 or 52) and they used to go to Switzerland together for "Winter sports in winter, climbing in summer" (chapter 1). But that Friday, the weather – with yet further snow likely – had prevented Burnaby from visiting Trevelyan.

There was no telephone in Sittaford which Burnaby could use for checking that all was well with "his old friend" and, since there was no chance of driving a car in the snow, he was determined to walk to Exhampton to check for himself, even though the snow would start again in an hour. Ignoring protests by the others, Burnaby insisted and, putting on his overcoat and lighting his lantern, stepped out into the night, saying that he would drop into his bungalow for a flask and get to Exhampton in a couple of hours.

Just before 8 pm and with the snow having begun about an hour before, he stumbled up the path to the door of Hazelmoor. Unable to obtain any reply to his ringing and knocking, he enlisted the help of Constable Graves and Dr Warren but they too could not obtain a response.

However, they noticed that the French window to the study at the back of the house was open. On entering, they found Trevelyan, face downwards in the study. Beside the body was a dark green baize tube about two inches wide used along the bottom of the door for keeping the draught out – "a very efficient form of sandbag", which had fractured the base of the skull.

Dr Warren's initial opinion was that Trevelyan had been dead about two or three hours (chapter 3). Later he adjusts this slightly, saying (chapter 20) that he saw the body at 8 pm[1] and that Trevelyan had been dead at least two hours (i.e. by 6 pm) but he could possibly have been killed at 4 pm, with four and a half hours (i.e. 3.30) being the earliest outside limit.

The study was in a state of confusion, creating the impression that Trevelyan had been sandbagged during a burglary after the French window had been forced. However, this is dismissed by Inspector Narracott, who says that, although the murderer did enter by the French window (because there were damp patches in the study where the snow was trodden in by the murderer's boots whereas there were no patches in the hall), it had not been forced open but merely splintered later from the outside to give the appearance of forcing. Since the murderer was therefore admitted through the *unforced* French window, he must have been known to Trevelyan.

Who, then, are the suspects? Emily says in chapter 26 that

none of those at the séance could have killed Trevelyan. That seems right because, if the murder was committed between 3.30 and 6 pm and Exhampton is about a couple of hours from Sittaford in the snow, the séance at 5.25 provides an alibi for its participants. As for the Sittaford residents who were not at the séance, they are rightly dismissed as suspects in that chapter – Captain Wyatt (No. 2) and Miss Percehouse (No. 4) because they are invalids; and Mr and Mrs Curtis (No. 5) because they would only have gone to Exhampton "comfortably", presumably meaning not in a snowstorm.

So it seems that the suspects are more likely to be found by looking at the people who will benefit from Trevelyan's will. Although his servant, Evans, gets a legacy of £100, there are four relations who will each get one quarter of the estate, which is estimated at about £80-90,000. These four relations are his estranged sister, Jennifer Gardner, and the three children of his deceased sister, Mary Pearson, who are Jim, Sylvia and Brian.

First is Jennifer, who needs money for expensive medical treatment for her husband and has an unconvincing alibi. Second is Jim, who is engaged to Emily (which explains her role as detective) and who also needs money, after "borrowing" from his firm, whose books are about to be examined. He had actually visited Trevelyan on the afternoon of the murder and is arrested as the police's chief suspect in chapter 12. Third is Sylvia, who is married to Martin Dering. Emily regards Martin as "an ideal person for a murderer" and he, rather than Sylvia, is the real suspect from her part of the family. However, although his original alibi proves false, he never has a clear financial motive.

Fourth is Brian, who is thought to be in Australia but had sailed to England two months before. He too has no financial motive but he does have a rather more evocative role than the other three because he is involved in helping a convict to escape from Princetown prison on Dartmoor. The convict, Freemantle

Freddy, turns out to be Violet Willett's father.

Although Brian's boat from Australia had touched at Cape Town, no mother and daughter from South Africa were on board because the Willetts (under the name of Johnson) had, like him, embarked at Melbourne. On the boat, Violet and Brian had concocted a plan to help her father escape, which is why the Willetts wanted a house on Dartmoor for the winter. The escape took place on the Monday after the murder – we are not told how it was managed – but Freddy was recaptured on Tuesday night.

In the end, we learn that the murderer is not a family member but one of the séance participants after all – Major Burnaby. He achieved the seemingly impossible task of getting from Sittaford to Exhampton in the snow in only about ten minutes (leaving shortly after 5.25 and murdering Trevelyan at about 5.45) by using skis. He had gone to his bungalow after the séance, buckled on his skis and skied to Exhampton – down hill all the way – knowing that the impending snow would wipe out all his tracks.

He rapped at the French window and was let in by the unsuspecting Trevelyan, presumably after removing his skis. It is never made clear why Burnaby came in through the French window rather than the front door. This is surprising because Narracott makes quite a lot of the murderer doing this at the end of chapter 4, saying twice that there must be a "reason" for this "odd" decision and that it will perhaps "come to light in due course". But it doesn't.

Maybe Burnaby entered that way, leaving damp patches in the study (where the melted snow was trodden in by his boots) rather than leaving them in the hall, to support the impression of a burglar forcing the French window. (The reason why there were no damp patches in the hall, despite Jim visiting that afternoon, is that he removed his boots at Trevelyan's request, leaving them on the doorstep.)

Then, while Trevelyan's back was turned, Burnaby sandbagged

him, after which he had plenty of time before 8 pm to clean the skis, put them away in the cupboard in Trevelyan's dining room (which contained Trevelyan's similar possessions, including his skis), force the French window and make it look as if there had been a burglary. Then, just before 8 pm, he went out, made a detour and came into Exhampton, "emitting the loud sighing gasps of an utterly exhausted man" – which is nicely written because the author is not saying that he *was* exhausted but that this is how he *appeared* – before enlisting the help of Graves and Warren to find Trevelyan.

All very clever, provided no suspicion was aroused by the skis which he had put in the cupboard – and it is, of course, the use of skis that is the memorable ingenuity on which the relatively simple sandbagging murder is founded. It provides one of the author's most unforgettable solutions. However, Burnaby was lucky because, if Jim's unexpected visit to Trevelyan that afternoon (which finished at 5.15) had occurred only an hour later, this could have been very inconvenient.

Burnaby's decision to check that Trevelyan was all right, which was thought foolish in view of the awful weather, could also have been considered suspicious if there had not been a reasonable excuse for him to appear so upset. This excuse was provided by the séance's message that Trevelyan had been murdered, although, even then, Emily thought that Burnaby got the wind up "rather easily" (chapter 15). She says (chapter 30) that Burnaby "deliberately engineered that table-turning" and "created the impression that Captain Trevelyan was dead". However, the way in which he "engineered" the spelling of the alarming words is never explained, although one assumes that he just shoved the table repeatedly with his hands or feet so as to make it rock.

Oddly though, it was not Burnaby who suggested the séance. Ronnie Garfield suggested it, supported by Violet, while Mr Duke was content to go along with it. Since the séance gave Burnaby the excuse to go to Hazelmoor, perhaps he had intended to suggest it if Ronnie had not, but he could hardly rely on the others agreeing to participate in this important step in his murder plan.

Least convincing of all is his motivation. Although Emily could eventually work out *who* had killed Trevelyan, she could not think *why*. However, she went to see Inspector Narracott and Mr Duke, who turns out to be an ex-Chief Inspector from Scotland Yard, "...and we got the thing clear" (though quite why they had any greater insight than her in relation to the motive is not explained).

The answer is that Trevelyan had entered, and won, a newspaper football competition using Burnaby's name and address. Trevelyan's servant, Evans, had previously explained (chapter 5) that Trevelyan entered competitions in other people's names because he thought that people with common names and addresses were more likely to win than 'Trevelyan of Sittaford House'. He had even won a competition in Evans's name from 85 Fore Street, Exhampton. However, although 'No. 1 The Cottages, Sittaford' does sound less grand than Sittaford House, Burnaby is hardly a common name.

Nevertheless, on the morning of the murder Burnaby received a letter from the newspaper telling him that he had won the £5,000 prize. Burnaby wanted this money badly because he had invested in some rotten shares and had, so Emily tells us, lost "a terrible amount of money". Emily suggests that the idea to kill Trevelyan must have come into Burnaby's head quite suddenly – perhaps when he realised that it was going to snow that evening. If Trevelyan were dead, he could keep the money and no one would ever know.

One really does wonder whether Burnaby would murder someone in order to retain a newspaper prize. Murders are, of course, committed for lesser reasons in real life but the motive seems very weak for a Christie novel. In fairness to the author, though, £5,000 in 1930 was, 90 years later, worth about £330,000 in 2020.[2] But there are still three other weaknesses.

First, Trevelyan was Burnaby's old friend, as we are repeatedly told. Second, we are given no clues that Burnaby wanted money badly or had lost a terrible amount. And, third, Emily says that the murder plan came to Burnaby after receiving the letter about the prize. But in chapter 8, when Enderby presented Burnaby with the cheque on Saturday morning, Burnaby "was completely taken aback" and told Enderby that he had not received the newspaper's letter the previous day (Friday) because Sittaford was ten feet deep in snow. The reader is therefore entitled to assume, particularly since Burnaby "was" completely taken aback, that he did not know of the prize – said to have motivated the murder on Friday – until *after* Trevelyan was murdered.

Nevertheless, Emily says in chapter 30 (disarmingly hidden away in brackets) that Burnaby had lied when saying that no letter had arrived on the Friday morning, adding that Friday was the last day things *did* come through. However, nowhere else is this expressly stated in the narrative. The nearest one gets is Mrs Curtis saying in chapter 13 "Cut off from the world we've been since Friday morning" but a reader would have to be inspired to interpret this as meaning cut off after the post had been delivered, but not until then.

Finally, in what appears to be an attempt to bolster Burnaby's financial motive, his friendship with Trevelyan is belittled by adding a touch of jealousy. In the final chapter, Miss Percehouse says "Friends indeed! For more than 20 years Trevelyan has done everything a bit better than Burnaby … I can tell you it's a difficult thing to go on really liking a man who can do everything just a little better than you can". However, we had been given no clue that Burnaby felt like this about Trevelyan.

Plot

The novel was published first in the United States as *The Murder at Hazelmoor* (the word '*The*' being dropped in many later editions). It was the first of the author's novels to be given a different title in the United States than in the UK where it was then published as *The Sittaford Mystery*.

Although the actual murder takes place at Hazelmoor, the UK title seems arguably better, not only because the murder has its origins in Sittaford but also because there are two other mysteries in the story and Sittaford is the location of both of them. One is how the "spirit" at the Sittaford séance could have known that Trevelyan had been murdered while the other is the Willetts' mysterious renting of Sittaford House for the winter.

The murder plan is highly memorable for three things – snow, séance and skis. First the snow, which provides the setting and appears to deprive those attending the séance of the opportunity for committing the murder. Second the séance, which provides an engagingly intriguing opening, gives the story an unusual element of mystification and provides Burnaby not only with his excuse for visiting Trevelyan in the awful weather but also with his alibi. And third the skis, which provide the story with its unforgettable solution.

The author also does well in conjuring the remote moorland village, desolate snowbound scene and desperate escaped convict. However, vast tracts of the story are pure padding or repetition, spinning out the story, particularly with the rather boring Trevelyan family suspects and the mystery of the Willetts. And padding is the enemy of pace. It is as if the author, having hit upon her great idea (the ski solution), then struggled from about chapter 11 onwards to create more than a mildly entertaining plot for the remaining 20 chapters.

Even Emily, despite her pluck and determination, is not only less engaging than the principal amateur sleuths in the author's other detective stories but also lacks the appeal of some of the author's thriller heroines, maybe because she has more common sense. In particular, it is noticeable that, when the pace picks up at last in chapter 24 (even if only temporarily), this is one of Narracott's rare chapters.

However, padding and repetition are not the only problems. There is also a little cheating – not only where Burnaby "was completely taken aback" but also where we are told that, as he came into Exhampton just before 8 pm, "He was numbed with cold" when in fact he had spent a couple of hours indoors at Hazelmoor (chapter 30). It's a pity that the author wasn't as clever there as she was in the immediately preceding sentence, noted earlier, in which Burnaby *appears* exhausted.

There are also minor errors or inconsistencies, which reveal a lack of care or interest beyond the great idea. For example, chapter 4 says that Evans got married a month ago and left Hazelmoor at 2.30 on the afternoon of the murder, while the next chapter says that he was married *two* months ago and left at *2 pm*. And chapter 16 says that a convict last escaped from Princetown 20 years ago while the next chapter says it was two. But perhaps the point is better illustrated when we try to get clear who lives in which bungalow.

Chapter 1 tells us that Duke's house is last in the row (No. 6) and that Rycroft lives next door to him (so he must be in No. 5). However, when Emily and Enderby are driven up to Sittaford for the first time (chapter 13), the car stops at No. 5, which they are told is owned by Mrs Curtis, who confirms that Duke is next door at No. 6. So, where, we wonder, is Rycroft's bungalow if Mrs Curtis is in No. 5? Thankfully, this is clarified in chapter 13 when we learn that in fact he lives at No. 3. Indeed, the numbers of the bungalows of all the residents are given in chapters 12 and 13. Thus we know that Captain Wyatt lives in No. 2 even though chapter 18 says that he lives in No. 3 (an error that has been corrected in later editions).

None of these points turns out to matter, although there is a particularly noteworthy example of carelessness in chapter 16 when Rycroft tells Emily that he has written a full account of the séance for the Society of Psychical Research: "Five people present, none of whom could have the least idea or suspicion that Captain Trevelyan was murdered". Why "five" when there were six including Burnaby, who has not yet been exposed? The error is immediately repeated by Emily: "It was not so easy to suggest her own idea to Mr Rycroft that one of the five people might have guilty foreknowledge, as he himself had been one of them".

This does seem an astonishing mistake but it is not just a typographical error because, when Emily and Rycroft (one member of the séance) have a discussion about Garfield (another member) and then the Willetts (two more members – bringing the total to four), she then remembers "the hitherto unmentioned member of the séance" – Duke (i.e. the fifth member). It seems that Burnaby (who would have made the number up to six) has been completely forgotten and yet, as we have seen, it must have been his engineering of the table that explains the mystery of the "spirit" being able to indicate that Trevelyan had been murdered.

As for the mystery of the Willetts, we are told in chapter 1 that they had been renting Sittaford House for two months following enquiries made on their behalf by a house-agent at the end of October. In fact, it's not quite two months by the time of the murder on 14 December.[3] But the time of year is relevant to the core of the Willetts mystery, which is why they would want to rent a house on Dartmoor for the winter. This is regularly questioned by the other Sittaford residents, with the Willetts' behaviour always described as "mad", "funny", "curious", "odd", "fishy", or "queer", or in some equivalent way. This occurs in about 15 conversations between chapters 1 and 21 and is the most obvious example of repetitious padding in the story.

Another example of padding concerns the questionable status of Mr Duke whom we are led to believe might be "a sinister stranger" in chapter 15 and then in a further half dozen such references. However, the most incongruous examples of padding occur from about chapter 21 when, just as the padding about the Willetts is abandoned, some rather curious red herrings are introduced instead. Their purpose seems to be to arouse our suspicions about Sittaford residents but they turn out to be entirely irrelevant, such as Rycroft being related to Martin Dering.

There is, however, a chance of drama towards the end, on the Friday one week after the murder, with Rycroft's suggestion that the séance should be repeated. After some initial reluctance, the participants (Rycroft, Ronnie, Burnaby and the two Willetts but with Brian replacing the absent Duke, and Enderby watching) take their places round the table at 5.25. Rycroft asks "Is there anyone there?" – at which point Narracott, Emily and Duke arrive and Burnaby is charged with the murder.

The purpose of this second séance is never made clear. Presumably Rycroft is not genuinely hopeful of some specific psychic result, such as the naming of the murderer, as Ronnie suggests. But it also seems unlikely that the séance was staged at the police's request, given that Burnaby does nothing at it to cement proof of his guilt. Either way, the abrupt ending of the second séance (before it really even starts) means that it does not fulfil the promise of theatre that we had expected when Rycroft made his suggestion.

Clues

Assuming, as we surely must, that the message from the "spirit" at the séance was a contrived (rather than supernatural) event, the starting point has to be the 'séance' clue, which tells us that someone at the séance must have known about the murder. So, this person was either the murderer himself or, since that seems impossible, he somehow knew that the murder would be, or had already been, committed, perhaps because he was in league with the person who actually carried it out.

But what clues tell us how it was carried out? As to this, the two main clues are first, of course, the skis and, second, the boots (in fact ski boots) which lead Emily to the skis. However, consistent with the author's focus on her one memorable idea and on padding, these two clues, combined with Burnaby's prowess at winter sports and the run to Exhampton being downhill, are the only clues of any real substance to the murderer. Even then, the reader would do extremely well to spot their significance because the 'boots' clue has a frustrating omission and is most unpersuasive while the 'skis' clue, although the most memorable, requires inspiration rather than deduction to conclude that Burnaby used them to commit the murder.[4]

The skis are first mentioned in chapter 5 when, in the cupboard in the dining room at Hazelmoor, Narracott finds "two pairs of skis, a pair of sculls mounted, ten or twelve hippopotamus tusks, rods and lines and various fishing tackle including a book of flies, a bag of golf clubs, a tennis racket, an elephant's foot stuffed and a tiger skin". The skis are not mentioned again until chapter 28 when Emily looks in the cupboard and sees "the skis, the sculls, the elephant's foot, the tusks, the fishing rods". Finally, they are mentioned again in chapter 30 when Emily provides her explanations.

Until then there is nothing to suggest that the skis have any significance to the murder plan – except perhaps one thing. When the skis (and other items) are first mentioned in chapter 5, Narracott regards it as funny that Trevelyan had removed his most precious possessions from Sittaford House (to Hazelmoor) when he was only letting it for a few months and when they could have been locked up there instead of being carted expensively to Hazelmoor. So we, as readers, should perhaps assume that these possessions are at Hazelmoor for a reason relevant to the murder. The question therefore is: why are they there?

The problem for readers is that the skis are just one of the items moved to Hazelmoor. Why should we focus on the skis rather than the other items, particularly when, as part of Enderby's misdirection in chapter 21, he doesn't even mention the skis but describes Trevelyan's things as "his elephant's trotters and his hippopotamus's toothy pegs and all the sporting rifles and what nots"? So even readers who are on notice that Trevelyan's possessions could be relevant would do well to focus on the 'skis' clue because it is so concealed. On the other hand, the skis are the one item connected with snow – but will readers make that connection?

The reason that Emily does so begins with her learning in chapter 28 that Evans has noticed that a pair of Trevelyan's boots is missing from Hazelmoor. She decides that "She *must* know why these boots were missing … she felt powerless to put them out of her mind". In chapter 13 she had reflected that boots "might help one to do a murder". But her reflection at that stage cannot seriously be treated as a clue and, even 15 chapters later, her emphasis on the 'boots' clue seems disproportionate to the reader whose likely disbelief is unashamedly recognised by the author in writing that the boots "were soaring to ridiculous proportions, dwarfing everything else to do with the case".

However, prompted by spotting a little pile of soot in the bedroom chimney grate at Hazelmoor, Emily finds the boots hidden up that chimney. She considers the case in detail and an "idea" takes shape. She hurries to the cupboard in the dining room where Trevelyan kept his prized possessions – including the skis – and bends down, boots in hand. In a minute or two she stands upright, having worked out who killed Trevelyan, though not yet understanding why.

We are not told how Emily knew that the dining room

cupboard was the place to look for skis. She had only ever taken "a quick look" in the dining room and there was no reference then to the cupboard. Moreover, it is very strange that the skis (and other items) were still in the cupboard at all because the solicitor, Mr Kirkwood, had told us in chapter 28 that "all" Trevelyan's effects had been removed from Hazelmoor.

Nor are we told, at least at that point (chapter 28), why the boots caused Emily to go and look at the skis. In chapter 30 she explains that the boots were ski boots and that this had made her think of skis. However, we had not been told before that the boots were ski boots.

This key fact in Emily's thinking had been omitted, so making her revelation about them feel frustrating. It is not as if the boots had merely been referred to previously as, for example 'a pair of boots' (with the word 'ski' inadvertently omitted). Rather, they had been particularly described in chapter 28 by Mrs Belling and Mrs Evans respectively as "a pair of boots Miss the thick kind you rubs oil into and which the Captain would have worn if he had gone out in the snow" and as "Big ones, they were, and he wore a couple of pairs of socks inside them". So there was every chance to add that the boots were ski boots.

Nevertheless, Emily, knowing (unlike readers) that the boots were ski boots, looked in the cupboard. There she found two pairs of skis, one pair longer than the other. Trevelyan's boots fitted the long pair but not the shorter pair where the "toe-clip things" were adjusted for much smaller boots. So the shorter pair of skis belonged to a *different* person.

Precisely how Emily deduced that these shorter skis belonged to Burnaby and had been used by him in his murder plan is not explained – only that she had her "idea". Not even the police would have been likely, as she admits, to bother whether Trevelyan had one or two pairs of skis in the dining room cupboard. And, if they had shown an interest in one pair being shorter than the other,

Burnaby could have said that he had left them with Trevelyan on a separate occasion. Moreover, Evans, who was alert enough to notice that a pair of boots was missing, and so would presumably have spotted an unexpected pair of skis, did not comment upon them, which suggests that their presence was unsurprising.

Nor is it at all obvious why Burnaby should have hidden Trevelyan's boots up the chimney. Had he not done so, Emily would not have found them and he would not have been caught. The detection therefore hinges on the hiding of the boots and so one hopes for a compelling reason for Burnaby to have done this. Emily's answer is "I suppose that he was afraid the police might do exactly what I did. The sight of ski boots might have suggested skis to them. So he stuffed them up the chimney. And that's really, of course, where he made his mistake, because Evans noticed that they'd gone…". But this really is most unpersuasive since it is not at all clear why the sight of Trevelyan's ski boots would suggest the use of skis to the police any more than the skis themselves which Narracott had actually seen in the cupboard in chapter 5.

In chapter 30 Emily describes Burnaby as "an expert on skis". We aren't told how *she* knows this but the clue for *readers* is presumably that Burnaby tells the Willetts that he used to go to Switzerland with Trevelyan and do winter sports in winter (chapter 1). A nicety of this 'winter sports' clue, beyond Burnaby claiming he is now too old for that sort of thing, is that Violet then asks him about the Army Racquets Championship, at which he blushes, so directing us away from winter sports.

Despite Burnaby's expertise at skiing, his achievement in reaching Exhampton in his thick clothing in ten minutes – at an average speed of 36 miles per hour – could be regarded with great scepticism were it not for the 'downhill' clue telling us of the "steady descent" from Sittaford to Exhampton. This starts in the book's third paragraph with "Up here, in the tiny village of Sittaford". And the point is then clued quite openly on a few further occasions, but cleverly, in sentences that seem to be pure scene-setting or description and so don't apparently reveal how significant the point will be, making this good 'downhill' clue the best in the book.[5] However, even going downhill, Burnaby's achievement is impressive.

Beyond these clues and perhaps his "cynical smile" during the table-turning, Burnaby, who describes himself as an "obvious" rather than "clever" person in chapter 15 (by way of misdirection), is not well clued as the murderer, particularly in relation to his financial motivation. We know that he and Trevelyan entered competitions in other people's names but, although we also know that Burnaby was "credulous" in money matters and bought and sold shares, usually at a loss, we get no clue that he had lost a "terrible" amount of money. The fact that he could not afford to offer a job to Evans is hardly a clue that he was in such financial straits as to need to commit murder.

As for Burnaby being jealous of Trevelyan, Miss Percehouse says in the final chapter "I told you Burnaby was a jealous man". She had indeed told us (chapter 17) that Burnaby had a "jealous disposition" but there was nothing to suggest that this 'jealousy' clue extended to his best friend. Indeed, Trevelyan's success in winning three novels in a Railway Pictures Names Competition (the one he had entered with Evans's name and address) was matched by Burnaby winning three books in a crossword competition.

It is not really surprising that Emily identifies Burnaby as the murderer before Narracott, who has a frustrating habit of not asking the questions one would expect him to ask. For example, not pressing Burnaby on the significance of 5.25 in chapter 6 or Jim Pearson on why he so urgently wanted to see Trevelyan in chapter 10 or Violet on why she fainted at the mention of "young Pearson" in chapter 14 (itself a nice piece of misdirection because we think of Jim while Violet is thinking of Brian). Of course, if he had obtained the answers straightaway, the padding of the story would be reduced. Narracott's technique looks subtle but the author's real purpose seems to have been to enable the issues to be revisited at later stages.

In chapter 14 Narracott deploys his "red herring" by asking the Willetts about the table-turning when his real aim is to find out why they came to Dartmoor. In the end, it is the Willetts themselves who are the red herring since their reasons for coming are unconnected to the murder, which is something of a surprise given the amount of speculation about their presence in Sittaford. Indeed, Emily had concluded in chapter 18 that there *must* be a link between the Willetts and Trevelyan which would provide "the clue to the whole mystery", a conclusion which seems reasonable, but wrong.

There are clues to the Willetts' real role and their connection to Brian, such as the 'label' clue from their luggage bearing the name of Mendle's Hotel in Melbourne (chapter 17), suggesting that the Willetts are from Australia, not South Africa. Miss Percehouse also notes that Mrs Willett calls "Coo-ee" to Violet, which, she says, is "more typical of Australia than South Africa" (chapter 17). However, it is odd that no mention is made of the name of the luggage owner on the label (presumably Johnson, the name under which the Willetts sailed), which should itself have aroused suspicion, and stranger still that no one spots the Willetts' accent as Australian, a failure which is not really glossed over by merely describing Mrs Willett as having "a distinct Colonial accent" (chapter 1).

The starkest clue about the Willetts' real role is the breakdown in Mrs Willett's appearance after the convict is recaptured and her decision to forego the rest of the winter in Sittaford. However, a neater clue is the 'Princetown' clue. One of Narracott's underlings says to him in chapter 27, in relation to where Brian was staying, "Quite right, sir. But it wasn't the Duchy at Princetown, it was the hotel at Two Bridges".

Why, we wonder, should Narracott have initially guessed that Brian might have been staying at the Duchy at Princetown? It is then that we remember that Princetown has been mentioned more than half a dozen times – all, of course, in the context of the escaped convict. So some readers will rightly assume that Brian, who had had a meeting with Violet in chapter 22 in the garden of Sittaford House, was staying near the prison (in fact, at the hotel at Two Bridges) because the convict has a connection with the Willetts.

Finally, we are presented (from about chapter 21 onwards) with a series of curious red herrings about Sittaford residents which are completely irrelevant to any part of the mystery and seem to be introduced purely as further padding. They are as slight as Ronnie dropping his stick when hearing that Narracott has been seen in Sittaford (chapter 21); Captain Wyatt dropping a glass of whisky on learning that Emily is Jim's fiancée (chapter 21); Ronnie going into Exeter to meet a "fellow" (chapter 22) who turns out to be Jennifer Gardner (chapter 25), who is his godmother (chapter 31); Ronnie's apparent snooping at Hazelmoor on Wednesday afternoon (chapter 23); and, strangest of all, the relationship between the Derings and the Rycrofts, which is referred to on no less than three occasions (chapters 24, 27 and 29) but without its purpose ever being made clear.

7

Why Didn't They Ask Evans?

Solution

This is a thriller in which the dying words of Alan Carstairs are "Why didn't they ask Evans?". Carstairs, who appears to have walked inadvertently over the cliff edge at the seaside town of Marchbolt on the Welsh coast on 3 October, utters his dying words to the Vicar's son, Bobby Jones, who finds him while he is looking for his golf ball.[1]

When Bobby talks to his childhood friend, Lady Frances (Frankie) Derwent, about the incident, she wonders whether anybody had *pushed* him. She persists with what Bobby thinks of as "Frankie's amazing theory" (chapter 7) and in chapter 9 (out of 35) they at last embark on their adventure, which is constructed around solving the mystery of Carstairs' dying words.

We finally learn in chapter 32 that the reason why the villains didn't ask Gladys Evans – the parlourmaid at Tudor Cottage – to witness the will of the millionaire John Savage (but instead sent out for Albert the gardener) was because Evans (unlike Albert and the other witness, Rose the cook) would have spotted that the person executing the will in favour of a lady called "Mrs Templeton" was not in fact Savage (who was found dead next morning) but an impersonator pretending to be him.

"Mrs Templeton" and the impersonator, who are in fact Moira

Nicholson and Roger Bassington-ffrench respectively, are the two principal villains, although there are two others, Leo and Amelia Cayman.

Roger had met Moira while he was in the Colonies but he was now back in England, at his family home, Merroway Court, in the village of Staverley in Hampshire. Moira had been an accomplished criminal in the Colonies and, in order to escape the police there, had married Dr Jasper Nicholson, a Canadian, who was coming to England to open a sanatorium for nerve patients. While looking for premises, Moira suggested the Grange which, conveniently for her and Roger, was only three miles from Merroway Court.

The villains commit three murders, the first being that of Savage prior to the start of the narrative. Moira, who was still involved in criminal activity, made several trips to Canada after her marriage, with her gullible husband believing that she did so to "see her people". She travelled under false names and, while travelling as Mrs Rose Emily Templeton the previous November, met Savage, a millionaire with no near relations (only distant cousins in Australia), and he became very attracted to her.

So the villains concocted a plan which involved inducing Savage to stay as a guest at a cottage acquired by the "Templetons", Tudor Cottage in Chipping Somerton. There Moira acted as "Mrs Templeton", with Mr Cayman acting as her unfeeling husband, and Savage came more and more under her influence.

During his third stay he apparently went up to London early one morning to consult a cancer specialist, having been uneasy about his health. Although the specialist said he was not suffering from cancer, he refused to accept this advice and on his return to Tudor Cottage, sent for a solicitor from a respectable firm (Mr Elford), who there and then drew up a will under which £700,000 was left to "Mrs Templeton" with the remainder to charity.

The will was signed and witnessed and that night it appears that Savage took an overdose of chloral, leaving a letter saying that he preferred a quick, painless death to a long, painful one. About two months later, "Mrs Templeton", having inherited under the will, disappeared, ostensibly abroad, though in reality back to the Grange. In fact, Savage had been murdered – given the chloral overdose while drugged. Although that makes the murder seem straightforward, some ingenuity was required to engineer a situation in which Savage could genuinely appear to have left £700,000 to Moira.

What happened was that, before his apparent visit to the cancer specialist, he was drugged and put in the attic at Tudor Cottage (presumably by Moira and Cayman). He was then impersonated by Roger during that visit and when executing the will in front of Elford. Neither the specialist nor Elford had met Savage – nor had the two employees at Tudor Cottage who were asked to witness the will – Rose Chudleigh, the cook, and Albert Mere, the gardener. Leaving the residue to charity also seemed clever because it looked "respectable and unfishy" and meant that the charities would probably resist any attempt to contest the will. Roger then forged the suicide letter and Savage was killed, although we are not told which of the villains did this.

However, Savage had a friend, Alan Carstairs, a Canadian explorer, to whom he had written about "Mrs Templeton", enclosing a snapshot of her (as we learn in chapter 34). When Carstairs heard about Savage's death and his will, he was incredulous, being certain that Savage wasn't worried about his health. He regarded the will as very uncharacteristic because Savage did not like charities and had strong opinions about money passing by blood relationship. Carstairs didn't believe that Savage would have left £700,000 to "Mrs Templeton", however attracted to her he was.

So he came to England from Africa and consulted a solicitor (Mr Spragge) about the validity of the will but was advised that nothing could be done. He also telephoned some friends, the Rivingtons, who happened to be going to lunch with the

Bassington-ffrenches and they invited him to accompany them. While at Merroway Court, he saw on the piano a photograph of the woman whose snapshot Savage had sent him (Moira alias "Mrs Templeton") and he asked a lot of questions about her, presumably spotted by Roger.

He then went to Chipping Somerton, knowing (from Savage) that this was where "Mrs Templeton" had lived, and started to poke about. He was pursued by Roger, who was concerned that, if Carstairs tracked down Evans and she identified "Mrs Templeton" as Moira, "matters were going to become difficult". Carstairs had to be suppressed.

In fact, Gladys Evans, who came from Wales, had returned there after the tragedy and married. She was living in Marchbolt (Bobby's home village), which is where Carstairs' inquiries then led him. While he was there, walking by the cliff edge, Roger came up behind him and pushed him over. He fell 40 feet and broke his back. No ingenuity was required for this.

However, just before he died, he uttered his final words to Bobby, who then drew a handkerchief from Carstairs' pocket to put over his face. As he did so, out came a photograph. He looked at it – it was of Moira (not that Bobby would have known Moira or "Mrs Templeton") – and replaced it. Roger then appeared at the top of the cliff and, with Bobby having to leave, offered to stay with the body until help arrived. Before Bobby left, Roger gave him his name but why he would wish to reveal his true identity (and so lead Frankie and Bobby to Merroway Court) is not clear.

While tending the body, Roger removed Carstairs' photograph of Moira and substituted a photograph of Mrs Cayman; and it was through that photograph that Carstairs was identified when Mrs Cayman and her husband materialised to identify him (falsely) as her brother, Alex Pritchard, recently returned from Siam. The inquest verdict was "Death by Misadventure".

Thus the villains seemed to have taken care of matters before

Bobby and Frankie were prompted into action by two things. First, by Bobby seeing Mrs Cayman at the inquest (chapter 4) and thinking that this was not the woman he had seen in the photograph and later realising (chapter 7) that the photograph found in Carstairs' pocket was not even the one he had seen there.

Second, by the villains' attempt to murder Bobby (which would have been their third murder) by poisoning his beer with morphia after he had told the Caymans of Carstairs' dying words. The words troubled the villains because, although Bobby did not realise this, Evans was now Mrs Roberts, who 'ran' the Vicarage in Marchbolt for Bobby's family. Frankie tells him that this was "dangerous" for the villains: "You and Evans were actually under the same roof", the point presumably being that, if Bobby realised this, he would ask Evans about the dying words and perhaps start to understand the murder plan.

The successful third murder – that of Roger's brother, Henry, who owns Merroway Court – is not part of the main mystery about Carstairs' dying words, although we do not appreciate this until later. Roger, in explaining his motivation (in chapter 34), says that he had two ambitions – to own Merroway Court and to have an immense amount of money. While the Savage and Carstairs murders flow from the second motive, the murder of Henry – and a couple of attempts at murdering his young son, Tommy (which, if successful, would have added to the murder count) – flow from the first.

In chapter 22, while Frankie and Roger are in the garden at Merroway Court, they hear a shot. They rush to the house where they find Henry's study door locked but, going outside and round the terrace to the study window, they see Henry sprawled on his desk, a bullet wound visible in his temple and a revolver on the floor. Roger breaks the window and they step inside just as Henry's wife, Sylvia, and Dr Nicholson come hurrying along the terrace.

Nicholson also steps into the study, bends over the body and

pronounces death as instantaneous. The door key is found in
Henry's pocket. He had been addicted to morphia (having been
introduced to it by Roger) and a suicide note explains that his
addiction is too strong for him to fight. The inquest verdict is
"Suicide while of Unsound Mind", as it had been with Savage.

Readers suspect murder but, since Frankie was with Roger
when the shot was heard, the only realistic suspect appears to be
Nicholson, who had appeared on the scene suddenly. Perhaps he
shot Henry, locked the study door on the way out and put the key
in Henry's pocket when examining the body. However, if he had
fired the shot and gone out through the study door, Sylvia would
have seen him whereas she says that she saw him coming up the
drive as Roger and Frankie ran round the terrace.

So Bobby and Frankie leave it as suicide. There is no
investigation or mystification of the sort that one might expect
in the classic locked-room detective story and so no sense of
ingenuity, and it is only through Roger's explanation in chapter 34
that we learn how the murder was carried out.

While he and Frankie were in the garden before the shot, he
left for a few minutes, ostensibly to telephone Nicholson. In fact,
he went to the study and, as an aeroplane flew noisily overhead, he
shot Henry, forged the suicide note, wiped the fingerprints from
the revolver, pressed Henry's hand around it and let it drop to the
floor. He put the key in Henry's pocket and went out, locking the
door from the outside with the dining room key which fitted the
lock and leaving a "neat little squib arrangement" in the chimney
timed to go off four minutes later, which it duly did as he talked
to Frankie.

While this could have been a clever little mystery if it had
been turned into one, our frustration that it wasn't is compounded
both by the coincidental aeroplane noise which gave Roger his
opportunity and the absence of any clue either to the dining room
key or the neat little squib.

However, it is easy to discern why the author included this almost entirely tangential sub-plot in the story, namely to throw suspicion for *all* the wrongdoing in the direction of Nicholson. If he were not a genuine suspect, the only other candidate for the role of the real villain would be Roger since the Caymans are so obviously villains that they must be mere henchmen.

Between chapters 7 and 12 Frankie and Bobby clearly regard Roger as the villain, principally for the excellent reason that no one else could have swapped the photograph in Carstairs' pocket – although there are also other obvious reasons such as his unconvincing explanation for being in Marchbolt on the fatal evening, his status as a "ne'er-do-weel", his access to Henry's morphia for poisoning Bobby and his possible involvement in Tommy's "accidents". Indeed, by chapter 12, when Frankie is due to meet Roger, she thinks she is about "to meet a murderer face to face".

However, by the end of that chapter, having now met the "charming" Roger, Frankie thinks that he couldn't be a murderer. And, as she becomes more sensible of his charms from chapter 13, she becomes more inclined to acquit him. But, whenever she thinks he's innocent, she is faced (in chapters 13, 14, 16, 17 and 20) with the fact that only he could have swapped the photograph, although he then produces an explanation in chapter 21. He admits taking the photograph (to protect Moira from publicity about it being in a dead man's pocket) but denies putting Mrs Cayman's photograph there, which suggests (incorrectly) that Carstairs had it on him as well as Moira's photograph.

All the while, from chapter 13, as Frankie inclines to acquit Roger, Nicholson, who appears in chapter 14, becomes the alternative villain. Sylvia doesn't like him and Frankie thinks he is "sinister", an adjective used a handful of times between chapters 14 and 26, along with "suspicious", "very jealous", "a very queer man" and "a dangerous criminal". He gives the barmaid at the Anglers'

Arms "the shivers", cross-examines Frankie intently about her arrival at Merroway Court, looks "daggers" at her and has the most disagreeable smile.

Moreover, his sanatorium, the Grange, sounds sinister. There are "very queer goings on" there, with moanings, shrieks and groans (chapter 15) and Bobby is aware of a strange, evil atmosphere. He and Frankie conclude that Nicholson is the head of a dope gang, with access to morphia, and they note that he was not at Staverley (so could have been at Marchbolt) on the day Bobby was poisoned when a car like his, a dark blue Talbot, was seen in the vicinity.

Then, in escalating his prospective villainy, a frightened Moira says in chapter 18 that he supplies Henry's drugs and that she is afraid he is going to murder her. When she later disappears, Bobby thinks that he is at the bottom of this. There is even the prospect, before Henry is murdered, that, if he were to go into the Grange for his drug-taking, Nicholson would do away with him.

And, when Henry is killed (in chapter 22), although Bobby and Frankie at first conclude that Nicholson cannot have done it because of Sylvia seeing him on the drive, Frankie later has the "monstrous idea" that she could have been in it with him. And in chapter 26, after all this misdirection, Nicholson is expressly described, in Bobby's thinking, as "the villain of the piece".

But, even though Frankie refers to Roger's "innocence" in chapter 27, we still think that the photograph in Carstairs' pocket was very probably swapped by him. So, by chapter 28, when Bobby has been knocked out, driven to Tudor Cottage and held captive in the attic, along with Frankie, who has been lured there by a forged letter in Bobby's handwriting, we still can't be sure who is the villain. And, when the villain's heavy, ponderous tread is heard mounting the stair, we do wonder whether Roger or Nicholson will open the attic door.

At first, it appears to be Nicholson because, although he is wearing a hat pulled down over his eyes, strong glasses and a heavy overcoat with the collar turned up, his voice would have betrayed him anywhere. However, after Bobby and Frankie are rescued by Bobby's friend, Badger Beadon, and the villain knocked out, he is revealed as Roger, impersonating Nicholson.

Having said so much about Roger and Nicholson, one must not forget that Moira too is a villain. She poisoned Bobby's beer with morphia and may have administered the fatal dose to Mr Savage. However, her role as a villain is well concealed until after Roger has been identified (chapter 28) and even after the mystery of Carstairs' dying words has been solved (chapter 32).

Her apparent vulnerability, and therefore probable innocence, is made clear when we first meet her in chapter 14 in which she is described as slightly nervous, gentle, fragile, very sad and terribly delicate. By chapter 18 she has graduated to being terribly nervous, terrified, terribly frightened and afraid of being murdered by her husband because he wants to marry Sylvia.

By chapter 23 Bobby feels that Moira's life is "hanging by a hair", following which she disappears and is later found drugged at Tudor Cottage with morphia or opium (chapter 30). So, even when Frankie and Bobby find her at the Marchbolt Vicarage in chapter 33, we still don't suspect her, even though we can't work out why Roger (who is known to be a villain by then) would have drugged her. In fact, she had injected herself with morphia, on realising that Roger had been knocked out, so as to appear innocent. Nevertheless, although her villainy is an unexpected final twist, it is subsidiary compared with the Roger/Nicholson issue and the mystery of Carstairs' dying words.

Plot

The title is engaging and intriguing, perhaps even the author's best, and has a convincing answer. The story itself is readable, has an enticing opening and moves at a good pace, with Frankie being charmingly portrayed. There is even an in-joke, with chapter 33 entitled "Sensation in the Orient Café", which is resonant of the Poirot novel earlier that year, *Murder on the Orient Express*.

However, as a light-hearted thriller, the story is never particularly mystifying because readers are kept continuously informed of the thought processes of Frankie and Bobby about the likely guilt of Roger or Nicholson. And, although chapter 15 says that the photograph had disappeared "mysteriously" (from Carstairs' pocket), there's no real mystery about that. Indeed, there is a fair argument that the title is the most memorable aspect of the novel.[2] One does feel that, if the essential mystery (of Carstairs' dying words) had been converted into a detective story with proper detectives, and without all the coincidences allowed in thrillers, a rather good novel could have been written.

There are two main keys to the plot's structure. The first is the to-ing and fro-ing, from as early as chapter 7 through to chapter 28, about whether Roger or Nicholson is the villain. This is interspersed with Frankie and Bobby's adventures, the genuinely surprising revelation in chapter 18 that the woman in Carstairs' photograph is Moira, the tangential murder of Henry (which sits uneasily within the main plot) and the gradual exposition of the story of Savage and the Templetons.

A peculiarity of this first structural key is that we learn in chapter 28 – with seven chapters still to go – that Roger is the villain before Frankie and Bobby even start to focus properly on the mystery of Carstairs' dying words. In the event, although they do solve it, the truth is that they just have a clever theory and no evidence that Savage or Carstairs were murdered. Were it not for Roger's written confession in chapter 34 and Moira dragging Roger into it at her trial, the authorities would have had to build a case from "Mrs Templeton" being Moira and from Roger's presence in Marchbolt.

The second main structural key is, unfortunately, coincidence. One has to wonder how the plot would have been constructed at all without three principal coincidences – ignoring relatively minor ones, such as the noisy aeroplane and, in chapter 24, Frankie's newspaper happening to contain an article about Savage which enables her to make important suppositions about what Carstairs had been doing

The first coincidence is that, having begun with Carstairs' dying words to the Vicar of Marchbolt's son, we find, some 32 chapters later, Frankie and Bobby heading back to Marchbolt because Evans (now Mrs Roberts) works in the Vicarage there. In fairness, since this device is the premise of the author's story – even being published in the United States as *The Boomerang Clue* – this coincidence is acceptable. This is much less so of the other two.

The second coincidence occurs when Frankie, prompted by the newspaper article, goes to see her father's solicitor, Mr Spragge, to ask him where to inspect Savage's will. Spragge turns out to be the very lawyer whom Carstairs had consulted about the will's validity and Frankie charms him into telling her Carstairs' story of Savage and the Templetons. Frustratingly, the coincidence of Carstairs, fresh from Africa, happening to choose Spragge from all the lawyers in London remains unexplained because Carstairs "couldn't remember just who it was" who advised him to consult Spragge (chapter 25). Surely a plausible reason could have been produced, especially since it is directly as a result of Spragge knowing Carstairs' story of Savage and the Templetons that Frankie gets to learn of it.

The third coincidence is crucial to Carstairs' detection. Although he had the snapshot of "Mrs Templeton" sent to him by Savage, he would not have known who she *really* was, even if he had spoken to Evans because Evans didn't know Moira Nicholson. But he learns Moira's name when he sees her photograph on the Bassington-ffrenches' piano on being taken to lunch with them by the Rivingtons and realises that she is the same woman as the one in his snapshot.

Of all the houses in England to which Carstairs might have been taken in order to lunch with people he had never even met, it is extraordinary that this one should have on its piano a photograph of a neighbour who turns out to be the one woman in England for whom he is looking. At least Frankie recognises this coincidence, which directly enables Carstairs to identify Moira as "Mrs Templeton", as "pure chance".

Roger says in his confession that Carstairs "had a photograph of Moira – he'd got it from the photographers – presumably for identification" and that it was this photograph which he had taken from Carstairs' pocket. This is surprising, given that Carstairs already had a snapshot of "Mrs Templeton" from Savage, which readers would have assumed was the photograph taken by Roger. Since Carstairs already had Savage's snapshot, would he really have gone to the trouble of obtaining a second photograph of Moira from her photographers?

It doesn't seem that Roger is simply referring to one item (treating the photographer's photograph and Savage's snapshot as one and the same) because the photograph is "from the photographers" and the snapshot, which he mentions twice in his confession, is one "that Savage had sent him". So, he seems to be referring to two separate items. But, if so, where is Savage's snapshot since there is no reference to it being in Carstairs' pockets as well? Surely he would not have disposed of this key clue. One is left feeling that there was probably only one photograph – the snapshot from Savage.

As well as the coincidences, there are some other, less significant, elements of the plot that don't really work. First, is the explanation for Carstairs having no luggage, not even a knapsack, when he was (according to his "sister", Mrs Cayman) on a walking tour in Wales. She tells the coroner that he didn't like knapsacks and that "He meant to post parcels alternate days. He posted one the day before he left with his night things and a pair of socks, only he addressed it to Derbyshire instead of Denbighshire so it only got here today".

The coroner's response "Ah! That clears up a somewhat curious point" is bewildering since this explanation raises more questions than it answers. For example, where was he going to post the parcels to? And where from? Would he really adopt such a potentially unreliable scheme just to avoid carrying a knapsack? What if the parcels didn't arrive? How did a parcel addressed to Derbyshire manage to get that day to a dead itinerant in Marchbolt (which must be in Denbighshire on the north Wales coast)? And, if he had received that parcel, how would he have carried the contents for the remainder of the tour? The author does not do herself justice in trying to explain this curiosity.

Another oddity is Mrs Cayman's questioning of Bobby in chapter 5 about whether her "brother" left any last words. It is odd that she asks at all, given that Bobby's inquest evidence did nothing to prompt such a question. Indeed, he had still completely forgotten the words when Mrs Cayman asks him. Her questioning turns into a self-inflicted wound because, purely as a result of it, he does later remember the words and writes a letter to Cayman, so leading to the attempt to poison him and thus to his investigation with Frankie.

With regard to the letter, the author goes slightly awry on dates. Carstairs died on 3 October (chapter 19) – a Wednesday (chapter 9). We know (chapter 3) that Bobby went to London next day (Thursday 4 October) and returned two days later (Saturday 6 October), with the inquest being "tomorrow" – 7 October. On that basis, however, the letter which Bobby wrote to Cayman *after* the inquest cannot be dated the "6th instant" (chapter 5).

After Bobby remembers the dying words in chapter 5, he and Frankie wonder who Evans might be on various occasions before finding out in chapter 32. Given their natural focus on Evans, it is extraordinary that, when Rose (the former cook at Tudor Cottage) tells Bobby that the parlourmaid was called Evans in chapter 31, he doesn't immediately tell Frankie (or the reader) about this. Surely, instead of just looking "preoccupied", he should be shouting "Eureka" even if he does not understand Evans's significance. But it is only later in the chapter, when he is well into a conversation with Frankie and she wonders why the villains didn't ask the parlourmaid, that Bobby tells her that the parlourmaid's name was Evans. Frankie gasps – just as one would have expected Bobby to do when speaking to Rose.

Finally, the most dramatic moment in the book does not relate to the revelation about Evans but to the heavy, ponderous tread of the villain mounting the stair to the attic, which means that we are about to learn who the villain is. After the door swings slowly open, the next sentence reads " 'And how are my two little birds?' said the voice of Dr Nicholson".

Naturally, the question arises, given that it turns out to be Roger speaking, whether this is fair. If there were no more to it than that, it would be fair: the author has deliberately referred to "the voice of" Nicholson, not Nicholson himself. No doubt Roger captured Nicholson's voice perfectly and "the voice of" Nicholson does not necessarily mean his *actual* voice.

The problem is that there *is* more to it than that because the person who enters the room is then repeatedly described as Nicholson when in fact he is not. We are told that "Nicholson" says "Your tolerance of morphia was … regrettable" and "Moira is still alive" without any reference to "the voice of" Nicholson. Indeed, there are various specific references identifying the man as Nicholson: "Nicholson put the candle down", "Nicholson picked up Frankie", "Nicholson walked to the door", etc. The author could and should have written this more carefully.

There are a couple of other situations which show similar carelessness. In chapter 22, Henry's suicide note is recited in the following way "*I feel this is the best way out,* (Henry Bassington-ffrench had written)". That is not right because Henry had not written it. And it is unnecessary anyway because it is obvious that the note purported to be written by him. Then in chapter 27 Bobby is supposed to have written a note to Frankie. Although the note was forged by Roger, the narrative says "*Dear Frankie* (wrote Bobby) *I'm on the trail ...*". That too is not right because Bobby had not written it and even more unnecessary because the forged letter actually ends "Yours ever, Bobby".

Clues
Although Carstairs provides the 'dying words' clue (discussed below), the main clues *for* him, and for Frankie and Bobby, about the identity of the villains are the photographs of Moira – the one removed from his pocket by Roger (the 'swapped photograph' clue) and the one he sees on the piano at Merroway Court (the 'piano photograph' clue).

As for the 'swapped photograph' clue, Bobby sees the photograph of an unknown woman (Moira) in Carstairs' pocket before Roger tends the body and yet the only photograph found on the body by the police is of a different woman (Mrs Cayman). Without revisiting here whether the 'swapped photograph' was Savage's snapshot of "Mrs Templeton" (the 'snapshot' clue) or a second photograph which Carstairs obtained from the photographers, it will be obvious to readers that either way only Roger could have made the substitution and, as we saw earlier, this is repeatedly made plain by Frankie and Bobby, for whom this is the main clue about Roger. Moreover, when Bobby learns that the woman in the swapped photograph is Moira, this also provides a connection between Carstairs and her.

As to the 'piano photograph' clue, this is the main clue about the identity of the villains for Carstairs. When he sees that the woman in the photograph is the woman in Savage's snapshot of "Mrs Templeton", he asks a lot of questions and learns that she is really Moira. He then goes to Chipping Somerton, knowing (from Savage) that this is where "Mrs Templeton" lived, to find an explanation for her having been left so much money.

Frankie learns of Chipping Somerton from Spragge but, before that, readers expect to get a clue about location (in chapter 24) from the names on the open page of an ABC railway guide in the Caymans' London house, which Frankie regards as having "possible significance". However, we aren't told that one of the names was Chipping Somerton until Frankie works out (chapter 27) that the Caymans had gone there – so nothing is made of this 'railway guide' clue.

While there, Carstairs presumably learns that Evans did not witness the will and, puzzled by this, goes to Marchbolt to enquire further. But he never sees Evans before uttering his dying words. This is unfortunate because she is the clue to whom Bobby must be referring when he says in the final chapter that it was queer that "the clue to the whole thing should have been in the Vicarage".

Strictly, however, Evans herself is not really a 'clue' (whether a 'boomerang' clue or otherwise). The clue, rather, is in Carstairs' dying words in which she is mentioned, described by Frankie in chapter 8 as "the '*Why didn't they ask Evans?*' clue". That clue (the 'dying words' clue) has two elements – Carstairs' question, which gives us the puzzle in the book's title; and its answer, which is more important since, if we can work it out, that will solve much of the puzzle by telling us why Evans was not asked to witness the will.

So, how do we work out the answer to the 'dying words' clue? This comes with the 'parlourmaid' clue given to us by Frankie in chapter 32. She puts both hands over her eyes (to help herself think) and, after remaining still for a minute or two, she explains that a parlourmaid waits at dinner and so would have recognised a house guest such as Savage (whereas the cook and gardener would not because they stay in the kitchen or outdoors). When one has the 'parlourmaid' clue, then one can start to think seriously about the answer to the 'dying words' clue and the probability of impersonation.

However, the structure of chapter 32 is such that we are presented with the solution to the 'parlourmaid' clue – that Evans, as a parlourmaid, would have known that the testator was not Savage – only two sentences after learning about the role of a parlourmaid and therefore have no chance to wonder about the clue, which is a pity because it is the most imaginative one in the novel.

Had we been given that chance, we might have been able to solve the 'dying words' clue before its solution was revealed because in chapter 28 we had been given the 'impersonator' clue (with Roger pretending to be Nicholson at Tudor Cottage) and the 'forger' clue (with Roger having forged Bobby's handwriting on the letter tricking Frankie to go there). Those clues indicate that Roger could have impersonated Savage and forged his will.

There had seemed to be a further potential element to the 'impersonator' clue in chapter 15 when Bobby learned that, while he was in London, a "tall, stooping gentleman with pince-nez" (as Mrs Roberts describes him) had called at the Vicarage asking for his London address. No further reference is made to this incident beyond Bobby telling Frankie about it. Nicholson wears pince-nez (chapter 26) and so readers are presumably intended to be misdirected into believing that he was the man. But it was surely Roger since he wore pince-nez as a disguise in the attic and was tall (chapters 2 and 12). But we never get the 'tall gentleman' clue confirmed.

Although the 'impersonator' and 'forger' clues come too late to confirm Roger as a villain (since they are only given to us at the moment of Roger's exposure), Frankie and Bobby did not need them to realise in chapter 28 that the man who mounted the attic stair and used Nicholson's voice was Roger. So, what clues did *they* use? There are two stages to the identification.

The first is Bobby's realisation, after the man has left the room, that he could not have been Nicholson because the man's ear lobes were not joined to his face whereas Nicholson's were. Bobby had noticed Nicholson's ears in chapter 26 but the 'ear lobes' clue is hardly a clue for readers since nowhere in the description of the man who enters the attic room is there any reference to his ears until *after* Bobby's sudden realisation.

The second stage is, if the man is not Nicholson, who *is* he? The answer, says Bobby (who answers first in chapter 28), is Roger. He simply says that they had spotted the right man at the beginning and had been led astray. Frankie, however, produces a clue, saying that it must be Roger because the man who had come up to the attic had referred to Frankie having taunted Nicholson about accidents (in chapter 27, after Henry's inquest) and Roger had been the only other person present when she had done this.

The word "taunted" seems strong when all Frankie had said to Nicholson was "I think it's a pity to go in too much for accidents – don't you?". But again, the problem is that there is no time to consider, or even spot, the 'taunting' clue because Frankie and Bobby's conversation moves so quickly. After the paragraph in which Bobby realises that it's not Nicholson, it takes only four sentences to decide that it is Roger.

There are, as we saw earlier with the to-ing and fro-ing, some other clues against the "ne'er-do-weel" Roger and the "sinister" Nicholson. These are all very obvious, save for a couple which are a little more subtle, one being Bobby's remark in chapter 26 that "As the villain of the piece, Dr Nicholson seemed regrettably careless" – raising doubts as to whether Nicholson is in fact the villain of the piece.

The other comes in chapter 21 after Roger says that he did not recognise the dead man as Carstairs (despite the lunch at Merroway Court) because he never saw the dead man's face, over which Bobby had placed a handkerchief. Frankie thinks "If *I'd* found a photograph of somebody I knew in a dead person's pocket, I should simply have had to look at the person's face. How beautifully incurious men are!". The subtlety comes in the speed at which Frankie's point is dismissed as a simple masculine lack of curiosity, perhaps causing some readers not to dwell on the 'dead man's face' clue. But those who do dwell, for just one moment, as Frankie should have, will realise that she was obviously right and that Roger's behaviour is not credible.

Related to the 'dead man's face' clue is a newspaper cutting which Frankie shows Sylvia and Roger in chapter 13 about the cliff edge "accident" at Marchbolt. Frankie had had no involvement in this and it had taken place over three weeks before and yet, surprisingly, Sylvia and Roger do not question her reasons for possessing such a cutting. Instead, Sylvia remarks that the man in it looks very like Carstairs – and thus it is that this 'newspaper cutting' clue gives Carstairs' name to Frankie.

Roger, however, says that there isn't much real resemblance, which leads Frankie to elevate the 'newspaper cutting' clue into a double one in the final chapter by saying that Roger's comment gave him away because it showed that he *had* seen the dead man's face. However, Roger was *not* comparing the picture of the dead man in the cutting with the dead man himself. He was comparing the picture in the cutting with the man, Carstairs, whom he had met at lunch, which reveals nothing about whether he had seen the *dead man's* face. So Frankie's second part of the 'newspaper cutting' clue doesn't work.

Indeed, it will be apparent, from what has been said so far, that generally speaking this is not a particularly well clued book, even allowing for it being a thriller rather than a detective story, with clues either being obvious or explained without allowing readers the time to think about them. Similarly, the detection is not of a high standard. For example, Frankie and Bobby seem ponderous in chapter 7 in establishing that the motive for poisoning Bobby's beer must relate to the man who was pushed over the cliff. And later (chapter 23) Frankie, despite being unable to sleep all night after Henry's death, appears not even to have thought about whether he might have been murdered.

However, it is when identifying Moira as "Mrs Templeton" that she is at her least convincing. From the time that we had first been told about "Mrs Templeton" (by Mr Spragge in chapter 25) until Frankie's identification of her as Moira (chapter 33), we had assumed, prompted by Frankie, that "Mrs Templeton" had been played by Mrs Cayman. But in chapter 33 it comes to Frankie "in a flash" that Moira is "Mrs Templeton".

Bobby asks, entirely fairly, in the final chapter "How on earth did you spot Moira, Frankie?". She replies that "everyone" (by which she means the waitress at the Seven Stars and the former cook at Tudor Cottage) said that "Mrs Templeton" was "such a nice lady"; and "that didn't seem to fit with the Cayman woman" whom no servant would describe as nice. This is a weak explanation – and the 'nice lady' clue a correspondingly weak one.

Moreover, it is only a clue to "Mrs Templeton" *not* being played by Mrs Cayman. It does not explain why Frankie thought that "Mrs Templeton" *was* played by Moira. This is not clued at all. What Frankie says is "And then we got to the Vicarage and Moira was there and suddenly it came to me – suppose Moira was Mrs Templeton?". That, again, was the product of Frankie's inspiration – rather than clueing or detection.

Finally, although Frankie and Bobby know from chapter 32 why the villains didn't ask Evans, Bobby nevertheless says in that chapter that there is still one thing they must do: "Find Evans. She may be able to tell us a lot" – presumably giving them further clues, even though they are not needed by then. But after they return to Marchbolt, there is no scene in which they seek Evans's comments about "Mrs Templeton" or about the death of Savage and they do not even pose the question "Why didn't they ask you?".

8

Murder Is Easy

Solution

This is a detective story in which Luke Fitzwilliam and Bridget Conway investigate seven murders. Six occur in Bridget's village of Wychwood-under-Ashe, about 35 miles from London, and the other in London.

Wychwood is a picturesque and traditional village which could have made an ideal setting for a Jane Marple novel. But it is also remote and fantastic, with a reputation for witchcraft, folklore and superstition and with Bridget herself, aged 28 or 29, being regularly likened to a witch, with her pale face, hollow cheekbones, black eyes and black hair.

She is engaged to Lord Whitfield, a newspaper proprietor, who had been born as plain Gordon Ragg in Wychwood, where his father ran a boot shop. Having made his fortune, Whitfield returned to the village and bought the only big house, Ashe Manor.

Luke has recently retired as a policeman in the Mayang Straits. He lands in England on Derby Day[1], and, although he has come home "after many years" with a pension, he seems relatively young and hates the idea of Bridget marrying a man in his 50s.

On the train to London he meets an elderly lady, Miss Lavinia Pinkerton, who tells him that "a good many" murders have occurred in Wychwood. She wasn't sure first time but, after the fourth one, she *knew* because when she saw the "look on a person's face" – a special look given by the murderer to an intended victim – that victim would very soon be dead. Yesterday she had seen the murderer giving the look to Dr Humbleby and so she was going to Scotland Yard.

Luke thinks that she just has a vivid imagination but, when she is killed by a car as she crosses Whitehall (before reaching Scotland Yard) and Dr Humbleby dies on 13 June, he goes to investigate in Wychwood. He pretends to be writing a book on folklore but Bridget sees through the pretence and, on learning why he has really come, she participates in the investigation and in chapter 16 (out of 23) agrees to marry him instead of Whitfield.

Otherwise, Luke's most useful source of information appears to be a friend of Miss Pinkerton's, another country spinster, Miss Honoria Waynflete, probably aged under 60, who lives in a little house adjoining Wych Hall. She had lived in the Hall itself as a child, when her family were important in Wychwood, and had been engaged to Whitfield years ago when she was a "girl", though they never married. When the Hall was sold, Whitfield bought it, turning it into a library and museum, in which she acts as librarian.

As the investigation proceeds, Luke reckons that four people (in addition to Miss Pinkerton and Dr Humbleby) have been murdered – which is consistent with Miss Pinkerton's remark that she *knew* after the fourth murder, although she did not actually say that there had been *only* four.

First, over a year ago, was Lydia Horton, the disagreeable but wealthy wife of Major Horton. She had suffered from an illness (not clearly described) and been attended at home first by Dr Humbleby, who had argued with Horton, and then by his partner Dr Thomas as well as a couple of hospital nurses. She seemed to be recovering but had a sudden relapse and died of acute gastritis.

Second, in April, was Amy Gibbs who had been a housemaid at the Hortons before working for Whitfield. She had stayed out all night with the exquisite Mr Ellsworthy, the antique shopkeeper, who was said to dabble in black magic and hold queer ceremonies in the Witches' Meadow. When Whitfield spoke to her about this, she was impertinent and he gave her notice.

She then worked for Miss Waynflete where she got a nasty cough. Dr Thomas gave her a bottle of cough mixture but that night Miss Waynflete heard a choking scream from Amy's room. The door was locked on the inside but a passing constable climbed in through her open window. She had swallowed hat paint and died of oxalic acid poisoning. Since a bottle of red hat paint by her bed was about the same size as the cough mixture bottle on her washstand, it was thought at the inquest that in the dark she had put the wrong bottle by her bed to take if she felt ill. But Luke and Bridget wonder if someone had climbed through her window and swapped the two bottles.

Third was Harry Carter, landlord of the Seven Stars, although we aren't told when he was killed. He was going home, quite drunk, on a misty night, fell into the river and was drowned. Someone could have shoved him.

Fourth, about a month ago, was a nasty little boy, Tommy Pierce, who was sacked by Mr Abbot, the local solicitor, for reading a confidential letter, then from his job as a garden boy at Ashe Manor for imitating Whitfield. Miss Waynflete got him some window-cleaning work but he fell from the top window of the library and died. Again, someone could have pushed him.

The next victim, after Miss Pinkerton, is Dr John Humbleby, who had argued with Horton, Abbot and Whitfield. He died of septicaemia about a week before Luke arrived in Wychwood after, it is thought, scratching his finger on a rusty nail. It turned septic and he was dead in three days.

There is one further death after Luke's arrival – Whitfield's chauffeur, Rivers, who angers Whitfield by taking Carter's daughter out in Whitfield's Rolls Royce and is then impertinent to him after being fired. That night he is found dead by the gates of Ashe Manor whose pillars are normally surmounted by two pink stone pineapples, one of which is on top of him. Luke reckons that somebody had hit him with a sandbag and rolled the pineapple onto him to make it look as if the wind had blown it down on him.

In chapter 14 Luke decides that the murderer is Thomas, Abbot, Horton or Ellsworthy, each of whom could have been away from Wychwood when Miss Pinkerton was killed in London. What should surprise readers is that he does not list Whitfield as a suspect, even though he thinks (twice) that the murderer has "standing" in Wychwood. Although Whitfield was only a bootmaker's son, he now has "standing" and is surely an obvious suspect.

Nevertheless it takes Luke three more chapters to suspect him when Whitfield points out that, every time someone mocks or abuses him, they are struck down. As well as Rivers, Whitfield mentions Tommy, Amy and Humbleby and even adds (as we were not previously aware) that Carter had abused him and that Mrs Horton had been rude to him. Only then does the "monstrous … incredible suspicion" leap to Luke's mind.

He remembers Horton saying that Whitfield had sent down grapes and peaches for his wife; that Whitfield allowed Tommy to clean windows at the library; and that Whitfield had held forth on his visit to the Wellermann Kreutz Institute with its serums and germ cultures just before Humbleby died of septicaemia. Luke now thinks that everything points plainly in one direction and that he had been a fool for not suspecting.

Readers will agree that he had been a fool but not that everything points in one direction. For example, we had been told (chapters 6 and 13) that anyone who climbed through Amy's window had to be reasonably active or athletic, which does not match our impression of Whitfield whose figure "ran mostly to stomach" (chapter 3) and was "pot-bellied" (chapters 15 and 17).

What is more important, however, is Whitfield drawing so much attention to his motive for murder. Surely he would not have done so if he was guilty. So his behaviour will, paradoxically, have the opposite effect on a good many readers to the one it has on Luke. It is the pivotal moment because, while he now focuses on Whitfield, those readers will look elsewhere.

In doing so, they cannot ignore that the victims (other than Miss Pinkerton) irritated Whitfield before dying. They may therefore wonder if someone is killing people known to have irritated him in order to make him look like a murderer. If they do, and then consider who has a grievance against *him* (rather than the victims), they should alight upon Miss Waynflete, who has not until then been a suspect but who does turn out to be the murderer.

Her grievance was revealed in chapter 15 when Luke had asked Whitfield why his romance with her had ended. Whitfield said that they had argued over her canary: "...one of those beastly twittering canaries – always hated them – bad business – wrung its neck". Whitfield thinks she has never forgiven him. In chapter 18 she explains that she broke off the engagement because she was frightened that he had enjoyed wringing the canary's neck.

However, in chapter 21, just before she is about to murder Bridget, Miss Waynflete reveals that it was Whitfield who had jilted her because of "that ridiculous business with the bird" (which we later learn she had in fact killed, causing him to terminate the engagement). She swore she would "pay him out" for "daring to jilt *me*". That was the start of it and, since Whitfield broke off the engagement when she was a "girl", she must have nursed her grievance for 30 years or more. And then he bought Wych Hall and patronisingly offered her a job in her own home. "How I hated him then!", she says before explaining that she wanted him to suffer for crimes of which he was innocent.

Her comments about paying him out and hating him suggest

that her motive was revenge or hatred. However, it is also clear from that chapter and the number of murders that she was "mad", "insane" and a "homicidal maniac". But whether her behaviour is explained by insanity or revenge or hatred, it would surely have been more convincing if she had simply killed Whitfield than embarked on such an extensive implication plan with seven other deaths.

As to killing the seven, she sat by Mrs Horton's bedside slipping arsenic into her tea and told the nurse how Mrs Horton had complained about the bitter taste of Whitfield's grapes – though the nurse never repeated this. Then, when Amy was dismissed by Whitfield, Miss Waynflete employed her. After changing the bottles (as Amy snored), she turned the key, which was on the inside of the lock, from the outside with pincers (to show that she could not have entered the room). When Carter lurched about in the fog, she pushed him from the bridge and later she pushed Tommy off the window-sill.

When she saw that Miss Pinkerton knew she was the murderer, she followed her to London and, unnoticed, pushed her under a Rolls Royce. She told the woman next to her that the car's number was FZX 4498 (Whitfield's car), hoping she would repeat it to the police, which she did. With Humbleby, she ran the point of her scissors into his hand and, acting distressed, put on a dressing, which she had infected with the discharge from the painful ear of her Persian cat, Wonky Pooh. She knew that Whitfield had talked about his visit to the Institute with its germs, cultures and bacteria and she tried to get people to remember that visit and connect it with Humbleby's death.

Strangely, she does not say anything about murdering Rivers. Presumably she just sandbagged him and rolled the stone pineapple on top of him. If so, then that murder plan required no real ingenuity, just a certain amount of strength – and the same is true of the murder plans for Carter and Tommy.

The murder plan for Miss Pinkerton would also have required a little strength and some luck because the car might not have killed her – though we have the extra element of implicating Whitfield with the wrong number after the car didn't stop. Similarly, the murder plan for Mrs Horton involved an attempt to implicate Whitfield by referring to the grapes but it is otherwise straightforward. The murder plan for infecting Humbleby, again involving an attempt to implicate Whitfield (by referring to the Institute), is rather more inventive, though, as Miss Waynflete herself concedes, "Of course, it *mightn't* have worked – it was just a long shot".

That leaves the murder plan for Amy, which has two elements of ingenuity. First is the hat paint, intended to implicate Whitfield. As Bridget says in chapter 6, people *did* paint hats about 20 years before, changing the colour each season, but hats were now thrown away when out of fashion and so Amy would not have used hat paint. In particular, she would not have used *red* hat paint and worn a scarlet hat because she had red hair – which a man wouldn't realise. The rather clever deduction from this is that the hat paint must have been substituted by "a man of moderately old-fashioned outlook". However, Miss Waynflete's attempt to implicate this sort of man fails again because, unsurprisingly, the rather clever deduction isn't made at the inquest.

Second is her use of pincers to lock Amy's door from the outside. She says that she got the idea from reading crime books but one rather suspects that it is not as easy to do this as she implies. So, even if we had been told that she possessed pincers, we would feel a bit sceptical about this, which slightly undermines the only potentially mystifying incident in the story.[2]

Overall, therefore, there is not much ingenuity in the seven murders, although, in fairness, the author's focus is on quantity rather than quality with her "homicidal maniac". Miss Waynflete's cleverness comes rather from not apparently having a motive for any of them, from selecting victims who (save for Miss Pinkerton) have irritated Whitfield and from trying to implicate him.

She does so again with her final attempt when she takes Bridget for a walk in chapter 21. When they rest and she wrongly thinks that the sleepy Bridget has drunk her drugged tea, she produces Whitfield's Moorish Riff knife. Wearing gloves and trying not to obliterate his fingerprints, she says that she hates Bridget because of her engagement to him and that she will be the crowning proof against him, with her throat cut with his knife.

Readers who had suspected Miss Waynflete after the pivotal moment may well think that Bridget does so as well, *before* going on the walk, because of her reactions. Thus, she pours Miss Waynflete's cup of tea out of the window, presumably because she suspects that it's been drugged. Then, when Wonky Pooh scratches her hand, she refuses iodine, presumably because she suspects that it's been infected. Then, before they start their walk, she notes that Miss Waynflete puts on gloves. Readers will presume that she thinks that Miss Waynflete wants to avoid leaving fingerprints but this time we are actually told what Bridget thinks, namely that they could be going to Bond Street. But surely, after rejecting the tea and iodine, this cannot be *all* she thinks?

And yet it is because, only when they are resting and Miss Waynflete suggests that Bridget is sleepy, does a "flash of comprehension" pass through her brain, succeeded by one of contempt at her own "density". To the surprise of surely many readers, she had not rejected the tea or the iodine for fear of drugs or infection since she had not realised that anything would be contemplated against her or so soon. She had merely "a dim suspicion" of the truth.

Her "density" seems greater when we learn in the final chapter that she had been thinking in chapter 20 (*before* the walk) that, if Whitfield wasn't the murderer – which she *knew* he wasn't – the answer seemed clear: it was someone who hated him – "Honoria

Waynflete, of course". That clarity is hardly "a dim suspicion". Although the author attempts to make sense of Bridget's "flash of comprehension" by having her play down how much she knew until Miss Waynflete's revelation, the attempt to reconcile her being both clear and dense at the same time is unpersuasive.

Nevertheless, having comprehended the situation, she and Miss Waynflete struggle and Luke arrives just in time to rescue her. It is then confirmed in the final chapter that there was insanity in Miss Waynflete's family and that she, not Whitfield, had wrung the canary's neck, which is a surprise because of his words "one of those beastly twittering canaries – always hated them – bad business – wrung its neck". But, although the words "always hated them" give the impression that he killed the canary, he did not actually say *who* did so or that this was why he thought Miss Waynflete had never forgiven him.

Plot

In the United States version entitled *Easy to Kill*, numerous sentences from the original version are deleted, characters' names are changed (Pinkerton to Fullerton; Whitfield to Easterfield), the more graphic descriptions of Ellsworthy's queerness are omitted and chapter 14 is split into two chapters. However, none of the changes affects the plot or the theme of the story, which is that murder is *easy*. But what makes it easy?

One factor, so Miss Pinkerton tells us (chapter 1), is that it is very easy to kill so long as no one suspects you and, as Miss Waynflete says (chapter 21), you can't suspect anyone of murder if there isn't a motive. Another, so Dr Thomas tells us (chapter 8), is that it is quite easy to get away with it if you are careful and, he says, a clever man is extremely careful. A further factor suggested by Miss Waynflete (chapter 21) is organisation. And the final factor, so Mr Jones, the bank manager, admits (chapter 11), is probably luck.

Those four factors are mentioned at different places rather

than in a composite list, although the word "easy" does appear nearly ten times when Miss Waynflete tells Bridget about her murders. She says it was "easy" to take Whitfield's knife, to arrange an accident, to make him believe that anyone who went against him suffered, to manage all the murders, to give Carter a push and to shove Miss Pinkerton under the car. And Bridget found it "easy" to get Miss Waynflete to boast about her cleverness.

During her boasting, she says "I'm always lucky" and she refers to the Rolls Royce not stopping and to Luke witnessing Whitfield's anger with Rivers. But in fact she was not always lucky: the nurse never repeated Mrs Horton's complaint about the grapes; Amy's inquest didn't spot that she wouldn't use hat paint; and Whitfield, his chauffeur and his car had alibis when Miss Pinkerton was killed. It was also hard to get Luke to suspect Whitfield – a point she makes herself, very fairly because a frustration about the plot is that Luke is so slow in keeping up with it – shown in his failure to list Whitfield as a suspect and then to realise that he's too obvious, as also is Bridget who, despite having her "clear" answer, only had "a dim suspicion" of the truth.

By then, we are in the odd position of having had the solution revealed by the murderer rather than the detectives.[3] However, Luke and Bridget do at least admonish themselves for their foolishness as they go along and Luke, having thought at the end of chapter 7 that "This job isn't going to be exactly easy", admits in the final chapter "Well, I am not much of a policeman!". But he does rescue Bridget and so doesn't need any help from Superintendent Battle, who arrives in Wychwood in chapter 21 but makes only a fleeting appearance, without conducting any investigations before the murderer is revealed.

The story's events all take place in June but we are only given one date – that Humbleby died on 13 June, "over a week" after Derby Day (chapter 2) and "about a week" before Luke arrived in Wychwood (chapter 3). So, doing one's best to make sense of the timing, it seems that the Derby was on Wednesday 4 June, that Luke arrived on Wednesday 18 June and that the climax, with Miss Waynflete's exposure, was on Thursday 26 June.[4]

Not only is that climax mildly exciting but the exposition from the moment of Luke's arrival in England on Derby Day is especially good: the initial conversation between Luke and Miss Pinkerton on the train is most engaging and we have the promise of an intriguing investigation by Luke after he learns of the deaths of Miss Pinkerton and Humbleby.

Apart from those opening two chapters and Luke's visit to Scotland Yard (chapter 18), the rest of the story is set in Wychwood, whose English village atmosphere is really well conveyed. One scene, Major Horton's positive description of life with his disagreeable wife in chapter 11, is particularly enjoyable. An oddity is Bridget's suggestion in chapter 3 that there are about six women to every man in Wychwood. That is not true of the people we meet; the numbers of men and women are almost exactly the same.

When Luke arrives in Wychwood in chapter 3, he asks about the men in the village and is told about Abbot, Thomas, Ellsworthy, Horton and Mr Wake, the rector. He is not told then about Mr Jones, the bank manager, or Amy's young man (Jim Harvey, the garage mechanic), although he is told about them in time to add them to the list of seven suspects which he prepares in chapter 7 (misdirecting us away from Miss Waynflete). The churchwarden, Mr Hobbs, isn't on the list because Luke is not told about him until chapter 9.

He also writes out a list of victims – Amy, Tommy, Carter, Humbleby and Miss Pinkerton. He then adds: Mrs Rose? Old Ben? After a pause, he adds: Mrs Horton? Bridget had mentioned Mrs Rose, the laundress, to him in chapter 4, and in chapter 5 Mr Wake suggested more names – "old Bell and that child of the Elkins" and poor old Ben Stanbury. We later hear of one further death in chapter 9 (Tommy's sister, Emma Jane).

By chapter 14 Luke has reduced his victims to six (Mrs Horton, Amy, Carter, Tommy, Miss Pinkerton and Humbleby) – omitting five deaths of which he was aware – and his suspects to four (Thomas, Abbot, Horton and Ellsworthy), which seems odd, partly because he had eliminated Thomas (chapters 8 and 11) and partly because, although he had eliminated Jones (chapter 11) and Jim Harvey (chapters 11 and 13), he had never eliminated Wake.

In chapter 14 ('Meditations of Luke') he considers whether each of his four suspects could have murdered each of his six victims. This further misdirecting analysis (away from Miss Waynflete) of 24 possible hypotheses (in fact it is only 23 because he fails to consider Abbot murdering Mrs Horton) tends to ramble and it would take a very patient reader to follow the 23 permutations knowing that all of them, except perhaps one, must be wrong; and that they probably all are because he has omitted Whitfield.

Moreover, even if his basis were reliable, his 23 hypotheses lack structure. He says he will consider the victims in "chronological order" but he considers Humbleby before Miss Pinkerton and varies the order for considering Tommy and Carter. And, although he usually addresses both motive and means for each hypothesis, there are omissions – such as *why* Thomas would have murdered Mrs Horton or *how* Abbot could have murdered Humbleby.

One imagines that many readers, faced with Luke's unreliable approach, stop following the meditations, which means that their purpose of misdirection away from Miss Waynflete is undermined. Indeed, the volume of text devoted to Luke's unstructured thought processes, and his slow-wittedness as a detective, are factors which, along with the limited mystification, prevent the plot living up to the promise of the opening two chapters.

Clues

Although the story's theme is that murder is easy, there is an underlying motif of witchcraft. It is first seen in Luke's claim to be writing about folklore and then in Wychwood's reputation; and it continues with Ashe Ridge brooding over the village; with the Witches' Meadow and Midsummer Eve; with Bridget being regularly likened to a witch (a "Witch without Broomstick", as chapter 3 is entitled); with Luke becoming "bewitched" by her; and with Ellsworthy and his black magic and queer ceremonies.

Perhaps this symbolism should have made readers think about Miss Waynflete reminding Luke of a goat. After Bridget realises that Miss Waynflete is the murderer, her most dramatic thought – as if it were the main clue – is "God! how like a goat she is! A goat's always been an evil symbol!" – and she is right since the goat has long been associated with witchcraft and satanism.[5]

When Luke meets Miss Waynflete, he thinks of her as the complete country spinster – her thin form, tweed coat and skirt, grey silk blouse, cairngorm brooch, felt hat, pleasant face, pince-nez, intelligent eyes – and, tagged onto the end of that list, she reminded him of those nimble black goats seen in Greece; her eyes held that quality of mild inquiring surprise. For those readers who do not spot the 'goat's eyes' clue among the long list of her features, there is another reference a few pages later and again in chapter 13.

Only the most astute reader would spot that, because there are three goat references, Miss Waynflete must be evil and therefore the murderer. Indeed, such a reader would need to be very astute, given that in chapter 13 her eyes are described as "so like an amiable goat's" – which is rather misleading. But, for any astute readers who do spot the 'goat's eyes' clue, it is quite a strong pointer to Miss Waynflete in a book with a witchcraft motif.

Luke, however, focuses on his suspects and victims. There are many links between them: Horton, who had inherited money on his wife's death, had argued with Humbleby; Humbleby, who had also argued with Abbot, disliked Thomas and objected to his interest in his daughter; Thomas, whose position was improved by Humbleby's death, had attended Mrs Horton and prescribed Amy's cough mixture; Amy, who had been sketched by Ellsworthy and stayed out all night with him, had gone walking with Carter and worked at the Hortons' when Mrs Horton died; Mrs Horton, who had amply provoked her husband, had swallowed a nostrum of Ellsworthy's; Ellsworthy had a sketch of Amy with a red cross over her face and a note saying "Settle with Tommy Pierce"; Tommy, who had imitated Ellsworthy, had been sacked by Abbot; and Abbot, who had visited Mrs Horton just before she died and been visited by Amy, had been abused by Carter for speaking to his daughter.

But these interlocking connections, although well constructed, don't seem like clues because they are stated so openly as simple facts – so openly that they are surely going to be red herrings. The biggest occurs in chapter 16 when Ellsworthy returns home from a nocturnal ceremony on Midsummer Eve in a "delirium of mad excitement", with his hands stained red. We learn in the final chapter that he and his friends had sacrificed a cock.

Luke's suspects in chapter 14 are all men. That is unsurprising because of the repeated indications that the murderer is a man, even though Miss Pinkerton never actually told Luke whether her suspect was a man or woman.

It would have been difficult, and sounded unnatural, for her not to use 'he' or 'she' when talking about her suspect to Luke in chapter 1 were it not for the author's clever device of introducing the point by reference to the Abercrombie case. Thus Miss Pinkerton starts by referring to Abercrombie, saying that "...*he'd* poisoned quite a lot of people … a special look that he gave any one…" before going on to refer, in the context of the Wychwood murderer, to "The look on a person's face…". This not only conceals the gender of that "person" but her two references to "he" suggest that she means a man (although in fact she was referring to Abercrombie).

So Luke tells Bridget in chapter 6 that Miss Pinkerton spoke of "the look in his eyes when he was measuring up his next victim". Luke's use of the word "his" (twice) is important because he has fallen into the author's trap of making us think that the murderer is a man. In fact, there had been no further references to 'he' before chapter 6 but in that chapter Luke starts in earnest to build on Miss Pinkerton's early references and to deceive readers (and himself) into thinking that the murderer is a man.

Thus he says that "*a man*" wouldn't realise that you don't wear a scarlet hat with carroty hair and that he is after "a certain man – a secret killer – a man here in Wychwood ... that man killed Amy Gibbs". The chapter has other references to "man" before Luke refers to "the look in his eyes" and thinks that the "man" Miss Pinkerton suspected was at least her social equal.

By the end of chapter 6 readers should be in so little doubt that the murderer is a man that it only takes the occasional further reference to consolidate this – "...he *must* definitely be mad" and "The man's been too careful" (chapter 10); and (because of the 'hat paint' clue) "...it was a man and a man of moderately old-fashioned outlook ... a reasonably athletic man" (chapter 13).

However, when Luke says that Miss Pinkerton had *told* him that the murderer was "A man with a certain look in his eyes" (chapter 13), some readers may spot that he has gone too far. They may recall that Miss Pinkerton never *said* "man" or be prompted to look back at what she did say. Luke even backtracks slightly in chapter 14 when, after saying "man" a couple of times, he refers to Miss Pinkerton giving him "a picture of a man" and "the impression ... of a very normal man" (in other words, only a *picture* or *impression*).

But, even if Luke is backtracking slightly at that stage, Miss Waynflete is not and she tells him in chapter 15 that "...*he'll* know.

He'll realise that you're on his track … he's a very clever man … he's got a great deal of experience". Then in chapter 18, while at Scotland Yard, Luke refers to "a man who's done a round half-dozen murders at least" as well as to "he" and to "his".

Naturally, with the author practising such a thorough deception with the 'man' clue, many readers will not spot that it is false before chapter 20 when Bridget gets Luke to go over what Miss Pinkerton had said. Whenever he pauses or she interrupts, she asks him to go on, doing so more than half a dozen times, making plain the importance of Miss Pinkerton's exact words, which he finally says were "The look on a person's face…".

By then it should be clear that Bridget is checking whether Miss Pinkerton had referred to a man (rather than a person). She confirms this in the final chapter, explaining that she made Luke repeat Miss Pinkerton's exact words because she "…remembered that Miss Pinkerton had definitely spoken of a *man* as the killer" (although this is odd because nowhere had Miss Pinkerton said that).

Therefore, by chapter 20, readers should spot that the murderer could be a woman and that the shift from the 'man' clue to the 'exact words' clue makes this pretty likely. So, we need to look more closely than we perhaps have at clues pointing towards Miss Waynflete (in addition to the 'goat's eyes' clue).

She does behave questionably in chapters 5, 13 and 15 (appearing puzzled, disappointed and nebulous, and having an "expression" of "impatience and something closely allied to it"). But this seems to be explained later by her belief that Amy was murdered and then by her frustration at Luke's failure to suspect Whitfield. So, we must look elsewhere for clues.

A clear impression is created of her as a most unlikely suspect. Her pleasant face beams encouragingly upon Luke and she seems to become his confidante almost as much as Bridget. She also appears disarmingly honest when telling him that Miss Pinkerton thought something odd was going on in Wychwood.

However, she cannot be excluded on those grounds because, while her insanity is not directly clued before the climax, the author does flag that a lunatic could be the "last person you'd ever suggest" and that a murderer can be "a nice gentle wouldn't-hurt-a-fly type of man" (chapters 6 and 8). Other examples of the 'last person' clue are Thomas saying "...a homicidal lunatic may be the most difficult thing on this earth to spot..." and, of course, Miss Pinkerton saying in the opening chapter that the murderer is "just the last person any one *would* suspect", which is a significant pointer towards Miss Waynflete.

Her social standing is also relevant because (as Luke reminds us in chapters 6 and 14) Miss Pinkerton suspected a man who was "at least her social equal" and Miss Waynflete suspected a man of "high standing". In the latter chapter it is easy to be misled into wondering who Miss Waynflete suspects – and away from her. But she is at least the social equal of Miss Pinkerton. As Tommy's mother, Mrs Pierce, says, Whitfield is not really gentry, "...not like Miss Waynflete, for instance, and Miss Conway" (chapter 9). This 'social standing' clue is subtle because we focus on *Whitfield* (since he is really the subject of Mrs Pierce's observation) rather than on Miss Waynflete being "gentry".

Looking more specifically at the individual murders, there are so many interlocking connections, as we have seen, that Miss Waynflete's employment of Amy and Tommy is not of itself of any special assistance except perhaps on one point. This is that Amy was killed in her house. But that happened in a room which appeared locked from the inside and, even if some readers might have wondered whether she had somehow locked it from the outside, there was no clue that she had any pincers.

However, one connection does give us a clue, which is Horton telling Luke (chapter 11) that Whitfield sent grapes and peaches to his wife and that "the old tabbies" (Misses Pinkerton and Waynflete) used to come and sit with her. This 'tabbies' clue is quite good, perhaps the best among a rather uninspired group, because readers will wonder if Whitfield's fruit is a clue to Mrs Horton's poisoning while the key fact is Miss Waynflete sitting at her bedside, which is when she put arsenic into her tea.

Otherwise there are no real clues to Miss Waynflete having murdered Amy, Carter, Tommy or Miss Pinkerton. As for Humbleby, the nearest we perhaps get to a clue is Wonky Pooh's ears having been rather painful lately (chapters 5 and 21). But this 'Wonky Pooh' clue doesn't really help readers because there is no reference to the septic discharge or the piercing with scissors or Miss Waynflete's dressing until she reveals she's the murderer.

As for Rivers's murder, one imagines that Miss Waynflete, with her "thin form", would not have had the strength to hit Rivers fatally and then move the pineapple. But in fact she turns out to be "very strong", although again we don't learn this until she reveals she's the murderer. Indeed, even in that chapter, she is "a skinny frail old pussy" and "a slender-built, frail creature".

So, if the individual murders don't really help, then who could realistically be "just the last person any one *would* suspect"? The only candidates are really Bridget – where there is no hint of a motive – and Miss Waynflete – where readers do get the hint of a motive with the 'canary' clue.

In chapter 15, when Whitfield says "Don't think she's ever forgiven me", readers will assume that the reason for her not forgiving him is that he killed her canary whereas the real reason is that he broke the engagement after she killed it. But the *reason* is not what matters in this context. What matters about the 'canary' clue is the *fact* of her not forgiving him because it means that she is the only living person known to have a grievance against him.

So it is through this process of elimination, rather than inspiring clueing, that the solution is likely to be spotted by readers. As for it being spotted by Bridget, Miss Pinkerton and Luke, they each suspect Miss Waynflete for *different* reasons. But they do so on the basis of knowledge or instinct which is not shared with readers until the murderer is revealed or not shared at all.

In Bridget's case, the 'canary' clue points her towards Miss Waynflete, but not in the same way as it hints to readers. She was not present (unlike readers) when Whitfield said "Don't think she's ever forgiven me" and so her suspicion does not come from the grievance element of the 'canary' clue. Rather, it comes from having a very strong sense of Whitfield's true personality – "I knew him so *well* … I knew him in and out", as she says in the final chapter, adding that it worried him even to kill a wasp and that he didn't shoot because seeing things killed made him feel sick. So she knew that Miss Waynflete had lied about the canary, which made her wonder if she had told other lies. But readers are not given any clue that she thought this.

She does say in chapter 20 that she is thinking of something which Mrs Humbleby once said but we never learn what clue she got from her. In chapter 22 Mrs Humbleby does tell Luke that she and Miss Pinkerton had both thought that Miss Waynflete was very wicked and capable of terrible things. So *perhaps* she had earlier said this to Bridget but, if so, that would be another reason why Bridget's mere "dim suspicion" doesn't make sense.

As for Miss Pinkerton, it seems that "She guessed", as Miss Waynflete says in chapter 21. Miss Waynflete adds that, when she looked at Humbleby, wondering how to kill him, she found Miss Pinkerton watching her and saw that she knew.[6] But Miss Pinkerton never describes what it was about Miss Waynflete's look that gave her away.

Finally, as for Luke, he does give us some description of the murderer's look. He remembers in chapter 22 that, when Miss Pinkerton had said "The look on a person's face…", her own face had changed as if she was seeing something clearly in her mind. Just for a moment it had been quite different, the lips drawn back with a queer, almost gloating look in her eyes. He wonders if Miss

Pinkerton had reproduced the look she had seen on the murderer's face. And he thinks that the look on Miss Waynflete's face had been like that when she had looked at Bridget in the drawing-room at the Manor.

This 'Pinkerton look' clue is the one that at last points Luke at Miss Waynflete. But, even if Miss Pinkerton had reproduced Miss Waynflete's look so as to reveal her as the murderer, readers would have found it difficult to match the two looks without knowing how Miss Pinkerton had *actually* looked on the train and how Miss Waynflete had looked at the Manor.

Despite Luke's graphic description in chapter 22 of Miss Pinkerton's look on the train, this is not what we had *actually* been told in chapter 1. There Miss Pinkerton trembled a little and her cheeks lost some of their colour. But that is it. Although Luke refers much later (chapter 20) to Miss Pinkerton looking "like someone who had really seen something almost too horrible to speak about!", one gets the impression there that her face showed horror, not madness of the sort conveyed by Luke in chapter 22.

Even if Miss Pinkerton had reproduced a look of madness, the clue would be incomplete without some indication that Miss Waynflete's face had had a similar look. But, when we go back to see what look Miss Waynflete gave Bridget at the Manor (chapter 19), we find only a "reproachful glance".

Perhaps Luke meant to refer to the look which Miss Waynflete gave her in chapter 21 while she and Luke were at her house. There her "expression" (which is not actually described) reminded him of "someone or something that he had seen not long ago" but he could not pin down the elusive memory. Since readers do not know what "expression" he was seeing, they would do well to match it to Miss Pinkerton's ostensible look of madness rather than just to, say, Miss Waynflete's own "expression" of "impatience and something closely allied to it" that he could not quite place in chapter 15.

9

And Then There Were None

Solution

Eight invited guests come to Soldier Island, over a mile out at sea from the fictional village of Sticklehaven in Devon, on 8 August. A married couple are already there – not the mysterious hosts, Mr and Mrs U. N. Owen – but a butler and cook, Mr and Mrs Rogers, newly engaged by an agency to staff the island's only house. These ten people are alone on the island. By the evening of 11 August all of them are dead.

After a good dinner on the first night, they hear The Voice, coming from a gramophone record played by Mrs Rogers on Mr Owen's written orders. It makes accusations against all ten, each of whom has deliberately, recklessly or vindictively caused or contributed to the deaths of others.

As the victims die one by one – and realise that one of their ever-decreasing group must be U. N. Owen, who is executing justice for their past wrongs – each member of that group becomes a suspect and/or detective as well.

Although there is no traditional detective, the main character seems, until the solution, to be Vera Claythorne. She dwells anxiously on her past crime on noticeably more occasions and at noticeably greater length than any other character; she appears to be the last survivor; she provides the climax to the island narrative by hanging herself, kicking away the chair on which she stands; and it is her chair that creates the puzzle because, although she had appeared to be the final victim, someone had put it back against the wall before the ten dead bodies were found on 12 August.

So, what has happencd? The puzzle is only solved at the end with the murderer's confession. In it he says that, having decided to commit murder on a grand scale, a rhyme of his infancy came into his head – that of the ten little soldier boys whose number diminishes one by one and ends, when the last one has hanged himself, with "And then there were None".

In chapter 2 Vera sees the rhyme framed in her bedroom. It also hangs in the other bedrooms. And on the dining-room table are ten china figures. One of the story's motifs, used for the first five victims but not consistently thereafter, is that each death is accompanied by the disappearance of a china figure.

Another motif is that the murderer tries to kill the victims in ways that match the nursery rhyme. Thus, the first soldier in the rhyme "chokes his little self" and so, shortly after The Voice is heard, Anthony Marston, who had killed two children by driving recklessly, chokes to death.

The second soldier "overslept himself" and so Ethel Rogers doesn't wake on the second morning. She and her husband had deliberately withheld amyl nitrate from a lady for whom they were caring and benefited on her death.

The third soldier, travelling in Devon, "said he'd stay there" and so it is with General John Macarthur, who had deliberately sent his wife's lover, who was one of his officers, on a wartime reconnaissance mission, knowing he would die. Weighed down by his misdeed, he says that no one will leave the island. He is struck on the head before lunch on the second day. So he stays in Devon *because* he's killed, which is an imaginative attempt at matching the rhyme.

The fourth soldier "chopped himself in halves" and on the

third morning Thomas Rogers's head has a deep wound from a heavy chopper.

Vera then looks forward to the fifth verse, asking if bees are kept on the island because "a bumble bee stung" the fifth soldier. On the third morning Miss Emily Brent, having just seen a bee, dies after feeling a prick in her neck. She thinks she has been stung by the bee, which is another imaginative attempt to match the rhyme. A servant girl, whom she had vindictively sacked for becoming pregnant, had taken her own life by throwing herself into a river.

Next, as the soldiers go in for law, the sixth "got in Chancery", meaning the Lord Chancellor's Court of Chancery, with its Dickensian reputation for entangling parties in never-ending disputes until its jurisdiction was transferred to the new High Court of Justice in 1875. The sixth victim is a retired judge, Mr Justice Lawrence Wargrave, who had vindictively turned a jury against Edward Seton at his trial for murder and sentenced him to death. On the third evening, in another imaginative attempt to match the rhyme, Wargrave is found in his chair, dressed as a judge in a wig and scarlet robe, with a round stained mark in the middle of his forehead, having, as Dr Edward Armstrong pronounces, been shot.

Armstrong, who had been drunk when operating recklessly on a patient who then died, is the next victim. In the seventh verse, when the soldiers are at sea, "a red herring swallowed one". Armstrong unsuspiciously swallowed a red herring by entering into an alliance with the murderer and was deceived into meeting him at 1.45 am on the fourth morning at the cliff edge. The murderer pushed him off the cliff and he was drowned (or "swallowed") as a result of the red herring. Since one cannot literally be swallowed by a red herring, this is about as valiant an attempt as one could make to match the rhyme.

The next victim – though he is killed before Armstrong is

found on the rocks – is William Blore, a former police Detective Inspector, who had deliberately or vindictively perjured himself to convict an innocent man, who later died in prison. In the eighth verse, the soldiers walk in the Zoo and Vera suggests "We're the Zoo" because those remaining were, in the atmosphere of fear the night before, "hardly human any more" and "reverting to more bestial types". In the verse "a big bear hugged one" and, as Blore reaches the house at lunchtime on the fourth day, a large marble clock shaped like a bear drops from Vera's window, crushing his head.

When Armstrong is found on the fourth evening while the sun is dropping, it seems that two people remain, each suspecting the other – Vera and Captain Philip Lombard, who had been lost in the bush with his men (21 African natives) and had, as a matter of self-preservation, cleared off with all the food, deliberately leaving them to die. He had brought a revolver to the island and, as he and Vera drag Armstrong clear of the sea, she takes it from his pocket and shoots him. In the rhyme the ninth soldier got "frizzled up" while "sitting in the sun".

This leaves Vera, who had been the nursery governess of a boy whom she had deliberately allowed to go swimming, knowing he would drown, so that her lover would come into the boy's money. Having shot Lombard, she returns to the house, dropping the revolver at the top of the stairs. In her room, she sees a rope with a noose, hanging from a hook in the ceiling, and a chair on which to stand. Like an automaton, recalling the child's murder and the final verse in which the tenth soldier "hanged himself", she climbs on the chair, puts the noose round her neck and kicks the chair away. That concludes the island narrative.

Then in an Epilogue, Assistant Commissioner Legge and Inspector Maine discuss the position. We learn that Fred Narracott, the Sticklehaven boatman, responding to SOS signals flashed by Lombard, Vera and Blore on the fourth morning, had taken some men out in a boat next day and found the bodies. No one else was there. And no one could have left before they arrived. "The only explanation possible", says Maine, is that the murderer was one of the ten.

In considering which one, the police do have diaries and notes of some victims showing that the first six died in the order: Marston, Mrs Rogers, Macarthur, Rogers, Miss Brent, Wargrave. So Maine reviews whether Armstrong, Blore, Lombard or Vera could have killed the others before committing suicide.

Armstrong can't have done so because his body had been dragged by someone away from the sea. Blore wouldn't have killed himself with a block of marble. Lombard can't have shot himself on the seashore because the revolver was upstairs. And Vera can't have hanged herself last because – as Maine now reveals, to our great surprise – someone had put her chair back against the wall. "But in that case", so the Epilogue ends, *"who killed them?"*.

Readers have some advantages over the police. We know that Lombard and Vera dragged Armstrong away from the sea. We know they were alive after Blore. We know that Vera shot Lombard, although we can't see how she can have shot Wargrave because at the time she was upstairs screaming in the dark. We know that she did kick the chair away when hanging herself. And we know that none of Armstrong, Lombard or Blore can have pretended to be dead before moving Vera's chair because we were told, as facts, that Armstrong had a "hideous drowned face", that Blore's head was "crushed and mangled" and that Lombard was "dead – shot through the heart…".

Nevertheless, those advantages do not really help. So we have a wonderful puzzle whose breathtaking solution would remain a mystery if it were not explained in a confession, which follows separately after the Epilogue and is found in a bottle at sea, signed by Lawrence Wargrave, the sixth 'victim'. He did not die until after Vera's hanging when he shot himself with the revolver.

In the confession he explains that, on hearing how often "murder" was committed which the law was unable to touch and that untouchable cases of deliberate "murder" were going on all the time, he decided to execute justice himself and that, on remembering the rhyme, he began collecting his victims. He tabulated information about their 'murders', jobs, holidays, skills, friends and colleagues and concocted a bait for each. His plan was complete when he received medical advice that he had a terminal illness: he did not want to suffer a slow and protracted death.

He used an accountant called Isaac Morris to acquire the island for him. We know (from the Epilogue) that Morris provisioned the island and made all the necessary arrangements (including, presumably, the engagement of Mr and Mrs Rogers), acting for the imaginary "Mr Owen"; that the gramophone record with The Voice was supplied to him by a theatrical effects firm (who understood it to be required for the performance of a play); and that he told the mainland villagers that, because of an experiment, any signals from the island were to be ignored (which meant that no boat would come to the rescue, even without the storm, which broke at lunchtime on the second day and made boating impossible) – although Narracott overrode this instruction on the fifth day.

Before leaving for the island, Wargrave killed Morris with barbiturates. Morris had done a vital job in covering Wargrave's tracks; and, of course, Wargrave must kill him. But, oddly, this is not why Wargrave says he did so. Rather, he says "I needed a tenth victim". But one does wonder why, since the 'need' for a tenth victim only comes from the rhyme, which already works so well with Wargrave as the sixth 'victim' before he later becomes a suicide victim when he is the tenth to die. Even the sixth verse matches *his own* 'death', not Morris's, and in his first clue (to be considered later) he claims to be unique among "the ten people on the island" and so he is not there treating Morris, who was not murdered on the island, as one of the ten. One imagines that very few readers think of Morris as one of the ten little soldier boys.

After hearing The Voice, Wargrave suggested to the others that the murderer must be a "madman" or "lunatic" – an idea they later echo about a dozen times. But his confession doesn't admit insanity and his motivation may rather be that of a 'sadistic fanatic' since he does admit to taking a "sadistic" delight in seeing or causing death and he is, as Maine says, a "fanatic" about justice.

In the tension after The Voice, he added potassium cyanide to Marston's glass and, when Mrs Rogers was given brandy after fainting, he added a lethal amount of chloral hydrate. Next day he struck Macarthur, perhaps with a life preserver (a short, weighted club).

He then embarked on the key element of his plan – appearing to be a victim – which needed an ally to say he was dead. He chose Armstrong and "hinted" to him that he had a scheme to trap the murderer. He doesn't say that he told Armstrong then what the plan was but he knew himself because by tea-time he had taken some of Miss Brent's wool and a scarlet bathroom curtain in order to portray a judge, and hidden them in the drawing-room for his 'death' scene.

On the third morning he killed Rogers. He also put chloral hydrate into Miss Brent's coffee to make her drowsy and, having presumably released the bee, injected cyanide into her neck with a syringe taken (we aren't told when) from Armstrong's room. Then the five remaining guests (including Wargrave) each submitted to a personal search by the others. Lombard's revolver was not found because Wargrave had taken it after Rogers's death and hidden it.

He then told Armstrong that it was time to carry out his plan to pretend to be a victim, which might rattle the unknown murderer and enable Wargrave to spy on him. Armstrong was keen. After lunch, the five sat in the drawing-room, with only one person leaving at a time. By 5.45 it was already dark because of the continuing storm and because there were no lights without Rogers to start the engine. Lombard suggested trying to start it but Wargrave (cleverly wanting to minimise the light) said it was better to use candles.

At 6.20 Vera went to her room and, as she entered, a draught from the window blew out her candle. Some seaweed hanging from the hook in her ceiling touched her throat. She screamed. Armstrong rushed up the stairs with Blore and Lombard, who thought Wargrave was with them. In fact he had stayed downstairs, applied some red mud to his forehead, put on the red curtain as a scarlet robe and the wool as a judge's wig, and posed as a murdered man.

When the others came down, they saw him in his chair, with two candles burning either side of him. Armstrong waved the others back and raised the wig revealing the "round stained mark" in the middle of his forehead. He pronounced that Wargrave had been shot, with, it was assumed, Lombard's missing revolver, which had not been heard in the howling wind and noise. Wargrave was carried up to his room and laid on his bed.

Wargrave had arranged the seaweed but he doesn't say when – perhaps when leaving the drawing-room alone. It was presumably also then (again he does not say) that he returned the revolver, which Lombard later found in his room. What is harder to say is when he told Armstrong the detail of his plan. The only reference to it in the confession *before* the personal search is his 'hint' to Armstrong that he had a scheme. Yet *after* the personal search, when he told him that "we must carry our plan into effect" (as if the detail had already been agreed), it is hard to see when they could have discussed it since all five then searched the house for the revolver, being "careful to keep together", and then sat together in the drawing room, with only one person leaving the room at a time, save when all five of them went to the kitchen. So maybe, rather than just 'hinting', Wargrave explained the plan before the search; there would have been an opportunity to do so when he told Armstrong that there were "several things we can do" in chapter 10 part 3.

Anyway, at 6.20, when Vera screamed, Armstrong knew what to do in accordance with his alliance with Wargrave. But, oddly, Wargrave says that he chose Armstrong because he was gullible and would find it inconceivable that a man of Wargrave's standing should be a murderer. Surely this is not as good a reason as Armstrong being a doctor, and therefore the only person to examine him closely, which he only mentions later as a sort of bonus.

Having executed the plan, Wargrave now had to kill Armstrong, who had "swallowed" the red herring of Wargrave's fake alliance with him. This "resulted", says Wargrave, in him being "swallowed" when, having unsuspiciously agreed to meet Wargrave at the cliff top early on the fourth morning, he was pushed off and drowned.

And then, says Wargrave, there were three people left (Blore, Lombard and Vera) who were so frightened of each other that "anything might happen – *and one of them had a revolver*". He watched them from the window and, when Blore came up for lunch, he had the bear clock ready – though the murder plan sounds unreliable because it depends on real accuracy and on the victim being under the window. Then he saw Vera shoot Lombard – a murder he did not have to commit himself.

Since Wargrave says "anything might happen", and it happened to be Blore who came up for lunch, he may not have minded whether he killed Blore or Lombard with the clock – though presumably he wanted Vera to be last since the hook was in her ceiling. But one wonders what he would have done if the clock had missed Blore or if Vera had not shot Lombard or, more likely since Lombard had the revolver (before being pickpocketed), if he had shot her.

However, Vera did shoot Lombard and, as soon as Wargrave saw this, he arranged the noose and chair. He thought that the consciousness of her guilt about the drowned boy, her nervous tension after shooting Lombard and the hypnotic suggestion of the noose, chair and rhyme would cause her to hang herself. His impressive psychoanalysis of her likely reaction proved correct since, instead of rejoicing in the "glorious sense of safety" which she now felt, she hanged herself as he stood in the shadow of her wardrobe. If she had not, he presumably had a plan for hanging her himself.

He then set the chair against the wall. After tossing the bottle containing his confession into the sea, he lay on his bed. The weight of his body was on his glasses, which were attached to a fine elastic cord, which he had looped round the door-handle and then attached, not too solidly, to the revolver, which he was holding. With his hand covered by a handkerchief (so as not to erase the fingerprints left by Vera when shooting Lombard), he pressed the trigger; and the revolver, pulled by the elastic, recoiled to the door and then, jarred by the door-handle, detached itself from the elastic and fell. He would be found on his bed, shot through the head in accordance with the records kept by his fellow victims, with the elastic hanging innocently from the glasses, the revolver just inside the door and an unremarkable handkerchief on the floor.

Wargrave's overall plan, making it appear that he was the sixth victim, is brilliant. It also accords with the diaries and notes of the others looked at by the police, who do not even review him as a suspect. However, he had to rely on playing dead convincingly while the others carried him up to his room (what if he'd been dropped?) and later on the revolver recoiling to the door with a fine elastic cord, even though the cord was attached to it "not too solidly" so that it could detach itself when it jarred on the door-handle.

Plot

The novel was first published in the UK in November 1939. It was originally titled *Ten Little N*****s*[1] because its plot was constructed around the British nursery rhyme of that name, which was a popular music hall song adapted in 1869 by Frank Green from an American comic song called *Ten Little Indians*.

In the United States, where the word 'n*****' had been regarded as racially offensive for many years, the novel's first edition published in January 1940 was titled *And Then There Were None*, with the closing lines of the nursery rhyme thus replacing the opening ones. This is a better title, not just for racial reasons, but because, in conjuring up a mysterious ending, it engages the reader's curiosity immediately. The 'n***** boys' of the rhyme were called 'Indian boys' and 'N***** Island' was called 'Indian Island'; and the Pocket Book paperback reprints (1964–1986) were actually titled *Ten Little Indians*. But modern United States editions use 'soldier boys' and 'Soldier Island'.

Although the novel was published first in the UK, the story began with a serialisation in the United States in *The Saturday Evening Post* from 20 May 1939 in seven weekly parts. The title was *And Then There Were None*, with 'Indian Island' being called 'Injun' Island' and the 'Indian boys' being 'Injun boys'. In the UK, it ran in the *Daily Express* from 6 June 1939 in 23 daily parts with the title *Ten Little N*****s*. Both serialisations concluded on 1 July.

Over time, UK public opinion became more sensitive to the racial offence caused by the title and in 1985 UK publishers began to change it to *And Then There Were None*. Even then, in that reprint, the island was still called 'N***** Island' and the nursery rhyme still had 'n***** boys'. However, modern UK editions use 'soldier boys' and 'Soldier Island'.

Modern UK editions also make a couple of other related changes. First, in chapter 1 part 8 Blore originally thought of N***** Island as resembling a man's head with "negroid lips". That crude resemblance is simply omitted in modern UK editions. In the United States serialisation, the resemblance was also simply omitted, but it then resurfaced in the novel's first edition (and, for example, 1944 and 1966 editions) as a man's head with "an American Indian profile", before then being omitted again in modern United States editions.

Second, in chapter 2 part 7 of the UK editions, Wargrave originally thought "N***** Island, eh? There's a n***** in the woodpile". That was solved in modern UK editions by changing those words to "Soldier Island, eh? There's a fly in the ointment" – but, of course, that phrase does not work so neatly (even if it is less jarring to modern ears).

However, the United States position is more striking. In the serialisation, the sentence was simply omitted. But in the novel's first edition (and 1944 and 1966 editions) the change was made to a surprising hybrid "Indian Island, eh? There's a n***** in the woodpile", thus retaining the very word which, given the other changes, one would have expected to be changed. However, modern United States editions have the same change as in the UK editions.[2]

Turning to the opening chapter, it quickly engages us with its enticing exposition of the characters' reasons for going to the mysterious Soldier Island. And it ends excellently, just after Blore reckons that a drunken seaman is nearer to the day of judgment than he is, with "But there, as it happens, he was wrong…". By then we are hooked on the story, which is compellingly readable throughout, very skilfully mingling a selection of the characters' thoughts and feelings into the factual narrative.

A sense of foreboding is conjured almost immediately. When Vera first sees Soldier Island, there is "something sinister" about it; mention of the Owens, whom no one has ever seen, has a "curiously paralysing effect" on the guests; Narracott warns that the island can be cut off for a week or more; Macarthur feels uneasy; Mrs Rogers looks frightened; Vera is faintly disturbed; and then The Voice from the gramophone record (nicely titled *Swan Song*, meaning a final performance before death) leaves everyone in "petrified silence".

And the situation worsens as victims start to die, china figures vanish, Narracott's boat doesn't come, a search of the island proves fruitless, a storm breaks and the characters realise that U. N. Owen "is one of us...". With the scene set this way, almost exactly halfway through the book, the suspense and menace are then maintained wonderfully well as further victims die and the remaining characters suspect one another during the ominous darkness of the third day which permeates the second half of the story.

Then, when Armstrong is found dead, and Lombard and Vera realise that they alone remain, the final (pre-Epilogue) chapter begins memorably with "Aeons passed... worlds spun and whirled... Time was motionless...". We still don't know who will survive. And when neither of them does – as the rhyme correctly predicted – the story seems to end without a solution.

The UK first edition dust jacket says that "Ten Little N*****s is certainly the greatest story that the Crime Club has ever published. We believe it may come to be considered the greatest crime problem ever devised in fiction" (the Crime Club being an imprint of Collins, the author's publishers since 1926).

Interestingly, although the *solution* is thoroughly original, the idea of an unknown host isolating a group of people and then killing them off one by one had been used in the United States nine years earlier in a murder mystery entitled *The Invisible Host*. There is no suggestion that Agatha Christie was aware of the story and it is most unlikely that she could have been since the book did not have a UK publication and 'foreign' works were by no means as readily available then as they are today.

In that novel, eight invited guests come to a New Orleans

penthouse apartment, 22 floors above the street, for an evening party. Staff are there to serve dinner, with instructions from an anonymous host who is not apparently present. After a good dinner accompanied by a storm, a voice coming from the radio warns the guests that they cannot escape through the electrified doors and that anyone who loses a game with Death will die. After the second death, a guest suggests (correctly) that the murderer is one of the remaining six. After the fifth death, two of the three remaining guests establish that the other one is the murderer. After he dictates a confession, they persuade him to kill himself (rather than be tried and hanged) and to allow them to leave.[3]

Readers of that novel will have wondered how the radio was rigged and how some of the deaths occurred. But otherwise there is no mystification about the howdunnit because no attempt is made to rise to the far superior plotting challenge which Christie set herself of concealing the murderer in a decreasing group of suspects which finally reaches zero, in accordance with the structure of a nursery rhyme, without the solution being apparent or absurd.

The key to achieving this is Wargrave pretending to be dead with the help of a doctor whom he kills and later killing himself in a way that implicates Vera.[4] With that key in place, the author can construct a plot based on the rhyme. And she does this beautifully, having thought carefully about how and where to assemble and isolate ten people; what personalities and past wrongs to allocate to them; how and when they should die; and how Wargrave's plan and suicide should work. The result is a story in which the individual murder plans are less important than the brilliant ingenuity of the overall plan for killing everyone in a way that seems mystifyingly incapable of solution.

However, having solved that plotting challenge, she still faces others – one of which is to match the deaths to the verses, where she is not always helped by the wording. Only four help her directly – choking, chopping, oversleeping and hanging (Marston, Mr and Mrs Rogers and Vera). She faces hurdles with the other six. With four (Macarthur, Brent, Wargrave and Armstrong), she does, as we have seen, as imaginatively and valiantly as one could expect.

With Lombard, one has to persuade oneself that "frizzled up" equates to 'shot'. Perhaps she wants us to treat "frizzled up" as slang for 'shot' (rather like 'burned'). Or perhaps being shot was not as important as Lombard being (as the rhyme says) "in the sun". Although the sun was "dropping" when Vera shot him, it had "enveloped them in a golden glow", possibly giving readers a sense of 'frizzling'. Whatever the answer, having Blore "hugged" by crushing him with a bear clock is the least convincing of Wargrave's attempts at matching.

She also has some of the characters trying to match the deaths to the verses. Vera notices a similarity with the rhyme after the first death; Armstrong and Lombard do so after the second; Vera seems convinced of the connection after the fourth when she anticipates the bee for the fifth; she matches the red herring of the seventh verse with Armstrong; she anticipates the eighth with "We're the Zoo"; and she remembers the tenth before hanging herself. But, although the relevance of the sixth is spotted *after* Wargrave's death, neither she nor anyone else anticipates it *beforehand*, even though its references to "going in for law" and "Chancery" identify the next victim more obviously than any other. Had she done so, the characters may, to Wargrave's frustration, have protected him.[5]

Another challenge relates to Vera hanging herself. This is mainly one of making readers believe that she would really do it, which the author does well by having her dwell on her past crime so anxiously; and by Wargrave's impressive psychoanalysis. But there's a subsidiary issue of how Vera is going to do it, which is solved by having a "big black hook" in her ceiling.

But who installed such a hook, strong enough to take a body's weight? Perhaps it was there before 'Mr Owen' acquired the house – but, if so, why? Using it to hang, for example, a light fitting of a size requiring such a strongly fixed – and inelegantly black – hook seems unlikely in a bedroom. So presumably Wargrave asked Morris to get it installed. But Morris must have wondered why, since he wasn't asked to hang anything from it.

A more significant plotting challenge is the ending. Wargrave's confession follows separately after the island narrative and the Epilogue. The Epilogue is integral to the story because the facts and ideas discussed by Legge and Maine, such as the chair being put against the wall, complete the puzzle. But the confession is just a device to reveal the solution and comes across as an artificial postscript, like an answer section at the back of a puzzle book. One wonders if the solution could have been constructed into the narrative so as to make the novel a coherent whole.

The author did achieve coherence when adapting the novel into a play in 1943. There Wargrave confesses and explains his villainy to Vera *before* her intended hanging rather than as a postscript. The play, however, has a different drawback, which is that his plan fails because, as he is about to hang Vera following his confession, he is shot by Lombard (who had survived being shot by her). Although Lombard then tells her of an alternative rhyme ending "We got married – and then there were none", the fact is that there are two left at the end, not "None".

One can understand why, in 1943 wartime, an uplifting ending might have seemed more appropriate than a successful villain. But, as indicated earlier, the novel is so brilliant because the suspects *do* reach zero, with the result that there *are* "None" left – which is, really, the whole point of the plot.[6]

Subject to the postscript ending of the novel[7], its plot is brilliantly clever, meticulously planned and excellently constructed, leaving the reader with an unarguable sense that there is something really very special about this story.

Nevertheless, some minor points should be mentioned. In chapter 3 Wargrave says that the Christian names, Una Nancy, are reasonably clear in Miss Brent's letter but the letter only has the initials. In chapter 12, after her death, a sixth china figure is thrown out but it should be the fifth. In chapter 13 Vera cries out that Lombard had said that Wargrave was the murderer that morning but he did so the previous day. And in Wargrave's confession he says that he had mentioned undergoing an operation but he hadn't mentioned this.

Clues

There are two types of clue in this story. First are three clues which, according to Wargrave's confession, the police might spot if they are clever; and second are other clues available to the police and/or the reader. The fact that Wargrave refers to clues, when he didn't need to leave any, is a recognition by the author of the importance of providing clues in a puzzle.

Wargrave's first clue is that the police are perfectly aware that Seton (the man Wargrave hanged after turning the jury against him) was guilty and, therefore, know that one of the ten people on the island (Wargrave) was not a murderer in any sense of the word. So, paradoxically, says Wargrave – because he can be distinguished from the other nine because they were all murderers whereas he was not – he must logically be the island murderer.

It is hard to believe that the police would seriously regard such 'logic' as a clue. But, analysing this 'past wrongs' clue seriously, Wargrave is not really distinguishable from the other nine because not every one of them is in fact a 'murderer' – which is the key word that he uses in his clue to distinguish himself from the other nine as well as being the very source of his motivation where, as noted earlier, he uses the word "murder" twice.

Under English law, 'murder' requires not only an act or omission that is *unlawful* but also death to be caused *intentionally*.[8]

Of course, the other nine all deliberately, recklessly or vindictively caused or contributed to the deaths of others. But this does not make each of them a 'murderer'.[9]

In Miss Brent's case, taking the clearest example, although her "hardness" (to use Vera's word) drove the servant girl to take her own life, she had not acted unlawfully or intended the girl to die. Maine says it was "not a nice business", but not "criminal" (let alone 'murder'). For her to be a 'murderer', 'murder' would have to be broadened to cover vindictiveness resulting in death.

If the definition of 'murder' was broadened to try to make all of the nine 'murderers', the clue still wouldn't really work if this then made Wargrave a murderer too, in that broadened "sense of the word", because he still couldn't be distinguished from the others.

But he does not regard himself as a 'murderer' in "any" sense of the word because Seton was guilty – and we know from the Epilogue that evidence turned up after his hanging which proved his guilt beyond any shadow of doubt. Indeed, Armstrong thinks in chapter 4 part 1 that Wargrave knew something about Seton before the case – a thought which, oddly, is never followed up but which may explain Wargrave's attitude towards Seton.

However, we are also told that at the time of the trial nine out of ten people believed Seton was innocent and that Wargrave's summing up had been vindictive. Indeed, we know that Wargrave himself thought that he had "cooked Seton's goose all right!" (chapter 5 part 3).

Nevertheless, it's hard to get away from the fact that Wargrave turned out to be right about Seton. So, if it were ever realistic to charge a judge with 'murder' under the *existing* law, based on his summing up, then – after taking into account that Wargrave was right, along with the later evidence and his genuine belief that he had acted correctly at the time – a jury may well accept that he had acted lawfully and so was not guilty of 'murder'.

However, if the definition of 'murder' was broadened – for example, to cover vindictiveness resulting in death (to catch Miss Brent) – could Wargrave himself then be a 'murderer' in that "sense of the word"? If he were charged with 'murder' in the vindictiveness "sense" and the jury were directed to consider only the evidence known at Seton's trial and to assess whether Wargrave's summing up had been vindictive by reference to it, they might well conclude that he had been vindictive, and that this made him as guilty of 'murder', in that "sense", as Miss Brent – and in fact more so because he actually intended Seton to die – thus again making him *indistinguishable* from the others as a 'murderer' and meaning that the 'past wrongs' clue doesn't work.

Indeed, if one were to get a clue from the suspects' past wrongs, a better way of distinguishing the murderer may be to ask if any suspects have *already* been punished by the law, so that no more justice is needed. Marston is the only one. He says in chapter 4 part 2 that his licence was suspended for a year but Maine says in the Epilogue that he was fined. Either way, he has been punished in accordance with the law at the time (though Maine thought he should have been banned).

Another way of distinguishing the murderer may be to ask if any suspects genuinely seem to believe that they have not acted wrongly – Miss Brent is only one (other than Wargrave, but he also knows he "cooked Seton's goose"). So, looking at the characters' past wrongs actually points as much towards Marston or Miss Brent as Wargrave.

Wargrave's second clue lies in the seventh verse of the rhyme ("A red herring swallowed one"). Vera describes this as "the vital clue" but she misinterprets it, saying that Armstrong, whose body has not yet been found, is not dead and that his disappearance is just a "red herring".

Wargrave, however, explains the clue by saying that "Armstrong's death is associated with a 'red herring' which he swallowed – or rather which resulted in swallowing him!". He says that at that stage some "hocus-pocus" is clearly indicated (presumably by the words 'red herring') and that Armstrong was deceived by it and sent to his death.

The words 'red herring' may attract readers who are actively looking for clues and they may even expect some "hocus-pocus", especially with Vera referring to "the vital clue". Nevertheless, interpreting the 'red herring' clue as Wargrave suggests requires those readers to be very astute.

First, they must deduce that the effect of the "hocus-pocus" was to deceive one of the characters, which requires reading the verse ("A red herring swallowed one") the wrong way round ("One swallowed a red herring") and then conclude that, by swallowing it, this "resulted" in the red herring swallowing him. And, second, they must deduce that the character was Armstrong, when Blore, whose body is found before his, seems to be the seventh victim. The author may have made a valiant attempt to link Armstrong's death to the rhyme but treating it as a clue goes too far.

Nevertheless, Wargrave treats it as a double clue – not limited to the *howdunnit* (the deception of Armstrong) but extending to the *whodunnit* (who fed the red herring to Armstrong?). Wargrave's answer to that is "For that period there are only four persons left and of those four I am clearly the only one likely to inspire him with confidence". But this is not right.

As far as readers (and the police) are concerned, Wargrave is *dead* by the seventh verse; there are only *three* alive to inspire Armstrong – Blore, Vera and Lombard. And, even if Wargrave might still be alive, he was not the only one likely to inspire Armstrong since, when Armstrong wanted a consultation in chapter 7 part 2, he thought about Wargrave but actually chose Lombard. So, even though the 'red herring' clue may be "vital", it is a very difficult one.

Wargrave's third clue is "symbolical. The manner of my death marking me on the forehead. The brand of Cain". This refers to the mark which God put on Cain after he had murdered his brother Abel (Genesis 4: verses 8–16). Wargrave doesn't say why the brand of Cain is a clue. Presumably he means that, after he had shot himself in the forehead, he would be found with a mark like Cain's, meaning that he too was a murderer, like Cain. Again it's hard to believe that, if someone is shot in the forehead, the police would seriously think of Cain and regard that person as a murderer.

But, even analysing it seriously, the 'brand of Cain' clue is a very weak one because it is not known whether the mark was put on Cain's forehead (or some other part of his body) – it does not say so in Genesis, or definitively in any other authoritative work – and so readers are unlikely to assume that such a mark is the brand of Cain or a clue to Wargrave's guilt.[10] Moreover, the *purpose* of the brand was not strictly to mark Cain as a murderer but (verse 15) to warn anyone who might think of slaying him, while he roamed the earth as a fugitive, that God would avenge the slaying seven times over.

So Wargrave's three clues do not help us with the *whodunnit*. But the police have a fourth clue, which does – the 'gramophone record' clue considered in the Epilogue. They know it charges "*indictments*", which is a good legal word, and does so in legal-sounding language and then ends "*Prisoners at the bar, have you anything to say in your defence?*". So surely the most likely character to have prepared the speech is the judge. The clue is just one of the elements of the 'judge' clue pointing to a judge being the murderer.

There are others which might link the murders to a judge, such as Mrs Rogers thinking The Voice was "*like a judgment*"; Wargrave referring to "the execution of justice" by U. N. Owen for offences which the law cannot touch; Lombard plumping for Wargrave as the murderer because as a judge he had played God Almighty and might want to be "Executioner and Judge Extraordinary"; and Armstrong thinking of Wargrave as "A hanging judge", which resonates with Vera's hanging.[11]

Of those, the police have only the 'gramophone record' clue but Maine still spots the motive – "Some fanatic with a bee in his bonnet about justice. He was out to get people who were beyond the reach of the law" – at which point Legge says "Just for a minute I felt I'd got somewhere. Got, as it were, the clue to the thing. It's gone now". Of course, he did nearly have "the clue to the thing" – the killing of people who were beyond the reach of the character most associated with the law (and whose first name even begins with the letters L A W).

Other information is also known to the reader but not the police. In particular, readers know what a number of the characters were thinking about their visit. It doesn't matter what they *tell* other characters because they could be lying or how they *behave* because they could be acting. Nor that they feel 'disturbed' or 'uneasy' because the murderer could feel like that. What matters is whether they have thoughts or feelings (of uncertainty about the visit or financial hardship) which are inconsistent with them being Mr Owen and able to organise and finance such a house party – as seven of them do.

Vera thinks it is "Really a great piece of luck getting this job" and wishes she "knew what they [the Owens] were like". Lombard, who is "literally down to his last square meal!", wonders "What exactly was up?". Miss Brent appreciates *"getting a free holiday"* with "her income so much reduced". Macarthur "hadn't got it clear who this fellow Owen was"; "the whole thing was deuced odd!" and a "Damned curious business the whole thing!". Marston wonders "Who *were* these Owens?" and what Badger "could have been thinking about to let him in for this". Armstrong "was anxious to find out a little about these people who owned Soldier Island". And Rogers mutters "That's a rum go! I could have sworn there were ten of them [china figures]" and "No more china-soldier tricks tonight. I've seen to that...".[12]

As for the other three, we can't eliminate them from suspicion because of the 'thoughts' clue. Blore does wonder on the third night where the revolver is but this doesn't stop him being the murderer (because someone else might have taken it). What stops him is his head being crushed before Lombard and Vera die.

We get no thoughts from Mrs Rogers. She and Rogers had inherited money and so their present roles as servants may, like her frightened appearance, be an act. So, strictly, we can't eliminate her, although it seems extremely unlikely that she could pull this off without her husband's involvement.

Nor can we eliminate Wargrave. He does say to Armstrong "Don't understand this place" (chapter 2 part 7) but he could be tricking him. And, cleverly, although he gives the impression that he was invited by Constance Culmington, he never *thinks* of her as his *host* but just as the sort of woman who would buy an island and surround herself with mystery, whereupon he nods "in gentle approval of his logic" – his "logic" being in selecting a person whom he can plausibly pretend invited him. And, similarly, when he later "reflects" on her (chapter 2 part 7), he just thinks she is "undependable".

There are other clues pointing to Wargrave, even if only seen with hindsight. The police know he could be "vindictive" but readers have additional elements of the 'malevolence' clue: he looked "with active malevolence" at Blore; he "dwelt malevolently" on a Harley Street interview (which is *possibly* a hint that he was not just ill but seriously so, thus partially explaining his motive); his mouth was "cruel and predatory" when smiling about Seton's goose; and there was "a faint malicious pleasure" in his voice after the island search proved fruitless. Lombard did have an "almost cruel mouth" while Miss Brent had "malicious" eyes in Armstrong's dream and Vera thought her "terrible". But no one else is described with Wargrave's degree of malevolence.[13]

We also get the 'control' clue. Since the murderer could not know how nine confused and scared strangers would react, he would need to control almost everything they come to realise about their predicament. And Wargrave does this, taking "charge of the proceedings" in chapter 3 part 3 and getting Rogers to tell the others what he wants to convey about Mr Owen. His control during that first evening might seem explicable (and so perhaps not a clue), in view of his social standing and reputation, were it not for two things which jar.

First, when The Voice recites the indictments – the accused's full names, dates and victims – it seems amazing that anyone could absorb the detail, especially if in shock or personally accused. Yet Wargrave, who has only met the others that afternoon, spots that The Voice did not accuse Mr Davis (the false name initially used by Blore) but did accuse William Henry Blore. Second, after then suggesting that U. N. Owen is, by a stretch of fancy, "UNKNOWN", he says that Owen is "probably a dangerous homicidal lunatic", which is oddly prophetic when no one has yet been killed or even directly threatened.

Then, on the second day, Wargrave "assumed command with the ease born of a long habit of authority" and continued to exercise control. It is Wargrave who says that Owen's scheme is the execution of justice; who concludes that "Mr Owen is one of us..."; who analyses whether anyone can be eliminated from suspicion; who proposes that any drugs and firearms should be collected and that the remaining five should submit to a personal search; and who directs that the drugs are locked away. Until his 'death', just about the only step he had not initiated was the search of the island (which Lombard proposed) but, as he says in his confession, he had anticipated a search being made.

For readers who identify Wargrave as the most obvious suspect for the *whodunnit*, the puzzle is still very much a *howdunnit* because we thought he was dead before the last four victims were killed; and he was certainly dead when the men arrived. The short answer to the *howdunnit* is that he was in fact still alive. That makes sense of Vera reckoning, when she and Lombard were alone, that there was "someone watching and waiting" (chapter 15 part 2) and her thinking, just before her suicide, that the house didn't seem empty.

So, if the murderer was still alive, the first *howdunnit* question is: which characters, based on the physical descriptions *in the narrative*, might have been alive to put back Vera's chair? Not, as we saw earlier, Armstrong with his "hideous drowned face", or Blore whose head was "crushed and mangled", or Lombard who was "dead – shot through the heart...". We can also exclude Marston with his "face contorted, turned purple ... blue twisted lips", and Rogers with the "deep wound" in the back of his head, and Miss Brent whose face was "suffused with blood, with blue lips and starting eyes" ("starting", not "staring", is in nearly all editions).

As for the other three (Mrs Rogers, Macarthur and Wargrave), each was examined by Armstrong. With Mrs Rogers, we are told that Armstrong "lifted the cold hand, raised the eyelid". She could perhaps have been alive if her "cold hand" had been dipped into iced water but two chapters later the narrative does refer expressly to Armstrong looking down on "the peaceful face of the dead woman". With Macarthur, we are given no facts about Armstrong's examination but we are excluding Macarthur anyway with the 'thoughts' clue. That only leaves Wargrave, thus providing yet further support for him as the most obvious suspect for the *whodunnit*.

But, in relation to the *howdunnit*, he was examined by Armstrong and pronounced dead. So, the second *howdunnit* question is: what clues do we get that he could still be alive despite Armstrong pronouncing him dead? One is the 'red herring' clue which, as we saw earlier, is a double one – the *howdunnit* aspect being the deception of Armstrong into Wargrave's pretended alliance. Another is Armstrong examining Wargrave in the candlelight, giving us a 'candlelight' clue about the reliability of his examination, especially with the others waved back. And, third, is Wargrave being pronounced dead by Armstrong rather than in the narrative. Although Armstrong "lifted the lifeless hand" in the narrative, the author has been particularly clever with the word "lifeless", which gives the impression of death and yet also means "apparently dead" or "lacking vitality".[14] So, very astute readers might spot how Wargrave could still have been alive to put back Vera's chair.

One also wonders if there is a 'Zoo' clue in Vera's idea that she, Blore and Lombard make up the Zoo of the eighth verse. Blore is a beast waiting to charge – a wild boar; Lombard is lithe and graceful – a panther but with a wolf's face; and Vera is like a bird with its head dashed against glass. The only other character described like an animal (a reptile in fact) is Wargrave – a tortoise, with a frog-like face. Is this a clue that he too was part of the Zoo and therefore still alive at the time of the eighth verse?

More substantial support for Wargrave still being alive comes with Maine saying that the revolver was found "just inside the door at the top of the stairs – Wargrave's room". This is significant because there was no reference to *his room* when Vera actually dropped the revolver – just to the top of the stairs.

However, the 'Wargrave's room' clue doesn't tell us how he could have shot himself in a way that wouldn't look suicidal but implicate Vera with the fingerprints. In his confession he says that he used his glasses, a cord and a handkerchief. But no reader could work out what Wargrave actually did because there is no reference in the Epilogue to those three clues.

So readers are in an odd position. The *whodunnit* is clued at least with hindsight, pretty clearly, not by Wargrave's clues, but by other clues, which either help directly (such as the 'gramophone record' and 'control' clues) or assist with a process of elimination. But the *howdunnit* remains mystifyingly difficult to solve, even making us doubt the *whodunnit* despite the revolver being in Wargrave's room. Which brings us back to clues known to the police. They must have found the cord, glasses and handkerchief and so they have some clues which readers don't.

10

N Or M?

Solution

This is a Second World War thriller set in the spring of 1940, prior to Germany's anticipated invasion of England, in which Tuppence Beresford inveigles her way into an assignment which her husband, Tommy, is undertaking for Mr Grant of the Ministry of Requirements.

The assignment is to go to Leahampton on the south coast to identify N or M, which are codenames for Hitler's most trusted agents. A German message decoded at the start of the War had said "*Suggest N or M for England. Full powers –*". The mission in England for N (known to be a man) or M (known to be a woman) is to organise a Fifth Column of people to assist an invasion.[1]

The two main puzzles are (1) which of N or M is the German agent sent to England (the question in the book's title) and (2) which character is N or M? Both questions are confused by the possibility that, despite the word 'or' in the coded message (and in the title), *both* N *and* M are in England.

In order to solve them, Tommy (calling himself Mr Meadowes) stays at the *Sans Souci* guesthouse in Leahampton where he finds, to his surprise, that Tuppence (calling herself Mrs Blenkensop) is also a guest. She had overheard Grant instructing Tommy and was determined to participate.

The proprietress of *Sans Souci*, Mrs Eileen Perenna, is the main suspect. The other residents, who are also suspects, are her daughter, Sheila, and her guests – Mrs O'Rourke, Major Bletchley, Carl von Deinim, Alfred and Elizabeth Cayley, Miss Sophia Minton and Mrs Millicent Sprot who is accompanied by her two-year-old daughter, Betty, but not by her husband, Arthur, an insurance clerk, who has remained in London.

Other suspects are Tony Marsdon who is a colleague of the Beresfords' daughter, Deborah, in the "coding department"; and a Polish refugee called Vanda Polonska, who is seen near *Sans Souci* four times but whose real aim is to kidnap Betty, which she does, resulting in a dramatic chase to the cliff edge where she is brilliantly shot dead by Mrs Sprot.

The final suspects are Commander Haydock, a retired naval man, and his manservant, Appledore, who live nearby at Smugglers' Rest, overlooking the sea. In chapter 5 Haydock tells Tommy how useful his house would be to an enemy – perfect for signalling out to sea; completely isolated; and with a path to a cove below for landing a motor-boat. Many expensive gadgets had been installed by the previous owner, Hahn, who had been exposed as a German agent four years before by Haydock, who then bought the house.

Tommy reckons, when visiting Smugglers' Rest for a second time in chapter 9, that Appledore might be German. So he decides to check how Haydock and Appledore react to the letters N and M and he gets his chance when Haydock moans about forms that ask idiotic questions. Tommy responds "I know. Such as 'What is your name?' Answer N or M".[2] This apparently innocent reference causes Appledore to spill crème de menthe over Tommy – so angering Haydock who subjects Appledore to a stream of abuse.

Then, when Tommy is in the bathroom washing it off, his foot skids against a bath panel, which slides out, exposing a wireless. So he decides that Haydock is N – and that Hahn had been sent first to prepare the house and draw attention to himself, before being unmasked by the gallant Haydock who, as agent N, was now ready to carry out Germany's plans.

Tommy, who then leaves Smugglers' Rest, is knocked unconscious on the driveway of *Sans Souci*. He is right that Haydock is a German agent. But readers may wonder whether he is actually N because, if so, we have the answers to the two main puzzles by chapter 9 of this 16-chapter book. Surely he can't be the *whole* solution since neither he nor Appledore, who remained at Smugglers' Rest after Tommy departed, can have knocked him unconscious. Who then might have done?

At the time, a bridge game was being played at *Sans Souci* by Tuppence, Mrs Cayley, Miss Minton and Mrs Sprot. Mrs Sprot, returning to the bridge table breathless after taking a telephone call in the hall, says that, while she was on the telephone, Mrs Perenna came into house "out of breath", though Mrs Perenna says that she had just gone outside to look at the weather.

As for the other *Sans Souci* inhabitants, Tuppence says that three had been out. Oddly, she omits Sheila, who went to the pictures, though she is right to omit Carl, who has by then been arrested as a German agent (wrongly, in fact, because he is neither a German agent nor the real Carl but someone in Intelligence who had taken his place).

The three are Major Bletchley, who had gone to the cinema alone and describes the picture in such detail as to suggest that he is establishing an alibi; Mr Cayley, who had, unusually, gone for a walk instead of remaining in his chair on the terrace; and Mrs O'Rourke, a terrifying woman, who returns, looking sly and malicious and swinging a hammer, which she says she found on the drive. So, various suspects might have hit Tommy, who awakes three chapters later to find himself imprisoned in a cellar at Smugglers' Rest (before being found by Albert Batt, who had helped the Beresfords in earlier stories).

Meanwhile Tuppence is startled in Leahampton by Tony

Marsdon, a colleague of the Beresfords' daughter, Deborah. Deborah had told him that "someone" had seen her mother in Leahampton and that this was "odd". So he has, he tells Tuppence, come to warn her about this because he knows, unlike Deborah, about the vital job she is doing there.

But Tuppence is suspicious and tricks him – although readers don't know this – by pretending that she and Tommy communicate with a slogan: "*Penny plain and tuppence coloured*".[3] Marsdon, using that bogus 'Penny plain' slogan, tricks Tuppence (so he thinks) into going to Yarrow and thence to Dr Binion's surgery in Leatherbarrow. But, in fact, she is tricking him because his use of the bogus slogan has, unknown to readers, revealed to her that he is luring her into a trap, but one which she enters willingly to expose the enemy.

At Dr Binion's surgery the person who enters the room is Haydock, who says that, unless Tuppence tells him what she knows, he will have Tommy, his prisoner, killed. Her response is "*Goosey, goosey gander!*"[4], which has a "magical" effect – enraging Haydock who repeatedly demands to know where Tuppence has hidden "it" – though neither readers nor Tuppence know what "it" is since she had not taken or hidden anything.

He gives her three minutes to tell him and, as the time ticks by, she sees everything in a "flash of bewildering light" and brilliantly realises who is the pivot of the enemy organisation. And, with two seconds to go, Haydock is himself shot as Grant rescues her. They speed to *Sans Souci* and she runs up to the Cayleys' room where she finds Betty's tattered picture book of *Goosey Goosey Gander*, which contains, in invisible ink, a list of all prominent people pledged to assist an invasion. This was Haydock's missing item.

However, it is not the Cayleys who are German agents. The real German agent didn't know that the book had been hidden by Betty in the Cayleys' room. But she is standing in the doorway as Tuppence turns to Grant and says "*Let me introduce you to M*! Yes.

Mrs Sprot!"

Mrs Sprot is, as Grant says, very dangerous and a very clever actress. Not only is she M but she – not Mrs Perenna or Mrs O'Rourke – knocked Tommy unconscious. Haydock had telephoned her when Tommy left Smugglers' Rest and she ran out into the drive with the hammer, which was why she was breathless when returning from the telephone to the bridge game. And, in an earlier episode, she – not Mrs Perenna or Mrs O'Rourke – was on the telephone extension in Mrs Perenna's bedroom when Tuppence, listening on the hall telephone, heard a reference to "the fourth" (which we learn is the date fixed for "the big attack on this country").

However, it is her true relationship with Betty that is the key to the main episode – Vanda kidnapping Betty and then being shot by Mrs Sprot. In Tuppence's "flash of bewildering light" she realised that Betty wasn't Mrs Sprot's child and that Vanda was her real mother.

Vanda had come to England as a penniless refugee and allowed Betty to be adopted by Mrs Sprot, who wanted camouflage for her spying. But Vanda hankered for Betty and 'kidnapped' her. Mrs Sprot insisted that the police weren't to be involved in hunting for Vanda but, says Tuppence, she roped in Haydock to help (though in fact that was Bletchley's idea). When they found Vanda and were within 20 yards of her, she was at the cliff edge, with Betty held close to her chest. Just as it seemed as if she would jump over with Betty or throw Betty over, Mrs Sprot shot her through the head with a pistol and Betty wriggled out from underneath her.

It was a miraculous shot. Mrs Sprot claims at the inquest that she was not used to firearms (but in fact she was a very fine shot) and didn't mean to kill Vanda. She adds "Oh dear – I feel as though I'd *murdered* someone" and, although exonerated, that is what she had unlawfully done, knowing that Vanda was not really going to let her own child be killed.

No clever murder plan is involved; it is a spur of the moment reaction to the kidnapping, though Mrs Sprot deserves credit for her repeated insistence on not calling the police (who might have stopped her shooting or even found Vanda before her), for taking Bletchley's pistol from his room before setting out on the hunt and for her brilliant shooting. The ingenuity of the murder comes rather in it not being clear that a murder has even been committed.

However, we do not get a complete explanation of this episode because it's not entirely clear *why* Mrs Sprot shot Vanda. Tuppence says that she "absolutely had to shoot" her because she "was *the child's real mother*". But that doesn't explain *why* Mrs Sprot "had to shoot". If Vanda was still alive to reveal that Mrs Sprot was Betty's adoptive mother rather than her real one, would that really have led others to think that Mrs Sprot had just adopted Betty as "camouflage" because she was a German agent? That sounds most unlikely. Maybe her worry was that her "camouflage" – extending not only to Betty but also to her children's books – was so important to her spying effectively that she could not risk losing it.

Were it not for her performance during this episode, Mrs Sprot would be a most unlikely suspect. Indeed, Tuppence says "I suspected everybody here except Mrs Sprot!". Not only is she portrayed as a meek, fussy, frightened, brainless creature but she is well hidden by Betty's "camouflage", which is really why Tuppence never considered her seriously.

Mrs Sprot's role in the telephone call about "the fourth" made from Mrs Perenna's bedroom is also well hidden. As Tuppence goes up the stairs and sees Mrs O'Rourke with her frightening smile, Betty darts along the landing to Mrs Sprot, who then burbles about laundry prices and electric irons. Her normality is contrasted with the tension created by Mrs O'Rourke and she doesn't even seem to be a suspect despite being on the landing.

Equally, even though she was breathless when returning to the bridge game, the possibility that she has been up to anything nefarious is wonderfully disguised by Tuppence's exasperation at the ceaseless reiterations of the bidding, and the finger-pointing (by the meek Mrs Sprot) at Mrs Perenna. With Major Bletchley, Mr Cayley and Mrs O'Rourke all behaving suspiciously and with some good misdirection towards "an odd noise" heard by Mrs Cayley (after Mrs Sprot's return), Mrs Sprot is not remotely a suspect for having knocked Tommy unconscious with the hammer.

However, she (and Haydock) were lucky. From the moment Tommy found the wireless until he left Smugglers' Rest, Haydock was with him all the time – meaning that he didn't telephone Mrs Sprot until Tommy had left. But what if she had been unavailable then, perhaps engaged with Betty, or unable to find a weapon in the short time that it would have taken Tommy to walk from Smugglers' Rest to *Sans Souci*?

As for Haydock himself, he is also pretty well concealed in terms of character, as the man mocked because of "his German spy complex" before his persistence exposed Hahn. But is he actually N or just an important German agent? The only time he is referred to as N is when Tommy, after finding the wireless, thinks he is. But we later learn that Tommy jumped to various wrong conclusions about Mrs Perenna, Carl, Vanda and Bletchley.

So, was he wrong again? Oddly, we are never expressly told if Haydock was N. Our instinct is that the author intended him to be N and Mrs Sprot to be M. However, there is a good argument that, since Mrs Sprot is M (end of chapter 14), Haydock cannot logically be N because we are looking for N *or* M (not N *and* M).

We know this because (a) that is the book's title (b) Grant's agent, Farquhar, said just before he died "*N or M*" and (c) the coded message said "*Suggest N or M for England*" – to which Grant says "Unfortunately we don't know *which*". Moreover, since the coded message would hardly have suggested sending N to England if he was already there, Haydock could not be N unless the message was sent at least four years ago since he was already in England by then, exposing Hahn.

If it was sent then (but took some years to locate or decode at the start of the War) and Haydock was N – meaning that N *and* M were sent over – the author has tricked us with the very title of the book. That may be fair. However, one would then expect Tommy, Tuppence or Grant to comment on the inaccuracy in Farquhar's dying words and in the coded message. But they do not.

Plot

Given the author's liking for nursery rhyme titles, it is perhaps surprising that this book is not called *Goosey Goosey Gander*, which was first published as a nursery rhyme in London in 1784. Not only does Betty's battered copy of that story contain the details about the Fifth Column but those words lead to Tuppence's "flash of bewildering light" and are the first ones she uses when explaining her inspired flash to Tommy. Instead, the author has opted for a title which, although less characteristic, is quite intriguing.

The plot is really pretty simple, the only real plotting question being whether to delay exposing Haydock until the scene in Dr Binion's surgery or to make his guilt pretty obvious much earlier, as she does, with the "completely unforeseen accident" of Tommy skidding against the bath.

Indeed, too many potential plotting difficulties are overcome by accidents and coincidences, such as Tommy being awake after a prolonged unconsciousness just as Albert hums a tune outside the cellar of Smugglers' Rest (so enabling him to be rescued). These coincidences are particularly frustrating when they actually help solve the puzzles, such as Tuppence being seen in Leahampton by "someone" known to Deborah (so prompting Deborah to mention this to Marsdon, and to his attempt to trick Tuppence); and Tuppence saying to Haydock "*Goosey, goosey gander!*", which turns out to be the title of the Germans' missing book.

In fact, however, what appears to be the biggest fluke of all, "a perfectly incredible fluke," says Tommy – the shooting of Vanda by Mrs Sprot – is not a fluke after all because she is a very fine shot, which is a nice touch.

There are other nice touches, the first being to call the guesthouse *Sans Souci*, the French for 'without worry', since the supposed carefree nature of the house contrasts well with the worrying done inside; another, with the goose motif in mind, is describing Mrs Cayley as someone "with never boo to say to a goose"; and another is Bletchley's name – since Bletchley Park was Britain's code-breaking centre during the War – which apparently led MI5 to investigate the author out of concern that she knew about this top secret centre before they concluded that her use of the name was a coincidence.[5]

However, one does wonder about the Germans' elaborate process for getting Tuppence to Dr Binion's surgery. She has to go to Yarrow, pretend to be a German agent who has landed by parachute dressed as a nurse (for which she gets kitted out) and then walk five miles to Leatherbarrow. Tuppence doesn't "see the point of all this rigmarole" and nor will readers, who may wonder why they didn't just knock her out (as they had done with Tommy) and take her to the surgery.

Although Haydock says that they didn't want her friends to trace her too easily, the "rigmarole" actually has the opposite effect by giving Tuppence the chance to step in an aniseed-smelling puddle, enabling Grant's dogs to follow her and for him to rescue her.

Having said that, the story is quite readable. Although Tommy and Tuppence are rather more staid than the young adventurers of *The Secret Adversary*, they are still engaging. And, although the exposition feels false (as they complain to each other about being seen as too old to assist the War effort), this is short-lived and Grant arrives before they finish complaining. After that, the book continues at a reasonably good pace, although the shooting at the cliff edge and the climax seem a bit melodramatic.

The story also has elements of mystification, with the kidnapping of Betty, in particular, seeming to make no sense at all since the Sprots have no money and are not employed by the government. The trick with the bogus 'Penny plain' slogan is also mystifying for those readers who spot that someone (Tuppence or Marsdon?) is playing a trick. And, of course, one wonders why the story is titled *N or M?* if Haydock is N *and* Tuppence is still after M.

Although the plot is rather lightweight as a thriller, it does do quite well in chapter 1 in conjuring up the atmosphere of the early stages of the War and of England's poor preparation, with multiple references to mismanagement and lack of organisation.

We are not told precisely when in the spring of 1940 the story is set but Tommy does say in chapter 1 that things look bad in France, which means that the German invasion, which began on 10 May, had started by then. By chapter 5 things are going "very badly" in France and the story takes us through the evacuation of Dunkirk (26 May to 4 June), the impending fall of Paris (14 June) and the capitulation of France (22 June).

Later that day, in chapter 9 part 2, we are told – as Tommy walks home from Smugglers' Rest before being knocked unconscious – that there was a pretty bad air raid on Southampton two nights ago, which fits the 22 June timeline very nicely because the first bombs did indeed fall on Southampton on 20 June, with no further bombs falling there until August.

It is after that, in chapter 11 part 1, that Grant tells Tuppence that "the big attack on this country" is fixed for "the fourth of next month" and, since France has capitulated by then, he must mean 4 July – although a "big attack" on that date is a fictional prospect created by the author. He adds that this is "a week exactly" ahead, which suggests he spoke to her on 27 June. But actually he did so *before* Tommy was found in the cellar (which would have been on 24 June, two days after he was knocked unconscious on 22 June, as just noted). So, "the fourth" was not exactly a week ahead – but ten days.

However, the story does have one very notable timing prediction. In chapter 3, Mr Cayley says "This war is going to last at least six years" and then "I give it six years". In fact, the War in Europe lasted until 8 May 1945. Bearing in mind that Cayley was making his comment in May 1940 in a story that was first published in March 1941 (in the *Redbook* magazine in the United States, prior to its hardback publication there) and therefore written even before that, the prediction by Cayley – and the author – is most impressive.

Cayley also reckons that Germany can hold out practically indefinitely – "with Russia behind her". Readers who know that Germany and Russia were enemies in the War might be surprised at Russia being "behind" Germany but in fact they had signed a pact in August 1939. Germany later broke it, causing Russia to join the Allies, but that did not happen until 22 June 1941. So Cayley was entitled to assume that Russia was behind Germany in a story written before 22 June 1941 – and, coincidentally, reviewed in the *New York Times* and *New York Herald Tribune* that very day.

Finally, there are a couple of minor errors. In chapter 5 part 1 Tommy thinks that Carl had said to *Tuppence* that he was working on decontamination experiments. In fact, Tommy had been told this *himself* – and by *Grant*. Then in part 5 Tommy agrees to play golf with Haydock at about 6 pm "tomorrow". However, it is "tomorrow" when Mrs Sprot realises at nearly 7 pm that Betty has disappeared and yet Tommy is at *Sans Souci* when the note is found. What happened to the game of golf?

Clues

The initial clues simply lead to *Sans Souci*. Just before dying, Grant's agent, Farquhar, said "*N or M. Song Susie*" and, since there was a guesthouse called *Sans Souci* in Leahampton, to which he had a return ticket in his pocket, the guesthouse becomes the focal point of the story – though Grant does recognise that interpreting the 'Song Susie' clue is "all guesswork".

At *Sans Souci* readers receive numerous red herrings relating to suspects who turn out not to be German agents. The first of the two most notable ones is Betty calling Mrs O'Rourke 'Nazer', which, of course, turns out not to be a clue to Mrs O'Rourke being a Nazi but just a word Betty uses if she doesn't like someone. The second is Tuppence thinking that Carl's story about coming to England to escape Nazi persecution sounds "as though he had learned it by heart". In the end we find out that he *has* learned it but that this is not a clue to him being a Nazi but to his not being the real Carl.

As to the clues that *do* identify the German agents and explain the kidnapping, readers are in a better overall position than Tommy or Tuppence. This is because the story is structured so that – with the exception of the clues arising from the hunt for Vanda (at which Tommy, Tuppence, Haydock and Mrs Sprot are all present) – Tommy has very little to do with Mrs Sprot while Tuppence has nothing to do with Haydock until the denouement. It is therefore unsurprising that, when Haydock comes into Dr Binion's surgery, he is not the person that Tuppence half fancied she might see (Mrs Perenna).

Tommy, however, should probably have done better with Haydock against whom the main clue is Smugglers' Rest itself, whose usefulness to an enemy is as much a clue against Haydock as it is against Hahn and a pretty obvious one at that. Of course, some readers will think that Haydock can't be a German agent when being so open about the suitability of his house. But many others will surely spot that the Hahn episode was manufactured to provide Haydock with cover and credibility.

Were it not for the 'Smugglers' Rest' clue, Haydock seems a rock solid citizen until four clues come in such quick succession during Tommy's second visit that readers are likely to suspect him. However, although Tommy deserves credit for spotting or generating all these clues, it is only *after* he has skidded and exposed the wireless that he sees their significance.

First is the 'Fritz' clue, relating to Appledore, who could be German, as Tommy spots when thinking "You could call that fellow Fritz easier than Appledore…" – fair-haired, blue-eyed and betrayed by the shape of the head.

Second is the 'head shape' clue, relating to Haydock. When Tommy thinks that Germans like Appledore are often betrayed by the shape of the head, he wonders where else he had seen such a head lately. But that is hardly a clue for readers because it is not until *after* he has exposed the wireless that we learn about Haydock's head: "The shape of the head – the line of the jaw – nothing British about them".

Third is the 'spilt drink' clue – when, at Tommy's mention of N or M, Appledore blunders by spilling crème de menthe on him. Plainly, Tommy's words have real significance for him.

Fourth is the 'abuse' clue – Haydock's abusive reaction to Appledore's blunder. Readers will assume that his anger derives not from concern about his guest but because the blunder has revealed that N or M is significant.

This fourth clue is the most important because the first and third – the 'Fritz' and 'spilt drink' clues – are just ones against Appledore (who could be an agent while Haydock is not), while the second – the 'head shape' clue – although a clue against someone in addition to Appledore (if 'head shape' is a valid clue at all), does not indicate Haydock to readers. The 'abuse' clue, however, is not only a clue against Haydock but it also causes one to look anew at the first three clues and to assess all four as a body of material pointing to him.

As for Tuppence, she says that two things made her suspicious about Marsdon. First, although he claimed to have met her before, she became sure that this was untrue. But she does nothing to clue this for readers. Second was his suggestion that she pretend to Deborah (who was wondering where she was) that she had joined Tommy "in Scotland or wherever he is". Since Marsdon had claimed to know about the vital job Tuppence was doing in Leahampton, most readers will surely spot that he should also know that Tommy is there and not in Scotland or anywhere else.

Although this 'Scotland' clue is obvious textually, some readers may already have suspected Marsdon because of earlier clues unknown to Tuppence. In chapter 10, when Deborah tells him that someone has seen Tuppence in Leahampton, he pauses "suddenly" and then "sharply" says "Leahampton?". He asks her "casually" what Tuppence did in the last War and is told that she did "something in the sleuthing line". Next day, Deborah's photograph of Tuppence disappears: who other than Marsdon might have taken it?

Although Tuppence doesn't have those clues, she lays her trap for him with the 'Penny plain' slogan, which she pretends she and Tommy use for communicating. He falls into the trap by sending her a letter from Penelope Playne, assuming that she will think that its instruction to go to Yarrow is from Tommy. She receives it at breakfast in chapter 13 and reads it after thrusting aside a Bonzo postcard from 'Maudie' saying that all is well. As she later explains, her real code for communicating with Tommy was, "of course", a Bonzo postcard, not the 'Penny plain' slogan.

That sounds straightforward but the combined 'Bonzo postcard' and 'Penny plain' clues create more issues than any other clues in the book (even ignoring the inconsistencies as to whether "Plain" should have a capital or small P), although they are almost entirely redeemed by a cleverly crafted paragraph.

First, for Tuppence to tell us in chapter 15 that the real code was "of course" a Bonzo postcard is extremely cheeky because readers were not told this before Mrs Sprot's exposure. The Bonzo postcard received in chapter 13 is the only one received, let alone mentioned, in the story.

Second, readers do not know, either when Tuppence tells Marsdon about the 'Penny plain' slogan or when she receives the letter, that she is tricking him with a bogus code. Since readers also know nothing about the significance of the Bonzo postcard, they are therefore likely to assume that the letter, not the postcard, is from Tommy when it is not.

That is fair concealment and misdirection. What makes it rather unrealistic, however, is that she thrusts aside the Bonzo postcard, which at last indicates that Tommy is safe (after escaping from the cellar), as if it had no significance at all. Naturally, one expects a trained agent to show no reaction to important news. But Tuppence, who has been very upset by Tommy's disappearance, wanting to know where he is "with a pang", is not trained. So it would have been more realistic if her instinctive reaction had been a little more positive, without actually giving away the significance of the Bonzo postcard.

Third, we have the different spellings of the first part of the slogan. When Tuppence tells Marsdon about it, the spelling in the novel is 'Penny plain', although, of course, she does not actually spell the words for him. When she then receives the letter, readers will note that the spelling is 'Penelope Playne', particularly since it is immediately juxtaposed with Tuppence thinking "Good old Penny Plain!". The 'Penelope Playne' spelling is even repeated for readers when Tuppence leaves the letter on her dressing-table. Those readers who spot the differences will wonder what clue they are getting from the different spellings.

They may think that the letter is still a genuine request from Tommy (or even Marsdon on his behalf) asking Tuppence to go to Yarrow, with 'Playne' being the spelling which he normally used, albeit wrongly. Or it may have been written by Tommy under duress, with a deliberate misspelling by him as a warning for

Tuppence. Or there may be some other explanation.

But, in the end, nothing turns on the different spellings. Although the slogan is then referred to on two more occasions (using the 'Plain' spelling), no explanation is given for the difference. Since nothing turned on it, because any letter from Penny Plain, however spelled, would have given Marsdon away, it does seem odd to have used them.

Fourth and finally, we come to the cleverly crafted paragraph, which occurs straight after Tuppence has received, but not yet opened, Marsdon's Penelope Playne letter. The paragraph contains two textual clues which might cause some extremely astute readers to spot, first, that the Penelope Playne letter had *not* been sent by or on behalf of Tommy and, second, that the Bonzo postcard *had* been. It is worth setting out the paragraph, which is referring to the Penelope Playne letter, in full to show the two textual clues:

> *This was no communication from Douglas, Raymond or Cyril, or any other of the camouflaged correspondence that arrived punctually for her, and which included this morning a brightly coloured Bonzo postcard with a scrawled, 'Sorry I haven't written before. All well, Maudie', on it.*

That paragraph has been so well crafted that the two textual 'camouflaged correspondence' clues are not at all apparent other than on a careful re-reading. The first clue is that the Penelope Playne letter was *not* "…any other of the camouflaged correspondence that arrived punctually for her…", meaning that it was *not* a camouflaged letter from Tommy or Grant. The second clue is that "the camouflaged correspondence … included this morning a brightly coloured Bonzo postcard", meaning that the Bonzo postcard *was* part of the usual camouflaged correspondence from Tommy or Grant and was therefore telling her that Tommy was well.

When, following Marsdon's letter, Tuppence goes to Yarrow and thence to Dr Binion's surgery, she sees everything in her "flash of bewildering light", as Haydock threatens to shoot her. So, what precedes that inspired flash? She later refers to three things, in the following order, when explaining her thinking: (i) Haydock's rage when she says "*Goosey, goosey gander!*"; (ii) the face of his subordinate, Anna, reminding her of Vanda; and (iii) a nagging recollection stirring in her brain about Solomon.

First, she says "*Goosey, goosey gander!*" to Haydock because it is the only phrase she can think of which is "both childish and rude". Although this is sheer luck (and so rather unsatisfying), she sees that it *means* something to him, and he angrily demands "Where is it? Where have you hidden it?". At first, she doesn't realise that he means Betty's book. So, what prompts her to make sense of this coincidence? We are not told. But, since *Goosey Goosey Gander* is the book whose title Betty had gurgled when coming out of the Cayleys' room, wanting to play hide-and-seek, shortly before Tuppence went to Yarrow, readers may *perhaps* see how she could have thought that this tattered book was Haydock's missing item.

And, if it was, then presumably (again we are not told) she realised from this 'Goosey Goosey Gander' clue that, if a child's book contained information important to a German agent, a mother would surely know this and so must be a German agent herself. As to which, readers may recall a clue in chapter 7 that Betty had a duplicate set of children's books, with the dirty and worn editions replaced by new cleaner ones, causing Tuppence to be amused by Mrs Sprot's fear of germs – the 'hygienic mother' clue. Since Mrs Sprot was a hygienic mother, why would she retain tattered books if she had a new set?

The second thing preceding Tuppence's inspired flash is that, as Anna talks about her son being killed in the last War, her face reminds Tuppence of Vanda – the same frightening ferocity and singleness of purpose of a mother deprived of her young. This 'deprived mother' clue connecting Anna and Vanda is a brave one because it nearly gives the game away that Vanda may be Betty's deprived mother, thus explaining the kidnapping.

But it doesn't give it away entirely because we know from the inquest into Vanda's shooting that she had also been deprived of *other* children who had been killed in Poland, which could explain why her face looked like Anna's. In order to tie Vanda to *Betty*, we need the third thing that preceded Tuppence's inspired flash – the 'Solomon' clue. But, in order to understand that clue, one needs to deal first with the 'miraculous shot' clue.

Haydock had not dared shoot at Vanda because he might hit Betty. He even murmurs "Bloody miracle. I couldn't have brought off a shot like that... A miracle, that's what it is". The miraculous nature of the shot is confirmed by Tommy description of it as "a perfectly incredible fluke".

The 'miraculous shot' clue is a double one. First, it is quite an obvious clue to Mrs Sprot being a trained shot. Few readers will be put off by her claiming to be unused to firearms or by Tuppence later suggesting, most unpersuasively, that it was sheer ignorance of the shot's difficulty that made her bring it off.

However, it is the second element of the clue which leads into the 'Solomon' clue. Just after Tommy says that he wouldn't have risked firing, he adds that it was "Quite Biblical. David and Goliath". Something twangs in Tuppence's brain but then it's gone, though she thinks it was to do with Solomon (David's son). Any reader who pauses to think about Solomon is misdirected away from his most famous quality – his wisdom – by Tommy referring instead to cedars, temples, wives, concubines, Jews and the tribes of Israel.

Nevertheless, when Tuppence is later threatened by Haydock, her brain has a nagging recollection of Solomon and she later explains the 'Solomon' clue to Tommy. She reminds him of the two women who came to Solomon with a baby, each claiming it was hers, and of Solomon saying "Very well, cut it in two". This enabled him to identify the true mother because the false mother said "All right" while the real mother, unable to face her child being killed, said "No, let the other woman have it". Tuppence says that it ought to have been plain that Mrs Sprot couldn't have risked firing at Vanda if Betty had been her child. It meant that Betty wasn't her child. Vanda was Betty's real mother, which was why she had kidnapped her.

This clue to the main episode is probably the best in the book because of its clever combination of two biblical stories – the unlikely success of David against Goliath (reflected in the miraculous shot) and Solomon's Judgment in 1 Kings 3:16-28 in which he settles the baby's true maternity. But it is not easy to spot that Vanda is the real mother from this 'Solomon' clue because the narrative says "It seemed clear that she was threatening to throw the child over the cliff" (supplemented five times by Tommy, Haydock and Mrs Sprot saying that she was about to do this or to jump with Betty) – and yet the whole point of the Solomon story is that the real mother was *not* willing to let her child be killed whereas Vanda did seem willing. This apparent contradiction is explained by the author cleverly using "seemed" in the narrative, which might cause a particularly astute reader to realise that it deliberately avoids saying that she was *actually* going to kill the child.

Tuppence goes on to say that she ought to have got a "hint" from the likeness between Vanda and Betty. She felt that Vanda's face was "somehow familiar" in chapter 4 and wished she could remember who it was that Vanda reminded her of in chapter 8. But this 'Vanda likeness' clue does not help readers because, although her face is described a handful of times, Betty's face is not described beyond saying that she has "large round eyes" and a "dazzling smile". Indeed, all the descriptions of Vanda's face –

which was "not human" and "disfigured" – sound most unlike the little we know about Betty's face.

Tuppence's next clue is what she describes as Betty's "absurd play with my shoelaces", immersing them in water and prodding them. She had earlier decided that Betty must have seen Carl doing this because he was arrested after being found with a supply of secret ink concealed in a shoelace which was soaked in water to release the ink. But this incriminating evidence had been planted upon him and Tuppence now suggests that it was more likely that Betty would have seen Mrs Sprot doing this – not Carl.

An oddity about the 'shoelaces' clue is that, when Grant tells Tommy about it, something "stirred in Tommy's mind" and Tuppence asks if he can "remember" what Betty did with the laces. But he was not in Tuppence's room when Betty did this. This was only seen by Tuppence and Mrs Sprot.

After Betty's kidnapping, there are some rather obvious clues to Mrs Sprot's intention to shoot Vanda – insisting that the police weren't to be involved; taking a pistol from Bletchley's room which "may come in useful" without asking him (and risking his refusal); and, of course, the 'miraculous shot' clue, which is completely out of character for the meek Mrs Sprot whose response to the kidnapping up to that point has been to go "meekly" into the house, to cry out "weakly", sob "wildly", "collapse" into a chair, moan "faintly" and "cling" to Tuppence.

As for Mrs Sprot making the telephone call about "the fourth" and knocking Tommy unconscious, we are so comprehensively misdirected away from her being on the landing just after the call, and from her being breathless when returning to the bridge game, that only the most astute readers would have spotted the 'landing' and 'breathless' clues – though clues they are.

Indeed the 'breathless' clue is a good one, not only because of its concealment and misdirection (noted earlier) but because the author plays fair by having Tuppence think, in relation to

Mrs Perenna, that one does not get "out of breath" looking at the weather. That seems to be a clue just against Mrs Perenna while in fact the same clue applies to Mrs Sprot since one does not get out of breath making a telephone call.

Overall, the story has a good number of clues for a thriller, including the good 'breathless' clue, the clever 'Solomon' clue and the cleverly crafted 'camouflaged correspondence' clues linking the 'Bonzo postcard' and 'Penny plain' clues. Some of the clues, though, are either too obvious in implicating Haydock, Mrs Sprot and Marsdon (as with the 'Smugglers' Rest', 'miraculous shot' and 'Scotland' clues) or have, as we have seen, a weakness of some kind.

There are perhaps two other clues, after the shooting, which are not referred to in Tuppence's explanations. One, which she mentions in chapter 8 (though without treating it as a clue) is that Mrs Sprot isn't interested in finding the reason for the kidnapping. This seems odd, perhaps suggesting she *knows* the reason.

Stranger still is the behaviour of her husband who, despite rushing down from London after the shooting, simply goes back that day. But does that actually provide a clue? We don't know because we are not told whether he was an innocent man, really married to Mrs Sprot and content for Betty to be adopted without appreciating his wife's real purpose, or whether he was also an agent – and perhaps not even married to her.

11

The Body In The Library

Solution

This Jane Marple novel opens with Dolly Bantry, wife of Colonel Bantry of Gossington Hall, being awakened on 22 September by the housemaid, Mary, crying "Oh, ma'am, oh, ma'am, *there's a body in the library*".

Dolly asks Miss Marple, whose village of St Mary Mead in Radfordshire is nearby, to help in an investigation in which four senior policemen are involved – Inspector Slack; Colonel Melchett, the Chief Constable of Radfordshire; Superintendent Harper from the adjoining county, Glenshire; and Sir Henry Clithering, a former Metropolitan Police Commissioner.

The body on the library hearthrug is that of a girl reckoned to be 17 or 18, with unnaturally fair hair, a heavily made-up face and blood-red nails. She had been drugged and strangled between 10 pm and midnight with the waistband of her poor quality evening dress of white spangled satin.

She is soon identified as Ruby Keene by her cousin, Josephine (Josie) Turner, a dance and bridge hostess at the Majestic Hotel in Danemouth about 20 miles away (in Glenshire)[1], where Ruby was also a dance hostess.

In fact – although we don't learn this until the final chapter (chapter 18) – the body is not 18-year-old Ruby but a Girl Guide aged 16, Pamela Reeves, who had been wrongly identified by Josie as part of a complex double murder plan in which both Ruby and Pamela are killed.

Although the murder plan is complex, the motive for murdering Ruby will seem obvious to readers on learning (chapter 6) that Conway Jefferson, an elderly, wealthy invalid staying at the Majestic, had become so fond of her that he had decided to adopt her and made a new will leaving her £50,000. His intended generosity is pivotal because, if the £50,000 passes to her when he dies, this will seriously reduce the residue of his estate.

When he was invalided in an aeroplane accident eight years ago, his wife had also been killed in the accident, as had his son and daughter who were both married. So the residue will be shared by his widowed son-in-law, Mark Gaskell, and widowed daughter-in-law, Adelaide Jefferson. They are therefore the two obvious suspects. And their motive for murdering Ruby before Jefferson dies with a reduced residue is repeatedly reinforced (in chapters 7, 9, 11, 12, 13 and 14) by Harper, Clithering, Miss Marple and even Mark and Adelaide (who is concerned not just for herself but for her son Peter, aged about nine).

Nevertheless, although there are two murderers, and one is Mark, the other is not Adelaide, but Josie (who wrongly identified Ruby). Josie in fact married Mark a year ago, but secretly because Jefferson (who still regards Mark as his deceased daughter's husband) would have been "furious" if he had remarried (chapter 14). Indeed, we only learn that he had done so in chapter 18 and that Josie therefore shared his motive.

Until then, it had seemed that she was angry with Ruby for getting killed since, as her cousin, she might have benefited if Ruby was alive to inherit Jefferson's money. So Ruby's death seemed contrary to her interests. Indeed, Harper and Melchett don't even mention her when reviewing alibis and motives in chapter 11. But for Mark, with his obvious motive, a simple murder plan would not resist scrutiny. It has to be ingenious and depend on an unimpeachable alibi.

He is staying, with Adelaide (and Peter), at the Majestic with Jefferson. On the fatal evening, after dinner, he takes his car for a spin, having arranged to play bridge later with Jefferson, Adelaide and Josie. He returns while Ruby is doing her 10.30 pm exhibition dance with Raymond Starr, the hotel's tennis and dancing pro. Ruby then dances with George Bartlett, a hotel guest, and the foursome start their bridge game at about 10.40. Ruby yawns as she dances. Then she says she has a headache and goes upstairs.

At midnight, with none of the bridge foursome having left the table, Ruby does not appear for her second exhibition dance with Raymond. So he goes with Josie up to Ruby's room to find her. The pink, foamy dress in which she had been dancing is lying over a chair. But Ruby has vanished.

The key aspect of that narrative, in relation to Mark, is that he was playing bridge from 10.40 (when Ruby was *seen* alive, dancing with Bartlett) until after midnight – and yet Dr Haydock (correctly) twice puts the time of death of the body in the library at between 10 pm and midnight. And Adelaide and Josie have precisely the same alibi. "Alibis", says Harper (chapter 11), "That's what we're up against" and it is indeed the alibis that make the puzzle difficult.

So, how did they work? The short answer is that Mark and Josie had a double murder plan. As well as killing Ruby, they would murder a second victim *before* Ruby's 10.30 exhibition dance – Pamela Reeves, who would be tricked by Mark into having a 'film test' and made up to resemble Ruby. Mark would strangle the 'fake' Ruby (Pamela) in a cottage near Gossington Hall, so implicating its owner, a film set decorator called Basil Blake.

Josie would later identify Pamela's dead body as Ruby and, since the 'real' Ruby was alive at about 10.40, she must have been killed *after* that, while the murderers were playing bridge. After the bridge game, when alibis were not under scrutiny, Josie would murder the 'real' Ruby, who in the meantime would lie drugged in Josie's hotel room, and her unidentifiable body would later be found in a burnt-out car and assumed to be Pamela.

We are not told whether the murderers wanted to implicate Blake from the outset and so chose the film angle *or* chose the film angle because it would be irresistible to Pamela and then realised they could make Blake the scapegoat. Either way, an unexpected twist occurs when Blake finds the 'fake' Ruby (Pamela) dead in his cottage at 2 am and moves her to the Bantrys' library as a revenge prank on the Colonel. So, to Josie's surprise, she finds herself identifying the body, not at Blake's cottage, but in the library which, despite providing the initial focus, actually had no part in the double murder plan.

Looking at that plan in more detail, as Miss Marple does in chapter 18, she refers first to the selection of Pamela. She must have been chosen as a girl who would look like Ruby when her dark-brown hair was bleached and when she was, like Ruby, heavily made-up. Although Dr Haydock would spot the "unnaturally" fair hair, Ruby too had bleached hair (chapters 3 and 9).

Pamela is approached by Mark, claiming to be a film producer from Lemville Studios (where Blake works), and he invites her plausibly for a film test. She can't resist and, after a Girl Guide rally, goes to the Majestic where Mark introduces Josie as a studio make-up expert. We are not told when she arrives but it was not late (because she had pretended to be going to Woolworths and her parents expected her home for supper). This allows enough time for Josie, who must have had the knowhow, to bleach Pamela's hair in a way that will not look recent and to make up her face and varnish her nails. She then drugs her – in an ice-cream soda, suggests Miss Marple – and she goes into a coma.

An unavoidable problem which the murderers face in making her resemble Ruby is that they cannot put her into Ruby's pink dress because Ruby is wearing it. So, instead, she is put into Ruby's dress of white spangled satin. She is then moved to one of the empty rooms opposite Josie's bathroom (which were only opened and dusted once a week) before being put in Mark's car, which he takes out for a spin after dinner (again we are not told what time). He drives to Blake's cottage where he strangles the still unconscious Pamela at or after 10 pm (Dr Haydock's earliest time). Then he drives back, returning while Ruby, *still alive*, is doing her 10.30 dance with Raymond.

Readers may wonder (since Miss Marple does not explain) why the murderers drugged Pamela instead of just killing her after making her up. The answer must be that the murder needed to occur late enough for it to fall within the range given by Dr Haydock (10 pm to midnight). That range was not only consistent with Ruby being alive at 10.40 but would also allow Mark to kill Pamela at about 10 pm and still have time to be back for Ruby's dance. Since the murder plan depends crucially on this, it is surprising that Miss Marple does not grapple with the point in her explanations.

Nor does she comment on Dr Haydock's range. Although 10 pm to midnight is correct, it seems surprising that he would give an earliest time so close to the actual time of death, rather than suggesting, say, 9 pm to 11 pm.

Instead, she moves on to explain that Josie had instructed Ruby that, after dancing, she was to change (in her room), go into Josie's room and wait. So, after dancing with Bartlett and yawning (having been drugged, Miss Marple suggests, in her after-dinner coffee), Ruby goes up to her room to change.

Readers may wonder (since again Miss Marple does not explain) why she had to change (out of her pink dress) before going to Josie's room. Presumably the purpose was to overcome the unavoidable problem that the dead Pamela would be wearing a different dress (the white satin one) from the pink one which

Ruby was wearing that evening. But, if the pink dress were found *in Ruby's room*, she must have changed out of it herself before vanishing, so explaining why the body in the library, which is supposedly hers, is not wearing that dress.

When Ruby does not appear for her midnight dance, Josie goes up to Ruby's room with Raymond to "look for her" (Miss Marple's quotation marks). Ruby is not there (having gone to Josie's room) but they see the pink dress. However, nobody goes into *Josie's* room – except Josie, who probably finishes off the drugged Ruby, with, Miss Marple suggests, "an injection, perhaps, or a blow on the back of the head". The word "perhaps" indicates that, unusually, we don't learn how the principal victim was killed.

Then, says Miss Marple, in the early hours Josie dressed Ruby in Pamela's clothes, carried her down the side stairs and "fetched" Bartlett's car – a Minoan 14 (a fictional make) – from the hotel courtyard. She drove Ruby to a quarry about two miles away, set the car alight and walked back to the hotel. The charred body is later found in the car with two of Pamela's items (a shoe and a Girl Guide's button), suggesting that she was in the wreckage.

Pamela's friend, Florence Small, then reveals that Pamela had had a film test with a producer from Lemville Studios. So Blake is arrested by Inspector Slack, who thinks that he committed both murders and knows that he has no alibi. But Blake claims that, on arriving at his cottage at about 2 am, he saw a girl on the hearthrug, strangled, and was worried that his wife, Dinah, would think he had killed her. So he moved the body to the Gossington Hall library because Bantry always sneered at him as artistic and effeminate.

When the real culprits are finally exposed, it is a genuine surprise to learn that Josie murdered Ruby (and that Ruby was in the car) and that Mark murdered Pamela (who was really the body in the library). Equally surprising is that they are married since they had betrayed not the remotest hint of this.

The actual murders are straightforward – killing two drugged victims – but the overall planning, in order to provide unimpeachable alibis, is most ingenious – although it does require the murderers to act with precision timing and to appear relaxed at bridge despite the incredible callousness of murdering an innocent schoolgirl just to provide an alibi for the principal murder.

The murderers' ingenuity is apparent in (i) delaying Pamela's murder to a time falling within Haydock's range; (ii) using the empty room to keep Pamela unseen until Mark could drive to the cottage; (iii) ensuring that his drive back to the hotel after strangling Pamela would work in terms of distance (from the cottage), speed (of his car and driving) and timing (so that he could kill Pamela at about 10 pm and still be back for Ruby's dance at 10.30); (iv) making Ruby change out of the pink dress in *her* room; (v) making her wait in Josie's room because *nobody but Josie* went into it when looking for Ruby; and (vi) giving Ruby the right dose of the right drug so that she would not go to sleep before her 10.30 dance but would do so before becoming restless in Josie's room.

There are, however, occasions where we are not told how potential difficulties were overcome. How did Mark get into Blake's empty cottage with Pamela's body?[2] How did Josie 'fetch' (get into and start) Bartlett's car? And how could she, after sitting up until 2 am (chapter 3) pretending to wait for Ruby, have got through the door to the side terrace with Ruby's body if, as the night porter says (chapter 6), the door was locked at 2 am?

One point which Miss Marple does explain is what she calls "the discrepancy of the nails", which Josie was "very thorough" to foresee. This is a reference to the body in the library, Pamela, having bitten nails whereas Ruby had long ones. To get round this, Josie managed, before dinner on the fatal night, to catch one of Ruby's nails in her shawl and break it. This provided an excuse for pretending that Ruby had then trimmed the other nails to give an even appearance and could therefore, despite her normally long nails, still be the body in the library with its short nails. To support the pretence, Josie must have trimmed the drugged Ruby's nails and put the clippings in the wastepaper basket in her room because they are later found there.

Breaking a nail on a shawl does not sound reliable but, more importantly, close cut nails and bitten nails are "quite different" says Miss Marple. The bitten nails gave away that the body in the library wasn't Ruby so that Josie, in wrongly identifying it, was involved – which makes her selection of Pamela not as "thorough" as Miss Marple suggests.

The ingenious murder plan also required some luck – that Mark was not seen getting Pamela's body from the empty room to his car or, later, into Blake's cottage; that Ruby was compliant enough to go to Josie's room (she was not invariably obedient, with Josie "always" ticking her off for overdoing her make-up); and that nobody except Josie went into her room to look for Ruby.

Finally, there was some bad luck – Blake moving the body to the library where Miss Marple saw the fingernails. She, however, indicates that moving the body gave the murderers a different problem – it "delayed things considerably" so that, instead of Blake being the first suspect, "…interest became focused much too soon on the Jefferson family". But this is not really right because Melchett questions Blake in chapter 2 before Jefferson is even mentioned in chapter 3. Any 'delay' was caused, rather, by Josie, surprisingly (in retrospect), scorning three chances to implicate Blake in the latter chapter.

Plot

The iconic title, described as a 'cliché' in the author's Foreword[3] and noted as an Ariadne Oliver story in *Cards on the Table* (chapter 2), conjures a welcome expectation that this will be a classic detective story. This is initially fulfilled by the library, which speaks of tradition and familiar use. But we quickly realise that this is not going to be a classic country house murder story since the body is unknown to the Bantrys and there are no other family members or guests at Gossington Hall.

Nor is it much of an investigation into events in St Mary Mead since after chapter 4, only three of the remaining 14 chapters are set there or in the adjoining town of Much Benham. The other 11 chapters are set in or near the rather less classic town of Danemouth.

However, the book is very well structured, both in relation to the gradual revelation of information about the characters and the intricate plotting of the ingenious double murder plan. Although it is her shortest novel to date – only about two-thirds of the length of her longest novel to date, *Death on the Nile* – it is most absorbing and densely packed with evidence.

There are two main elements of mystification. One is how the obvious suspects – Mark and Adelaide – got their opportunity to murder Ruby during the bridge game (although the author has cleverly sent us down the wrong path with Adelaide). The other is how Miss Marple seems to understand the murder plan so quickly, with even the reason for the body being in the library coming from her ideas and intuition rather than classic detection.

Many readers will be happy with her operating this way but a detection technique that relies so much on instinct does result, as we have seen, in her not dealing with some aspects of the murderers' *thinking*. It is good, however, that she is so inspired because she refers (chapter 8) to "a great possibility" of the crime never being solved "like the Brighton trunk murders".[4]

In the Foreword the author explains how she came to write a story to fit the clichéd title, with an orthodox and conventional library, an improbable and sensational body and an elderly crippled man as the pivot. She also lists the roles of some of the characters: a tennis pro, a young dancer, an artist, a girl guide and a dance hostess, which we can recognise as Raymond, Ruby, Blake, Pamela and Josie. She does not identify roles for Mark or Adelaide.

Chapter 1 then has an excellent opening in which Dolly's "dream state" is well depicted before it is interrupted by Mary's breathless, hysterical voice. It is certainly within the top three of the author's best openings, perhaps even the best, and it provides an appetising start to the puzzle.[5]

The novel then flows most readably. So it is only a minor issue when we can't understand why Miss Marple thinks in chapter 8 that the body was in the library as a result of a "very careful plan" going wrong "because human beings are so much more vulnerable and sensitive than anyone thinks". But her thinking becomes more of an issue in chapter 9 when it seems unjustified for her to "expect" that the body in the burnt-out car is the missing Pamela and "*must* be connected" to Ruby's murder.

She may be right about Pamela going through Danemouth after the Girl Guide rally but she hasn't been told that the body is a girl or where the car is, let alone that it is near Danemouth. And, as for the two bodies being "connected", she hasn't been told that the car is missing from Ruby's hotel. Nevertheless, the book remains highly readable, though less pacey from then, until the end.

By the start of chapter 13 readers may well sense that Miss Marple hasn't appeared much in the story. She saw the body in the library in chapter 1; she met Josie there in chapter 4; and she flushed with pleasure at meeting Clithering in chapter 8. But in the first 12 chapters she appears in well under 30% of the book. After that she is much more involved, appearing in over 70% of the remaining six chapters.

In chapter 15 she even visits the Vicarage of her previous novel and speaks to the Vicar's wife, Griselda. When she has gone, the maid announces to "the most influential parishioner (who didn't like children)" that Griselda is in the drawing room. Who is this parishioner? Intrigued readers are left to guess.[6]

In chapter 17, although Miss Marple knows the solution, she wants to be "doubly sure". So a trap is laid which ends with Jefferson looking grimly "at the murderer of Ruby Keene". We are not told then that this is Josie but have to wait, still guessing, until the final chapter. That is much better than *The Murder at the Vicarage* where Miss Marple suddenly names the murderer.

Clues

The starting points for the clueing are the financial motive and the 'fingernails' clue. The motive, for which no credible alternative is suggested, leads directly to Mark and Adelaide, who are "extremely hard up" (chapter 11). Although Adelaide has a dual financial motive (because of Peter), Mark is "of course", as Miss Marple says (chapter 18), a much more likely suspect, as a gambler without a high moral code, which is repeatedly made plain, even by Mark.

Although he is the most likely suspect, Miss Marple knows that Josie must be involved because of the 'fingernails' clue, which has three elements – the fingernails on the body in the library, which remind her of a village parallel; the fingernail torn by Ruby on Josie's shawl; and a confirmatory element, the nail clippings in Ruby's wastepaper basket.

After viewing the girl's body in chapter 1, Dolly asks Miss Marple whether it reminds her of anything. She says, "No, I can't say that it does – not at the moment". But then she says that, because the girl bit her nails and her front teeth stuck out a little, she was reminded of Edie Chetty, who was fond of cheap finery too. When her response is set out that simply, it seems surprising that readers could miss that the girl in the library bit her fingernails.

However, this element of the clue is about as excellently concealed as it could be. First, despite a pretty thorough description of the body, we are not told then that the nails were bitten – only when Miss Marple compares the girl to Edie. Second, readers may skip over the parallel because she starts her answer so negatively

("No, I can't say that it does – not at the moment"). Third, when she mentions the "cheap finery", Dolly asks about this and so it is the body's dress ("very tawdry satin – poor quality") – not the fingernails (or teeth) – that becomes the focal point. Fourth, readers may be put off by Dolly feeling that the "village parallel didn't seem to be exactly hopeful" – though it turns out to form part of the book's most important clue.

The second element, the torn fingernail, is not referred to until chapter 9 when Adelaide's son, Peter, refers to Ruby catching her nail in Josie's shawl and tearing it. However, readers may not focus on Ruby therefore having long fingernails because Peter moves on to refer to Bartlett's shoelace. But the point is flagged again by Miss Marple who says that, if a nail was torn off, the others might have been clipped, so as to match.

In order to confirm that Ruby normally had long nails, she asks Clithering whether nail clippings were found in her room. When she learns of the ones in Ruby's wastepaper basket in chapter 13 – and so has the third element of the clue – she says "Then that's that…". Most readers will assume that she means that the short fingernails on the body have been satisfactorily explained (by the clippings) without actually providing a clue after all.

However, those words are also capable of the opposite interpretation. Since the clippings confirm that Ruby did indeed have long nails and since, as Miss Marple says, "*Bitten* nails and close *cut* nails are quite different!" (chapter 18), her words "Then that's that…" did *not* mean that the body *was* indeed Ruby but that the body, with its bitten nails, *could not* have been Ruby, who had been wrongly identified by Josie. Surprisingly, however, she does not refer to the nail clippings or her words in chapter 18.

The importance of the 'fingernails' clue, which is the best and most memorable in the book, is confirmed by Harper saying in chapter 18 that the bitten nails were the "only real proof" that Miss Marple had. However, she says that she had more than that because the girl in the library had teeth that stuck out whereas Mark had said that Ruby's teeth ran "down her throat". Readers would do very well to recollect where either of these two contradictory points comprising the 'teeth' clue were made.

The point about *the body* comes during Miss Marple's parallel with Edie Chetty. It therefore benefits from the same four concealment features as the 'fingernails' clue. But, unlike the nails which are revisited in chapters 9 and 13, there is not one further reference to *the body's* teeth until chapter 18.

The point about *Ruby* comes when Mark says she had a "thin ferrety little face, not much chin, teeth running down her throat, nondescript sort of nose..." (chapter 9). Only the most astute reader would have spotted this one reference to Ruby's teeth (*and* been able to visualise what Mark meant) and realised that, unlike her other facial features, it was important and to be contrasted with teeth that stuck out. If anything, readers are more likely to notice Mark describing Ruby's nose as "nondescript" when in chapter 3 we were told that she had a "*retroussé*" (upturned) nose.

In fairness, we were warned in chapter 9 (by Clithering, Adelaide and Miss Marple) that Mark said too much – meaning there would be a clue in something he said. What is odd, though, is that his comment about the teeth *precedes* Peter telling us about the torn fingernail and so provides an earlier clue that the body is not Ruby. Yet, unlike the second element of the 'fingernails' clue, Miss Marple does not react to it.

In chapter 18 she says that "for certain reasons, I was of the opinion that a *woman* was concerned in this crime". She doesn't clarify the "reasons" but presumably she means the 'fingernails' and 'teeth' clues which caused her to disbelieve Josie's identification. She does, however, indicate that she gave us a clue about her disbelief when saying in chapter 13 that "...everybody has been much too *credulous* and *believing* ... When there's anything fishy about, I never believe anyone at all!".

Nevertheless, readers who had paused to wonder about her 'credulous' clue would have done very well to realise that she meant we shouldn't trust Josie's identification of the dead girl. Indeed, our assumption that Josie had *correctly* identified Ruby seemed confirmed by Miss Marple saying in chapter 8 that the reason why Josie had looked "definitely *angry* with the dead girl" was "no doubt" because, as her cousin, she had been looking forward to doing very well out of Jefferson's affection for her.

However, Miss Marple's undoubted belief about the cause of Josie's anger starts being eroded in chapter 9 when Josie says, with what seemed "undeniable sincerity", that she never dreamed of Jefferson taking such a fancy to Ruby. If Josie was indeed sincere, and so *not* party to a family plot to obtain Jefferson's money (and Miss Marple expressly indicates that she wasn't in chapters 12 and 18), there must be some other significant reason for her looking "really angry", "very angry" and "definitely angry" about Ruby because so much is made of the 'anger' clue (chapters 3, 4, 7, 8).

In chapter 18 Miss Marple gives two reasons. One is her point (noted earlier) that, because of the body being moved to the library, interest became focused much too soon on the Jeffersons (rather than Blake), which was, she says twice, to "the great annoyance" of the murderer. However, although Josie does seem to try to minimise focus on the Jeffersons in chapters 3 and 4, there is no "great annoyance", let alone anger, on those occasions. The references to her anger in the early chapters relate not to any focus on the Jeffersons but to Ruby and her disappearance and death.

Miss Marple's second reason is that Josie cherished such "bitter anger" against Ruby that she couldn't hide it – "even when she looked down at her dead" – because she was "hard as nails, and *all out for money*". It's not clear how Miss Marple knows that Josie couldn't hide her anger when looking at Ruby's body: Miss Marple wasn't with Josie at the mortuary; and, when they were together (in the library in chapter 4), Josie was looking down at the hearthrug, *not* the body, which had been taken away.

Nevertheless, it is Josie's desire for money that correctly explains the 'anger' clue – not anger at *Ruby's death* causing the demise of a family plot but anger at *Ruby herself* for her effect on Mark's inheritance. However, the fact that Josie was "*all out for money*" should surprise readers because the only indication that she gave about her financial motivation was her natural wish not to lose her job after hurting her ankle.

Mark and Adelaide's financial motives are, however, never in doubt and Miss Marple says that it was "annoying" that both had alibis. But then she says "…soon afterwards there came the discovery of the burnt-out car with Pamela Reeves's body in it, and then the whole thing leaped to the eye. The alibis, of course, were worthless". Despite the words "of course", it would be very surprising if any reader deduced that, because of the 'burnt-out car' clue, the alibis were worthless, let alone that the whole thing "leaped to the eye".

This is because the alibis relate to the time when *the body in the library* was killed. In order for the burnt-out car to affect *those* alibis, there would need to be a realisation that the person thought to be the body in the library (Ruby) is in fact the body in the car. But it is plain that Miss Marple does *not* know this at the time of "the discovery of the burnt-out car" because at that point she actually suggests, as we saw earlier, that it is Pamela in the car.

She then goes on to say, "I now had two *halves* of the case, and both quite convincing, but they did not fit". She adds that "The one person whom I *knew* to be concerned in the crime hadn't got a motive", thus indicating that the two halves are the person whom she knew to be concerned in the crime (Josie) and the motive (money). So the puzzle for her is not a *whodunnit* in relation to Josie but a *whydunnit* – she must "fit" Josie to a motive.

The main clue for that is the 'Somerset House' clue. Blake's wife, Dinah (who uses her maiden name, Lee), asks how Miss

Marple knows she is married to Blake: "…you didn't go to Somerset House?" (where public records of births, marriages and deaths were kept until the 1970s). Miss Marple says she didn't but knew they were married because they quarrelled like married people. Her comments on quarrels, followed by Blake's arrival, his story about moving the body and his arrest all conceal the marriage connotations of Somerset House.

But we do know that Dinah has given us a clue of some kind because Miss Marple has "an idea that something you said – just now – may help". And Somerset House is mentioned again when she tells Dolly that they would have a good idea about the murderer "if we went up to Somerset House". This might get some readers wondering whether a couple could be married. If so, what clues did we have before then that the couple could be Mark and Josie?

We know (from chapter 12) that Miss Marple told Dolly that Mark wouldn't remain a widower but that he had told Clithering that he didn't want to marry again. In reconciling those two statements, some readers might wonder if he was already remarried. And we know from Edwards, Jefferson's valet (chapter 14), about Jefferson being "furious" if Mark remarried – which might get those readers wondering if he had remarried in secret. However, those hints relate just to Mark – not a relationship with Josie – although we do get the 'Golden' clue in chapter 8 when Miss Marple compares Josie to Jessie Golden, an "ambitious" baker's daughter, who "…married the son of the house…" (as Josie, in effect, did by marrying Mark).[7]

As for the *howdunnit*, readers should be surprised when Miss Marple says in chapter 18 that it was Josie's "plan throughout" since her comment in chapter 12 that Josie had one of those minds that "…never do foresee the future and are usually astonished by it" suggests that she would not be a good planner. Nevertheless, we do get various clues to help us with, as Miss Marple puts it, "tracing out the course of events".

Pamela's friend, Florence Small, gives us the 'film test' clue by telling us that Pamela was going for a film test with a producer, who was "absolutely businesslike about it all", meaning that he had spoken "plausibly" (as Miss Marple says in chapter 18) – like Mr Cargill, the builder, to whom she had compared Mark in chapter 9. Florence's story is extracted at her second interview after a couple of good observations, one by Harper who suggests that Pamela was not going to Woolworths, as she had pretended, because girls prefer to go shopping *with* someone (rather than alone) and the other by Miss Marple, who selects Florence for a second interview because at her first one she had, like her own maid Janet, relaxed too soon when leaving the room.

We were also told that the empty room used for Pamela was only dusted once a week and how Ruby's room was well placed (near the staircase, obscure corridor and unfrequented side terrace) for leaving the hotel unseen; we were told by Bartlett (twice) that Ruby yawned; we were told that Mark went out in his car after dinner and returned while Ruby was doing her 10.30 dance; and we were given enough information about likely distance and speed to establish that he could have driven back from the cottage to the hotel by then.

We also get some clues, in addition to the 'fingernails' and 'teeth' clues, that the bodies may not be the ones we think. Thus, when Melchett, Harper and Slack examine the bathroom between Ruby's room and Josie's room in chapter 7, why is so much made of the beauty aids that women use, particularly those having "to ring a change" with their appearance? And why, when burning a car to render the charred body inside unidentifiable, would one overlook the shoe and button? Perhaps they were left deliberately by someone who *wanted* the body to be identified as Pamela.

However, a more strongly flagged *howdunnit* clue relating to the swapped bodies – with three times more references than the 'fingernails' clue in chapter 13 – is the 'old dress' clue. This concerns the poor quality white dress on the body in the library, which had reminded Miss Marple of Edie Chetty who was fond of cheap finery too. Miss Marple says that the "old dress" was "all wrong" because it was shabby and rather worn whereas Ruby belonged to the class who wear their *best* clothes, however unsuitable, for an occasion. So, if she had had a date (after her 10.30 dance) – with Blake or someone else – she would have kept on her best pink dress instead of changing into an old one.

Assuming that Miss Marple is right, the body in the old dress in the library is unlikely to be Ruby's. Surprisingly, however, despite her regarding the 'old dress' clue as "important" in chapter 13, she does not mention the significance of the pink and white dresses at all in relation to the *howdunnit*, let alone interpret the clue, during her chapter 18 explanations.

Absence of explanation and interpretation is, as we have seen, her approach to some other points as well, even her ambiguous words "Then that's that..." about the nail clippings. Her approach is one of the three most noticeable aspects of the clueing. The second is how openly some significant murder plan clues are flagged for us, making them less intriguing – not just the motive and the 'old dress' and 'Somerset House' clues but also the 'fingernails' clue, which despite its initial excellent concealment, is emphasised in chapters 9 and 13. The third is that some of the clues are not so much ones which Miss Marple is seen to *receive* but are insights which she *gives* to readers.

This applies less to the murder plan (although the 'credulous' and 'Golden' clues are examples there) than to the body ending up in the library and it begins with the 'unreality' clue. In chapter 1 Miss Marple had "understood" what Dolly meant when saying that the dead girl "doesn't look real at all" and had "nodded" when Dolly said "It just isn't true!". Her understanding and nodding are hints about the unreality of the situation, which she builds into a clue in the final chapter when saying that a body in the library was "altogether too like a book to be *true* … it made the wrong pattern – it wasn't, you see, *meant*…".

This leads to the conclusion that "the *real* idea" had been to plant the body, not in the library, but elsewhere, which is what she had hinted when saying in chapter 8 that a "very careful plan" had gone wrong. So, with the 'unreality' clue and with Bantry refusing to hear a good word about Blake and the body being dressed for a party of the sort Blake gave, she feels able to say, even before the end of chapter 1, that Blake is "the only possible explanation".

There seems to be support for the 'unreality' clue in chapter 4 when Josie says "None of it seems real, somehow" and "I just *can't* understand it! I *can't*!". But Miss Marple goes further in chapter 18, interpreting her words to mean that "*she* knew, none better" that the body should have been in Blake's cottage because she was "completely puzzled at finding the body where it was". Setting aside that she did *not* find the body "where it was" (because by then it had been taken away), Miss Marple gets much more than readers are likely to get from Josie's words since she may well just be naturally puzzled that her cousin's body was in a library belonging to people she didn't know.

What Miss Marple says at the time (chapter 4) is that she can explain the body being in the library and she refers, without clarification, to Tommy Bond and the schoolmistress who went to wind up the clock and a frog jumped out. The 'frog' clue, with its sense of surprise and schoolboy prank, hints that Blake put the body in the library to startle Bantry; and in chapter 18 Miss Marple says that Tommy had the same idea – he was a sensitive boy and the teacher always picked on him – so he put a frog in the clock and it jumped out at her.

Then at the end of chapter 8, when Miss Marple refers to the "very careful plan" going wrong, she provides another clue about the body being in the library by saying, again without clarification, that the plan went wrong because "human beings are so much more vulnerable and sensitive than anyone thinks". What we are left to assume about the 'vulnerable' clue – although this is never made clear – is that Miss Marple is perhaps hinting that Blake had moved the girl because he was vulnerable to Dinah thinking he had killed her and sensitive to Bantry's sneering.

As for the existence of a "very careful plan" (the implication plan), she relies – in addition to Josie's anger and puzzlement – on two clues. First is the 'film man' clue, with Josie asking Raymond, while they look for Ruby, whether she is "with that film man" in a rather obvious attempt to implicate Blake. Second is the 'snapshot' clue, with Edwards having seen a snapshot of an unknown man (in fact Blake) which Josie had slipped into Ruby's handbag. But readers would have done quite well to identify the unknown man as Blake since Edwards says he had "rather untidy hair" whereas in chapter 2 we were told that Blake's "somewhat long" hair was "straight".

Finally, there is never any serious consideration of Bantry as a suspect, even though he doesn't have an alibi and had dined at the Majestic and sometimes even gets, as Dolly says, a little silly about pretty girls who come to tennis. But she's not troubled about that. "After all," she says, "I've got the garden".

12

The Moving Finger

Solution

Superintendent Nash, with some limited but crucial support from Miss Marple, investigates an outbreak of poison pen letters in the market town of Lymstock which apparently lead to the suicide of Mrs Mona Symmington and the murder of her maid, Agnes Woddell.

Their text, whose "foul" tone is of a sexual nature, is composed of individual letters cut out of an 1840 book of sermons and gummed to sheets of paper. The envelopes are typed on a Windsor 7 machine, well worn, with the *a* and *t* out of alignment, from the office of Mona's solicitor husband, Richard, who had given it to the Women's Institute where it was fairly easily accessible. The letters, posted locally or hand delivered, were of local provenance.

The story is narrated by Jerry Burton, who has rented a house in Lymstock with his pretty sister, Joanna, in order to recuperate in the countryside after a flying accident. Their house, Little Furze, belongs to Miss Emily Barton who has moved to rooms kept by her old parlourmaid, Florence. Her maid, Partridge, agrees to stay on at Little Furze for the Burtons.

The Symmingtons have three children – a girl from Mona's first marriage, Megan Hunter, aged 20, and two young boys of their own, Brian and Colin. As well as the maid Agnes, their household comprises Rose, the cook, and the boys' beautiful nursery governess, Elsie Holland.

Mona is neurotic and suffers from attacks of neuralgia. She takes cachets for her nerves and goes upstairs after lunch to sleep. She is usually up again by 4 pm, often coming down for the afternoon post delivered at about 3.45.

On the afternoon of her death she was, so it was thought, alone in the house since it was Rose and Agnes's day off; and Symmington, Megan, Elsie and the boys were out. When Symmington returned from the office at about 4.50, he called out for Mona and, since she didn't answer, he went up to her bedroom where he found her dead.

It seems that an anonymous letter, asserting that Colin was not Symmington's child, had come by the afternoon post – the envelope was on the floor and the letter screwed up in the fireplace. She must have read it and in her agitation fetched some cyanide from the potting shed, dissolved it in water and drunk it after writing 'I can't go on' on a torn scrap of paper found by her hand.

At the inquest, four days later, Dr Owen Griffith, who had moved to Lymstock from "up north" (as he puts it) five years ago with his sister Aimée, suggests that the shock of receiving the letter may have induced the neurotic Mona to take her own life, feeling that her husband might not believe her if she denied it. So the verdict is 'Suicide whilst temporarily insane'. But Griffith's view is not the prevalent one in the village: Partridge, Joanna and Aimée all think that Mona would never have killed herself unless the letter was true; and the village women whisper that there's "No smoke without fire" (chapter 6 part 1).

A week after her death, on Agnes's next day off, she rings Partridge at breakfast time and asks to consult her. So she is invited to tea at Little Furze but does not arrive and is found murdered next day in the Symmingtons' understairs cupboard. She had been stunned by a blow on the head before a kitchen skewer was thrust into her skull.

Mona's letter was not the first. About three weeks before her inquest, Jerry had received one, after being in Lymstock for two weeks. Two days after the inquest we learn that Symmington had received a letter about two months before. So, we can work out that he received his letter, which is the earliest of which we learn, about three weeks before Jerry and Joanna's arrival.

Joanna also receives a letter. So do Mr Pye; Emily Barton; Beatrice Baker, the Burtons' daily help, and her boyfriend, George; Symmington's clerk, Miss Ginch; Agnes's boyfriend, Fred; Dr Griffith, his sister, Aimée, and some of his patients; Maud Dane Calthrop, the vicar's wife; Mrs Mudge, the butcher's wife; Jennifer Clark, barmaid at the Three Crowns; Mr and Mrs Beadle at the Blue Boar; the (unnamed) bank manager; and, finally, Elsie.

There is no indication that Agnes, Rose, Megan, Partridge, Mrs Baker, Florence, the Rev. Caleb Dane Calthrop, Mrs Cleat (the local 'witch') or anyone else received letters.

Although it was initially assumed that Mona's letter had come by post, we learn that it hadn't – it had a used stamp and faked postmark – suggesting that it was left by hand. We also learn that Mona had not been alone in the house since Agnes had quarrelled with Fred and returned home. Nash thinks that she waited at the pantry window for Fred and saw Mona's letter being delivered without realising what she'd seen. Yet the more she thought about it during the week, the more uneasy she grew, and so she wanted to consult Partridge. However, she never left the house for the consultation because she was still in her cap and apron when found.

It appears – as it had in Mona's case – that she had been in the house alone. Nash thinks that the murderer rang the doorbell, batted her on the head, stabbed her and bundled her into the cupboard where Megan found her next day.

So, who are the suspects? Since the letter writer may have

written to himself or herself, all the villagers named so far are suspects save for those who are mentioned only fleetingly. One can also eliminate Jerry and Joanna because the letters started about three weeks before their arrival and he expressly states near the outset of his narrative that they knew no one in Lymstock.

So the suspects are Miss Barton, Partridge, Beatrice, Symmington, Megan, Elsie, Rose, Miss Ginch, Dr Griffith, Aimée, the Rev. Dane Calthrop, his wife Maud and Mr Pye, but not the villagers' own suspect, Mrs Cleat, since she never appears.

The number is reduced in chapter 6 part 5 by Inspector Graves, an expert on anonymous letter cases. He can match the Lymstock letters to two other cases – a local one involving a milliner woman; and an outbreak in Northumberland written by a schoolgirl, which Griffith remembers from his practice up north. Graves then pronounces that in his opinion the Lymstock letters were written by an educated woman, of middle age or over (oddly, since the writer in the second case was a schoolgirl) and probably unmarried.

The idea that the writer is a woman is then repeatedly drummed into readers. Although the writer is referred to as 'Poison Pen' a handful of times (giving no clue as to gender), there are nearly 90 occasions after Graves's pronouncement when the word 'woman' (or an equivalent such as she, lady, her, hag, spinster, female or maid) is used to describe the writer; and that figure doesn't include occasions where a specific name is used, like Miss Barton or Miss Ginch.

Nash limits the suspects further in chapter 8 part 2 by establishing that there are two definite times on which to focus: the letter to Mona must have been delivered between 3.15 and 4 pm; and Agnes was killed between 2.50 and 3.30. He is then asked by Jerry in chapter 9 part 7: "And who remains?".

The answer is that those without an alibi are (1) Miss Ginch (2) Aimée (3) Miss Barton and (4) Mr Pye. Although Graves had suggested a middle-aged spinster, Joanna says that Pye "*is* a middle-aged spinster" and Nash says he has "an abnormally female streak in his character". Jerry asks whether it is just those four, to which Nash says "Oh, no, no, we've got a couple more – besides the vicar's lady", who, he says, *could* have done it (though Maud's later engagement of Miss Marple makes this most unlikely).

As to his "couple more", frustratingly, we never find out who they are. Jerry thinks they might be Partridge and Mrs Cleat but his choice seems odd since Graves had described the writer as "educated". And Miss Marple eliminates Mrs Cleat on the basis that, as a witch, she could just "ill-wish" Agnes to waste away and die naturally – which is not sound reasoning because, even if Mrs Cleat had that facility, Agnes had to be killed straightaway, not "waste away", or she would have had time to consult Partridge.

Which brings us back to Nash's four suspects (1) Miss Ginch, who worked in Symmington's office with the typewriter before he gave it to the Women's Institute (2) Aimée, who has known Symmington for years because 'Dick' used to stay up north (3) Miss Barton, in whose house, Little Furze, Jerry finds the book of sermons used for the letters and (4) Mr Pye, who is rather "*frightening*" and might hate all the "normal" happy people and take "a queer perverse artistic pleasure" in being spiteful.

However, even when one adds Partridge and Maud to those four, as Jerry does in chapter 10 part 1, this is misdirection because the murderer is not on his list. It is understandable that Symmington and Griffith are not there – they are men and Nash says they are "all right" in terms of alibis. But readers may find the absence of Megan and Elsie less understandable.

Admittedly, they are young whereas Inspector Graves had said that the writer was of middle age or over. But Megan, whose real father may have been to prison, hates everyone in Lymstock because she's not wanted (Symmington hardly notices her and Mona had neglected her) and says she's going to "make them all sorry". And Elsie might have wanted Mona dead if, as the gossip suggests, she had envisaged becoming the second Mrs Symmington.

Indeed, Elsie receives the final anonymous letter, which tells her to leave the Symmingtons' house because she's not stepping into Mona's shoes. That letter was sent by Aimée, who was seen typing it at the Women's Institute, and Nash charges her. The pages cut from the book of sermons are found at her house and a heavy pestle, with which she is assumed to have stunned Agnes, is missing from Griffith's dispensary.

We later learn that she wrote to Elsie because she loved Symmington and, since she was hoping to become his second wife, was upset by the gossip about Elsie. So, why not frighten her away with an anonymous letter? But readers will rightly doubt that Aimée wrote the other letters as well since – unlike all of them – the *letter* to Elsie, not just the envelope, was typed, even though she could have gone on using the cut-out pages found at her house.

And, indeed, she turns out to be just a one-off letter writer. The real 'Poison Pen' is Symmington himself. He was, Miss Marple explains, a rather dry repressed man, tied to a neurotic wife, when a radiant young nursery governess came along. She says that, when gentlemen fall in love at a certain age, it's "quite a madness"; and because his qualities were "all negative", he couldn't "fight his madness". He wanted to marry Elsie – but also keep his home, his children and his respectability. Only Mona's death would solve his problem.

In order to prevent suspicion falling on himself as the husband, he chose a "very clever way" by creating a death which seemed only incidental to a non-existent letter writer. And "the clever thing" was that the police would suspect a *woman* because, by cribbing and mixing up expressions from letters by women in the local (milliner) and Northumberland (schoolgirl) cases, his letters represented a woman's mind – although we are not told how he got to examine those letters, which would hardly be readily available. He then typed all the envelopes before giving the typewriter to the Women's Institute and cut the pages from the book of sermons while at Little Furze one day, knowing that people don't open such books much.

Then, with the smoke screen of 'Poison Pen' well established, he put cyanide in Mona's top cachet to take after lunch on a day when everyone would be out in the afternoon. He got home at about the same time as Elsie, called up for Mona, got no answer, went up to her bedroom (with the anonymous letter, which Mona had never received), dropped a spot of cyanide in the plain glass of water which she had used for the cachet, threw the crumpled letter into the grate and the envelope onto the floor and put by her hand the scrap of paper in her handwriting saying 'I can't go on', which was part of an ordinary message of hers which he had come across and torn off for the day of the murder.

However, he couldn't foresee Agnes returning. She waited at the window for Fred. But *no one* came – not the postman, nor anyone else. It took her days, being slow, to realise that that was odd – because Mona should have received a letter by hand. Symmington must have heard Agnes at breakfast time ringing Partridge to say she didn't understand something. He couldn't take a chance – Agnes has seen *something*, knows something – and so must be killed. But the 'something' she has seen is 'nothing'. Killing someone for seeing nothing is an imaginative motive and the most satisfying puzzle point in the story.[1]

Miss Marple imagines that he killed her before going to the office. He opened and shut the front door, as if he had gone out, then slipped into the cloakroom. When only Agnes was left in the house, he probably rang the front-door bell, slipped back into the cloakroom, came out and hit her on the head as she opened the door and then, after killing her and hiding her body in the cupboard, hurried to the office.

He then got a chance to make himself safe on learning that Aimée had been seen writing the letter to Elsie. He hid the cut-out pages at Aimée's while the police were charging her and probably pinched the pestle that day. But Miss Marple, who was already "sure" he was the murderer, intervenes. Although we aren't told precisely what she does, Jerry sees her speaking to Megan and later coming out of the police station. The result is a trap laid for Symmington into which he falls by trying to kill Megan.

Until Miss Marple's intervention, his smoke screen had deceived the villagers and police, as had his quite clever murder plan for Mona. Agnes's murder did not require any real ingenuity but he deserves credit for acting quickly. However, he made a potential error by putting her body in the cupboard which was used for "fishing-rods and golf clubs and things". Since his purpose was to delay it being found (so making it harder to fix the time of death), that purpose could well have been defeated because Elsie and the boys had gone fishing that afternoon. Surely, at some point after returning at 4.50, they might have put the fishing rods back in the cupboard and seen the body.[2]

However, the real problem, both for Symmington and the puzzle generally, is that, since this is a Christie novel, *readers* (rather than *villagers*) will be sure that Mona was murdered and that the suicide note is fake, even if they are not sure why. And, if it was murder, those with the best opportunity to poison Mona in her bedroom are those in her household – Symmington, Megan, Elsie, Rose or Agnes – two of whom, Megan and Elsie, have rather obvious motives based, respectively, on hatred and ambition, while the two servants, Rose and Agnes, have no known motive. That leaves the husband to whom readers are pointed with clues from, as we shall see, Jerry, Maud, Nash and Miss Marple.

Plot

Anyone expecting to read a Miss Marple novel is likely to be disappointed. Until the very end, this hardly seems like one of her novels at all. She doesn't live in Lymstock and doesn't appear until chapter 10 part 1 of this 15-chapter story – about 75% of the way through – after Maud has called in "an expert".

She then disappears quickly, at the end of part 1, before reappearing very fleetingly in chapter 12 part 3 to speak three sentences about Maud, none of which affects the plot. She then reappears on three short occasions in chapter 13 part 4 and, finally, for the whole of chapter 14 to explain the solution to Jerry, Joanna and Maud. In total she appears in only 7.5% of the novel and, most strikingly, is not even present when we learn the identity of the killer, which is revealed by the trap rather than by her.[3]

Nash appears in nearly 20%. But before her intervention he clearly believed that Aimée had written the letters. When he charges her, he does so for "the letters" (i.e. not just the one to Elsie) and, when Griffith asks if she was responsible for "those letters", he replies that there is "no doubt of it, sir".

The novel's title comes from the start of one of the four-line poems of the 11/12th century Persian, Omar Khayyam, translated by Edward FitzGerald in 1859, which begins "The Moving Finger writes; and, having writ, Moves on…". As in the poem, a single finger is used in the novel (according to Inspector Graves) but on a typewriter – not, for example, on a wall or in sand – perhaps, he suggests, by someone "who can type but doesn't want us to know the fact". His point, which does not turn out to be significant (except for the title), is presumably that a typist using just one finger leaves a different (heavier) indent on paper than a regular typist who uses all the fingers.

We are not given any dates but can work out that the story covers nearly seven weeks in the spring. Although there is reference to the War, it is never given as the reason for Jerry's flying accident. However, since Miss Barton says "A flying accident? So brave, these young men", his "accident" might have been caused by the War.

Otherwise, we know very little about Jerry, or Joanna, which is surprising when he's the narrator. But he does write in quite an enjoyable style. And he captures some characters really vividly, describing characteristics perceptively and recording some notable lines, such as Nash suggesting breakfast because "Murder is a nasty business on an empty stomach" and Maud commenting that the letter about her husband is absurd because "Caleb has no taste for fornication. He never has had. So lucky, being a clergyman". His most amusing writing comes in Mrs Baker's ramble (chapter 4 part 1), including when she pauses and the next paragraph reads "Unable to find her way out of this sentence, Mrs Baker took a deep breath and began again".

However, a weakness of Jerry's narrative is that Lymstock, despite being "full of festering poison" (chapter 6, part 5), never feels as poisonous or scary as it perhaps should – in fact, it seems to be an agreeable village. And Jerry does behave surprisingly sometimes. We would have expected him to do more than just go to bed after Agnes disappears, especially when he seems so agitated about it; his love for Megan seems unlikely; and his casual dismissal of the two murders near the end ("…what the hell? we've all got to die some time!") jars when we have spent the story identifying with him as someone we like.

More generally, although this is quite a likeable novel[4], one feels that it is some way from being one of the author's strongest puzzles. One reason is that it takes time to get going. By the end of chapter 3, readers will probably think that we have spent long enough on the letters; and, when we finally learn of Mona's death in chapter 5, we already feel that either a death or the detective should surely have been in the puzzle by now. And, just as it should be reaching a peak of mystification, the whole of chapter 11 and the first part of chapter 12 are dedicated to Jerry falling in love with Megan, making one feel that the puzzle has rather lost its way.

But the main reason is probably that no real mystification is generated, either by the anonymous letters (which do not create the same interest as a good murder plan) or by the police investigation (which seems plodding when we reckon that they should be focusing on murder) or by the real sleuth (since, when Miss Marple does at last appear, her detection is so opaque as to seem non-existent).

Instead the author relies, quite successfully, on "misdirection". Miss Marple says "You've got to make people look at the wrong thing and in the wrong place – Misdirection, they call it, I believe" (chapter 10) and "Misdirection, you see – everybody looking at the wrong thing – the anonymous letters..." (chapter 14). What "everybody" – readers and villagers – should have looked at was not the letters but the motive behind them since, while Symmington's smoke screen is the novel's cleverness, his motive is really its cornerstone.

And, just as he uses misdirection with the letters, so the author uses it with the letter writer's gender; with the letter writer's assumed insanity (the word 'lunatic' is used about ten times); with Agnes's call to Partridge perhaps being overheard at the Symmingtons' house by Elsie or Rose (without mentioning Symmington); and with Jerry listing his six suspects on separate lines (without mentioning Symmington) in both the UK and United States editions.

In the United States, after serialisation in *Collier's Weekly*, the novel was published in July 1942, prior to the UK edition in June 1943. Although the United States edition has the same title, it is rather different from the UK edition, right from the first sentence about the anonymous letters, which are not referred to until about the 50th paragraph of the UK edition. The most obvious difference is that it has only eight chapters (not 15). The omissions are almost all in chapters 1 and 2, which replace chapter 1 to chapter 6 part 2 of the UK edition. Thereafter, the text is almost identical but the chapters are structured differently, each being of similar length, presumably for the original eight-part serialisation in the United States.

The omissions in the United States edition are essentially of characterisation, description, reflection and conversation. The effect is to remove about 40% of the equivalent sections in the UK edition and to make the whole book shorter by about 15%. The purpose was presumably to reduce text in order to get the murder story underway much more quickly than in the UK edition but at the expense of passages such as Mrs Baker's monologue.

One also wonders, in view of the toning down of Ellsworthy's queerness in the United States version of *Murder is Easy*, whether Mr Pye is similarly treated. In fact, he is still "extremely ladylike"; lives in "hardly a man's house"; is "a middle-aged spinster" who might take "a queer, perverse, artistic pleasure" in writing the letters; and has an "abnormally female streak". The only alteration made to accommodate American sensibilities is to change Maud's reference to her husband's lack of taste for "fornication" to "flirtation".

Clues

In chapter 8 Jerry says "I believe that if I had given my mind to it, I could have solved the whole thing then and there". We will consider later whether Jerry could have done that with the clues which he then had. But it is probably best to start where Miss Marple begins her explanations.

She says "The truth was really so very obvious. *You* saw it, you know, Mr Burton". Of course, Jerry says he didn't. However, she persists: "But you did. You indicated the whole thing to me … To begin with, that tiresome phrase 'No smoke without fire."

Jerry had "indicated" that phrase because in Miss Marple's

first scene he had told her that it had been used *ad nauseam* (about whether the letters were true) and that he had dreamed of it.

In fact, he had had two dreams. In the first, as he drops off to sleep in chapter 8 part 1, the words dancing through his mind are "'No smoke without fire'. No fire without smoke. Smoke … Smoke? Smoke screen … No, that was the war – a war phrase. War. Scrap of paper … Only a scrap of paper…". In the second, in chapter 9 part 7, as sleep is near, he repeats to himself "No smoke without fire. No smoke without fire…That's it … it all links up together".

So, how does the 'No smoke without fire' phrase act as a clue to the letters being, as Miss Marple calls them, a "smoke screen"? Jerry says that he mixed up the phrase 'No smoke without fire' with War terms such as 'smoke screen'. And, as seen in the quoted passage, he did indeed convert 'No smoke without fire' via the word 'smoke' to 'smoke screen'. The author even tries to give credibility to the way his dream evolves by inverting the phrase in the second sentence of the first dream to 'No fire without smoke', thus allowing the last word of the inverted phrase ('smoke') to lead into the next word ('Smoke').

But this is most unpersuasive. Although Miss Marple tries to legitimise Jerry's dream process about the 'smoke' clue by saying that he had "proceeded quite correctly to label it for what it was – a smoke screen", the fact is that the phrase is not intended to suggest a smoke screen. The phrase simply means that, where there's a suggestion that something bad is true, there is probably a good reason for the suggestion. So, the link between the phrase and the smoke screen doesn't really work. Moreover, Miss Marple credits Jerry for making a jump he never made because he did not actually "label" the phrase as a smoke screen. As he says, he just got them "mixed up".

Having described the letters as a smoke screen, Miss Marple then says that "the whole point" was that there *weren't* any anonymous letters because they "weren't real at all". She explains that any *woman* writer from Lymstock would know about its scandals and have used them in the letters; and that a genuine woman writer "would have made her letters much more to the point". Yet, as we had learned from Maud, Griffith and Graves, the letters didn't seem to *know* anything – there was not much accurate or intimate knowledge behind them, just blind spite and malice. Maud even says, "That's what is so curious…" – thus telling us that there is something wrong about the letters.

In fact, Miss Marple's 'unreal letters' clue is a double one. Their lack of knowledge and gossip tells her not only that they weren't 'real' and therefore a smoke screen but also that, since men aren't interested in gossip in the same way as women, they were really created by a man, who had cribbed them from letters written by women in the two other cases.

But there is a curiosity with the clue. Having said that a genuine woman writer would have made her letters much more to the point and gossipy (than Symmington's letters), Miss Marple says five paragraphs later that his letters "definitely represented a woman's mind". But how can that be so if they weren't like a genuine woman writer's letters would have been?

There is a further clue in relation to the letters. In chapter 9 part 1 Nash says that the envelope containing Joanna Burton's letter was "actually addressed to Miss Barton, and the '*a*' altered to a '*u*' afterwards". Jerry says "That remark, properly interpreted, ought to have given us a clue to the whole business". This explicitly flagged clue should set readers thinking. But thinking what?

Although Miss Marple doesn't deal with this quite clever 'altered envelope' clue, the deduction must be that, since the envelope was originally typed before the Burtons came to Lymstock and since the typist cannot have wanted to risk accessing the typewriter at the Women's Institute just to type a new envelope for Joanna, it was originally typed while the typewriter was still at

Symmington's office.

Before considering who typed it there, readers may wonder whether the deduction is confirmed by Jerry's envelope also having had its typewritten address altered. But we are not told. Nevertheless, since Symmington would sensibly have given away the typewriter *before* starting to send the letters – as Miss Marple later confirms he did – and since he started sending them at least three weeks before the Burtons came to Lymstock, he *must* have altered Jerry's envelope to avoid accessing the typewriter at the Women's Institute.

However, there is an oddity. It is all very well for 'Miss Barton' to be altered, unnoticed at first, to 'Miss Burton'. But it is quite another to alter 'Miss' to, presumably, 'Mr' on Jerry's envelope without this being noticed, particularly since he looked at the envelope at some length – assuming, of course, that his letter was in an envelope originally addressed to Miss Barton; if it wasn't, it's not clear who the original typed addressee could have been.

Readers who aren't deflected by that oddity from pursuing the deduction should then wonder who could have accessed the typewriter in Symmington's office. Only two such people are named in the story – Symmington himself and Miss Ginch – and we are told that the typewriter was given "by him" to the Women's Institute. Since the 'altered envelope' clue is therefore, as Jerry says, "a clue to the whole business", it is surprising that Miss Marple doesn't deal with it in her explanations. Perhaps she was unaware of it.

Next we have Symmington's motive derived from his infatuation with Elsie. There are really three elements to the 'Elsie infatuation' clue, namely (using Miss Marple's adjectives) the neurotic wife, the repressed husband and the radiant governess. So, how well are these elements clued?

We know that Mona is neurotic, hysterical, nervy, weepy and in poor health. But we believe that Symmington copes with that because he was "the sort of man who would never give his wife a moment's anxiety" and "not one to set the pulses madly racing". Indeed, Jerry feels sure he is a "kindly man" (twice) and a good father to the two boys; and we are told by Griffith and Miss Barton that the Symmingtons were devoted to each other and to the children.

Even Miss Marple says, when noting that his qualities were "all negative", that he was devoted to his children. So, beyond his lack of interest in Megan and one remark by Aimée that he "could be very jealous", it's not clear where Miss Marple finds his total negativity. Therefore, although she says during her explanations that the first person one thinks of in such a case is the husband, that does not, on its own, suggest a promising line of enquiry.

As for Elsie, she is clearly beautiful – "a goddess ... a glorious, an incredible, a breath-taking girl!". But one wonders if she is sufficiently clued to support the motive since, when she spoke, "the magic died completely". Jerry adds that she is a "nice healthy-looking well set-up girl, no more" and "just a nice kind girl", while Joanna says (twice) that she's good looking but has no "S.A." (sex appeal). Her beauty is also contextualised by Joanna being "probably the most attractive thing that had been seen in Lymstock for many a long day".

So, one feels that, despite Mona's nerves and Elsie's beauty, Symmington's motive, although certainly credible, is weakly clued. There may be gossip about *Elsie* becoming the next Mrs Symmington. But Symmington *himself* never provides a positive clue about his infatuation, which is a pity because, as noted earlier, his motive is really the cornerstone of the novel.

Instead, we receive a *negative* clue – the 'no Elsie letter' clue. Although Elsie gets Aimée's anonymous letter in chapter 13, she had not had one by chapter 8 part 3, causing Nash to say "... why the devil hasn't she? ... she's just the meat an anonymous letter writer would like" and Miss Marple to say "Now that's very interesting. That's the most interesting thing I've heard yet" – clearly flagging this as a clue for readers. She even describes this in her explanations as "the most important thing of all", saying that Symmington "gave himself away" by being unable to write a foul letter to the girl he loved.

The reason why Miss Marple has to emphasise the 'no Elsie letter' clue must be that, since Symmington doesn't demonstrate any affection for Elsie, it is the only clue to his motivation. But the significance of his failure to write to her seems to be more in Miss Marple *asserting* that it is "very interesting" than in the failure itself – after all, 'Poison Pen' had not written to, for example, Megan or Partridge; and might just not have written to Elsie yet.

Nevertheless, prompted by Miss Marple's assertion, readers should look for a suspicious explanation for the failure and they are helped by another of her assertions. In chapter 8 part 2, Nash had told Jerry that "we're up against someone who's respected…". So Jerry tells Miss Marple that Nash had "stressed respectability". She says "Yes. That's *very* important", with "*very*" in italics, plainly emphasising Nash's 'respectability' clue. And when Jerry first met Symmington, he was described as the "acme of calm respectability".

Miss Marple also advises Jerry, in response to one of his many references to a 'lunatic', to "look for somebody very sane", to which he responds "That's what Nash said" (although actually he hadn't). In retrospect, her 'sanity' clue looks slightly odd – not because we ever thought that the letter writer was a lunatic (of course, we didn't) but because of her expressly referring, in the context of Symmington's motivation, to his love for Elsie being "quite a madness" and to him being unable "to fight his madness".

Turning from the murderer to Mona's 'suicide', the main clue that she was murdered is the torn scrap of paper with the words 'I can't go on' written on it. Miss Marple says that a 'scrap of paper' was "all wrong" because people don't leave suicide notes on torn scraps of paper – they use sheets of paper and often an envelope too.

She adds that Jerry *knew* it was wrong – again giving him undue credit, which he again rejects. In fairness to him, though, the words "…Scrap of paper … Only a scrap of paper…" had danced through his mind in his first dream and so he must have been wondering, subconsciously, why Mona had left a suicide note on "only" a scrap of paper.

Some readers will also have been wondering this but, for those who aren't, the 'scrap of paper' clue is supplemented by another clue in the form of a message left by Joanna in chapter 9 part 7 on the telephone pad. It reads "*If Dr Griffith rings up, I can't go on Tuesday, but could manage Wednesday or Thursday*". Jerry worries about the message but, as he falls asleep before his second dream, he can't think why – so telling us that the telephone message is a clue.

When he then tells Miss Marple in chapter 10 about mixing up "No smoke without fire" with "Smoke screens, scrap of paper, telephone messages", he adds "No, that was another dream". What he means is that "telephone messages" were not in his first dream but the precursor to his second. He is right about that. But what the author has done is get him to juxtapose "scrap of paper" and "telephone messages" when talking to Miss Marple, even though he thought of them on *separate* occasions, as a way of connecting the 'telephone message' clue to the 'scrap of paper' clue.

Miss Marple makes quite a fuss about what the telephone message said. Although Jerry doesn't set it out again, but just repeats it "as best I could remember it", Miss Marple "nodded her head and smiled and seemed pleased" with its "actual words", which is a clear indication for us to look back at them.

In chapter 14 Jerry recalls that Joanna's message had said "Say that *I can't go on* Friday" (he gets the day wrong) and sees that the connection is the wording 'I can't go on', also written on the scrap of paper torn from a similar message of Mona's. The combined 'scrap of paper' and 'telephone message' clue is rather good, the best in the book despite the contrived juxtaposition, even though a scrap of paper should be spotted as wrong for a suicide note anyway.

The only further clue that Mona may not have killed herself is Nash's suggestion to Griffith in chapter 9 part 7 that a suicide victim would take an overdose of something soporific rather than prussic acid.[5] Although Miss Marple doesn't mention the 'prussic acid' clue and Griffith is a bit dismissive of it – because prussic acid would be more dramatic and certain than barbiturates – some readers may well see merit in Nash's point.[6]

As for Agnes's murder, Miss Marple says about its timing in chapter 10 part 1 that Agnes must have been like her own maid – slow to take things in. Later she uses her 'Agnes slowness' clue to explain why she took a week to ring Partridge. But we had an idea she was slow before the clue, Nash having said in chapter 8 part 2 that she "*didn't realise what she had seen. Not at first…*".

What will be apparent generally about the clues is how many are emphasised by the characters because the facts on their own may not be suggestive enough for readers without prompting. This rather unsubtle approach is true not only of Jerry and Miss Marple's discussion about her main 'smoke' clue; but we also have Jerry explicitly flagging the 'altered envelope' clue and worrying about the 'telephone message' clue; and Maud being curious about the 'unreal letters' clue; and Nash suggesting the 'prussic acid' clue. And Miss Marple herself tells us that the 'respectability' clue is "*very* important"; seems pleased with the 'telephone message' clue; and says that the 'no Elsie letter' clue is "the most interesting thing" she's heard yet.

But what is even more noticeable is that, when Symmington falls into the trap by trying to kill Megan, he is exposed without any apparent detective work on Miss Marple's part. Maud may claim at the start of chapter 14 that "I was quite right to call in an expert" but Jerry's reaction is to stare at her and say in surprise "But did you? Who was it? What did he do?". These questions are entirely reasonable in the light of Miss Marple's apparent contribution.

Indeed, when reading her explanations, one could fairly assume that she had solved the puzzle on her first appearance in chapter 10 by simply asking Jerry about his dreams. Or, more impressively still, that she had solved it with effortless brilliance before even appearing in the story (having had the background from Maud) and that, rather than *getting* clues from Jerry's dreams, she was prompting him to *use* clues from them to solve the crimes for himself. In which case, the credit she gives him seems surprising because as late as chapter 13 part 5 he suspected Elsie, to which she reacts in chapter 14 by saying "Oh dear, me, no...".

With the truth being so "very obvious" to her, she must have convinced Nash of it and persuaded him to lay the trap. It was in those respects, rather than in any apparent detection, that her contribution was crucial. And the trap was necessary because of there being "no evidence against this very clever and unscrupulous man" – though other clues are later found in his office, namely the missing pestle with which he tried to incriminate Aimée, the skewer with which he killed Agnes and the clock weight with which he struck her.

Which brings us finally back to whether Jerry *could* really "have solved the whole thing then and there" by chapter 8. He was well aware of the 'no smoke without fire' phrase and he dreams of a smoke screen in that chapter. He had the 'unreal letters' clue, which might explain what the smoke screen was and possibly even that it had been created by a man. He had the 'scrap of paper' clue (albeit without the 'telephone message' clue) and so could have assumed that Mona was murdered. And, since she was poisoned in a household where there was only one man, he could have alighted on the husband, even though he didn't yet have the 'altered envelope' or 'respectability' clues.

But the question he would then face is *why* Symmington would have done this. He has two elements of the 'Elsie infatuation' clue (the neurotic wife and the radiant governess) but no indication that Symmington was tiring of Mona – indeed he knows of their mutual devotion – or of his infatuation with Elsie; and he doesn't get the 'no Elsie letter' clue until the end of chapter 8. So, he probably couldn't have solved 'the whole thing' but he could be pretty sure of the murderer, even if he didn't understand the motive.

13

Towards Zero

Solution

This is a detective story in which Superintendent Battle of Scotland Yard investigates the murder of Lady Camilla Tressilian at her house, Gull's Point, in Saltcreek. The house stands on a plateau of rock overlooking the River Tern with sheer cliff going down to the water.

Lady Tressilian, an elderly invalid, is murdered in bed between 10 pm and midnight on Monday 12 September. She is found next morning, struck twice on the right temple. A nine-iron golf club, known as a niblick, is found in her room with a blood-stained head and some white hairs sticking to it.

Since there was no space on the left side of her bed, the murderer must have stood on the right side, where it would have been awkward to deliver a right-handed blow. So, it appears that the murderer was left-handed, although the niblick was right-handed.

On her pillow was the tassel of a bellpull connected by wires that ran out of the room and along the ceiling to a bell that rang upstairs in the room of her maid, Jane Barrett. Barrett is found in a coma that morning, doped with barbiturates in the senna pod brew which she drank every night. It is assumed that she was doped so that she could not respond if Lady Tressilian rang the bell. Since an outsider would not have known about the bell or that Barrett took senna, and with the niblick being taken from the understairs cupboard, the murder was, as Inspector Leach calls it, an "inside job".

Setting aside the servants, there are six suspects. Five had been in the house on the evening of the murder, including her companion of nearly 15 years, Mary Aldin, aged 36. The other four are guests: Nevile Strange, aged 33, well-known as a first-class tennis player and all-round sportsman – golfer, swimmer and climber – whose guardian had been Lady Tressilian's late husband, Sir Matthew; Kay Strange, Nevile's current wife, aged 23; Audrey Strange, Nevile's first wife, aged 32, whom, we are told, he had deserted three years ago after eight years of marriage; and Thomas Royde, Audrey's cousin, who had been keen on her before she married Nevile. The sixth suspect, who is staying at the Easterhead Bay Hotel opposite Gull's Point on the other side of the river, is Ted Latimer, aged 25, who had been in love with Kay, and she with him, until Nevile came along.

At 10 pm Nevile quarrels with Lady Tressilian just before going over to Easterhead to play billiards with Ted. Next morning, after her body is found, he comes under suspicion not only because of the quarrel but also because the niblick is his (his fingerprints, and no one else's, are on it) and because in his wardrobe there is a dark blue suit with Lady Tressilian's bloodstains on it, while by his washbasin there are pools of water, suggesting that he washed the blood off himself hurriedly. In addition, he inherits about £50,000, being half of Sir Matthew's estate.

Nevile admits the quarrel but says he parted on friendly terms; that he then changed out of the blue suit he had worn at dinner (because it was raining and he was going over to Easterhead); and that he put on an older, grey pinstripe suit, so was not wearing the bloodstained blue one. He was then heard to leave by Hurstall, the butler, and Thomas at about 10.20 and caught the 10.30 ferry across the river. He could not find Ted at his hotel at once but from about 11.15 they drank and played billiards and both noticed a beastly smell. Nevile missed the last ferry. So Ted drove him back, leaving at 2 pm and arriving at about 2.30, having had to drive 16 miles all the way round the river.

When Barrett awakes from her coma, she says that, after drinking her senna, Lady Tressilian's bell had rung at 10.25 and that, on coming down, she had seen Nevile going out, wearing his grey pinstripe and banging the door. She went into Lady Tressilian, who was alive, although unable to remember why she had rung. So, with Nevile going across to Easterhead *before* she was struck, someone must have tried to frame him with the niblick and blue jacket.

However, the niblick is not the murder weapon because Battle finds part of the real weapon in a bedroom (we are not at first told whose) in which there is a steel fender whose left knob is brighter than its right one. The knob unscrews and has a bloodstain on it. The weapon was created by screwing the knob into the handle of a tennis racquet whose head was sawn off. After the murder, the murderer cleaned the knob (but not the stain on the screw) with some emery paper, later found in the wastepaper basket, and screwed it back. The handle and head of the racquet were rejoined with adhesive surgical plaster.

Battle then learns of a significant event which happened about five days before the murder. Mr Treves, a retired solicitor, who was staying at the Balmoral Court Hotel almost next to Gull's Point, had come to dinner. He told a story to the suspects (Mary, Nevile, Kay, Audrey, Thomas and Ted) of two children playing with bows and arrows. One had killed the other and was distraught. This was treated as an accident because the children were said to be unused to bows and arrows, but a farmer, who said nothing at the inquest, had noticed the surviving child practising with a bow and arrow *before* the accident.

So Treves thought that the 'accident' was an ingenious murder, planned in detail and committed by a child who hated the other and practised before the shooting. Treves says that the child (whose age and sex he does not give) is now grown-up, with a new name, but that he would recognise the little murderer because of a physical peculiarity (which he does not describe). Mary later suggests that he had said this as though he *had* recognised him.

When Treves returned to his hotel that evening, a notice read "Lift Out of Order". So he walked up the stairs, extremely vexed because, as he had told the six suspects after dinner, he had a weak heart and stairs were forbidden. He died that night and Dr Lazenby says that walking up three flights of stairs in his state of health would almost certainly have killed him.

Nothing had been wrong with the lift and so Battle rightly concludes that the 'out of order' notice had been hung on it to kill Treves by making him use the stairs. This would prevent him exposing someone whose later murder of Lady Tressilian was, like the child murder, "very carefully planned beforehand down to the smallest detail" and a "murder for pure hate". The murderer is, Battle suggests, a "maniac" under the domination of one fixed idea.

However, the murderer's hatred was not aimed at Lady Tressilian. Her death was (to quote Battle) "only incidental" to the murderer's "main object", which was to have the hated person framed and hanged for her murder. When Battle asks Nevile whether anyone hates him or has been injured by him, he replies that he has only injured one person – Audrey, when he left her for Kay. So she is the obvious suspect for having framed him out of hatred or revenge (and she receives the other half of Sir Matthew's estate).

In due course, we learn that a number of clues implicate her: the fender, with the cleaned knob and emery paper, was in her room; outside the window, in the ivy, was a pair of leather gloves, which fit only her, and the left one (Audrey is left-handed) was stained with blood; her fingerprint was on the adhesive surgical plaster; and her white hairs and powder were on Nevile's bloodstained blue jacket, suggesting she had worn it.

Audrey, afraid of being hanged, runs towards the cliff edge at Stark Head but is stopped by a guest at the Easterhead Bay Hotel, Angus MacWhirter, who had also tried, but failed, to commit suicide there eight months previously. Battle then arrests her for Lady Tressilian's murder and she reacts by saying "It's all true". In arresting her, Battle decides (because he has "to go by the facts") to disregard a revelation made just beforehand by Thomas that she hasn't got a revenge motive because Nevile didn't desert her. It was *she* who left *him*, running away with Thomas's brother, Adrian.

This gives us a previously unknown motive for Nevile. It was his love for Audrey that turned to hate when she left him for Adrian, who died later in a car accident (which he may have caused). Nevile had killed Lady Tressilian but his main object was that the woman who had left him should be hanged.

However, it is not clear that this will be the solution until MacWhirter claims in the final chapter to have been at Stark Head at about 11 pm on the night of the murder and looked over to Gull's Point where he saw a man climbing a rope hanging from a window into the river. The man can't have been Audrey, Mary or Kay – or Thomas whose right arm and shoulder are partially useless. That leaves Nevile and Ted, who were at Easterhead but not together until about 11.15. Before then, one of them, who wasn't seen between 10.30 and 11.15, might have been swimming over and back.

Battle then takes the suspects (except the arrested Audrey) out on a launch and, by pushing Ted overboard, establishes that he cannot swim (which seems unnecessary because he *was seen* at the hotel with a Mrs Beddoes), meaning that the murderer is Nevile, whom we know to be a fine swimmer and climber.

On the day of the murder – we are not told when – Nevile must have drugged Barrett's senna and doped Kay (who yawned after dinner) to stop her coming into his room. He must also have entered Audrey's room – again we are not told when – and taken the knob (and made the weapon) as well as taking (one presumes) her powder, the gloves (if they were hers, which she denies) and some adhesive plaster on which her fingerprint occurred naturally.

After the quarrel with Lady Tressilian, he changed out of his blue suit into his grey pinstripe and (one again presumes) left a rope, obtained at some point from the boxroom, hanging from his room into the river. Before leaving, he went to the passage outside Lady Tressilian's room and, using a pole with a hook (normally used to draw down the sash of an awkwardly placed window), rang her bell by pulling on the wires running along the ceiling. It was 10.25 and Barrett came down and, as he intended, saw him going out, banging the door, so as to be *heard* to leave by others in case Barrett didn't see him.

He was then seen to take the 10.30 ferry. But, before joining Ted at about 11.15, he stripped in the dark on some rocks, thrust his grey pinstripe into a niche there, swam across the river, climbed up the rope into his bedroom, leaving water on the floor, got into his blue suit and went to Lady Tressilian's room, with his weapon and the niblick.

He then hit her twice, doing so with backhanded strokes to make it look as if she was killed by a left-hander. He must then have smeared blood and white hairs on the niblick, which had his fingerprints on it, showing that someone had tried to incriminate him. Then he returned to his room, took off his bloodstained blue suit, went down the rope and swam back to Easterhead.

There he found that he had, unluckily, put his grey pinstripe on a decayed fish which had left a stained patch on the shoulder – and that it smelled. So, when at about 11.15 he found Ted, who noticed a nasty smell, he suggested that the hotel drains were faulty while Ted suggested that there might be a dead rat under the billiard room floor. Later, Ted drove Nevile back to Gull's Point.

Battle says that Nevile then had all night to "clear up his traces", including presumably reassembling the racquet and throwing it back into the cupboard under the stairs, returning the damp rope to the boxroom and putting Audrey's powder and white hairs (perhaps acquired when he caught his cuff button in her hair a few days earlier) onto the blue jacket which he put in his wardrobe. But one 'trace' which he did not clear up was the water by his washbasin, perhaps because, despite this being a clue to his swimming, it indicated that someone had made it look as if he had been washing off blood. Next morning, Battle says, Nevile returned the knob to Audrey's room and presumably, after cleaning it, put the emery paper in the wastepaper basket and planted the gloves in the ivy.

This is a particularly ingenious murder plan, albeit requiring real athleticism by the murderer. The ingenuity comes partly in the murder itself, with an unusual weapon enabling Nevile to strike backhanded and so brilliantly implicate a left-hander, and partly in the murder being committed by someone thought to be out of the house.

However, the ingenuity comes mainly in the way in which he creates a sequence of clues which will, first, make him the obvious suspect (before Barrett can give him an alibi), then, second, place him so triumphantly above suspicion (after she has come round) that no one will check exactly when he got to the hotel, and, third, implicate Audrey as the murderer who had tried to frame him. The doping of Barrett's senna is thus the cornerstone of the ingenious sequential clueing. But it does require Nevile to judge the right dose to ensure that she is still awake when Lady Tressilian's bell is rung but does not come round to give him an alibi until after he has been implicated.

Readers expect the murder plan to be particularly ingenious

because we are, unusually, privy (in the second part of the opening chapter) to the unnamed murderer, whose smile is "not quite sane", writing out "a clear, carefully detailed project for murder" some seven months earlier on 14 February. There we are told that the scheme was being worked out "meticulously"; that every eventuality and possibility was being taken into account; that it had to be "absolutely fool-proof"; and that, although it was not absolutely cut and dried (with "intelligent provision" for the unforeseen), the main lines were "clear and had been closely tested".

With such impressive claims – and Nevile himself asserting in the final chapter "I'd thought out every detail – every *detail!* I can't help what went wrong" – the author has set a very high standard against which his murder plan should be judged. In judging it as particularly ingenious, we probably have to accept that the main lines had indeed been "closely tested", even though we are not actually told this in relation to various points.

Thus one can almost envisage Nevile deciding that, as the core of the actual murder, he would hit Lady Tressilian with a backhanded stroke; and then choosing the knob as the operative part of his weapon and checking that it could screw into the handle of a racquet which could later be reassembled.

We also have to make other assumptions – that he had, in a rehearsal before February, swum across the river at night and climbed the rope (knowing it was in the boxroom); that he knew which bedroom he would be given; that he had checked the tides in September because we are told that even an enthusiastic bather can be swept down the river by the current; and that he knew that Ted, who would give him an alibi from 11:15, would book a room at the Easterhead Bay Hotel, such that his apparently innocent question "Latimer? Is he down here?" was one to which he already knew the answer.

He must also have been confident about getting Audrey to

agree that he and Kay could stay at Gull's Point while she was there in September. There is quite a bit of misdirection as to whether this idea was his or Audrey's, and one clever element of his plan was protesting so loudly that it was his idea that everyone thought it was hers. His further implication of her, by telling Battle that she was the only person he had injured, is clever too because he adds that she doesn't hate him. So he seems to be trying to avoid implicating her when he must know full well that this is precisely what he is doing.

Despite Nevile's cleverness, his behaviour after finding that his grey pinstripe smells of decayed fish is very strange. First, according to Battle, he wore his raincoat over his suit at the hotel while with Ted, presumably to try to mask the smell, which was "pervasive". Surely Ted must have thought it extremely odd that Nevile would keep on his raincoat indoors for nearly three hours, especially when playing billiards. Moreover, with the smell being pervasive, it is unbelievable that Ted would not have realised between 11.15 and 2.30 that it came from Nevile, rather than the drains or a dead rat, particularly on the 16-mile drive. One also wonders what Nevile did with the raincoat during the murder: if it was also put near the fish, it might have smelled as well.

Second, one assumes that, on returning to Gull's Point, he would be keen to deal with the stain and the smell. Yet there is no reference to him doing so. We are only told by Battle that he got the wind up about the suit "afterwards" and took it to the cleaners at the first opportunity. This opportunity cannot have arisen by the time Battle inspects Nevile's room since the suit is hanging over his chair. Oddly, there is no reference then to the pervasive smell and yet we know that the suit must still have smelled because it had a "particularly unpleasant smell" even after Nevile had taken it to the cleaners.

When he left it there, he used Angus MacWhirter's name which he had seen in the Easterhead Bay Hotel register. When

MacWhirter came to collect his own suit, he was given Nevile's in error and was astute enough to interpret the stain, deducing that there had been a swimmer who had climbed a rope. He was even willing, for Audrey's sake, to assert that he had seen this – though in fact he hadn't. Although Battle says that Nevile didn't give his own name at the cleaners "like a fool", one can understand him not wanting to have his name linked with a smelly, oddly stained suit during a murder investigation. But what would he have said about using MacWhirter's name if asked where the suit was?

In fairness to Nevile, it was very bad luck that he put the suit on a decayed fish; that the man in whose name he had left it at the cleaners had also left a suit there and was given Nevile's in error; and that he was so astute. Nevile also had two other bits of bad luck. First, that Thomas knew about Adrian and Audrey: "Didn't know anyone knew", he says. And, second, that, when Audrey admits "It's all true", she looks at Battle with the same eyes as his daughter, Sylvia, had done six months before when admitting to some thefts at school despite being innocent. Battle realises then that Audrey is innocent too.

Finally, as to Treves's bow and arrow story, Battle says that Nevile had been a bit unhinged mentally ever since he was a child. His physical peculiarity was that the little finger on his right hand was much longer than the little finger on his left. After Treves told the story, Nevile nipped down to his hotel and hung the notice on the lift. To murder someone by making them take the stairs is hardly a reliable plan – though, as Battle rightly says, it was resourceful and it might not have come off but it did. Certainly, it is most inventive.

Plot

The book has an intriguing title, which encapsulates the author's underlying concept for the story, which is explained twice – first by Treves, then by Battle. In the Prologue entitled "November 19th"

Treves says that detective stories begin in the wrong place because they begin with the murder whereas "the murder is the *end*" since the story begins long before that, with all the causes and events that bring certain people to a certain place at a certain time on a certain day – all of them converging towards zero – "*Zero Hour*".

Battle makes the point in similar fashion, derived indirectly from Treves, in the final chapter entitled "Zero Hour". He says that accounts of a murder usually begin with the murder itself but that that is all wrong; that the murder begins a long time beforehand and is the culmination of a lot of different circumstances all converging at a given moment at a given point, with the murder itself being "the end of the story"; and that "*It's Zero Hour now*".

The author adopts this 'convergence' concept by not beginning with the murder (as Treves and Battle had suggested was usual) but focusing instead on characters and circumstances as they converge towards Lady Tressilian's death over halfway through the book. But her murder is not the culmination of those converging events since, as Battle clarifies in the final chapter, his reference to "Zero Hour" relates to "*the murder of Audrey Strange*".

By then, further events have converged against Audrey and have just culminated in her being taken away by the police – presumably on a journey via the courts to the gallows. With her 'murder' being, so Nevile must think, 'the end of the story', just as he had planned, it is now "Zero hour".

The author's insightful *Towards Zero* concept works well and is not spoiled by the plan happening to fail through unforeseeable events. What the murderer could not have anticipated on 14 February was that, as well as the obvious characters (victim, suspects and policemen), others would converge – Treves, MacWhirter and a detective whose innocent daughter would admit to being guilty – or that they would participate in events culminating in his exposure.

Readers will assume from the early episode involving

MacWhirter's recovery from his attempted suicide that he will have a significant role when his nurse suggests that, just by *being* somewhere at a certain place at a certain time, he might accomplish something important. The episode ends with her perhaps seeing the picture of a man walking up a road on a night in September and thereby saving a human being from a terrible death – presumably a reference to MacWhirter walking up to Stark Head and preventing Audrey's suicide.

In addition to the Prologue, the book comprises a dedication to Robert Graves[1], a map of Saltcreek and just four unnumbered chapters. The first entitled "Open the Door and Here are the People" is in 11 dated parts, the second part being engagingly original in describing the unnamed murderer's approach to a very carefully planned murder.

The second chapter "Snow White and Red Rose" is in 12 parts leading to Lady Tressilian's murder. Until then, the pace may be too leisurely for some but the chapter reflects the author's concept and allows most of the characters to become well developed, the title neatly contrasting Kay (who has red hair) and Audrey (who has white hair and little colour). Thomas says "Red Rose and Snow White ... Like the old fairy story" – a reference to one of the German fairy tales, collected together in 1857 by the Brothers Grimm, of two sisters, Rose-Red, an outdoors girl, and Snow-White, more of an indoors one.

The third chapter "A Fine Italian Hand..." is in 16 parts and takes us through Battle's investigation until the police take Audrey away. In the fourth part, Battle says that the crime seems blunt, brutal and straightforward but that he glimpses "a fine Italian hand" at work behind the scenes – a reference to Machiavellian craft and deceit. In the sixth part, Kay sees Audrey's "fine Italian hand" behind Nevile coming to Gull's Point but in her case the repetition of this obscure expression seems unlikely and contrived.

The final, much shorter chapter entitled "Zero Hour" is in

three parts which cover the exposure of Nevile and explanation of his murder plan and end with Audrey and MacWhirter agreeing to marry.[2] Frustratingly, Battle's explanation of the plan is given in a rather disordered way and his failure to deal with it more chronologically results, as we have seen, in some of the timing being omitted (in relation to, for example, the senna, knob, weapon, powder, gloves and rope) and in readers having to make assumptions about what Nevile did when he "closely tested" the plan.

The plotting of that chapter is not therefore as good as the excellent plotting of the murder plan, or of Nevile's intricate sequence of clues or of the brilliant misdirection where the person being framed, Audrey, seems to be framing the real murderer. Despite that masterly plotting, this very good novel doesn't feel as superb as it perhaps should. It is hard to say exactly why this is but Ted's unbelievable failure to spot the source of the fishy smell does leave one wishing that the author had realised how frustrating this would be for readers.

There may be more general reasons as well. One could be that, after the murderer's very careful planning, we expect his project for murder to be not only ingenious and mystifying, as it is, but perhaps also to involve rather more subtlety than swimming a tidal river at night and using a rope to climb a sheer cliff in order to murder a bedridden old lady who has been like a mother to him, just to implicate someone else for her murder. His other two murders (with the bow and arrow and 'out of order' notice) have a much simpler ingenuity and feel more satisfying and memorable.

Another reason may be that the plan is worked out, not by Battle, but by MacWhirter making a real deductive leap from the smelly suit and then lying about seeing a man climbing a rope (which is a bit naughty anyway because in his first scene he had made clear that "I don't tell lies"). Although Battle does spot that Audrey is innocent, his reliance on MacWhirter for working out how Nevile is guilty perhaps ties in with what may be the final reason, which is that he is not as appealing as a detective as Poirot. This is a point which the author seems to recognise by having him mention Poirot three times

There are, however, some nice touches – Battle being asked if he's going to give Nevile "plenty of rope" and later suggesting to Audrey that the business is "fishy". The author also has some fun in the second chapter with her whites and reds, as she describes the suspects looking white or going red about 15 times. Gull's Point too is white, as is Lady Tressilian after Treves's death. The story ends suitably with Audrey going red, then white and then red again.

However, the way in which Nevile conceals, until he's ready to implicate Audrey, that she inherits under Sir Matthew's will seems rather feeble. On 19 April and 13 September he says that the money comes "to me and my wife", surely meaning that Kay, as his wife, will inherit and, indeed, she says so on 28 July and 13 September. But Battle asks Nevile for a second time on 13 September and, when he replies "My wife", Battle asks which one. He replies "I expressed myself badly" and he explains that he means Audrey, who is named as his wife in the will. But can the earlier misdirection towards Kay really be excused by Nevile *expressing himself badly*? He refers on three occasions to his "wife" – and his wife is Kay, whatever the position was at the time of the will.

Clues

As we have seen, Nevile sets a false sequence of clues which at first implicate him and then implicate Audrey. However, the real clues in the story are the ones which implicate him *actually*, rather than falsely, and it is those that now need to be assessed. The main one (if a motive can be found) is that he is an all-round athlete in magnificent health – specifically a first-class tennis player and a fine swimmer who has done some good climbs in the Alps.

The significance of the 'athlete' clue will not be apparent for some time but starts to become so when Battle describes Lady Tressilian's murder as "Brutal, masculine, rather athletic and slightly stupid". It is not clear why he regards brutally striking an old lady as "rather athletic" when he has no idea yet about the swimming or climbing. So readers may wonder about those words. They may even spot the connection with Nevile when Inspector Leach, on seeing his golf bag, thinks about "athletic chaps" and when Battle, referring to Nevile, says that "athletes" generally aren't brainy.

Battle is right about the murder being "rather athletic" because we later get clues which implicate an athlete – the 'damp rope' clue, used for climbing; the 'pools of water' clue, left on Nevile's floor after swimming; and the 'tennis racquet' clue used, with the 'knob' clue, for the weapon. The 'tennis racquet' clue does not of *itself* conclusively implicate a tennis player (since it might have been wielded by any left-hander) or Nevile specifically despite his fingerprints being on it (because its weight suggests that it belongs to Kay whose fingerprints are also on it). Indeed, after the police find the racquet thrown carelessly back into the cupboard under the stairs, Battle suggests that it was *Audrey* who used it to strike down Lady Tressilian and then implicated Nevile with the niblick.

However, we get an excellent additional clue – the 'backhand' clue – about the way in which the racquet might have been wielded, which not only explains part of the *howdunnit* but also makes the *whodunnit* pretty clear. The clue comes when we are told, just once, by Ted on 28 July, that "Nevile's backhand is good … It's better than his forehand." Although Battle later says that "Strange's backhand was always his strong point, remember!", readers would have done extremely well to "remember" that. But, if they had, they might have appreciated the clue's cleverness in the context of an apparently left-handed crime – assuming, of course, that Nevile *is* a right-handed tennis player (not just a right-handed golfer[3]) which we had not actually been told.

Similarly surprising is that we are not expressly told that Audrey is left-handed until Battle asserts this in the penultimate part of the third chapter. It seems that, despite all Nevile's planning, he is leaving it to Battle (and the reader) to spot this himself. Battle duly obliges. He sees Audrey with a cup and saucer in her right hand and a cigarette in her left, suggesting, he says, that she was more likely to be left-handed. He even thinks "Funny about that coffee cup". But, despite that prompt, readers would do very well to see his point unless perhaps they also spot that she keeps her pens to the left of her blotter.

Beyond the 'backhand' clue, until we can attribute a motive to Nevile, readers would again do well to interpret the other clues against him correctly. First is the 'September' clue – his suggestion to Kay of going to Gull's Point in September while Audrey is there. The difficulty with this clue is that it is not clear until *after* Nevile's exposure whether this was his idea or Audrey's or, therefore, which of them the clue implicates.

Then, at the end of dinner on the day of the murder, Nevile says he will visit Ted at Easterhead. This should strike readers as odd, not so much because he says it with "elaborate casualness" but because Ted plainly doesn't like him, later saying that Nevile seemed "quite glad of my company for once", the clever part of this 'Ted visit' clue being the words "for once". Then, after dinner Kay yawns ostentatiously. She may just have been tired. But Battle reckons that the 'Kay yawning' clue means that she had been doped, presumably to stop her disturbing the murderer's plans. If so, the person she was most likely to disturb was Nevile because of their connecting rooms.

A few readers may also wonder whether Nevile's reason for banging the front door when visiting Ted – the 'door bang' clue – was so as to be *heard* to go, as he was by Hurstall and Thomas. Indeed, he was *seen* to go – by Barrett. Her sighting of him explains the 'bell ring' clue – Lady Tressilian seemingly ringing her bell for Barrett but being unable to remember why. So, might someone else have rung it and, if so, how? That is explained by the 'window pole' clue, with a hook on its end, used to ring the bell so that Barrett would leave her room and spot Nevile going out while Lady Tressilian was still alive.

The other clue relating to Barrett is the drugging of her senna, which appears to be a clue against anyone in the household who knew her routine (rather than just against Nevile). One only realises that the 'senna' clue specifically implicates him if one spots, after she wakes and clears him, that she was drugged so that she could later give him an alibi.

As for the murder of Treves, it is interesting that, when he tells the bow and arrow story, each of Ted, Mary, Audrey, Kay and Thomas asks him a question or makes a remark and that only Nevile remains silent. It's hard to know if we are getting a 'Nevile silence' clue since his apparent disinterest in the story is never referred to as such. Anyway, the killer's identity depends most obviously on who had the opportunity to put the notice on the lift.

As to this, straight after Treves tells the story, Nevile invites Audrey outside but, although he goes out, she says she's going to bed. Kay and Mary follow, leaving Treves talking to Thomas while Ted goes out to the hall for some gramophone records. As he returns, Nevile strolls in, breathing deeply with his face looking "excited and unhappy", after which Thomas leaves the room, apparently to go for a walk. Treves then sets off for his hotel.

Of course, we don't know whether the ladies really went to bed or if Ted could have nipped to Treves's hotel while he was out of the room or what Thomas did on his walk. But the 'deep breathing' clue should make readers wonder what the athletic Nevile might have done to get out of breath while outside. What may, however, prevent them from suspecting Nevile is his invitation to Audrey to go outside with him. If she had accepted, he would not have had the chance to put up the notice.

What we do know from Treves is that the murderer has a "certain physical peculiarity". As we enjoy trying to solve the mystery of what this is, we note – though we have to do some re-reading for this – that each of the suspects has by then already been described with one (except Kay, who never is), meaning that the 'physical peculiarity' clue does not point to any person in particular.

Apart from Nevile's right-hand little finger being much longer than his left, we had been told that Mary had dark hair with one natural white lock across the front; that Thomas walked a little sideways, the result of being jammed in a door, leaving his right arm and shoulder partially useless; that Ted had an interestingly shaped head with a curious angle from the crown to the neck; and that Audrey had small hands and, as we later learn, a tiny scar on her left ear. But the 'little finger' clue is the relevant one, the others being red herrings.

It is not clear when Treves notices Nevile's fingers. We know that, as he looks out of the French windows over Mary's shoulder, he sees Nevile's hands trembling as he tries to free a cuff button caught in Audrey's hair. But, *before* that, some "absorption" holds Treves aloof – though Mary can't make out whether he is watching Nevile, Audrey or Thomas. He then tells her that he is a very shrewd observer; that sometimes one is placed in a position of responsibility; and that the right course of action is not always easy to determine. Those remarks suggest that he had identified Nevile during his "absorption" rather than when later seeing Nevile over Mary's shoulder.[4]

He then tells the bow and arrow story, after which Nevile looks "unhappy" on returning to the house. He had looked "troubled" when first appearing in the novel and after that he regularly looks unhappy or scared, not just after Treves's story. We notice this because we are watching out for someone who might have looked "not quite sane" while writing the murder plan; and Battle too focuses on insanity after his suggestion that the murderer is a "maniac".

The two people most implicated by the 'insanity' clue are Audrey and Nevile. Kay thinks that Audrey is "a little frightening"; Mary thinks she isn't normal; Thomas thinks that there's something wrong with her; and Audrey herself says she's not quite normal about some things.

As for Nevile, on the evening of the murder he is like "an unhappy little boy" and "very worried and unhappy-looking". Next day, his nerves are shot to pieces and he looks "scared as Hell". He is "frightened" when speaking to Battle; is "pale and worried" when interviewed; has "frightened horror-stricken eyes" when thought to be the murderer; and mutters "sulkily" when Thomas reveals that Audrey had no motive. However, it is never clarified whether Nevile's demeanour should be interpreted as a clue to his unhinged mental state or if he is just innocently unhappy and scared.

Also difficult is interpreting the significance of the smelly suit given by the cleaners to MacWhirter, particularly since we don't know that it was a grey pinstripe (or therefore Nevile's), only that it wasn't dark blue. The smelly suit does, however, provide a couple of clues. First is its unpleasant fish smell noticed by MacWhirter. But readers may not connect the 'fish smell' clue with the smell in the hotel because that was attributed to drains or a dead rat.

Second is the stained patch on the shoulder. Battle explains that you *step* on a decayed fish but you don't put your *shoulder* on it "*unless you have taken your clothes off to bathe at night,* and no one would bathe for pleasure on a wet night in September". So someone had gone bathing at night for a purpose. That sounds like a clever deduction from the 'shoulder stain' clue but it does include an assumption that the bather bathed *at night*, which is fair enough if Battle is implying that in daylight the bather would have noticed the fish.

MacWhirter then brilliantly "deduced", to use his own word, that the bather had swum across from Easterhead; had climbed a rope left hanging from a window; and had murdered Lady Tressilian. MacWhirter then pretended to have seen this, after finding the 'damp rope' clue in the boxroom, knowing that mere "deductions" would not carry weight.

By then, Thomas has revealed Nevile's motive for implicating Audrey, who ran off with Adrian. The 'Adrian' *whydunnit* clue is the most important in the story because at last it provides the athletic Nevile with a motive based on a mixture of hatred and revenge. It is also quite well concealed because, when Thomas makes the revelation, the emphasis is very much on Audrey *not* having a motive rather than on Nevile having one. But readers who do spot it may then look with greater suspicion at the other clues pointing to Nevile.

Those relating to athleticism point directly to him, including the excellent 'backhand' clue, which is the best in the book. However, the other clues are less direct, either because they do not implicate only him (such as the 'September'; 'physical peculiarity'; and 'senna' clues) or because they can be hard to spot, or interpret, since they could have an innocent explanation (such as the 'Ted visit'; 'Kay yawning'; 'door bang'; 'bell ring'; 'window pole'; and 'Nevile silence' clues). But those are legitimate clueing devices, in a story where the clueing generally is very good.

The key clue relating to Audrey comes when she reacts to her arrest by saying "It's all true" and Battle stares at her as though he can't believe his eyes. His staring disbelief seems to suggest a clue to Audrey's innocence – but how? For *Battle*, the clue is that she looked at him with the same eyes as his daughter, Sylvia, when admitting to the thefts at school despite being innocent.

But, for *readers*, the Sylvia episode had occurred so early in the story (and been referred to tangentially only once since) that they would do well to have remembered it. Even those who do will find the 'Sylvia' clue difficult to interpret because, although Battle says that Audrey looked at him with Sylvia's eyes, neither Audrey's eyes nor Sylvia's are described in the text beyond Sylvia becoming tearful.

Finally, we end with Poirot, who keeps coming into Battle's head after he has searched the suspects' rooms. He can't think why at first but it was because the left knob on the fender was brighter than the right one. He had thought unconsciously "That would worry old Poirot" and so he looked in Audrey's room for a second time and found that the knob was bloodstained. However, for readers wondering what Battle has in mind, there was no mention of the fender or its knobs when he first searched Audrey's room and so they could not have spotted that one knob was brighter than the other. But Battle, inspired by Poirot, did so. And it was lucky for Nevile that he did because, as well as being an actual clue (to the weapon), the 'knob' clue was a false one chosen by Nevile from Audrey's room as an integral part of his plan to implicate her.

ENDNOTES

Preface

1 Poirot's story has since been expertly analysed in Dr Mark Aldridge's very enjoyable *Poirot The Greatest Detective in the World* (2020).

2 Frustratingly, she does not say what the "one point" was but Dr John Curran considers some options in *Agatha Christie's Secret Notebooks* (p.234). More generally, in a Foreword written for the Penguin 1953 paperback edition (which has since appeared in some, but not all, editions), she does refer to "my sense of triumphant achievement". However, she also comments on all the research required, which suggests that her sense of achievement was in getting the book completed rather than in its 'dissatisfying' ending where she was, as we have seen, "… hampered by the gratitude I felt to Stephen…". He died in 1956 and so was still alive when she wrote the Foreword – but not when she wrote *An Autobiography* (1977) and so she might have felt less hampered in expressing her views then.

3 It would, of course, have been neater to have had 33 novels in the *Golden Age* and 33 in the *Modern Age* (rather than 34/32, as I have done). But there is no substantive justification for moving *Towards Zero,* which is a very good Golden Age novel, into the latter category – unless perhaps one regards the *Golden Age* as coming to an end about 80% of the way through it when we learn that Ted Latimer had failed to realise over more than three hours – including a half-hour car journey – that the pervasive smell of decayed fish came from Nevile Strange.

Chapter 1 - Miss Jane Marple

1   In Peter Keating's excellent *Agatha Christie and Shrewd Miss Marple* he takes great care (p.30, p.32, p.235) to place the novel in the context of the previously published Miss Marple short stories, rightly crediting (p.226) the work of Jared Cade in *Agatha Christie and the Eleven Missing Days* and Karl Pike. The 12 short stories were published in *The Royal Magazine* and *The Story-Teller*. The thirteenth short story *Death by Drowning* appeared in *Nash's Pall Mall Magazine* in November 1931. The other seven short stories (in addition to *The Thirteen Problems*) are listed here with details of their first publication: *Miss Marple Tells a Story* (May 1935, *The Home Journal*); *The Case of the Caretaker* (Jan 1942, *The Strand Magazine*); *The Tape-Measure Murder* (Feb 1942, *The Strand Magazine*); *The Case of the Perfect Maid* (Apr 1942, *The Strand Magazine*); *Strange Jest* (Jul 1944, *The Strand Magazine*); *Sanctuary* (Oct 1954, *Woman's Journal*); and *Greenshaw's Folly* (Dec 1956, *Daily Mail*).

2   Part IX section Two. A fourth is, however, suggested by Professor Bargainnier, who says (p.67) that Miss Marple has "antecedents" in Miss Amelia Viner, an elderly spinster of St Mary Mead, in *The Mystery of the Blue Train* (1928); and Professors Maida and Spornick refer (p.108) to Miss Viner as the "prototype" of Miss Marple. It's not clear whether they are right since *The Mystery of the Blue Train* was first published in *The Star* (a former London evening newspaper) in Feb 1928 in serialised form whereas the first of Miss Marple's Thirteen Problems (*The Tuesday Night Club*) had already been published in *The Royal Magazine* in Dec 1927. On the other hand, the author may have written Miss Viner's chapters before creating Miss Marple since she refers in *An Autobiography* (Part VII section Six) to writing "the best part of a new book, *The Mystery of the Blue Train*, while we were in the Canary Islands", where she went in "February" – presumably meaning February 1927 (rather than 1928, as some commentators have said) since *The Star*'s serialisation started on 1 Feb 1928, with the novel itself being published in Mar 1928. Either way, Miss Viner is not

mentioned in *An Autobiography*.

3 An article written by Agatha Christie entitled *"Does a Woman's Instinct Make Her a Good Detective?"* appeared in *The Star* in May 1928 to coincide with the publication of the sixth Miss Marple short story *The Thumb Mark of St Peter*, which was later to feature in *The Thirteen Problems*. I came across it in Tony Medawar's book *The Quotable Miss Marple* (p.148). He later told me that he identified it when, with Christie's daughter's permission, he was searching the records held by Christie's then literary agents. It is instructive that Christie felt the need to produce this particular article, which must have been written with Miss Marple in mind, in order to explain a detective technique based on instinct and to illustrate how ladies like Miss Marple can reach conclusions in that way. In the article (of about 700 words) she asks what a "woman's instinct" means. And her answer is "Shorn of all glamour, I think it comes down to this – women prefer short cuts! They prefer the inspired guess to the more laborious process of solid reasoning. And, of course, the inspired guess is often right". She gives the example of a fictitious Mrs Smith who is asked "How could you tell, my dear?". And Mrs Smith answers negligently: "I couldn't say. I just knew".

Chapter 2 - Tommy and Tuppence Beresford

1 The core of the *Partners in Crime* collection (20 of the 23 chapters) is based on 12 stories which had appeared in the weekly magazine *The Sketch* from 24 September 1924 to 10 December 1924, though the earliest story (on which chapters 20 and 21 of the book are based) had appeared in *The Grand Magazine* in December 1923 and the final story (on which chapter 19 is based) did not appear until December 1928 when it was published in the Christmas issue (called *Holly Leaves*) of *Illustrated Sporting and Dramatic News*.

2 Their physical descriptions are from *The Secret Adversary* chapter 1 and *N or M?* chapters 4 and 13. The descriptions

of, and quotations from, their lives up to the start of their first adventure are from *The Secret Adversary* chapters 1 and 4 and *N or M?* chapter 1. The descriptions of their personalities are from *The Secret Adversary* chapters 12, 16, 17, 18, 22 and 27 and *N or M?* chapters 1 and 3.

3 Professor Bargainnier suggests (p.78) that Tommy is 25 and Tuppence 20 in *The Secret Adversary* but he does not set out his reasoning.

Chapter 3 - Thrillers

1 The five quotations in this chapter from *An Autobiography* are, in the order they occur, from Part IX section Two; Part V section Five; Part VIII section Six; Part IX section Five; and Part VI section Four.

1 - The Secret Adversary

1 An audio-surveillance study produced by the CIA Historical Review Program in July 1996 says that from not long after 1892 newspapers were full of reports about the clandestine installation of concealed microphones, both by the police and private citizens; and that there is abundant evidence that in the First World War intelligence services made extensive use of microphones and clandestine eavesdropping. The author's merging of 'dictaphone' and 'microphone' seems strange, given that she was aware of the purpose of a dictaphone in *The Murder of Roger Ackroyd* – though perhaps she was not as clear about the terminology four years earlier when the present novel was published.

2 In chapter 7 Whittington tells Boris that 'Flossie' is a "marvel" who "gets the voice right every time". So we assume that Flossie, whoever she is, will do an impersonation later. But – unless Flossie and Nurse Edith are the same person – we never come across her.

2 - *The Man in the Brown Suit*

1 Anne doesn't say why she thinks this in chapter 15 but her view seems borne out by later occasions when he clasps her throat after chasing off her assailant (chapter 16), when he says he'll choke the life out of the scoundrel who caused her to fall down the ravine (chapter 25), when he says he could have put his hands round Nadina's throat and squeezed the life out of her (chapter 26) and when he tells Anne that, if she marries anyone but him, he'll wring his neck (chapter 27).
2 Race later appears in *Cards on the Table*, *Death on the Nile* and *Sparkling Cyanide*.
3 In the *Ackroyd* commentary, Van Dine's Rule 2 was also considered. But it was concluded that it was unsound because it undermined the very aim of a puzzle and so is not considered here.

3 - *The Secret of Chimneys*

1 A nice use of the name 'Battle' after two novels and one short story collection with 'Hastings'.
2 The Koh-i-noor is one of the world's largest diamonds. It was surrendered by the Maharajah of Lahore to Queen Victoria in 1849 after the British annexation of the Punjab. After she died, it was set as the centre stone in the crowns of Queen Alexandra (1901) and Queen Mary (1911) and currently adorns the crown of Queen Elizabeth (known as The Queen Mother) (1937). It is one of the British Crown Jewels which are kept securely in the Tower of London. That is where the Koh-i-noor would really have been when the novel was published in 1925.
3 It seems pretty clear that (fictionally) Varaga not only hid the diamond while at Chimneys but actually stole it from there as well, rather than from the Tower of London. Chimneys was "famous for its hospitality … there was hardly anyone of note in England – or indeed in Europe – who had not, at one time or another, stayed there" (chapter 3). So the diamond

may have been on loan there, as a display item for impressing foreign dignitaries. Indeed, Lomax, when referring to "that unfortunate disappearance" in chapter 3, goes on to say "Why, it happened while they were at Chimneys".

4 There is an interesting textual clue against Lemoine, which is so subtle that the author may well not have intended it. In chapter 18 we are told that the intruder of the second midnight adventure (whom we know to be Lemoine) "went over to the same bit of panelled wall he had been examining the night before". This 'panelling' clue tells us that the intruder was *the same person* during both midnight adventures. Then in chapter 19 Lemoine suggests that the person examining the panelling during the first adventure was King Victor. *If so*, it was therefore also King Victor who examined the panelling during the second adventure, when we know that the examiner was Lemoine. In which case King Victor and Lemoine would be one and the same person.

5 The apostrophe after E is not a textual clue, but just a punctuation error from the first edition narrative (which is repeated in the quotations from Anthony and Battle).

6 *Romeo and Juliet*, Act II, Scene ii: "What's in a name? that which we call a rose By any other name would smell as sweet".

5 - *The Murder at the Vicarage*

1 The creation, and elimination, of suspicion against the obvious suspect had previously been used in *The Mysterious Affair at Styles*, which also had two villains in league. The difference in the present novel comes in the two villains making confessions. That device had been used by the author in a Harley Quin short story *The Love Detectives* (originally titled *At the Crossroads*) in 1926.

2 Although not described as three 'stumbling blocks' in the text, the term – taken from Clement's question to Miss Marple in chapter 26 about whether Protheroe's note is "still a stumbling block?" – does describe them fairly.

3   For an illustrated history of the Crime Club, see Dr John Curran's *The Hooded Gunman*.

4   In *An Autobiography* Part IX section Two the author says she thinks that there are "far too many characters, and too many sub-plots".

5   The words 'On It' are not in all editions.

6 - *The Sittaford Mystery:*

1   However, the time taken in chapter 3 means that it would have been somewhat later than 8 pm that Warren saw the body because, after arriving "just before eight o'clock", Burnaby paused for "a few minutes" after ringing the bell; he rang again and then a third time, keeping his finger on the bell, which "trilled on and on"; he then knocked on the door "vigorously"; he then went "slowly" down the path and along the road in the snow a hundred yards to the police station, hesitated, "finally" made up his mind and entered; he then reported the position to Constable Graves, who, after Burnaby had displayed impatience at his "slowness", then tried to telephone Trevelyan; they then went almost next door to report the position to Dr Warren, who, after grudgingly agreeing to accompany them, dressed up warmly; the three of them walked, in the still falling snow, to Hazelmoor and rang the bell and knocked but got no response; they then went round the back and tried a side door on the way but it was locked; they "presently" emerged on the lawn, went to the open study French window, entered and saw the body. It is hard to imagine all these steps being taken in under 25 minutes, meaning that Warren would not have seen the body until perhaps 8.20. One focuses on this when reading chapter 3 in case the time of death is going to prove significant – which, indeed, it does (for the alibi) – although in fact the issue of whether Dr Warren was more likely to have seen the body at 8.20 rather than 8 pm does not itself turn out to be significant since in either case Trevelyan was murdered more than two hours beforehand.

2 See links on The National Archives 'Currency Converter' website e.g. Bank of England 'Inflation Calculator'.

3 The murder took place on "the 14ᵗʰ instant" (chapter 29). The "instant" must be December because it is "just before Christmas" (chapter 9).

4 Osborne says (p.91) that "...the solutions to its puzzles are not likely to be arrived at by deduction on the reader's part". At first, this looks complimentary (suggesting that readers will be outwitted by the author). But really he is criticising the clueing by indicating that the solution is unlikely to be arrived at by deductions that can be derived from the clues.

5 Chapter 1: Sittaford "was not in a valley … but perched right on the shoulder of the moor" with Exhampton being "a steady descent which necessitated the sign, 'Motorists engage your lowest gear', so familiar on the Dartmoor roads"; chapter 4: Narracott at Hazelmoor: "Outside was the snowy landscape. There was a fence … and beyond it the steep ascending slope of the snow-covered hillside"; and chapter 16: Emily in Sittaford: "...Sittaford House, and the dotted cottages beyond it. In the valley below she could see Exhampton."

7 - Why Didn't They Ask Evans?

1 Bobby has a reassuring name for a golfer – Bobby Jones having won seven Open Championships between 1923 and 1930.

2 Surprisingly, in the first edition of *Bloody Murder* (1972) Julian Symons in his chapter on the 1930s says about Christie (p.135): "It is on her work during this decade, plus half a dozen of her earlier and later books, that her reputation chiefly rests, perhaps most specifically upon *Peril at End House* (1932), *Lord Edgware Dies* (1933), *Why Didn't They Ask Evans?* (1934), *The ABC Murders* (1936) and *Ten Little N*****s* (1939)". By 1981 he has changed his position, describing *Evans* in *Tom Adams' Agatha Christie Cover Story* (p.126) as "the slightest of tales" and by 1992, in the third edition of *Bloody Murder* (p.136), he has omitted *Evans*, and lists only the other four novels.

8 - *Murder is Easy*

1 During the 1930s the Derby was always run on the first Wednesday in June. In 1995 the day was changed to the first Saturday in June.

2 Readers would feel a bit sceptical anyway. But, interestingly, Colonel Johnson says in the author's previous novel, *Hercule Poirot's Christmas* (in which pincers are also used), that "These sorts of tools aren't easy to manage" (Part 3 section VII).

3 The denouement doesn't feel quite as unusual as in *The Moving Finger* (see endnote 3 to the commentary on that novel) because readers will have no particular expectation with the single-appearance detectives in the present novel about how the solution might be revealed, whereas in *The Moving Finger* they would probably have expected it to be revealed by Miss Marple because of their knowledge of her from other stories.

4 This is based on Humbleby's funeral being on a Friday (according to the obituary notice); the tennis party being on Saturday (confirmed in chapter 16); chapter 13 taking place mainly "after church" (so on a Sunday); and Luke having no word alone with Bridget after the day of the tennis party until Midsummer Eve (chapter 16), so suggesting that Midsummer Eve (23 June) can't have been the day after tennis but Monday at the earliest. In the US edition *Easy to Kill*, Humbleby's death is given in the obituary notice as 12 June and Bruce Pendergast (2004) bases his timings on that date (p.174).

5 See, for example, Goya's 1823 painting, *Witches' Sabbath*.

6 After all, she had, as Luke says in the opening chapter, a "very suitable name" – no doubt a reference to the Pinkerton National Detective Agency founded by Allan Pinkerton in the US in the 1850s.

9 - *And Then There Were None*

1 Although, of course, the original title with its offensive third word is a matter of historical fact, I am conscious of its

impact and anxious not to give any offence unintentionally. Accordingly, I am redacting the word throughout.

2 Although the sentence is in chapter 2 part 7 of modern US editions (as it has always been in the UK), it was in chapter 2 part 8 of the first and 1944 and 1966 US editions (which split chapter 2 part 1 of the UK edition into two parts). And, although the wording of the sentence is changed in modern US editions, the phrase "n***** in the woodpile" is still used as the title of and within chapter 18 of modern US editions of *Dumb Witness*. Moreover, in 1931, in chapter 20 of the US first edition of *The Murder at Hazelmoor* (*The Sittaford Mystery* in the UK) Emily Trefusis was working "like the worst kind of n***** to find out the truth", although the offensive expression was changed to "working like fury" in the Dell edition of 1950 and to "working like a slave" in later UK editions.

3 *The Invisible Host* (1930) by Gwen Bristow and Bruce Manning, published by the Mystery League, Inc, New York. Some additional points may be worth making:

   a) The guests are known to one another, and to the host, whose motive is hatred. After dinner, the three staff are drugged while having their own meal and are harmlessly asleep before and during the murders. The radio is wired to some phonographs (gramophones) which are in the suite below the penthouse, along with three microphones and a series of records prepared in advance by the host in a disguised voice. Each phonograph can change its own records and is controlled by a switch in the penthouse, installed by an expert technician, who is told that the rigging is for a joke being played on friends. He is murdered before the party and is referred to (in chapters 4 and 10) as "the ninth guest", Death being "my guest of honor" (chapter 4).

   b) The novel was adapted into a Broadway play by Owen Davis entitled *The Ninth Guest*, which ran from 25 August 1930 for 72 performances at the Eltinge Theatre on 42nd Street. And the play was made into a film of the same name directed by R. William Neill (released 1934). In the film, Death is "the ninth guest" as well as "my guest of honor".

4 Some readers may be reminded of the Sherlock Holmes short story *The Problem of Thor Bridge* (1927) in which Mrs Maria Gibson makes her suicide look like murder by shooting herself with a revolver attached by string to a heavy stone, which she hangs over the parapet of the bridge. As she releases her grip on the revolver after shooting herself, it is whisked away by the weight of the stone, which disappears, with the string and revolver, into the water. Mrs Gibson wanted the revolver to disappear (unlike Wargrave) because it was one of a pair and she had earlier fired the other revolver in the woods without attracting attention and planted it among the possessions of the person she was seeking to implicate.

5 Perhaps this point was made to the author because in her play she does have Vera alerting Wargrave to the verse. He, however, diverts attention away from a judge being the next victim by saying that the term 'Chancery' can apply to a boxer (i.e. not just a judge) – which it did in bare knuckle boxing outside the Queensbury Rules. 'Chancery' was the term used for controlling headlock positions, enabling the holder to land punches on his opponent's head or body – a very effective technique, whose name derived from the slow and expensive court of the Lord Chancellor where litigants were, like the boxer's opponent, in "an awkward or helpless position" (see the website of the pugilism expert, Dan Kanagie). However, the context of 'Chancery' in the rhyme is expressly stated to be the law (not boxing) and so Wargrave's diversion doesn't really work.

6 Beyond saying this (and making the point in the previous footnote), I won't comment further on the play since I regard this as the preserve of Julius Green's very knowledgeable book *Agatha Christie – A Life in Theatre*. My focus is on the novel and so, although there are also various film and television versions, I will similarly refrain from commenting on those since I regard them as the preserve of Dr Mark Aldridge's equally knowledgeable book *Agatha Christie On Screen*.

7 My view is that chapter 16, with Vera on the chair, could have ended immediately before the very final sentence in which she

kicks it away. And that then, after having the same Epilogue text (but as an ordinary numbered chapter), there could have been a final numbered chapter, replacing the confession, in which (in a 'flashback' to Vera standing on the chair with the noose around her neck) Wargrave appears and explains his motivation, the murders of his victims, his pretended alliance with Armstrong and his intended suicide on his bed before he then kicks away the chair and ends the novel by putting it against the wall, prior to going to his bedroom to shoot himself. Having two of the characters still alive at the start of that final chapter, so that the island narrative is not yet finished when the puzzle is explained, but having both of them dying at the end (so that Wargrave's plan succeeds), seems less like a postscript and more like a genuine denouement.

8 In England 'murder' has never been defined by statute. But under English common law, reflected in Chief Justice Coke's *Institutes of the Lawes of England* (1628 onwards), 'murder' in 1939 was, and still is, causing a person's death (a) by an act which is unlawful (i.e. has no legal justification such as killing reasonably and proportionately in self-defence or in prevention of a crime) or by an omission which is unlawful because of a legal duty to act arising from a dependent relationship; and (b) with 'malice aforethought', which doesn't assume 'ill will' or 'nastiness' or require 'premeditation' (one can commit 'murder' impulsively), but means an actual (subjective) intention to kill or to cause grievous (really serious) bodily harm. (There have been legal cases since 1939 which have extended the meaning of 'malice' to include, for example, an objective test of intention – *Smith*, 1960 – or recklessness – *Hyam*, 1975 – but these have subsequently been held in, for example, *Moloney*, 1985 and *Frankland*, 1987 not to have represented English law.)

9 Not all the characters committed 'murder' technically. They fall into categories which look less 'murderous' as they descend a scale ranging from those who knew that they were letting people who depended on them die, by unlawfully and deliberately failing to help them, without inflicting direct physical harm themselves (Vera and Mr and Mrs Rogers, who wanted their

victims to die; and Lombard, who, although motivated by self-preservation rather than a desire to kill his victims, had intentionally left them to die); to those who caused death intentionally but in a way that would look lawful – Macarthur and Wargrave (though they are rather different cases: Macarthur guiltily dwelling at length – second only to Vera and noticeably more than the others – on having sent someone to his death for just having an affair; and Wargrave convinced he was right for ensuring that a murderer was executed); to those who caused death recklessly, not intentionally – Armstrong and Marston; and to those who did not intend or anticipate death but contributed vindictively to it – Blore and Miss Brent. (If Morris is, as Wargrave says, the "tenth victim" – rather than Wargrave himself – his dope peddling to a girl, who later committed suicide, was unlawful but her death was not intentional.) Although The Voice describes the charges against the ten characters in various ways ("killed"; "responsible for the death of"; "brought about the death of"; etc), the words do not accurately reflect differing levels of culpability with technical accuracy. Thus The Voice uses "guilty of the murder of", which sounds like the worst level, not only for Marston, who was tried for a less serious offence, but also for Wargrave, even though we know that he does not regard himself as guilty of 'murder' in any sense of the word. Moreover, although in his confession Wargrave says that he decided that his victims who had the lightest guilt should be killed first (and not suffer the prolonged mental strain and fear of the more cold-blooded offenders) and although he does then kill them in an order which may roughly reflect increasingly heinous behaviour, that order does not reflect an increasing likelihood of being found guilty of 'murder'. For a more detailed analysis of whether the ten islanders are 'murderers', see my article in *CADS 85*, May 2021, entitled *Cooking Seton's Goose* (or *Ten Little Murderers?*).

10 But the author clearly thinks that the mark was on the forehead because she makes the point again at the very end of Poirot's final novel, *Curtain*, when Hastings thinks that "*The mark on Norton's forehead – it was like the brand of Cain*".

11 Chapter 3 part 2; chapter 9 part 5; chapter 10 part 1; and chapter 2 part 6 respectively.

12 Vera: chapter 1 part 2 and chapter 2 part 5; Lombard: chapter 1 part 3; Brent: chapter 1 part 4; Macarthur: chapter 1 part 5, chapter 2 part 10 and chapter 5 part 5; Marston: chapter 1 part 7 and chapter 2 part 4; Armstrong: chapter 2 part 6; and Rogers: chapter 5 part 4 and chapter 10 part 7.

13 Chapter 2 part 2; chapter 2 part 7; chapter 5 part 3; chapter 9 part 2; chapter 1 part 2; chapter 6 part 1; and chapter 7 part 1 respectively.

14 Concise Oxford English Dictionary, 2011, p.823. On a related point, Panek (p.53) suggests there is a "miniscule" clue in Wargrave's death being described in "figurative language" while the rest are depicted in "physical detail". In fact, however, "physical detail" *is* given about Wargrave when Armstrong "lifted the lifeless hand"; and this is actually similar to the physical detail given about Mrs Rogers when Armstrong "lifted the cold hand, raised the eyelid".

10 - N or M?

1 During the Spanish Civil War (1936–39) General Emilio Mola said, as four columns of his troops approached Madrid, that they would be helped by a "fifth column" of supporters undermining the government inside the city. The expression became widely used, including in the UK where there were fears in 1940 of a Fifth Column of Nazi supporters sabotaging the country from within.

2 This refers to the answer to the first question in the Church of England Catechism, where the person being catechised is asked for his name (N) or his names (NN, which are contracted to M).

3 That slogan is based on an 1884 essay (*A Penny Plain and Twopence Coloured*) by Robert Louis Stevenson, written after visiting Benjamin Pollock's Toyshop in Hoxton, which sold sheets of characters and scenery for toy theatres. They cost

one penny when printed in black outline for colouring or two pence if already coloured.

4   In the first and later editions, one capital letter and one comma are used at this point. Different capitals and commas appear elsewhere in the novel, starting with 'Goosey Goosey Gander' (chapter 7), which is the format used in this commentary except when quoting actual text.

5   See Michael Smith's *Bletchley Park: The Code-breakers of Station X*; Shire Library, 2013.

11 - The Body in the Library

1   Gossington Hall is "eighteen miles or so" (chapter 3) from Danemouth and "some twenty" (chapter 6) or "about eighteen" (chapter 8) miles from the Majestic. A discordant reference in chapter 11 to Gossington Hall being "thirty-odd" miles from the Majestic is surely a mistake.

2   Perhaps the answer is in *The Murder at the Vicarage* chapter 12, where Redding says "...no one does lock up their house round here".

3   This Foreword does not appear in the first edition, being originally written (with Forewords for some other books) for the Penguin 1953 paperback edition. It has since appeared in some, but not all, editions.

4   Although the two trunk murders of 1934 were unsolved when the novel was published, Tony Mancini, who had been found not guilty of the second murder in December 1934, confessed to it in 1976.

5   The author told Nigel Dennis, who interviewed her for his article *'Genteel Queen of Crime'* in *Life* Magazine on 14 May 1956, that it was "the best opening I ever wrote" (p.97/98).

6   I have asked various Christie/Marple experts to identify this person but no one has answered with confidence. Any suggestions would be welcome.

7   Shaw & Vanacker suggest (p.82 and 87) that Josie had married Mark "for reasons of financial gain through possible

inheritance" and that, *before* the marriage, she had a "plan to get Jefferson's money". The novel does not expressly say this. But they may be right if the 'Golden' clue is a double one – not only to Mark and Josie being married but also to her having married him out of financial (not just social) ambition which extended to his inheritance from Jefferson.

12 - *The Moving Finger*

1 This is reminiscent of the motive for killing Mrs de Rushbridger in *Three Act Tragedy*, although she is murdered because she *knew* nothing, rather than *saw* nothing.

2 Credit for this point goes to Robert Graves who, in a letter to Christie of 18 June 1943 quoted by Laura Thompson (p.505), suggests that Elsie should have been arrested "for failing to report the presence of Agnes's body in the cupboard when she returned the fishing rods there".

3 Dr John Curran suggests in *Secret Notebooks* (p.382) that it therefore "has the most unusual denouement of any Christie novel".

4 In *An Autobiography* Part XI section Three, the author comments that, rather to her surprise, she is "really pleased" with *The Moving Finger*, which she must have held in pretty high regard since her comment comes immediately after saying that *Crooked House* and *Ordeal by Innocence* are the two detective books that satisfy her best.

5 Although Dr Kathryn Harkup does not analyse *The Moving Finger* in her very interesting book *A is for Arsenic*, she has kindly clarified Nash and Griffith's discussion of prussic acid for me. When Mona's cachet containing "cyanide" (chapter 6 part 1) – a salt referred to as "cyanide of potassium" (KCN) in chapter 6 part 2 – was dissolved in water, the KCN would have split to form K+ and CN- and it was the CN- unit which would have killed her. So, when Nash and Griffith discuss prussic acid, they are either using that term simply to mean 'cyanide' or, given that Christie knew full well the subtle differences between

the many different terms for cyanide and its compounds, to mean, more accurately, the lethal CN- unit that would have been produced when the salt was dissolved.

6 Especially where (as here) there was no immediate urgency of the sort faced by Edgerton in *The Secret Adversary*. In fact, however, for example, Wallace Carothers, the inventor of nylon, committed suicide by drinking potassium cyanide in April 1937.

13 - Towards Zero

1 Graves was a friend and neighbour of Christie's in Devon. In the dedication she asks him to restrain his critical faculties because the story is for his pleasure and *not* a candidate for his literary pillory! Notwithstanding the friendship and dedication, Graves was to write later, in the *New York Times Book Review* of 25 August 1957, referred to in Sanders and Lavallo (p.212) and Thompson (p.382), that "her English was schoolgirlish, her situations for the most part artificial, and her detail faulty".

2 The book ends (in the first and most subsequent editions) with MacWhirter telling Audrey that, when he stopped her committing suicide, "…you felt like a bird – struggling to escape. You'll never escape now…" to which Audrey, who has just agreed to marry him, responds "I shall never want to escape". However, I am grateful to an American Christie enthusiast, Christopher Chan of *The Strand Magazine*, for pointing out to me that in the 1991 edition published by Berkley Books, Audrey's response has been omitted so that the novel ends with MacWhirter's words "You'll never escape now", which sound unexpectedly possessive and threatening, whereas Audrey's response negates that tone, at least to some extent, even though their marriage still sounds rather like being in prison. Audrey's response is not omitted in all US editions but it is also omitted in the 1983 Bantam edition.

3 Internet searches confirm that right-handed golfers can be left-

handed tennis players.

4   Ramsey says (p.35) that *Towards Zero* "features strongly the
    idea of intense surprise when a person looks straight ahead of
    him over another person's shoulder and is shocked or stunned
    by what he sees" and Osborne says (p.200) that in it "a character
    looks straight ahead of him, over the shoulder of the person
    addressing him, and is affected by what he sees". Neither author
    identifies the incident to which they are referring but they must
    mean Treves looking over Mary's shoulder and seeing Nevile's
    hands trembling as he tries to free the cuff button. However,
    Treves does not react to what he has seen over the shoulder
    in a way that suggests "intense surprise" or that he has been
    "affected" or "shocked or stunned" and so the Ramsey/Osborne
    point is not clear.

BIBLIOGRAPHY

Books about Agatha Christie's novels or detective fiction

Aldridge, Mark: *Agatha Christie on Screen*; Palgrave Macmillan, 2016

Aldridge, Mark: *Poirot The Greatest Detective in the World*; HarperCollins*Publishers*, 2020

Anders, Isabel: *Miss Marple: Christian Sleuth*; Circle Books, 2013

Bargainnier, Earl F.: *The Gentle Art of Murder – The Detective Fiction of Agatha Christie*; Bowling Green University Popular Press, 1980

Barnard, Robert: *A Talent to Deceive – An Appreciation of Agatha Christie;* William Collins Sons & Co Ltd, 1980; Fontana Paperbacks, 1990

Barzun, Jacques and Hartig Taylor, Wendell: *A Catalogue of Crime;* Harper & Row, Publishers, 1989

Bayard, Pierre: *Who Killed Roger Ackroyd?*; English Translation, Fourth Estate, 2000

Bernthal J. C.: *The Ageless Agatha Christie*; McFarland & Company, Inc, Publishers, 2016

Bernthal J. C.: *Queering Agatha Christie*; Palgrave Macmillan, 2016

Brawn, David: *Little Grey Cells: The Quotable Poirot*; HarperCollins*Publishers*, 2015

Bunson, Matthew: *The Complete Christie*; Pocket Books, 2000

Cade, Jared: *Agatha Christie and the Eleven Missing Days*; Peter Owen, 1998, revised and expanded 2011

Campbell, Mark: *Agatha Christie*; Pocket Essentials, 2001, revised 2006 and 2015

Cawelti, John G.: *Adventure, Mystery and Romance*; The University of Chicago Press, 1976

Champigny, Robert: *What Will Have Happened*; Indiana University Press, 1977

Christie, Agatha: *An Autobiography*; HarperCollins Publishers, 1977

Cook, Cathy: *The Agatha Christie Miscellany*; The History Press, 2013

Cooper, John and Pike, B. A.: *Detective Fiction The Collector's Guide*; Scolar Press, 1994 Second Edition

Craig, Patricia and Cadogan, Mary: *The Lady Investigates*; St Martin's Press, New York, 1981

Curran, John: *Agatha Christie's Secret Notebooks*; HarperCollins Publishers, 2009

Curran, John: *Agatha Christie's Murder in the Making*; HarperCollins Publishers, 2011

Curran, John: *The Hooded Gunman*; Collins Crime Club, 2019

Edwards, Martin: *The Golden Age of Murder*; HarperCollins *Publishers*, 2015, Paperback 2016

Feinman, Jeffrey: *The Mysterious World of Agatha Christie;* Award Books, 1975

Fido, Martin: *The World of Agatha Christie;* Carlton Books Ltd, 1999

Fitzgibbon, Russell H.: *The Agatha Christie Companion;* Bowling Green State University Popular Press, 1980

Gerald, Michael C.: *The Poisonous Pen of Agatha Christie;* University of Texas Press, 1993

Gill, Gillian: *Agatha Christie – The Woman and her Mysteries*; Robson Books Ltd, 1990

Goddard, John: *Agatha Christie's Golden Age* (Volume I); Stylish Eye Press, 2018

Green, Julius: *Agatha Christie – A Life in Theatre*; HarperCollins Publishers, 2018

Grossvogel, David I.: *Mystery and its Fictions from Oedipus to Agatha Christie;* The John Hopkins University Press, 1979

Harkup, Kathryn: *A is for Arsenic: The Poisons of Agatha Christie*; Bloomsbury Sigma, 2015

Hart, Anne: *Agatha Christie's Marple*; HarperCollins Publishers, 1997 Edition

Hart, Anne: *Agatha Christie's Poirot*; HarperCollins Publishers, 1997 Edition

Haycraft, Howard: *Murder for Pleasure, The Life and Times of the Detective Story*; Peter Davies, London, 1942

Haycraft, Howard: *The Art of the Mystery Story*; Carroll & Graf Publishers Inc., 1946 with a new introduction in 1992

Keating, H. R. F.: *Murder Must Appetize*; The Lemon Tree Press Ltd, 1975 revised 1981

Keating, H. R. F. (Editor): *Agatha Christie – First Lady of Crime*; Weidenfeld and Nicolson, 1977

Keating, Peter: *Agatha Christie and Shrewd Miss Marple*; Priskus Books, 2017

Macaskill, Hilary: *Agatha Christie at Home;* Frances Lincoln Ltd, Publishers 2009

MacEwan, Peter, F.C.S: *The Art of Dispensing: A Treatise on the Methods and Processes involved in Compounding Medical Prescriptions*; published at the Offices of The Chemist and Druggist, 1888 (First Edition); 1900 (Sixth Edition); 1912 (Ninth Edition)

Maida, Patricia D. and Spornick, Nicholas B.: *Murder She Wrote – A Study of Agatha Christie's Detective Fiction;* Bowling Green State University Popular Press, 1982

McCaw, Neil: *Adapting Detective Fiction*; Continuum International Publishing Group, 2011

Medawar, Tony: *Murder She Said: The Quotable Miss Marple*; HarperCollins Publishers, 2019

Milne, A. A.: *The Red House Mystery*; Methuen & Co Ltd, first edition 1922, with Introduction added by the author, April 1926

Morgan, Janet: *Agatha Christie, A Biography*; William Collins Sons and Co. Ltd, 1984; paperback edition, 1997; and with an updated Foreword, HarperCollins*Publishers*, 2017

Morselt, Ben: *An A–Z of the Novels and Short Stories of Agatha Christie;* Phoenix Publishing Associates Ltd, 1985

Osborne, Charles: *The Life and Crimes of Agatha Christie;* HarperCollins Publishers, 1982 revised and updated 1999

Panek, Leroy Lad: *Watteau's Shepherds, The Detective Novel in Britain 1914–1940*; Bowling Green University Popular Press, 1979

Pendergast, Bruce: *Everyman's Guide to the Mysteries of Agatha Christie;* published on demand in cooperation with Trafford Publishing, 2004

Ramsey, G. C.: *Agatha Christie Mistress of Mystery;* Dodd, Mead & Company, 1967

Riley, Dick and McAllister, Pam: *The Bedside, Bathtub & Armchair Companion to Agatha Christie;* The Continuum International Publishing Group, 1979 Second Edition 2001

Robyns, Gwen: *The Mystery of Agatha Christie;* Doubleday & Company, Inc., 1978

Rodell, Marie F.: *Mystery Fiction Theory and Technique;* Hammond, Hammond & Company, 1954

Ryan, Richard T.: *Agatha Christie Trivia;* Quinlan Press, 1987

Sanders, Dennis and Lovallo, Len: *The Agatha Christie Companion;* W.H. Allen, 1985

Shaw, Marion and Vanacker, Sabine: *Reflecting on Miss Marple;* Routledge, 1991

Sova, Dawn B.: *Agatha Christie A–Z;* Facts on File, Inc., 1996

Symons, Julian: *Bloody Murder;* Penguin Books Ltd., 1972 and Third Edition 1992

Symons, Julian: *Tom Adams' Agatha Christie Cover Story;* Paper Tiger, 1981

Thompson, Laura: *Agatha Christie An English Mystery;* Headline Review, 2007

Thomson, H. Douglas: *Masters of Mystery – a Study of the Detective Story;* Collins, 1931

Toye, Randall: *The Agatha Christie Who's Who*; Frederick Muller Limited, 1980

Wagoner, Mary S.: *Agatha Christie;* Twayne Publishers, 1986

Wagstaff, Vanessa and Poole, Stephen: *Agatha Christie A Reader's Companion*; Aurum Press Ltd, 2004

Wells, Carolyn: *Technique of the Mystery Story*; The Home Correspondence School, Springfield, Mass, 1913 and revised edition 1929

Zemboy, James: *The Detective Novels of Agatha Christie: A Reader's Guide*; McFarland & Company Inc, Publishers, 2008, reprinted 2016

Index of Titles

The 13 novels analysed in the commentaries (but see Contents page for their commentary page numbers)

Other Agatha Christie books and stories

Works by other authors

Pendergast, Bruce, *Everyman's Guide to the Mysteries of Agatha Christie*: 329

Ramsay, G.C., *Agatha Christie Mistress of Mystery*: 338

Rodell, Marie F., *Mystery Fiction Theory and Technique*: 41

Sanders, Dennis & Lovallo, Len, *The Agatha Christie Companion*: 337

Shakespeare, William, *Romeo and Juliet*, 1595: 326

Shaw, Marion & Vanacker, Sabine, *Reflecting on Miss Marple*: 335

Smith, Michael, *Bletchley Park: The Code-breakers of Station X*, 2013: 335

Stevenson, Robert Louis, *A Penny Plain and Twopence Coloured*, 1884: 334

Symons, Julian, *Bloody Murder*: 328

Symons, Julian: *Tom Adams' Agatha Christie Cover Story*: 328

Thompson, Laura, *Agatha Christie An English Mystery*: 336, 337

Unknown, *Historic Homes of England*, fictional: 92

Van Dine, S.S., *Twenty Rules for Writing Detective Stories*, 1928: 42

ABOUT THE AUTHOR

John Goddard read law at Magdalene College, Cambridge.
He became a litigation partner at the City law firm Freshfields
but is now retired. He lives in Wimbledon with his wife Linda.
They have two adult children. And their cat Minnie is still
very chatty.

For further information about the author and the book,
see **www.stylisheyepress.com**.

Printed in Great Britain
by Amazon